THE TEMPTATION OF TRUTH

THE HOMETOWN HEARTLESS

BRIT BENSON

The Temptation of Truth

Cover Design: Kate Decided to Design

Photographer: Cadwallader Photography, LLC

Cover Model: Lex

Editing: Rebecca at Fairest Reviews Editing Services, Emily Lawrence at Lawrence Editing

Sensitivity/Authenticity Reading: Callie Puncochar, Rosie Alice

❀ Formatted with Vellum

PLAYLIST

Boyfriend – Dove Cameron
girls girls girls – FLETCHER
Birthday Cake – Dylan Conrique
Pretty Girls – Reneé Rapp
Silk Chiffon – MUNA, Phoebe Bridgers
Colours of You – Baby Queen
She – Dodie
So Hot You're Hurting My Feelings – Caroline Polachek
Cherry Bomb – Julianna Joy
Risk – Gracie Abrams
Constellations – Jade LeMac
Wanna Be Missed – Hayley Kiyoko
Hands to Myself – Selena Gomez
Love You For A Long Time – Maggie Rogers
The Louvre – Lorde
gold rush – Taylor Swift
The Giver – Chappell Roan
RAW NEXT QUESTION – KTLYN
Birds of a Feather – Billie Eilish
LUNCH – Billie Eilish

Kitchen Light – Xana
Crazier Things – Chelsea Cutler, Noah Kahan

For the extended playlist, visit
www.authorbritbenson.com

For Women.
To the person you are,
the person you've been,
and the person you've yet to become.

CONTENT NOTE

Please be aware, The Temptation of Truth contains some difficult topics that could be upsetting for some readers.

Topics that take place on page are: cheating; vulgar language; sexually explicit content; alcohol consumption; domestic abuse (emotional, verbal, and financial); weight shaming; manipulation; grief; discussions of fertility and unwanted pregnancy

Topics that are referenced but do not take place on page are: death of loved ones; fatal car accident; domestic abuse (physical)

PROLOGUE

I USED to be someone else.

Someone loud with wonder and hope. Someone with big plans and a restless need to see the world.

I used to dream of greenhouses and poetry and cities I couldn't pronounce. I used to write until my mind was calm and my hands ached for relief. I used to fear nothing.

Not losing people. Not losing myself.

Not never being found.

Then came grief, and with it silence. A yawning sea of darkness so wide and deep and heavy that it nearly swallowed me whole. It blotted out the sunlight. It cloaked everything in despair, sticky and thick, making movement difficult. Making breathing difficult.

When the dreams started to fade, I let them. I didn't reach for them. I didn't try to save them. I didn't try to save myself. I was content to drown in the darkness. To let it suffocate me.

And then...

Then came *her*.

I didn't mean to fall for her. I didn't mean to forget the ring or the promises I made while I was still too numb to understand them. I didn't mean to ache at the sound of her laughter, or yearn for the softness of her lips, or memorize the soft curve of her waist like it was mine to keep. Like it was made just so my hand had a place to rest.

I didn't mean for the dreams to return. I didn't mean for them to include her.

I didn't mean for any of it to happen, but it did.

And somewhere in that mess—somewhere amidst the stolen glances, the broken boundaries, and the overwhelming temptation of truth—I started to bloom again.

Not because she loved me.

Not even because she saw me.

Because I dared to grow toward the light.

I dared to breathe.

And it changed everything.

1

———

AURORA

"I can tell you're angry."

Brady sighs through his nose, his nostrils flaring with the action. He's wearing sunglasses, but the designer frames don't hide the harsh slant of his eyebrows or the tightness in his jaw. He doesn't respond, so I tear my eyes from the side of his face and look back out the window.

"I'm sorry." My voice is lower this time, less confident, but he hears me and sighs louder. "She said this could take time."

He still says nothing.

I lower my gaze to my ring finger and run my thumb over the silver band. The skin around it is puffy and an angry red color. The ring fit when he proposed, but it's too small now. I need to get it resized, but I keep forgetting. I'm in the garden every day, so I don't wear jewelry when I'm at home. It's not until we go out that I remember how uncomfortable it is to wear, and we don't go out often.

Eighteen months.

We've been married only eighteen months, but he acts like it's a sprint toward some constantly moving finish line. It's nothing new, though. He's always been like this. By the fifth date, he was talking about engagement. Once he'd bought the

3

diamond, he was planning the wedding. Now it's all about the happy family dynamic. House, check. House*wife*, check. Babies? Working on it.

I was swept up in it at first. I was desperate for something to pull me from the thick fog of sadness. Hungry for some semblance of security and the promise to be part of a family again. But I've been growing weary. I've been quietly questioning everything. Secretly, I wish he were, too, and that fills me with guilt.

I reach across the center console and rest my hand on his thigh.

"I'm sorry," I whisper. "It will happen."

He grabs my wrist and moves it back to my lap. "Do you even want it to?"

"What?" I furrow my brow and force a swallow. "Of course I do. Why would you even ask that?"

"Never mind. I don't want to talk about it anymore."

Brady jabs at the radio button and turns up the volume, but I can't hear the music over the echo of his question repeating in my ears.

Do you even want it to?

Do I?

An answer starts to form that makes my stomach cramp, but I force it away. It's just fear talking. It's just selfishness. It's not real.

Of course, I repeat to myself. *Of course I want it.*

How could I want anything else?

When my phone rings, I check the time on the stove.

I have fifteen minutes until dinner is ready. My uncle never calls for small talk, so the conversation should be quick. I take a seat at the kitchen island and answer.

"Uncle Wade, hey."

"Aurora. How are you?"

I can't help but grin at his familiar, all-business tone. My uncle is about as personable as a boulder, but he's still one of my favorite people.

"Great. How are you?"

"Good."

"What country are you in right now?"

"America."

"Oh," I say with a laugh. "This is a long break for you guys."

Uncle Wade works as the manager for a popular band called The Hometown Heartless. I never know where he is in the world, but the band's taken some time off recently. I'm not used to him being in one place for so long.

"It has been, but we'll be touring again soon."

"Oh? Where to?"

"You mean you haven't been keeping tabs on me?"

I can hear a hint of playfulness in his voice. It's rare, but he's always had a smile for me.

"I've no time to keep up with your jet-setting ways, Sawyer Wade Hammond," I joke, mimicking my mother's tone. "My life may not be as glamorous as yours, but I've been quite busy."

"Ah, you're writing again?"

The question is like a zap of static electricity. Not sharp enough to hurt—not physically, anyway—but I still wince.

"You know I'm not."

I can tell he hears the shame in my whispered words because he backs off and changes the subject. I'm grateful for it.

"Heartless are headed to Australia and New Zealand at the end of the month to kick off the tour for the new album."

I screw up my lips, trying to recall anything about the band's new music. Not that long ago, I'd have known everything about The Hometown Heartless, but they've fallen off my list of interests in recent years. I've had to prioritize other things.

"That sounds like fun. I've always wanted to visit Australia. Quokkas are so cute."

"Well, now you can."

I arch a brow. "Now I can what?"

"Visit Australia."

"How?"

"I have a proposition for you."

"Okay?"

My eyes narrow in question, and I sit up straighter. A proposition that would allow me to visit Australia? I'm intrigued, despite knowing I shouldn't be.

My attention darts to the timer on the stove, then out the kitchen window to the empty driveway. Brady isn't home yet, but my next sentence still comes out quieter, almost conspiratorial.

"What kind of proposition?"

"My lead singer's daughter tours with the band and does all her schooling online, but the high school courses have become more challenging. English is her worst subject, so Savannah is looking for a tutor."

A pause stretches between us, and when my uncle doesn't elaborate, I prod.

"What does that have to do with me?"

"I'm offering you the job."

My brows rise as I drop my attention to the island countertop, possibilities sparking in my mind. I've always wanted to travel. I had a savings account and a rough plan to go backpacking through Europe after college, but as with most things I used to want, the urgency and importance have dulled. The money has been repurposed, and the dream has been set on a metaphorical shelf to collect metaphorical dust.

"I've never taught before," I say absently, tracing my fingertip along the gray veining in the white marble.

"Brynn will be easy."

"I have no experience with high school kids."

"She's twelve."

My eyes widen. "She's *twelve*? And taking high school courses?"

"Ninth-grade English and literature courses. She's very bright for her age."

"Sounds like it. I don't have experience with twelve-year-olds either."

"She'll be easy," Uncle Wade repeats. "She's a hard worker. She studies. She wants to succeed."

I fall silent once more, toying with the offer despite the impracticality of it. I did some tutoring in college. Never anyone under eighteen and never ninth-grade material, but I was good at it. I enjoyed it. I'd be using my degree, too, sort of. It's not how I'd originally wanted to use it, but still. Literature is relevant.

"How long?" I ask, letting myself entertain the fantasy further.

"Thirty-two shows between five cities. Melbourne, Adelaide, Sydney, Brisbane, and Auckland. We spend roughly ten to twelve days in each city. It's eight weeks of touring total."

I jerk upright. "Eight weeks? I can't...I can't leave for eight weeks."

"Why not?"

I shoot from my chair and start to pace. "Well, Brady needs me here."

"Brady is an adult capable of taking care of himself, Aurora."

"We just got married, Uncle Wade."

"You could come home every other week. He could come visit you. You wouldn't have to be without each other for long periods. You should discuss it with him."

"That wouldn't work," I say with a shake of my head. I almost laugh at the idea of Brady taking time off work. "I can't."

"Why not?" Uncle Wade asks again.

"Because."

"Because *why*, Aurora?"

I huff but don't answer, so he continues.

"Because *you* don't want to do it? Or because you think Brady wouldn't want you to? If it's the latter, you won't know unless you discuss it with him."

I open my mouth to respond, but then I bite my tongue and swallow back the answer to his first question. Regarding the second...Well, just the thought of discussing this with Brady has my forehead creasing with worry. I can't tell Uncle Wade that, though. He's already not fond of my husband.

I could just tell him no and end it, but for some reason I don't. A simple *no* isn't good enough for me, I guess, and I'm not sure if it's to convince my uncle or myself. Instead, I run through other excuses in my head, each one sounding more ridiculous than the last. I don't want to fall behind on laundry? I don't own real luggage? I've got nothing to wear? My husband is in a rush to get me pregnant? The last one creates a sinking feeling in my stomach.

Traveling will be so much harder after I have a baby.

I stop at the window and look out at my garden, running my eyes over the colorful blooms. When we bought this house, the small plot of land was my favorite part, and over the last year, I've turned it in to something beautiful. Then I move my gaze to the potted orchid on the shelf in the living room. It's the only greenery I'm allowed to keep in the house. Of all the reasons I've considered, this is the one that hits me the hardest.

"My flowers will die."

"Couldn't your husband—"

"No," I say with a huffed laugh. "He definitely couldn't."

Brady in the dirt with the bugs? No. I couldn't trust him to water them, let alone do all the other things necessary to keep the plants healthy and thriving. Even in my imagination, the image is comical.

"Savannah will be paying you enough that you could hire a gardener."

The statement penetrates my thoughts and piques my curiosity before I can stop it.

"How much would she be paying me?" I cringe and shake my head. "Actually, don't tell me. I don't want to know."

"Aurora."

"Uncle Wade. Leaving the country for eight weeks is just not feasible for me right now."

He inhales and exhales deeply. "Aurora, forgive me if this comes off as an overstep—"

"Never stopped you before," I grumble, but he continues.

"—but I've watched you put everything you love on hold."

"We've only just gotten married, and marriage takes compromise."

"Compromise? And what has Brady compromised?"

"It's only been eighteen months," I snap. "After he gets established at work, it will be different."

"I'm not just talking about the eighteen months you've been married, Aurora, and you know it."

Despite his even, calm tone, the words still make me flinch. I'm twenty-three years old, yet he still has the power to make me feel like a scolded child. I grit my teeth and push through the shame.

"With all due respect, I am an adult, and my decisions no longer require your input. I don't need it or want it."

The last time we had a disagreement like this was when Brady proposed, and it went much the same way. Uncle Wade expressed his disapproval, and I told him that his opinion didn't matter; I was going to do what I wanted, regardless. This time, though, I hold back the reminder that he's *just* my father's brother and not my father. The memory of the hurt that flashed over his face is enough to have me biting my tongue as I brace myself for his retort.

Thankfully, before our conversation escalates into an argument, the timer on the stove goes off and releases me from the uncomfortably charged silence stretching between us. I crane my neck so I can look out the window, and sure enough, Brady's car is pulling in.

"I'm going to have to let you go. I'm sorry for snapping at you. I know you're only looking out for me."

He sighs. "You don't have to apologize for saying no, Aurora. I always want you to stand up for yourself, though I do wish you'd show the same tenacity when it comes to conversations with your husband."

My jaw drops, and I lower my voice to a whisper as I hear the garage door open.

"I didn't ask for your judgment."

"It's not judgment, Aurora."

"Auri, what's burning?" Brady's voice calls from the mudroom, and it startles me into action.

"Sorry, Uncle Wade. Love you. Bye."

I hang up, drop my phone to the counter, and rush to the oven. I'm pulling the lasagna out just as my husband steps into the kitchen. I set the dish on the stove and turn to him with a smile.

"Sorry. Some of the cheese dripped, but it's not burnt," I say before he can ask again, then I cross the floor and let him wrap me in a hug. "Welcome home."

Brady presses a kiss to my head before pulling away.

"I'm sure it will be amazing. I'm going to go change."

He leaves me to plate up our dinner while he changes out of his suit. Brady started at the tech startup company just before we got engaged, and he's already been promoted twice. If he stays on this trajectory, he could be a junior partner in the next three years.

He comes back into the kitchen as I'm filling water glasses, and he tells me about his day as we eat. When he asks about my day, it's on the tip of my tongue to tell him about my phone call with Uncle Wade. I almost do, but for some reason, I stop myself.

I turned the job offer down. There's no point in bringing it up, especially if it will increase the tension between the two most important men in my life. I miss the days when they got along. Back when Brady was just my friend and Uncle Wade was just my uncle. Back when things were easier. When the path forward was clearer, and I didn't feel so...*tethered*.

"Are we in the window?"

I blink out of my thoughts and look back at Brady. "Hmm?"

"Are we in the window? You ovulate this weekend, right?"

"Oh. Right." I take a sip of my water, then nod. "Yeah, we should be in the window."

"Great." He grins at me as he stands. "I'll clear the table. You go get ready."

I nod again, then head into our bedroom without a word.

I brush my teeth and strip out of my clothes, but instead of climbing into bed like usual, I go a little further. Just entertaining my uncle's proposal has left me feeling guilty, like I've betrayed my husband in some way, and this is the least I can do to make up for it.

I cover my skin with scented lotion, tear the tags off the silk nightgown he bought me for my birthday, and then pull it over my head. I swipe some red-tinted balm over my lips and give my cheeks a pinch to bring out a natural-looking blush. I fluff my hair, adjust my bangs, then survey myself in the mirror.

I look pretty—sexy, even—and it has my mouth curving into a genuine smile. I don't feel sexy often, if ever. Most days, my hands and clothes are covered in dirt from being in the garden. Most nights, being intimate with Brady is a clinical responsibility. It's like getting your car's oil changed or visiting the gynecologist. *Sexy* isn't useful or practical or necessary. But right now, I have to admit it feels good.

I glide my hands down my sides then back up, the smooth silk feeling sensual under my palms. My eyes flutter shut when my fingertips brush the underside of my breasts. My nipples harden, and I ghost my thumbs over the sensitive peaks.

Yes. This definitely feels good.

My pulse quickens as I run my hand back down my torso, stopping at my pelvis and teasing the band of my panties beneath the fabric of the lingerie. In my mind, the fingers that slowly inch lower belong to someone else, and my inhale is shaky as I press on my clit. The touch is delicate and soft, so very gentle, but it's not my touch.

It's not Brady's either.

That realization has my eyes flying open just as the bedroom doorknob twists, and my hands jerk to my sides. I whip around and face him as he steps into the bathroom.

His eyes heat as he drags them over me. It's been a while since I've seen that look on his face.

"You look hot."

My cheeks warm with a mixture of shame and arousal.

"Thought I'd try something new for you."

"I'm not complaining." He shrugs out of his shirt and pants, his penis already hard as he bares himself to me. "You can leave it on if you want."

I take a few calming breaths before following him to the bed. I lie down, and he crawls on top of me. His kiss is rough, the stubble on his chin and upper lip scratching my skin as he drags his mouth to my shoulder. I'll have a rash again.

"Try to come this time. It's supposed to help."

"It's not like I can just make myself come."

My husband pushes up onto his arms and looks down at me. "I read that it's mostly mental for women. Can't you just, like, *think* about coming?"

"Brady," I say on an awkward laugh. "You want me to manifest an orgasm?"

He grins. "Sure."

My brow furrows.

"Maybe you could...um..." I wiggle beneath him, heat rushing to my cheeks once more. "Maybe you could touch me? It might help."

"Yeah, I guess." He takes off my panties and settles between my legs. "Damn, Auri, you're already wet."

He sounds so pleased with himself as he presses more scratchy kisses to my inner thigh. I close my eyes and push down the guilt. He's right. I am already wet, but no matter how badly I wish it were, it's not because of him.

I try to stay present, try not to admit it to myself, but when Brady licks up my labia, swirling his tongue around my sensitive spot, it's not his mouth I'm picturing. Not his tongue or lips.

I try, I swear I do, but it's not him I see at all.

A voice inside me scolds that this is wrong—I shouldn't be picturing someone else when I'm with my husband—but I already welcomed the fantasy into my marital bed. I've opened Pandora's box, and I can't figure out how to close it again.

I grip my breasts and picture a different pair of hands.

I move my hips and picture rubbing myself on a different mouth.

And when I come, it's not my husband's head I imagine clamped between my thighs.

"Hell yeah, Auri."

Brady's deep, rumbling voice has my breath catching in my chest, shame washing over me, tensing my muscles. He lets out a celebratory whoop as my chest heaves, whispers of panic causing my stomach to flip.

"That's what I'm talking about." He notches himself at my entrance and pushes in swiftly. He drops onto his forearms and moves to take my lips, but I turn my head, so he buries his face into my shoulder instead. "God, yes, you're so wet for me."

He pumps as I attempt to breathe through my anxiety. I dig my fingers into his back, keep my mouth locked shut, and focus my stare at the ceiling. I don't trust myself to close my eyes again. I don't trust myself to do anything other than lie here until he's finished.

When Brady groans his release, I let loose a slow, shaky exhale and plaster on a smile.

"That's the one." He pulls out and plants a sloppy kiss on my cheek, then slaps my ass as he stands from the bed. "That's the one. I know it."

I don't move as he picks up his discarded shirt and wipes off his softening penis. When he smiles at me, I make myself smile back. I'm happy. I should be happy.

He checks his watch. "Fifteen minutes. You have to stay still for fifteen minutes. Let gravity do its thing."

I give him a thumbs-up. "Fifteen minutes. Got it."

"And I didn't miss tip-off!" Brady claps his hands once, bounces his eyebrows, then hurries out of the room.

I listen intently for the television. When sounds of sportscasters and bouncing basketballs filter down the hall, I sit up quietly and rush into the bathroom. Once I've peed, I clamp my eyes shut and fight back the sting of tears. My shame for what I've just done mixes with the sense of foreboding summoned by Brady's words.

That's the one.

I *should* be happy. Excited, even. This could be what we've been wanting. What I *should* be wanting. I should be excited, but I'm not. Not even a little bit.

In fact, I'm dreading it.

And not only am I so very *not* excited about a possible pregnancy, but the only time I've managed a real orgasm with my husband was because I was pretending he was someone else. Not the man I'm supposed to love and spend the rest of my life with. Not the man who wants to be the father of my children.

He deserves better. I'm a terrible wife.

The more I think about it, the more I start to spiral. Fear creeps in, seizing my body. My skin stretches and itches. My fingers tremble. My chest tightens as my breathing grows shallow. I begin second-guessing every decision I've ever made.

How did I get here? Is *here* where I want to be? Am *I* who I want to be?

Is any of this what *I* want?

It's about compromise, is all. We've only been married for eighteen months. It will get better. Marriage is all about compromise. I'm happy. I am. It *will* get better.

I have to beat back the memory of Uncle Wade's voice. *What has Brady compromised?*

No. I shake my head and attempt to take slow, deep breaths.

Brady loves me. He's always loved me. I love him.

I love him. I love him. I know I do.

It will get better.

I sit on the side of the tub and drop my head between my knees. I do my best to calm myself, but the walls continue to close in. The house, my life, this marriage—it all shrinks around me. Confining me. Trapping me. Suffocating me.

I love him. He loves me. I'm happy.

I'm suffocating.

Before I can overthink it, I sit upright and rush for the first lifeline that comes to mind. The first and only ray of hope in the thick, impenetrable darkness. I grab my phone, open a text thread, and send a message to my uncle.

ME

I'll do it. When do you leave?

2

MABEL

"Do you have to leave?"

I roll over and wrap my arms around Kat's waist.

"I was really looking forward to you coming with us. I'm going to be lonely without you."

She laughs and lies back down on the bed, turning to face me.

"I'll see you in Auckland."

"That's too far away." I poke my lip out in a pout, bringing a smile to her face. "What if you stay for a few more hours? Have coffee with me, at least. It will help soothe the ache of you bailing on our trip last minute."

My girlfriend's smile turns sympathetic. "You know I can't. I've got the event. I have to get to glam."

"The event with Kaz?" I try to keep the jealousy out of my voice, but the look on Kat's face tells me I did a shit job.

"Yes, with Kaz."

I purse my lips and nod slowly. Of course. She spends more time with him than she does with me, and while I know it's not the same, I can't help but feel envious at how open they can be. Kat and Kaz can grab coffee or attend premieres together, and it doesn't have to be a secret. Not like with me and her.

"Don't do this." She leans over and kisses me. "I was looking forward to Australia, too, but I can't turn down this brand event. I was lucky my manager could get me in. In a few weeks, I'm all yours again."

I release a slow breath and bounce my eyes between hers. She's got these dark brown eyes, so dark they almost look black, and impossibly long, full eyelashes. I run my gaze over her face, taking in each feature. It's no wonder she's a model. It's like she's molded from clay.

"Okay, you're right. I'm sorry." I kiss her again, then release her. "Have fun at your event. Laugh and smile for the cameras. Charm everyone. Then soon, you're mine again."

I watch as she climbs out of my bed and gets dressed, then shoves her long black hair into a baseball cap and slides on a giant pair of sunglasses. The extra precautions make me want to roll my eyes, but I don't. I'm just bitter, is all. It's important that she isn't spotted. I get it.

Just before Kat leaves, she turns that cover model smile on me. "See you soon."

I force a smile back. "I'll miss you."

"It's not that long," she says in a singsong voice. "It will be here before you know it."

Then she lets herself out of my bedroom. I listen as she moves through my house. The door to my garage opens and shuts, and soon, I get a notification that my private gate has opened.

If I check the security stream on my phone, I'll see the dark car pulling out of my driveway with Kat sequestered behind tinted windows in the back seat.

I'm alone again.

Aside from my band members and close friends, Kat's bodyguard might be the only other person who knows the extent of our relationship. That was going to change if she came on this trip with us, and I had Hammond draw up a non-disclosure agreement months ago just to make Kat feel safe. The crew, the Caveat boys, and everyone else coming on tour have already signed them, but maybe it wasn't enough.

Maybe Kat is bailing because she's still not ready for more people to know about us.

We've been off and on for three years, but as far as the world knows, we're barely acquaintances.

That's all I can think about as I get dressed in the silence and make a toffee latte. This espresso machine is one of the few luxuries I've splurged on outside of the necessities. Necessities being the house close to the rest of my band, my car, my drum set, and the occasional accessory for award shows and appearances. I have no issue dropping money on gifts, either, but most of my personal wardrobe is thrifted or discount brand, and I bargain shop literally everything else.

Kat makes fun of me, but I spent eighteen years counting pennies just to survive. After over a decade, it's a mindset I still can't kick. She grew up with an investment banker father and an actress mother. Frugality isn't in her vocabulary.

The espresso machine, though? I have yet to regret it.

I do a quick check of my email, and aside from an updated schedule from Ham, there's nothing of note. Except for the unopened message I have pinned to the top of my inbox, but I've been avoiding that one. My eyes stick on the bolded name of the sender, and the longer I stare, the more anxious I become, despite having a pretty good idea of what it says.

Something along the lines of, *hello...we've tried to reach you via phone...please contact us at...*

No, thanks. Not yet.

I sigh and shut my laptop with zero intentions of opening it again until tomorrow morning, then head to my studio space. Another big expense that I do not regret.

I take a seat behind my kit and pick up my sticks. I don't bother with backing tracks. I just close my eyes, create a beat in my mind, and play until the only thing left is the music.

Sav's house is a hive of activity when I let myself in the front door, and the tension in my body lessens the moment I'm hit with the noise.

Her house is never quiet. It's *never* been quiet where Sav is. She's always buzzing with energy, and for someone who hates being alone—who feels her skin start to crawl the moment silence descends—Sav is the most welcome kind of chaos.

I release a sigh of relief and start to kick off my shoes, then I'm nearly bowled over by her troublemaker of a dog.

Chaos. Always.

"Good God, Ziggs." I drop to my knees and give her some scratches while her whole body wags along with her tail. "You are such a menace, aren't you, you big moose. Yes, you are! You're a big lovable pain in the ass."

"Oh, you're talking to Ziggy. I thought the Caveat boys were here." I glance up and find Brynnlee, Sav's fiancé's daughter, smirking down at me. "Although you said lovable, so I guess I should have known."

I laugh and push to standing. Sav's soon-to-be stepdaughter is nothing but sass and snark these days. Twelve going on sixteen. I find it entertaining, but I know it's not always the case for her parents.

"You ever think you're too hard on them?" She curls her lip, and I laugh louder. "Okay. Point taken."

"Honestly, I don't mind Rocky and Beckett. Heck, even Crue is tolerable most of the time."

"But Ezra," I say knowingly as I follow her into the house.

"But Ezra," she says with a sigh, her voice matter-of-fact in her assessment. "He's the most irritating and immature person I've ever met."

I don't get a chance to respond because it's travel prep mode the second I step into the living room. Sav's on the phone giving orders to someone. Torren is loaded up with two duffel bags and two rolling suitcases, and Jonah is standing at the kitchen counter, cutting up some fruit for the two-year-old strapped into a booster seat beside him.

Torren glances at the door, then at me. "Kat outside?"

I force a smile and shake my head. "Nope. Something came up last minute. She'll meet us in Auckland."

I don't miss the sympathy in Torren's eyes or the complete *lack* of surprise. Everyone probably saw it coming but me. I'm grateful when he changes the subject.

"Your stuff loaded?"

"Already at the airfield."

He laughs. "Should have guessed. You're always the first ready."

"Hey, I only have to worry about me. I don't have to wrangle and pack for any significant others, kids, or pets."

"I miss those days."

"Liar."

He winks at me, then lugs the baggage out the door, so I join Jonah in the kitchen. Teddy, his daughter, is all smiles, with a face covered in goop. I give her some love, careful to miss the mess, then snag a grape from the bowl in front of Jonah.

"No Kat?" he asks.

I ignore his question and pop the grape in my mouth, then nod to the food-wearing two-year-old.

"Snack time?"

"First dinner."

"First dinner is my favorite dinner."

He gives his daughter some grapes just as Sav joins us. She plants a kiss on Teddy's head, making her giggle that adorable baby giggle, and then she turns her mischievous smile on me.

"Ham's going to meet us at the jet. He had to pick up his *niece* from the bus station."

My eyes go wide. "His niece? Why?"

"She's the tutor he found for Brynn."

"No shit." I bounce my eyes between Jonah and Sav. "We get to meet the mysterious niece?"

Jonah nods. "I'm surprised he's letting her come, considering Caveat Lover is touring with us."

Hammond's always been protective of his niece. So much so that we know very little about her. When we were first starting out, he'd leave to visit her several times a month. Then it transitioned to only holidays and touring breaks. I don't know when or if he's gone to see her recently, though. Not in the last year, at least.

"Those boys will learn quick," I say on a laugh. "Ham's nowhere near as tolerant of their shit as he was with you and Tor."

"Because he knew we were joking when we asked about her. Tor and I never would have"—Jo stops and flicks his eyes to Teddy before continuing—"*messed with* our manager's niece."

I can't help but smile at the way Jonah censors himself so he doesn't cuss in front of his daughter. It's adorable and vastly different from the guy he was just a few years ago. I always knew Jonah was a nurturer, but I can't say I ever thought he'd become a family man. Having seen him at his worst and struggle for over a decade, it's a really beautiful thing to witness.

"You sure about that?" Sav teases with an arched brow. "I don't remember you being very selective about who you *messed with*."

"Positive. Even when I was at my lowest, I respected Hammond too much. Torren did too."

"Wouldn't say the same for Ezra and Crue, though," I add.

"Beck and Rock are probably fine," Sav says, and I nod in agreement.

"If anyone's going to try to make a move on the boss's pride and joy, my money's on Ezra."

"Not Crue?" Jonah asks while taking the cutting board to Sav's sink and washing it off. "He *fancies himself a Casanova.*"

Sav and I both laugh at his botched attempt at an English accent.

"That was a terrible impression. You sounded like a leprechaun," Sav says.

Jo narrows his eyes at her, but then Claire comes into the kitchen and wraps her arms around his waist. The irritation melts from his features, and his expression goes all lovey-dovey. It always does when she's around.

"A leprechaun?" Claire tilts her head up to smile at him. "Were you mocking Crue's accent again?"

"He tried and failed."

Jo starts to flip me off but catches himself and puts his hand behind his back. Can't have Teddy learning how to flip people off at the ripe age of two. It makes my grin widen, and I stick my tongue out at him, then turn to Claire.

"We were talking about which Caveat boy is likely to make a pass at Ham's niece first."

Her brow furrows. "Hammond's niece?"

"She'll be tutoring Brynn in English," Sav explains. "She's nice. Kinda quiet and nervous, but I'm used to that."

I smirk at her. "Because you're such a big, breathtaking star?"

She throws a grape at me. I yelp and bat it away, making Teddy giggle again.

"Aunt Sav is such a bully," I tell the baby, giving a marginally clean spot on her forehead a little boop, then I look back at Sav. "That's why I'm the favorite."

"*Anyway*," she says with a dramatic sigh, trying like hell to suppress a smile. She likes to act like she's annoyed, but she's not. "I talked to her a few days ago just to go over expectations and stuff. She seems legit. Has a degree in English lit and creative writing."

"Where'd she go to college?"

Sav shrugs. "Does it matter? We didn't even finish high school."

I laugh. She's got me there.

"I still feel bad that I can't help," Jonah cuts in.

Sav turns to him. "Jo, you've been great. You did so much

more than you had to, but you've got a whole-ass kid now. You don't have time to tutor Brynn, and you shouldn't have to."

"What else do you know about her?" Claire asks.

"Not much, honestly. Her name is Aurora. She's twenty-three and fresh out of undergrad."

"Twenty-three? She's practically a baby." I always forget that Hammond's only in his early forties. He looks young, but he acts much older. I grab the last grape out of Jonah's bowl and shake my head. "We definitely need to keep her away from Ezra and Crue. We can't let them corrupt her."

Sav smirks just as Torren walks into the kitchen. "Who would have thought we'd become the mature, responsible ones?"

Tor throws his arm over my shoulder. "Not me."

"Not me," I chime in.

Jonah laughs. "I thought I'd be dead by now, so I definitely didn't see it coming."

I raise my brows and nod slowly. "I hear no lies."

We all were worried about Jonah for a while. We came close to losing him for good more than once. I shoot Claire a soft smile, and she returns it. We don't talk about it much, but we all know she saved him. I don't think anyone else could have done it but her.

Just before we climb into the SUVs to head to the airfield, Claire sidles up beside me and bumps my arm with hers.

"I'm sorry Kat couldn't make it. I know you were looking forward to it."

"What did Sav tell you?"

"Nothing, but Kat's not here, so I made an educated guess. Was I wrong?"

"No, you're not wrong." I sigh and attempt to force the disappointment from my voice. "It's fine, though. Her manager got her an invite to a launch party for a new makeup line. She wants to be a brand ambassador for them, so she couldn't turn it down."

I leave out the part that she'll be attending on the arm of

Hollywood heartthrob Kaz Storm. It goes without saying, though. If it's a public event, you can bet money that they'll be there together. Kaz and Kat, America's favorite celebrity "couple." The media loves to speculate about them. Are they dating or aren't they? Will they or won't they? The masses love them, and I admit that they photograph well together. Even if it sucks.

Claire gives me a small smile. "Well, that's good for her. I hope she gets the ambassadorship. Will she be meeting us after?"

"Not until Auckland."

She hums, her next words full of positivity. "We'll see her soon, then."

"Yep. Soon."

Claire climbs into one of the seven-seater SUVs with Jonah, Teddy, Callie, and Torren, while I get into Sav's SUV with her crew. It doesn't take long before the dark cloud surrounding my mood lifts. It's hard to be sad when you've got a sixty-pound menace of a dog snoring in your lap and your best friend cracking jokes beside you. By the time we're pulling up to the airfield, the disappointment of Kat's absence has been effectively pushed to the back of my mind. It will no doubt creep back to the forefront tonight when I'm alone, but right now it's family time.

"You sure you want to fly with them?" Brynn casts an annoyed glance at Callie's bandmates as they board their jet. The label has been chartering one for them now that they're too popular to fly commercial. And by *the label*, I mean Sav. "It's sixteen hours. You're going to go all smooth-brained from lack of stimulation. It might even liquefy and leak out of your ears."

Callie laughs as Torren pulls her carry-on from the SUV. "I used to travel the country in a van with them, Boss. I can handle a private jet."

"Yeah, but you didn't have any other options before. Now you have us."

"She's not wrong," I say with a grin.

"Well, I can't write another award-winning album if I don't spend time with my band, can I?"

Brynn arches a brow. "I *meeeean*, you won't know until you try. I believe in you."

"Goodbye, Brynnlee," Cal sings playfully before giving her a hug. "I'll see you in sixteen hours."

I throw my arm around Brynn and lead her to our jet. "You're stuck with me, kid."

"You're my favorite anyway."

I laugh. "Lies. Teddy's your favorite."

She doesn't bother denying it.

Just as we're getting to the boarding stairs, a car rolls up beside the SUVs and parks. It's Hammond, and Brynn slows her steps, her shoulders tensing.

"Think that's my new tutor?"

I can hear the nerves in her voice. "Yeah. You want to go say hi?"

She turns back to the jet quickly. "No, not yet."

"I heard she's nice, Boss. Sav says she's kind of quiet, though, so you might have to protect her from Ezra."

That perks her up, and she nods curtly. "You're probably right. Because those boys simply cannot be trusted."

"Speak the truth, girl."

I follow her up the stairs, then look at the car once more. Hammond is opening the door to the back seat, and I watch just long enough to see two feet in white ballet flats hit the tarmac, blue gingham fabric brushing mid-shin. A dress, I'm guessing. Before the tutor stands, I turn back around and step into the cabin.

White ballet flats and a blue gingham dress. Very Dorothy of Oz. I laugh and shake my head. I sure hope this girl has attitude. Otherwise, those Caveat boys will descend like winged monkeys.

Poor thing.

She's going to need all the help she can get.

3

AURORA

I STAND and stare at the two private jets looming intimidatingly before me.

Excitement and anxiety have been warring for control in my chest, but right now, anxiety is winning. Not for the first time since this whole thing started, I question my decision to come. Going on an international tour on a private jet with arguably the most famous rock band in the world? It was not, and has never been, on my bucket list.

I almost want to laugh. I'm without a doubt the *least* rock and roll person on this airfield. Even Uncle Wade is more rock and roll than me, and he doesn't wear anything except dress slacks and button-downs. I've never seen him in a pair of jeans. Ever. I'll probably stick out like a sore thumb the minute I set foot on that jet.

I tighten my grip on the planter in my arms and shift my weight in my ballet flats. It took nearly half an hour of scrubbing to get the dirt and grass stains from underneath my fingernails. I definitely should have worn something less...Well, less *this*. One look at me and it's obvious that I do not belong here.

I resist the urge to tug on the skirt of my dress as the last conversation I had with Brady swirls around in my head. At first, it didn't go well. The argument was heated. I cried. It was so bad that he slept on the couch for three whole nights. That alone was enough to make me want to walk it all back. I haven't slept without him in a long time, and everything about it left me feeling cold and lonely.

Days later, though, he hugged me and told me that he was sorry. He said I was right. I'd given up everything for him to follow his dreams, and it would be unfair to make me pass up this opportunity right now. The concession, the apology, had me soaring, but then his reasoning sent me right back down to Earth. I should do it now because after we have a family and he's promoted to partner, the opportunity will be gone.

He didn't say the quiet part, but he didn't have to. I heard it.

This is my *last chance* to travel. My *last chance* to use my degree. My *last chance* to have something that's *just mine*. To do something *for me*. After this, it's back to the pretty life he's planned for us, and the fact that scares me—makes me want to run away and never look back—fills me with guilt.

He loves me. I love him. I'm happy.

"I should go back," I say under my breath, and I can feel my uncle's eyes on me. "I think this was a mistake."

"Is that *you* talking, or is it fear?"

I glance at him. "Aren't they one and the same?"

"I don't think so. At least not the Aurora I know. The Aurora I know would be sprinting up those stairs with a smile on her face."

My eyebrows slant behind my sunglasses, and I look back at the jet. "That Aurora was young and fearless and naïve."

My uncle sighs, but I hear the smile in his voice when he replies.

"You're still young and fearless, Roar."

The old nickname turns the corners of my mouth up and succeeds in relieving some of the tension that's collected in my muscles.

"Young compared to you, maybe."

He narrows his eyes, but he doesn't comment on my teasing.

"Mistake or not, you're here now. Take a deep breath, square your shoulders, and get on that jet, Aurora Jade. You have a job to do."

"Did you just middle name me?"

My uncle gives me a ghost of a smirk, and then his face softens, taking on an expression that makes my brows jump. He looks so much like my father in this moment, and I hold my breath, prepping myself for something I know I won't like.

"She'd be proud of you. They both—"

"Don't."

I cut him off, my voice calm despite the screaming growing louder in my head. I move my eyes back to the jet and breathe through the ache his words conjured. Emotions I prefer to keep buried stir in my chest. I curl my toes in my flats and push my heels into the ground. My fingers twitch to reach for my necklace, but I tighten my grip on my planter instead.

"Just don't."

He's silent for only a few seconds before his stern, professional demeanor returns, and all traces of the loving uncle and grieving brother are gone. He checks his watch, and without another word, brushes past me. I keep my attention on his back as he walks up the jet stairs and disappears into the cabin, leaving me standing alone on the tarmac.

I close my eyes again and force myself back into the present, keeping the past in the past, where it belongs. Where it needs to stay.

"You're here now, Aurora," I whisper to myself. "Shoulders back. Chin up. On the jet we go."

I adjust the planter, take one last deep breath, then force my ballet flats to move until I'm stepping into the luxury interior of the private jet.

I do a visual sweep of the passengers inside. Each new yet familiar face spikes my pulse until I'm worried I'll pass out, and I avert my eyes quickly.

So much for the calm I'd cultivated.

I'm in a small, confined space with some of the most famous people in the world, and I'm a nervous wreck. When Sav Loveless, the lead singer of The Hometown Heartless, stands and approaches me, I have to bite the inside of my cheek so I don't gawk.

"Hi, Aurora. I'm Savannah. We spoke on the phone."

She sticks out her hand to shake mine as if this is just any normal introduction. As if she's just any normal person. *I* might be, but Sav Loveless certainly isn't. I'm still reeling from our phone call, but standing in front of her? It's surreal enough that all I can do is blink at her—for one breath, then two, then three—before I'm able to shake myself out of my trance.

Thankfully, she doesn't even blink at how I momentarily short-circuited. I'm sure she gets it all the time. I release my hold on my planter and mimic her gesture, forcing my hand out so I can take hers in a formal greeting. Her hand is small, but her grip is firm, and I don't miss the guitar string calluses on her fingers.

"Hi." I clear my throat. "Thanks for having me."

"Thank you for coming. You're really helping us out by being here, and we appreciate it. Let me introduce you to everyone before we have to strap in for takeoff."

"Sure. Thank you."

Sav turns to face the group, and when I do the same, I find all eyes on us. I want to shrink behind her, but I don't. I hug my planter to my chest and remind myself not to lock my knees.

"Guys, this is Aurora. She'll be tutoring Boss for a while. She just graduated college and has never traveled before, so help her out when you can. You know how overwhelming this whole thing can be."

"Wrap it up, Savannah, we've got to get in the air."

Sav arches a brow in the direction of my uncle, then gives him a saccharine smile and gestures in his direction with a sweeping palm.

"Aurora, you already know King Ham."

She curtsies, and I'm surprised by the urge to laugh. I have to hold my breath to keep it from slipping out. I recognize the way my uncle's eyebrow twitches. He's amused but trying to hide it. I was on the receiving end of that expression many times as a kid.

When Sav turns back to the rest of the cabin, Uncle Wade winks at me and makes his way to his seat. He knows I hate being the center of attention, so he's hurrying Sav along for my benefit, and I love him more for it.

"This is Torren King, Jonah Hendrix, Claire Davis, the little sleeping princess is Teddy, that bald giant is Red, the dog is Ziggy, this is my fiancé, Levi Cooper, and our daughter, Brynnlee—she's who you'll be tutoring—and Mabel Rossi is the one wearing sunglasses and big headphones because she finds us all insufferable on long-haul flights."

Brynnlee gives me a cautious smile before dropping her eyes to her lap, and weirdly enough, it makes me feel a little better. I think she's just as nervous as I am, so I decide to give her some space. I'll let her adjust to my presence before I bombard her with introductions and lesson plans. I need time to adjust, too. I wave hello to everyone else, giving each person a quick nod, but I let my eyes linger a little longer on Mabel, since she's sleeping and therefore the only one not looking back.

Of all the band members, her image is the clearest in my memory. Music videos, album covers, magazine rack displays. I even used to have a poster of the band on my bedroom wall. The drummer is never front and center, but she was always the first I saw. There's just something intriguing about her. Something that draws my eyes and my curiosity. Something that makes my stomach tighten and my heart kick up speed.

While everyone else is dressed down, Mabel looks ready for a photoshoot. Knee-high leather platform boots, fishnet tights, a distressed denim skirt, and a pink-and-black corseted top that shows off her tattoos.

My first thought is one of awe. She's so damn *cool*. It makes me feel even more out of place in my cotton dress and vegan leather ballet flats. Her black-and-pink hair is shiny and curled in loose waves, and I'd bet money that if I could see her eyes, they'd be winged with black liner. They usually are. I find myself wishing she weren't sleeping just so I could know for sure.

When my gaze drops to her plush, bright pink lips, she smirks, and my breath catches. I dart my attention to the ground in front of me and try my best not to burst into flames of embarrassment. Guess she wasn't sleeping after all. Now my heart is thrumming so loudly I can hear it in my head.

"Don't worry. I don't expect you to remember any of those names."

I blink out of my panic and nod awkwardly at Sav, then force a shaky laugh.

"Yes. Okay. Thanks."

"*Savannah.*"

Uncle Wade's voice mercifully serves as a stern reminder that we have to take off, so Sav dips her chin in his direction, then gives me a smile.

"Sit anywhere. We can chat later. Oh, and cool plant."

"Thank you."

Sav makes her way to a couch-type seating fixture on the side of the cabin with Levi and Brynnlee. Despite the open seat next to Mabel, I choose one of the empty chairs in front of her. I buckle quickly, then drop my head to the headrest.

Shoulders back. Deep breaths.

When the pilot announces that we're readying for takeoff, I move one of my hands to the armrest and dig my fingers into the plush leather. My intention was to watch out the window, but instead, the moment the jet starts to taxi, my eyes clamp shut involuntarily. The wheels rolling beneath me feel different than a car or a bus, and I immediately hate it.

I know what it means to fly. Yesterday, I was even excited for it. But it's no longer an abstract event now. It's real, and the fact that we're about to be air-bound suddenly has sweat dotting my hairline. Forty thousand feet above sea level in a tin can with wings is more terrifying than anything else has ever been. I should open my eyes to seek out the emergency exits or the oxygen masks or the life vests, but I can't. When the jet jostles slightly, I have to bite back a yelp.

It's official. I hate flying. This was a terrible idea.

"Rossi, sit down!"

"Sorry, Ham."

I hear my uncle mumble something about *grown fucking adults*, but then a body drops into the seat next to mine and all my attention zeroes in on it. My eyes fly open to find Mabel beside me. Her sunglasses are still on, but her giant headphones are around her neck.

"My first time flying was scary as fuck, too."

Her tone is kind, but her words float on a teasing lilt, and heat surges to my cheeks.

"What? No. I'm fine. I'm okay."

"Girl, I could see your hand white-knuckling the armrest from back there."

"Oh. I just..."

God, this is embarrassing. My face is on fire. Not only am I the least rock and roll person on this plane, but I'm also a giant baby. I try to force out an unbothered laugh, but it ends up sounding like a choked hiccup.

"I'm fine."

She smiles playfully. "Let's not lie to each other. Let's start our relationship on a foundation of truth."

There is no judgment in her voice, and it helps to dampen my embarrassment. I work to unclench my teeth and exhale slowly. Lying is useless, anyway. I'm a wreck.

"Right. Okay. Yes, I'm very nervous."

"It's okay to be nervous. Want to hold my hand? It might help."

She turns her hand over, so it's palm up in front of me. The offer makes my stomach flip, and on impulse I grip the armrest tighter.

"No. No, sorry, but no. That's okay. Thanks anyway."

She drops her hand back into her lap, and I can't help but follow the movement. Her nails are short and painted a dark, glittery black, she has a stack of gold and silver bracelets on her wrist, and a flashy pink diamond ring on her middle finger.

I bet her hand is soft. It looks like it is. I wonder if she has calluses like Sav. Surely, she would. She holds drumsticks for a living, and even though I know she wears fingerless gloves, the pressure from banging on the drums would still take a toll on her smooth, golden skin.

"I like your plant."

Mabel's voice startles me, and my eyes jump back to hers.

"What? I'm sorry. What?"

I can feel my cheeks heating once more. When the corners of her lips twitch, I glance away so I don't stare at them again.

"I said I like your plant. Orchid, right?"

I look at the planter in my arms and nod. I've barely let go of it since I left home.

"Phalaenopsis," I clarify, and then I wince. "Sorry, I mean yes. It's an orchid. A moth orchid. Phalaenopsis is the scientific genus. I always forget not everyone knows those." I laugh lightly at myself and run my finger over the smooth edge of the ceramic planter. "The family is Orchidaceae. It's one of the largest families of flowering plants. Over twenty-five thousand species, actually. That's through eight hundred or so genera—that's plural for genus—but this one, Phalaenopsis, is probably the most well-known. This particular plant is resting, but I'm—"

The jet picks up speed, stealing my words with my breath. I look quickly out the window, then shut my eyes once I see the world whooshing past in a blur.

"Oh, God."

"Breathe through it. It will be over fast."

"Think of England?" I say, forcing a joke to keep from doing what I want to do, which is whimper and squeak with every rotation of the wheels. And though I'm barely maintaining composure, Mabel's answering laugh gives me a small chill, anchoring me to the moment before I spiral into a full-blown meltdown.

"Exactly. Close your eyes and think of England."

I give her a small smile, but then the plane shakes violently, and my whole face scrunches into what I'm sure is a very unattractive expression of terror. Panic claws at my throat, and I reach desperately for Mabel, grabbing onto her forearm and holding tightly. She covers my hand with hers and speaks, her voice softer and closer than before.

"This is normal. It's the jet taking off and the wheels retracting. It's almost over."

"Are you sure?"

"Foundation of truth, remember? Only honesty here."

I jerk out a nod and try to focus on her thumb rubbing back and forth on my wrist. On her forearm under my palm. I knew she'd be soft. Soft and warm. Mentally, I zero in on each point of contact. I can feel the pads of her fingers—index, middle, ring, pinky—and the way they curve atop mine. The comforting weight of her touch.

I force a swallow and breathe until the jet has leveled out and the cabin no longer shakes.

"It's over now. When you're ready, it's safe to open your eyes."

I peek through my lashes until I'm brave enough to open my eyes fully, and then I turn my head toward Mabel.

"Sorry."

"What for?"

"Um...freaking out, I guess? Making you have to, um, *be here*."

She smiles curiously and scans my face, eyebrows slanting just slightly. "Babe, you don't have to keep apologizing. Not for this, and not for anything else."

I freeze.

She called me babe.

Mabel Rossi, drummer for the most famous band on the planet, called me babe.

My heart starts racing again, but this time it's not from fear. It's from...I don't even know. Something I can't analyze right now. My answering laughter is awkward, but I try to act like she didn't just make me dizzier with one little word.

One little word that means absolutely nothing.

"Oh. Right. Sorry. Thank you."

"Anytime." She leans forward, that small smile still affixed to her lips as she whispers to me, "And you don't have to apologize for apologizing, either."

Instinctively, I open my mouth to apologize again, but she arches a brow, and I snap it shut.

"Much better," she says, and her smile grows, stretching across her face and making her caramel-colored eyes crinkle at the sides.

I don't know when she took her sunglasses off, but I was correct in my earlier assumption. Thick black kohl lines her upper lids, flaring out into expertly drawn wings. She's calm, collected, and looks like she just stepped out of a magazine.

"Are you always this composed?"

The question slips from my lips before I can stop it, and my eyes widen. Thankfully, she laughs.

"Only when other people are around," she says, her voice low, like it's a secret. Her answer gives me pause, but then she turns on a charming smile that halts all deeper thought. "Hi. I'm Mabel."

"I'm Aurora."

"It's nice to meet you officially."

"You, too."

I realize as I look at her that there's green drawn under her lower lashes, giving her an almost ethereal appearance, and I find it difficult to look away. When my chest starts to tighten, though, I drag my attention back to my planter.

"You're getting some color back. That's a good sign. For a minute there, you were white as a ghost."

"Yeah, well, for a minute, I thought I might end up a ghost, so it's fitting."

Her musical laughter brings a small, pleased smile to my face, but I keep my eyes on my orchid. I don't trust myself not to make it weird.

Her thumb brushes over my wrist, reminding me that I'm still holding on to her, so I release her forearm and wrap my hand back around the planter. The ceramic cools my palms, but her warmth doesn't disappear. It sinks deeper into my skin.

"So anyway. The orchid."

"Hmm?"

"You were telling me about your orchid before takeoff."

"Oh. Right. My orchid."

I sit up straighter, grateful to be back in familiar territory. I can talk about plants. I'll just pretend she's one of the ladies from church and not some famous, gorgeous rock star, and it will be fine.

"So, this is Phalaenopsis, also known as a moth orchid. It's the most well-known of the orchids. This one will be pink when it reblooms. It was my mom's, but it's been resting...wait..." I turn to face her. "How did you know this was an orchid? There are no flowers. It's just stems and leaves."

Her smile quickens my pulse.

"I know a bit about orchids. I had a guardian who liked plants, and she loved orchids."

"A guardian?"

"Yeah."

"Not your parents?"

She arches a playful brow. "We getting personal already, Aurora?"

My eyes widen before I whip them back to my lap. "I'm so sorry. I didn't mean to—"

"It's fine. I'm kidding. No apologies necessary." She bumps my shoulder with hers. "I wasn't raised by my parents. I grew up in the system."

The system.

Foster care.

"Oh. That's nice." When she laughs, I cringe. "I didn't mean nice. I meant...Fine...Good? I don't know. I'm sor—" I catch myself before I apologize *again* and blow out a slow breath, willing the fuzz in my head to clear. "I'm not usually like this. I'm overwhelmed and tired, and the seats on the bus I took to Los Angeles made my neck sore, so I have a bit of a headache. And I think I'm hungry. And I'm overwhelmed. And tired. And, well, it's all making me more awkward than normal."

Not to mention her proximity and all the weird things *that* seems to be doing to me, too.

"Understandable. Luckily, these seats are much more comfortable than a bus, and they recline into beds." Mabel stands and steps into the aisle. "Get some rest. If you need anything, just ask. I'm right behind you."

She gives me one last smile, and then she disappears. When I take my first full breath since she sat down, I notice a floral scent lingering in her absence. I don't know how I missed it before. *Gardenia.* I inhale again, deeper this time, filling my lungs with the familiar scent. Gardenias love the Mediterranean climate out here, but they can be temperamental. They need specific conditions to thrive, so they're one of my favorite plants to grow. Every bloom feels like a reward.

My eyes fall to my orchid, and my stomach does another little flip. There are no blooms, but Mabel still knew what it was.

I know a bit about orchids.

My lips fight to curve into a small, strange smile. I shift in my seat. She didn't interrupt me when I started to ramble, either. And her touch was soft. Her skin was warm. She called me babe. She was so...so...

"Here."

I jump with a gasp, and Mabel laughs, holding something out to me.

"I didn't mean to scare you. I brought you these since meal service isn't for another hour."

I focus my attention on her outstretched hand. "Shortbread cookies?"

"Do you not like shortbread?"

"No, I do. Sorr—"

She arches her eyebrow again, halting the word before I can finish saying it. I bite my tongue, then fold my lips between my teeth before altering my response.

"I do like shortbread."

"Much better," she teases, then wiggles the package.

"Thank you."

I take the cookies, and when I look back to her face, that curious smile is back, and her caramel eyes sparkle in the soft cabin lighting. They look like amber gemstones. When my skin starts to tingle, I look away.

"You're welcome," she says finally. "There should be a blanket and pillow under the seat if you'd like to sleep."

Then she leaves me once again.

My exhale is audible as I drop my head back to my seat. I need to get it together before I make a fool of myself. I have no idea what's going on in my head, but whatever it is, it feels too obvious.

I stare at the ceiling for several breaths before I'm ready to move again. Gently, I place my orchid in the seat beside me, and then I open the cookies. They're just cookies, but for some reason, that weird smile returns as I bring one to my mouth. I take a bite, the corners of my lips twitching with the need to grin wider, and I let out a quiet laugh.

My anxiety is nearly gone, but the nerves swirling in my stomach persist. They feel different, though. Now they almost tickle instead of ache.

Now they almost feel like butterflies.

4

MABEL

MY BODY ACHES with exhaustion as I climb out of the rented SUV and walk into the hotel.

The Heartless jet is as comfortable as they come, but the flight from Los Angeles to Melbourne is always killer. I need a shower and a bed ASAP, and from the look of everyone else, I'd say they're in the same boat. The *I need at least forty-eight hours to feel human again* boat. I'm so grateful we don't play until Thursday.

My eyes rise to find Hammond's back as he leads us through the lobby and toward the elevator. My clothes are wrinkled, my hair is mussed, and I'm certain my makeup is smudged despite the touchup I did before deplaning, but Ham looks fresh as a spring daisy. Sixteen hours on a plane and not even his bespoke slacks have creases, let alone his suit jacket. I'm sure his beard is still perfectly manicured as well. Sorcery, I swear.

Then my attention falls to the woman beside him. *Aurora.* She's a curious thing, wearing her blue gingham dress and clutching that white porcelain planter. Replace the planter with a small dog, and she'd look like she was on her way to Oz. Fitting, actually, considering the situation.

I remember Ham saying once that she's his brother's daughter, and while Aurora's hair is blonde to his brown, I can still see the family resemblance. Apparently, the family has some good genetics in the appearance department. They have the same hazel green eyes. The same full lips. The same high cheekbones.

But where Ham's face could be carved from marble for how little his expression changes, Aurora's plays out like a film reel. I've never seen so many emotions pass over a face in such quick succession until our brief interaction on the jet.

Fear. Shock. Excitement. Interest. Embarrassment.

The memory of how pink she turned has my mouth curving up at the corners. If she doesn't get that under control, teasing her will become Ezra Hawke's new favorite pastime. He's a shameless flirt, and I can tell Aurora would be fun to flirt with.

Stepping out of the elevator onto our private floor, Ham starts handing out our room assignments and keycards. Aurora is down the hall in her own room. Jonah, Claire and Teddy are in one. Sav, Levi, Brynn, Zigster, and Red are sharing a suite, and Callie is rooming with Torren despite the rest of Caveat Lover being on a separate floor.

Ham sent the boys ahead of us with their own security guards, and I have a feeling it was to prolong the inevitable introductions with his niece. I laugh to myself at the thought. I hope I'm around when they finally meet. It's sure to be entertaining.

I'm taking my keycard from Ham when Aurora comes walking back to him with hers, planter clutched to her chest just like it's been since LA. I let my eyes scan over her. Her dress is rumpled, the curls in her blonde hair have fallen flat, and her makeup has worn off almost entirely, but even in the dimly lit hotel hallway, she's pretty. Beautiful, even. Softer than before, less tense. Her nerves must have calmed some. Conquered by exhaustion, no doubt.

"Uncle Wade, can I ask you something?"

A ghost of a smile passes over Ham's face. "What do you need, Aurora?"

"Can I get a new room? East or south facing, preferably? I don't mind being on a different floor if necessary."

Ham's eyebrow lifts, his head tilting to the side slightly. "Care to tell me why?"

She hesitates and flicks her eyes to me. I smile, and she looks quickly back to Hammond.

"I need better lighting. My room is too dark. East or south facing, if possible. Please."

For her orchid, I realize. She needs better lighting for her orchid. I check the number on my keycard, then scan the hall for my door.

"Mine might work," I say, glancing back between the two of them. "I haven't been in it yet, though. Want to come check?"

Her hazel eyes grow wide, and she bounces them to me, then back to Ham. He shrugs.

"Check it out, Roar. If it's good for your plant, you can swap."

Roar.

I like that. I also like that Hammond knew her request was plant-related. Every time I learn something new about our manager, it's like picking at an outer layer of an onion. I know there's so much more to him—we've all seen glimpses of it in the years we've been together—but he's too good at playing a one-dimensional business drone ninety-eight percent of the time. Sometimes I almost forget he's human.

I look back to Aurora.

"C'mon. I'm over here."

She flushes pink, the contrast making her eyes sparkle, and she follows me to my room. I push open the door and make a sweeping gesture with my arm.

"After you."

She shuffles past, and my phone buzzes just as I shut the door behind me. I pull it from my skirt pocket to find a text from Kat.

KAT

I got the ambassadorship!

I smile immediately. She wanted this so badly, and it looks like her attendance at the event sealed the deal. Then my happiness mixes with guilt. I shouldn't have gotten so upset about it. It's her job, after all. She's never expected me to skip a show. I shouldn't have whined about her going to a brand event.

ME

I'm so happy for you! Was it fun?

KAT

So much fun. My dress was divine.

ME

Pictures?

When she doesn't answer, I swipe out of the text thread, open a browser window, and search her name. Within a fraction of a second, photos of my girlfriend fill the screen in a sexy, low-back, yellow dress and sky-high, glittery stilettos. She's right. The dress is divine, but the photos only sour my mood.

There's not a single photo without Kaz. Red carpets and posed pictures are bad enough, but even the candid ones are tainted by him. His hands never leave her body. Her waist, her arm, the small of her back, dipping into the fabric so his fingers are just above the curve of her ass.

How much lower did they slip when the cameras weren't flashing?

"This is perfect."

My ears tune in to Aurora's voice, but my eyes stay on the phone, doomscrolling through photos of my girlfriend being felt up by a man half the world probably wants to fuck. I'm not usually a jealous person, but I'm so full of jealousy right now that I can practically taste the acidity on my tongue.

"Right here. I can put it right here. It can see the sun, but—"

"The sun can't see it."

"That's right. How did you know that?"

I look up from my phone to find her gazing at me with wide eyes. The soft sunlight is filtering through the windows, making

42

her look almost angelic, and again, I'm hit with how pretty she is. Aurora is an attractive woman.

"My guardian liked plants, remember? She used to say that a lot. *You need to put it in a place where it can see the sun, but the sun can't see it.*"

"That's right," she says again. "Did your guardian have a name?"

I smirk. "She did."

Aurora folds her lips between her teeth, but humor dances in her expression as she fights a smirk of her own. "Too early to ask that, too?"

"I gave you an answer," I say coyly. "If you're looking for a different answer, ask a different question."

"Fair enough."

The words are carried on a tinkling laugh, and the smile she'd been fighting breaks through. A full-faced smile with straight white teeth and sparkling eyes that crinkle at the corners. Even her nose scrunches, and my stomach does a little flip that startles me.

Aurora is a *very* attractive woman.

I wipe the smile from my face, slide my phone back into my pocket, then nod.

"It's settled then. We'll swap."

Her amusement flickers. "Are you sure? The other room really is quite dim. It's in the shadow of the other hotel tower. I could ask Uncle Wade to find me something else so you don't have to give this one up. We're here for ten days. You should be in a room you enjoy."

"I like dim lighting," I say, and I can't help the smirk that curves my lips. "Better to hide my poor decisions." She laughs again, cheeks flushing, and I wink. "I'll tell Ham to reroute the bellhops when they deliver our things."

"Okay. Thank you."

"See you later."

I take one last glance at her, then let myself out, releasing a slow breath the moment the door shuts behind me.

I was right.

Aurora would *definitely* be fun to flirt with, and it's reminded me that I once had something in common with Ezra Hawke. I used to be a shameless flirt, too, and my brief interaction with Ham's niece has already lit a familiar spark of excitement in my chest. A spark I haven't felt in a long time.

I roll my shoulders and make it all the way to my new room before I realize I never swapped keycards with her. I look down the hall, but instead of heading back to her room to get it, I walk to Sav's.

I'll get another keycard from Ham later. Right now, I'm feeling a little off-balance, and the distraction of my best friend's chaos is just what I need to set me right.

"Wait. I thought we were doing a destination wedding."

I wrestle the slobbery rope toy out of Ziggy's mouth and toss it across the room.

"I can't keep up. First, it was a small beach wedding in North Carolina. Then it was destination in the Scottish Highlands. But now you're thinking of doing it in LA?"

Sav groans and drops her head to the couch just as Zigs bangs into my leg with the rope toy clamped between her jaws. I swear, this dog never knows if she wants to play fetch or tug-of-war, so I grab the driest part of the rope and pull.

"I know. I know. But we can't decide. North Carolina would be nice because Mom's there, and we could use the beach house, but"—she grimaces—"*sand.*"

I laugh and nod. Sav hates the beach, so as soon as she suggested a beach wedding, I knew it wouldn't stick.

"And the Scottish Highlands are gorgeous, but I don't know if I want to coordinate a destination wedding. It would be a pain in the ass."

I shrug and toss the rope across the room again. "It's not like you'd have to do the planning, though. You can hire someone."

"Yeah, I guess."

"What do you think?" I turn to look at Levi. "You're the groom. Do you have a preference?"

He shakes his head. "Nope. I'd do it anywhere. I'd do it right here, right now. I just want to marry her. North Carolina. Scotland. LA. Makes no difference to me."

I smile. "That's a good answer."

"He's no help," Sav says with mock irritation before blowing her fiancé a kiss. "There are pros and cons to all of them. Doing it in LA would be so much easier, but—"

"But then she'd feel obligated to invite everyone she knows," Levi cuts in, and Sav flares her eyes.

"But then there's that."

"Never thought THE Sav Loveless would have so many friends," I tease.

Sav smirks. "Upside of sobriety is that I'm not going to take a swing at someone or fuck their boyfriend while on a bender. Downside is that I'm now more approachable and passably kind."

"I hope I'm alive when they make your biopic." Brynn throws herself onto the couch and drops her wet head into Sav's lap. "It's going to be so messy."

"You weren't supposed to hear that." Sav laughs and shoves Brynn's shoulder. "Get off. Your hair is soaked."

Brynn sits up with a loud, dramatic sigh.

"You forget I used to sneak-read every article I could find about you."

"I didn't forget," Sav says, shooting a glare at Levi. "I just choose not to think about it."

Levi shrugs. "Trust me. I'd have stopped it if I'd known."

I laugh. They're lucky Brynn is a good kid. If she wanted to break a rule or ten, they'd never know. She's too smart, and if she ever decides to use those smarts for the wrong things, Sav and Levi are going to be so fucked.

"How's the pool?" I ask, looking from Brynn to Red and back. "You weren't there very long."

"Unwanted guests," Red says.

Sav shoots from her seat and heads straight for the hotel phone. "I'll call hotel security." Savannah puts up with the paparazzi hounding her, but when they bother Brynn, she goes all snarly momma bear.

"Not paparazzi," Brynn says. "Worse. Caveat boys."

"Oh." Sav exhales, and I watch as she transitions out of fight mode and slinks back into her usual, laid-back self. Sharp as razor blades to smooth as water. "Well, that *is* unfortunate."

"I left once Ezra and Crue decided to have a cannonball contest."

"Smart," I say with a nod.

"Actually, Boss, this is great. You can meet with Aurora now." Sav plops back onto the couch and grabs her cell phone from the side table. "I'll text her. Go hose off and get dressed."

Brynn groans. "Sav, do I have to?"

"Brynnlee." Levi's tone bucks argument. "Your courses start in a week. You can't put this off."

"I hate new people," she grouses.

Sav and I share a glance as we both force down the instinct to laugh, then I throw my arm over Brynn's shoulder, ignoring her wet hair.

"Aurora is pretty cool, Boss. You don't have anything to worry about."

"You talked to her? What's she like?"

An image of Aurora fills my head, and my stomach does another little flip. I catch my eyebrows just before they slant downward.

What's she like?

Every word that comes to mind seems inadequate for some reason. Like no matter what I say, it will fall short, and that makes me uncomfortable. Nervous in a way that mirrors guilt. But I shouldn't feel guilty. Aurora is attractive; there's no denying that.

A lot of people are attractive. My whole band is attractive. My bandmates' partners are attractive. I am *literally* surrounded by attractive people all the time. It's just a fact, and there's nothing wrong with objectively acknowledging a fact.

I've done *nothing* wrong.

"Mabes." Brynn's voice pulls me from my thoughts as her hand waves in front of my face. "Earth to Mabel."

"Yeah?" I force a smile, ignoring Sav's eyes. I don't want to see any assumptions in them.

"I asked what Aurora was like."

"She's..." I shrug. "She's interesting."

Brynn frowns. "Interesting?"

"Yeah." I shrug again. "Interesting. Nice. She's nice."

I almost want to laugh. Of all the words flying around in my head, *interesting* and *nice* are what I chose. They aren't enough, but I don't offer Brynn anything else. I bite my tongue, then stand from the couch.

"I'm heading back to my room. I'll see you guys later."

Sav doesn't throw any questions at me, and that's nerve-racking. She's too good at reading me, and right now, I don't want to be read.

"Be nice to your tutor, Boss."

Brynn rolls her eyes, but she's smiling, so with a wave to the room, I let myself out of the suite.

Then I run smack into Aurora.

The collision knocks us both off balance, her breath leaving her on an *ooof*. My hands wrap around her biceps, and she grips my waist, her fingers sinking into the exposed skin where my corset doesn't reach my skirt. I feel heat radiate out from her touch, covering every inch of my body, and when her eyes pop open, she lets out a little gasp that I feel on my lips.

"I'm so sorry. I didn't mean to...I didn't see you...I should have been watching—"

"You're good. I wasn't watching where I was going either."

I should let go of her, but I don't, and she doesn't let go of me either. She just stands there, hazel eyes bouncing between mine, mouth open just slightly, pink blush spreading from her cheeks to her neck to her collarbone.

"Did I hurt you?" she asks on a breathy whisper.

"You didn't hurt me." I brush my thumb over the soft, warm skin on her arm. "I don't think you could if you tried."

Her mouth curves into a small smile and her expression lights with humor as her nose does that cute little scrunch thing again.

"Are you saying I'm not intimidating?"

I shrug. "That might be what I'm saying."

"I could be." She narrows her eyes, lips twitching like she's trying to keep her smile from widening. "If I wanted to be."

"I'll believe it when I see it."

We stay frozen like this, currents of *something* passing between us, the eye contact making my pulse speed up. I've always been a sucker for eye contact, and it's gotten me in too much trouble in the past. Then loud laughter sounds from beyond the door to Sav's suite, and we break apart. My arms drop to my sides as hers fold across her midsection, and she makes it a point to look at everything in the hallway except for me.

"Anyway. So. Um. Sav texted, so..."

"Right. You're meeting Brynn." I take a few steps backward so I'm no longer blocking her from the door. "She's nervous, so take it easy on her."

Aurora lets out a breath of laughter. "No worries there. I'm nervous, too." She brings her eyes from the carpet to my face. "I don't have much experience with kids."

"Honestly, that's probably a good thing. Boss isn't like most kids."

She glances at the suite door and nods, inhaling deeply through her nose before exhaling slowly, her pink lips forming a perfect little O.

"Any advice?"

"Just be yourself." I smirk. "As long as you don't want to be intimidating, you should be fine."

Another tinkling laugh from her. Another stomach flip from me. Then she turns back to face me and locks her eyes with mine.

"Thank you."

"Anytime."

"Oh, I almost forgot." She pulls a keycard from a pocket on her dress. "Here. I didn't realize I had it until I was leaving to come here. Otherwise, I'd have found you sooner."

I take the keycard, careful not to brush her fingers with mine.

"Thanks, *Roar*."

She blushes. "My uncle is the only one who calls me that."

"Do you not like it?"

"No, it's not that. I just...Well, I guess it sounds different when you say it."

I quirk an eyebrow. "Different good or different bad?"

She traps her lips between her teeth again before slowly rolling them free. Then her eyes flit shyly back to mine, and she gives me a small, almost playful smile.

"I haven't decided yet."

A smile of my own stretches across my face.

"Well, when you decide, let me know." I take a few steps backward, down the hall toward my room. "And don't worry about Brynn. I think you two will get along just fine."

I take three more backward steps, holding her eye contact, and then I turn. When I reach my door, just before I step inside my new suite, I glance over my shoulder to find her watching me. On impulse, I wink, and as I shut the door behind me, I swear I hear that tinkling little laugh again.

5

———

AURORA

"How's it going so far?"

Brady's words echo through the hotel bathroom as I finish getting ready for bed. I recognize the familiar gruffness of his voice. It's his *tired* voice, and if I closed my eyes, I could almost imagine him here with me. He doesn't sound nearly eight thousand miles away.

"Good," I say. "I met Brynnlee, the girl I'll be tutoring. That went...Well, it went fine."

He yawns, and his words tumble out with it. "Just fine?"

"Yeah. I mean, I don't think she's excited to be tutored, but she wasn't rude or anything. Just a little standoffish at first, but she warmed up to me by the end."

I turn off the bathroom light and pad my way to the bed in semi-darkness. My body longs for sleep. I'm surprised I made it through the day, to be honest, but I read that napping makes jet lag worse.

"She's going to love you. How could she not?"

"Thanks." I pull back the duvet, climb into the soft bed, and sigh as my head hits the pillow. "I think we'll get along okay. I actually ate dinner in the suite with her and her family."

"How was that?"

"Weirdly *normal*. I don't know what I was expecting—caviar and thousand-dollar bottles of champagne or something—but we ordered Margherita pizza. If I hadn't been in the presence of a modern-day rock icon, it might have felt like any other random day."

"Sav Loveless." Brady draws out her name. "I had the biggest crush on her in high school."

"I remember," I say with a laugh. "You almost peed yourself when you found out Uncle Wade was her manager."

"I didn't *almost pee myself*."

"Mmhmm, sure."

He chuckles. "So what's the queen of rock like?"

"Gorgeous. Intimidating. Larger than life. You know how her voice kind of *vibrates* through the radio? Well, it's like that in person, too, except...I don't know...*more*. She speaks and you can almost feel it in your chest. But she's also really kind and surprisingly down to earth. She was nice when we talked on the phone and all, but I wasn't sure how she'd be in person. I was afraid she might be a snooty, stuck-up celebrity, but she's not at all."

"Your uncle wouldn't have brought you on to work for someone who was snooty and stuck-up, Auri."

"Yeah, that's true. But still. I was worried, anyway."

My husband hums, and I can hear coffee brewing on the other end of the phone. He had to wake up two hours early so he could talk to me right before I went to bed. The eighteen-hour difference is going to take some getting used to.

"What about the guys? Torren King and Jonah Hendrix. You going to leave me for one of those tatted, broody rock stars?"

The teasing tone in Brady's voice has me rolling my eyes as I snuggle deeper into my pillow. "I have no interest in those guys, B, and they have no interest in me."

"I doubt that. You're hot."

I snort out a laugh. "Torren King is engaged to the lead singer of Caveat Lover, remember? Long red hair? Voice like an angel?

And Jonah Hendrix has a two-year-old with his girlfriend. Both of those very kind, very *beautiful* women are also on tour. I met them, too. Trust me, you have nothing to worry about."

He gives me the same playful *mmhmm* I gave him, drawing another little laugh from me as my eyelids grow heavier with exhaustion. Silence stretches between us for long enough that I'm seconds from slipping into a dream world before his next question pulls me back to the present.

"Do you miss me?"

"Yes."

My answer is immediate. I don't even have to think about it. It tumbles out of my mouth like a natural reflex, and it's not a lie. In this dark hotel room, with this giant, empty bed, I do miss him. I miss the comfort. I miss the security.

I don't tell him that I didn't think about missing *him* until he asked, though.

"Do you miss me?"

"Of course I miss you. You're my wife, and you just left me to fly across the country with some depraved rock stars."

The change in his tone has my eyes popping open and my brows furrowing. We were having such a good conversation before. Now the guilt is back, and my body has grown tight with tension.

"I'm sorry," I say, digging my fingers into the cool, softer-than-soft bedsheets and squeezing. "I just...I didn't want to pass up this opportunity. You said you were okay with it."

"I was. I am." Brady sighs. "It's just harder without you here. That's all."

I nod even though he can't see me, and my voice drops to a whisper that sounds timid even to my own ears.

"I'm sorry."

"If I change my mind, if I'm not okay with it anymore, will you come home?"

I want to say *no*, but something else has me telling him the opposite.

"If that's what you really want, I'll come home."

Brady goes silent for a moment, and when he finally speaks, his voice is quieter. "Would that be a selfish thing for me to ask?"

I want to say *yes.*

Yes, it would be selfish of you to ask me to leave. Yes, it would be selfish to take something away from me when I've given everything to you.

I want to say it, but again, I don't. Instead, I force a swallow and try to keep my voice from trembling.

"I don't know. What do you think?"

Another long pause stretches that has my stomach roiling with nerves, and I halt my own breathing so I can listen more closely to his. He's going to ask me to leave. I just got here, and now I'll have to turn around and go back home.

My muscles grow heavier, defeat mixing with the exhaustion. I look at the empty side of the bed. The blankets and pillow are smooth and untouched. The room is peaceful, so different from the bedroom I share with Brady back home. I usually fall asleep to the sound of my husband watching sports highlights on his laptop. Tonight, it's just quiet, and I was enjoying it. The thought of being alone, of being blanketed in silence, used to terrify me, but not tonight.

"It would be selfish," he says finally, catching me by surprise.

"What?"

"If I asked you to come back, that would be selfish."

"Oh." I blink. "Okay."

"I'm being an asshole."

"No. No, you're not. It's fine."

He sighs again, this time sounding more frustrated than tired, and I listen as he pours himself a cup of coffee. I don't have to be there to know that he's probably using the blue *Mr.* mug we got as a wedding gift. He uses it every morning.

"Look. Let's just forget I said that, okay? It's not like you're going to last the whole eight weeks anyway."

I frown. "What does that mean?"

"Oh, c'mon, Auri. I can't even get you to stay at a dinner party with my bosses longer than a few hours, and you haven't had a job in years. You can barely keep up with your chores most of the time. Being responsible for someone's education? No. Either you'll leave, or they'll send you home." He chuckles to himself, then I hear him take a sip from his coffee and swallow before the mug clinks back onto the kitchen counter. "I want you to enjoy this while it lasts. Forget I said anything."

Sometimes, I wonder if he knows how much statements like that hurt me. It doesn't matter if they're said with a smile or veiled as a good-natured joke. My confidence is already fragile. One underhanded comment from him can beat it down for days. I bite the inside of my cheek and close my eyes, giving my head a shake as if I can rattle the memory of his words from my mind. I can't, but I still try. Every time.

I don't want to argue with him. It never works in my favor, anyway. My stomach churns, and my forehead stays creased, but I force a lightness into my tone that I don't feel.

"Sure. Yeah. Forgotten."

"So what else have you done?"

"Not much, really. I've spent the majority of the time since leaving California in the air. I've only been on the ground for a handful of hours, and now I'm in bed about to crash."

"Eighteen hours in the future," Brady jokes. "I guess I'm in your past now."

I huff a fake laugh. "I guess so."

"What about the drummer? Mabel Rossi."

"What about her?"

"Have you met her yet?"

I lick my lips and open my mouth to speak, but nothing comes out. The question has me fumbling for words, and I don't understand why. I think about the jet. About the room swapping. About our exchange in the hallway outside Sav's suite. I mean to tell him, but I don't. Instead, I force a fake smile that he can't see, and I mention none of it. I lie. When I speak, I hope he doesn't notice the odd, high pitch or slight nervous shake to my voice.

"Not really, no."

"She's always been kind of mysterious, you know? I feel like she's the only one who hasn't been mentioned in some sort of scandal."

I swallow. "Huh. Yeah."

"She's hot, too, though."

I force another light laugh, but this one comes out wobbly. "I guess. If you like the pixie punk rock thing."

Brady chuckles. "Don't be jealous. There's nothing sexier to me than coming home to find my wife with soil stains on her knees and under her fingernails."

His playful jibe draws a genuine smile from me. "Yes, well, I could do a mean winged liner back in the day."

"Oh, I know. That's how you hooked me. With the purple streak in your hair, black eyeliner, and ripped skinny jeans. It only took me a few years to earn my way out of the friend zone."

I hum, my eyes fluttering shut as my body finally transitions out of fight, flight, or freeze.

"You're still my friend, B. My best friend."

"I'm just grateful the cool, popular, artsy girl finally gave the math nerd a chance. I'm so lucky."

"Well, it was bound to happen when there were only five hundred people in our town," I tease. "Statistics were in your favor." A long yawn escapes me, and with it goes the very last dregs of my energy. "I'm going to fall asleep. Talk tomorrow night?"

"It's a date." Unlike mine, his voice has grown more chipper. "Oh, and don't forget."

"Hmm?"

"You should take a test soon."

A jolt zaps through me, and my eyes snap back open. A test.

A *pregnancy* test.

"Right. A test."

"Tomorrow?"

I swallow. "Sure. Tomorrow."

"Love you."

"Love you."

"Good night, Auri."

We hang up, and despite the way my body yearns for rest, my mind can't seem to find it. When I finally do succumb to sleep, it's after hours of staring at nothing in the darkness.

6

AURORA

THE KNOCK on my hotel door breaks my stare off with the unopened pregnancy test box on the bathroom counter.

Thankfully, too, because I was giving myself a headache from how hard I was frowning. It's been three days since Brady reminded me to take it, and I still can't bring myself to do it. I've held him off by saying the one I brought with was damaged in travel, and I've been unable to buy a new one.

It's all lies, but the truth is worse.

I spit my toothpaste in the sink and tuck my toothbrush in my cheek as I make my way through the room. I ordered breakfast only ten minutes ago, but I guess promptness is a perk of traveling with celebrities.

I double-check to make sure my bathrobe is pulled tight so I don't scandalize a poor hotel employee, then plaster a smile on my face as I swing the door open. The moment the person in the hall is revealed, my eyes go wide, and my mouth goes slack.

I've been in Mabel Rossi's presence every day since arriving in Melbourne, but something about seeing her outside my hotel room at eight in the morning steals every thought from my brain.

"Minty fresh?"

She smirks at me with her head tilted to the side. It takes a minute to realize she's talking about my toothbrush, which is currently hanging precariously from my gaping mouth. I grab it quickly and hide it behind my back.

"Hi. Hey." I clear my throat. "What's, um, up?"

"We're doing family breakfast in Savvy's suite."

Her eyes drop down my body, surveying my pink fluffy robe covered in daisies, and the smirk grows into a grin.

"Sleeping Beauty. You can come in that if you want."

I clear my throat again and attempt to act more confident than I feel, hoping like hell the inevitable blush stretching from my cheeks to my neck doesn't give me away.

"Is everyone else stage-ready like you, or will casual suffice?"

"Is casual what you want?"

The flirtatious lilt to her voice causes a cool chill to dance over the back of my neck. My eyes fall to the plump pink smirk on her lips, and I blink. I search frantically for a witty response to a question I don't understand before Mabel finally takes mercy on me with a laugh.

"Everyone else is probably still in pajamas, so wear whatever you want."

"Okay. Sure. I'll be just a minute. You can come in if you want. Or I can just head down when I'm done?"

"I can wait."

"Okay." I open the door and wave her in. "Sure."

Mabel steps into my room, and I move to my suitcase, suddenly very self-conscious of, well, everything, and trying my best not to let it show. I dig through my clothes to find an outfit while being hyper-vigilant not to drop any underwear on the floor. That would be mortifying.

I haven't been alone with her since the day we landed, and we've only exchanged a handful of words since our encounter in the hallway. If I'm being honest, I've been avoiding her. Mabel Rossi makes me nervous, and I don't want to make a fool of myself. *Again.*

It hasn't stopped me from watching her, though. Usually

through my periphery or from beneath lowered lashes, I watch her from the moment she enters a room to the moment she leaves. It's almost impossible not to, and it makes being in this enclosed space with her that much more difficult.

Don't be awkward, Aurora Jade. Just act normal.

"How's the orchid? Does it approve of the room?"

I practically jump out of my skin when her question punctures my thoughts, and I whip around to find her smirking at me.

"Oh. Um. Yes? I mean, he can't talk, because plants can't talk, as you know. Well, not really, anyway...Though I do think they have ways of communicating without words. Drooping leaves and wilting and discoloration and....such...."

Her smirk grows into an amused grin, and my ears burn with embarrassment. I clear my throat, plaster on a plastic smile, and avert my eyes to the *non-talking* plant in question. So much for *act normal*. Good grief.

"The window placement is great. Thank you again."

I hug my clothes to my chest and purse my lips as I survey the flower, my attention focused on the small bud I've managed to coax from him. Just one. Only ever one. A small frown pulls my brows inward.

"Now if he'll just wake up."

"He?"

"Arthur Orchidaceae." I can't help but smile as I say it. "I know it's silly. My mom always had names for her plants."

"*Had?*"

Her voice is softer around the word. I force a swallow, then nod.

"Yeah. She passed away a few years ago, so I got custody of Arthur."

She's quiet for a breath, and I brace myself for one of the many platitudes I get when people find out my parents are dead. I hate it, but I'm used to it. I've realized in the last four years that people never say those things for my sake; they say them for themselves. Because they feel uncomfortable sharing space with my grief, and they want to feel helpful. They want to believe they've comforted me in some way.

I don't like it, but I understand it.

When Mabel does speak, I'm surprised to hear no pity in her tone. No fake positivity or cliché hope. Just that playful lilt that makes my stomach tighten and a welcome subject change.

"Sounds like Arthur is in recovery mode."

"Yeah."

Recovery mode. Him and me both. I sigh and frown harder, eyes sticking on the single bud.

"I didn't think he'd be this temperamental, but Arthur has been a bit of a diva lately. Honestly, I took a gamble even bringing him with me, but I don't feel comfortable entrusting him to anyone else."

"How long has he been resting?"

When I finally glance at Mabel, I find her thankfully studying the plant, not me. I scrunch my nose.

"I don't know if I want to tell you. Your guardian would think less of me."

"She would never."

I huff a laugh then walk to stand next to her. We're the same height, and I glance down at her shoes to find that while she's still wearing platform boots, they're not as high as the pair from yesterday.

I try my best to ignore the way she smells, but I fail. Gardenia and something sweeter. Something fruity. I'd normally associate gardenia with the older ladies at church, but not this scent. Whatever she's wearing, it's fresh and playful, like her. I want to drown myself in it. Growing up around flowers has given me a pretty keen sense of smell. Usually, I like it. Right now, I do not.

I widen the distance between us and give my head a shake before forcing myself back on topic.

"Moth orchids don't really go through periods of true dormancy, so that makes this extra weird, but Arthur has been *resting* for well over a year. I can get him to bud but not bloom. I think I've made him angry."

Mabel hums. "Not too angry. He's still alive."

I laugh again. "True. He's just throwing a tantrum, and I can't figure out why." I release a sigh. "Anyway. I'll get dressed."

I turn toward the bathroom, but I only get two steps before Mabel stops me.

"Aurora, you forgot something."

I look back at her. "What?"

I can tell she's biting the inside of her cheek, no doubt trying not to laugh at me, as she nods to the floor beside my suitcase. I can actually feel the color leech from my face before it flames back to bright red. Warm, to cold, to burning hot.

I already know what I'll find when I turn around, but I still have to choke back a shriek of horror when I see my granniest pair of cotton underwear splayed out on the hotel carpet.

Of course it's the period underwear. It couldn't at least be the cute little hipsters or the new silk bikinis. Nope. Of all the things to fall out of my suitcase in the presence of a rock and roll goddess, it's my high-waisted, greyish-white, old-as-hell pair of cotton briefs.

Oh, God.

Now she's going to think I'm dirty and disgusting.

I almost trip over my feet as I dive to pick them up and shove them back into the suitcase. I turn to her and shake my head.

"I own newer ones...nicer...better...I mean, these aren't my only...They're clean, I swear. And I do have other pairs...cuter...I just...They're just..."

Mabel's expression softens, and she gives me a one-shouldered shrug.

"They're just really fucking comfortable when you're on your period and feel like your uterus is being stabbed from the inside out by a drunk Gremlin holding a fist full of dull knives?"

My brows jump in surprise. "Yeah."

She pats her stomach. "I own a uterus, too, babe. I understand the luxury of a comfy pair of period underwear."

I stare at her for a few breaths as my brain labors to process the interaction. I feel like I've just run a mile in a pair of flip flops while spinning in circles, so it takes several moments before I'm finally able to form a coherent thought, but when my body finally transitions out of panic-mode, I laugh.

"Right. Of course. I'll just..."

I gesture to the bathroom once more, then duck inside quickly. As soon as the door shuts behind me, the scene replays in my head, and I have to cover my mouth to keep from laughing out loud again. I think about it over and over the whole time I'm changing out of my pajamas.

I own a uterus too, she'd said.

I don't know why I thought she'd judge me over something as trivial as underwear. She's not Brady. Just because he thinks they're gross doesn't mean Mabel would. Maybe I'd have known that if I had any female friends. The thought brings a frown to my face as I finish pulling on my clothes. It makes me wonder what other views of mine have been unfairly skewed.

I really need to get some friends.

Once dressed, I turn and survey myself in the mirror. I hadn't paid much attention to what I was grabbing, but there's no way my outfit could compare to what Mabel's wearing. While she's not in a leather miniskirt or hot pink sequins this morning, she still looks ready for a photoshoot. I run my eyes over my bare face and damp hair, then picture the gorgeous rock star currently standing on the other side of the door with her million-dollar blowout and perfectly winged eyeliner.

If she's not going to judge me over cotton granny panties, she won't judge me over a cotton sundress. I know this, but it doesn't eradicate the feelings of inadequacy that creep into my head.

I give myself exactly thirty seconds to feel out of place. Thirty seconds to internally panic about how I don't belong here and how I should have just stayed home. Then, when those thirty seconds are up, I meet my eyes in the mirror and whisper to myself.

"Shoulders back. Deep breaths. You're here now, Aurora Jade. Stop being a baby."

I smooth my hands down the skirt of my sundress, adjust the pendant of my necklace so it sits right between my collarbones, then I step back into the bedroom. Mabel has made herself comfortable, sitting cross-legged on the little loveseat by my window with my room service in front of her. Her eyes scan from my face to my toes and back, and then she smiles.

"You look good in green."

"Oh. Um, thank you."

I drop my eyes and try to suppress the goofy grin that wants to take over my face. Movement draws my attention back to her, though, and I catch her popping a berry in her mouth. I laugh.

"Are you eating my breakfast?"

Mabel smirks. "Want some?"

"Do I want some of the breakfast that I ordered for myself?"

"Do you?" She scoops a spoonful of yogurt from a glass parfait cup and holds it out to me. "It's pretty good."

I don't move right away, but I let my gaze stay locked with hers. The smirk on her pink lips grows slightly, and then I catch a flash of challenge in her amber eyes. The challenge is what sets my feet in motion. I close the distance between us slowly, until I'm standing over her, but when I reach for the spoon, she moves it away. I huff a laugh, and she arches a brow.

I know what she wants me to do, and the way my heart races makes me dizzy. I tell myself it's a little, harmless thing, but I have to remind myself to take slow, controlled breaths. I sink my teeth into my bottom lip, hesitating for a few seconds before finally sitting beside her on the loveseat.

I watch her attention drop to my mouth as I open for her, and I swear I see heat flash in her amber irises as I close my lips around the spoon. The cold yogurt hits my tongue, but I can barely taste the sweetness. I'm too busy staring at Mabel's expression as she slowly pulls the spoon back through my lips and watches as I swallow the yogurt. She looks from my mouth to my eyes and darts her own tongue out to swipe over her plump lower lip.

"Well?"

I nod and swallow twice more before I can respond. "Yum."

"You've got just a little..."

She brings her hand up slowly between us. When I don't flinch away, she rubs her thumb at the corner of my mouth, and my skin erupts in goosebumps from her touch. Then my stomach flips over on itself when she sucks her thumb between her lips and hums.

"Yum."

My inhale and exhale are shaky, and when I feel my face and neck heating, I break our stare and force out an awkward laugh. I can still feel her eyes on me, but I keep mine fixed firmly on the ground until she finally, abruptly, stands from the couch.

"C'mon, *Roar*. Let's go before Savvy sends out a search party. She's very impatient."

The rapid change of mood leaves me scrambling for a complete thought, and I'm slow to follow as she starts to leave. We're silent as we step into the hall. Thankfully, too, because I doubt I could carry on even the lightest of conversations.

What just happened? Was she testing me, pushing to see how I'd react? Or is that normal behavior between friends?

The way she fed me the yogurt. The way she smirked at me. The way she touched me. Her thumb on my lips. In her mouth. The tone of her voice when she said *yum*.

I replay the whole thing, then run through my memories, sifting for some comparable experience, but I come up short. I *really* need to find some friends. I've had no friendships, or even friendly interactions, with any other girls since high school, and nothing comes anywhere close to my interactions with Mabel.

It could be normal, I suppose. I'm probably over thinking it. I'm just being ridiculous and out of place, which is further proof that I don't belong here. Or...

Or...maybe...

I flatten my palm over my stomach and note the strange, tickling flutter of nerves.

Or was she *flirting* with me?

No. I almost laugh out loud. Definitely not. Mabel Rossi wouldn't flirt with me. She's a gorgeous, talented, famous rock star, and I'm, well, *me.*

I try to squash the thought, but it gets louder, demanding to be considered.

Maybe...

Everyone knows the drummer for The Hometown Heartless is queer. Mabel Rossi is attracted to women. I've seen pictures of her with girlfriends in the past, and even the big drum of her drum set is emblazoned with a glittery rainbow flag. I don't think she's dating anyone right now. Or, at least, I can't remember any recent pictures with a current girlfriend. If she's single, then maybe...

No. *No.* No.

That's ridiculous. She wouldn't flirt with me. She was just messing with me. Testing me, and I probably failed whatever it was. That's the only possible explanation, and I walked right into it.

I frown at the hotel carpet and keep my strides in time with Mabel's, trying and failing to ignore the sinking feeling in my stomach. Maybe I *am* just the butt of the joke. Maybe Brady was right. I don't belong. I don't—

"Be honest. Have I made you uncomfortable?"

My head jerks upward, my eyes colliding with Mabel's. From what I've learned about Mabel in the last few days, I shouldn't be surprised to see concern there, but I am. I bounce my attention to the hotel door behind her. We're at Sav's suite. Family breakfast. I take a deep breath, force a smile, and look back at Mabel.

"No, you haven't."

It's not a lie. She's made me feel a lot of confusing things in a short period of time, but none of them has been discomfort.

"Are you sure? Because it wasn't my intention. I was just teasing."

Teasing.

Just *teasing.*

Not flirting with me. Not making fun of me, either, but...

I resist the urge to frown, but I picture myself stomping on the embers of disappointment I feel glowing in the pit of my stomach.

"I'm sure," I say, my voice tight as I nod multiple times. "I'm not at all uncomfortable."

Mabel scans my face, the lines between her eyebrows deepening for a moment before she finally returns my nod.

"Okay." She gestures to Sav's suite door. "Sustenance awaits."

It takes a good ten minutes to settle back into my thoughts before I'm able to enjoy, as Mabel called it, *family breakfast.* I try my hardest to keep my eyes off her despite the strong force trying desperately to pull them in her direction.

I try but I fail.

I was just teasing, she'd said. Not flirting.

It shouldn't feel like a letdown. It shouldn't make my brows slant and my shoulders droop as if I'd been filled with the weirdest, most confusing kind of hope, only to have it popped in an instant.

I'm married. I have a husband. And moreover, I'm not even into women.

What happened with Mabel...

It was teasing. Playfulness between friends. Completely and totally normal. I'm just not used to it because it's been so long since I've had a friend outside of Brady.

Of course Mabel wouldn't *actually* be flirting with me. I'm definitely not her type, and I wouldn't even know what it felt like to be flirted with, anyway.

Of course I am not disappointed.

Because I feel absolutely no attraction, whatsoever, to Mabel Rossi.

7

MABEL

"How's Boss getting along with Aurora?"

Sav shrugs as we step onto the stage for sound check.

"I think she likes her. It's just the subject matter that she hates." She pauses to take her guitar from a roadie with a thank you. "They've decided to meet once a day for an hour and then plan additional help as needed. They had their first real tutoring session this afternoon, but I haven't had a chance to talk to either of them about it."

I fold my arms across my chest and watch as she hooks the receiver for her in-ear monitor on the band of her jeans, then checks the tuning on her guitar. We've been doing this for over a decade, so everything is like muscle memory at this point.

While I'm waiting for my own in-ear monitor, I pull my phone from my pocket and check my texts, but the messages I sent Kat last night are still unread. She's posted to her social media stories, so I know she's probably seen my texts despite the time difference, and her lack of response has my chest growing tight with anxiety. I pull up a browser and refresh my earlier page of search results, but no new photos pop up on the screen. I try not to acknowledge the small bit of relief at not seeing any new Kaz photos.

"Have you talked to Kat?"

I roll my eyes at the bite in Sav's question. She doesn't like Kat. She hasn't since the first time we broke up, and Sav's not great at pretending. I put my phone back into my pocket and give Sav a fake smile.

"Yes."

"She still coming for Auckland?"

"Yes."

"Hm."

I arch a brow, waiting for Sav to drop whatever snarky comment that's brewing in her head, but when she stays quiet, I sigh.

"*What*, Savannah?"

"I didn't say anything."

"You don't have to. It's all over your face."

She looks at me finally, lips pursed and eyes scanning mine before the tense set to her shoulders relaxes, and her expression softens from annoyed to concerned.

"You deserve better than what she gives you."

I huff out a laugh and twirl my ring around my middle finger.

"I'm serious, Mabes. You've wasted way too much time and energy on her as it is. What's it been, four years?"

"Three." *Ish.*

"Well, that's two and a half too many. The first time you broke up should have been the last time."

I tilt my head to the ceiling and close my eyes. This conversation isn't new. I don't want to have it again, but Sav can be so fucking stubborn. She won't stop until she thinks I've really *heard* it.

"Kat and I love each oth—"

She snorts, cutting me off, and my brows slant angrily.

"Don't be a bitch, Sav."

"Mabel, if Kat loves you, then her way of showing it fucking sucks. I know you think you're in love—"

"Don't be patronizing."

She swings her guitar off and sets it in its stand, then faces me with her hands on her hips, so I mirror her stance. With my platforms, we're the same height, so I'm thankfully not having to look up at her when she's on her soapbox.

"You're letting her walk all over you. You've sacrificed everything I know you want in a relationship to be with someone who gives you the bare minimum, and it's bullshit."

I shake my head and try hard not to dwell on the nagging truth in her words. Have I sacrificed everything? Does Kat give me the bare minimum? I shove the questions down and stand up straighter.

"Relationships in this business are hard," I say, working to keep my voice level and firm. "It's complicated."

"It's not that complicated."

Sav brings her hands in front of us and starts ticking off her fingers, her giant engagement ring sparkling in the stage lights as she does it. It just makes me angrier.

"She's always bailing on you. She won't go out in fucking public with you. You've had to spend your whole relationship underground, and you hate it. You're always bending over backward for her and making concessions and compromising what you want, and for what? A top secret rendezvous and a clandestine fuck once a month?"

I flinch and grit my teeth.

"Lower your voice," I hiss. She scoffs, but I push forward. "Our relationship could ruin her career."

"That's bullshit." Sav rips her hand through her long silver hair, her nostrils flaring and eyes flashing with anger as her whispered words lash between us. "It's homophobic bullshit peddled by her homophobic manager and perpetuated by her own internalized homophobia. Everyone on Earth knows you're bisexual, and it hasn't affected your career at all."

My eyes sting. My chest hurts. The only thing keeping me from storming off or shouting in her face is the absolute pain I see in her eyes. She doesn't get joy out of this. She's not saying it to hurt me, even though it does.

"That's different, and you know it."

"It's not different, though. It's not. There are a lot of successful queer fashion models. She might get some media heat at first, but her career would be fine. If she loved you—really loved you, like loud and proud and not in secret—she'd do it."

"You have absolutely no idea what you're fucking talking about, Savannah. You have no idea how scary it is to come out. It's terrifying."

"You came out at sixteen—"

"To you! I came out *to you*. I didn't have a family or a community or a career to worry about shunning me, and I was *still* scared shitless. Kat doesn't know how her family will take it. She doesn't know how it will affect her standing in the industry. And regardless of whether *you* think her career will be fine, not everyone can handle media backlash the way you do. Not everyone was born with your *no fear, fuck it all* kind of attitude. You can't expect Kat to take that kind of risk or make that kind of sacrifice until she's ready. Fuck, even after I came out it took me a while to get comfortable with myself. Do you remember how long it took me to actually date someone? How hard it was for me to be openly queer, even around Jo and Torren?"

Sav frowns, sadness passing over her expression as she scans my face. Then she nods.

"I remember," she says on a resigned sigh. "You're right. I don't understand. I will never fully understand. But can I expect her to at least rearrange her schedule so she can keep a date with you?"

"It was a brand deal. It was important."

"I'm not talking about just this time, Mabel. There is *always* something. There is always something more important, or more urgent, or more exciting than you."

My jaw drops. I feel tears start to well in my eyes as a

matching glitter fills Sav's. When I hurt, she hurts, and vice versa. It's always been like this.

"That's low, Savannah."

She blinks and a single tear rolls down her cheek, but she doesn't look away from me.

"You deserve to be a priority, Mabes. You deserve to be *the* priority. Top fucking priority. I hate watching you let yourself be put dead last, and I hate her for doing it. I know you're not happy. She keeps hurting you over and over, and you deserve so much fucking better. You deserve the world."

I close my eyes against the sting of tears and shake my head, taking deep, measured breaths. She acts like it should be simple. Like the choice should be blinking neon and obvious. But not all of us find our soulmate in middle school like she did. Not all of us have the universe on our side. She just doesn't get it.

"It's not that easy, Sav. She just...She just *can't* right now."

"Yeah, well, if she wanted to, she would."

Sav's voice trails off, and I don't respond. I have nothing else to say. I just stand in front of her with my eyes closed, focusing on the movement happening all around us. I can hear Jonah and Torren at their instruments. Can hear roadies moving around, prepping for the show in a few hours. Hammond's voice is a low hum from somewhere offstage, probably talking on the phone. But Sav and I just stand in silence, and despite the fight we just had, I'm glad she's not walking away. She knows how much I hate being alone.

And deep down, I think I know she's right.

I deserve better than what Kat is giving me. Maybe I'm hoping that if I subject myself to Sav's verbal ass beating, I'll finally wake the fuck up.

I haven't yet. But maybe I will.

Approaching footsteps pull me from my thoughts, and I open my eyes just as a roadie steps in front of me. I take my in-ears with a thank you, then turn back to Sav. Her expression has softened, and it makes me want to hug her.

"I love you. I don't mean to be a bitch. I'm just protective. I don't like seeing you like this."

That brings a small smile to my lips. Even if she's a pain in my ass, it's fucking amazing having someone who is permanently in my corner. We went through a rough patch for a while, as a band and as a family, but her loyalty and love have never wavered, and neither has mine. The world may know her as Sav Loveless, badass rock star. But to me, she'll always be Savannah Shaw. My sister. My best friend.

"I know," I say with more exasperation than I feel. "I'm used to it." She narrows her eyes, so I roll mine. "I love you, too, Savvy."

With the conversation over, I turn toward my drum set, but my eyes land right on Aurora. She's standing in the wings offstage in a blue cotton dress, frozen like an animal in flood lights. Our stares lock for three whole breaths before she drops her head and bolts from sight.

I'm certain she witnessed my argument with Savannah, but I'm hoping she was too far away to hear much of it. It's not that I don't trust Ham's niece; it's that I find it hard to trust *anyone*. In this industry, you can never be sure of someone's intentions, and I've worked too hard to keep my name out of any scandals.

I'm going to have to run damage control.

I throw myself behind my kit and slump into my seat with a groan.

Kat. Another email from my lawyer. Now this fight with Sav. I'm already exhausted, and it's only the first show of the tour. I adjust my transmitter and put in my ear monitors, and while I don't miss a single beat through sound check, I've mentally checked out.

God, I hope I don't feel like this for the entire fucking tour.

8

———

MABEL

"I'm sorry."

Instead of following Sav toward the dressing rooms, I slow to a stop and turn to face Aurora. I thought I'd have to hunt her down, but she came to me. I arch a brow, and she lets out a cute little huff of laughter.

"I *am* sorry," she insists. "I didn't mean to eavesdrop."

I nod slowly. "I was wondering if you heard anything."

"Not a whole lot. I think it was just the end bit—just a few words—and not enough to really know anything. I just wanted to tell you that. I didn't hear a lot, and I didn't try to. I just want you to know that."

I lean my shoulder on the wall and watch her expression as she rambles. The worry I feel of being overheard is dulled by just how entertaining I find her. She really, truly has no poker face, and it makes her far too fun to play with. She wears every emotion on her lips, in her eyes, in the rise and fall of her brows and cheeks, in the tightening of her jaw and the quiver of her chin. And that blush? It's so fucking cute. It makes me want to draw more from her. To make her feel everything so I can observe the way it transforms her expression. It takes effort to keep myself from teasing her even now.

73

"You didn't do anything wrong. You have no reason to apologize."

"But...When you saw me, you looked so...Angry? Concerned, I guess? I don't know. I just...I just want to make sure it's not because of me, or that I'm at least not adding to it. Whatever it is."

"I'm not angry with you," I reassure, then I lean in a little closer. "I would like to know exactly what you heard, though."

She drops her gaze to the floor. "I heard Sav say something about how you deserve to be a priority..."

She pauses and brings her eyes back to meet mine.

"*And...?*" I press, noting how her brows slant as she whispers her next words.

"And...I heard you say *she can't right now.*" Her eyes bounce between mine. "Were you talking about your girlfriend?"

The question feels wrong, for some reason, and I hesitate to answer.

Maybe it's the hint of disappointment I hear laced throughout her curiosity. Maybe it's the loyalty I feel toward Kat. Or maybe it's something else. Something being stirred up inside my chest by those wide, hazel green eyes and that pretty face that reads like a flashing neon sign.

I don't want to think about it, so I smirk and deflect.

"More personal questions, Roar?"

Her flush deepens, and she drops her eyes to the floor again. This time, though, it's not from shyness, and I immediately feel terrible. Teasing is one thing, but causing her to feel shame or regret? That's the opposite of what I want to do. Even before she can open her mouth to apologize *again*, I rush to fix it.

"Hey, I was just kidding. You didn't do anything wrong. I'm sorry."

She blinks a few times, her hand reaching to grasp the pendant of her necklace as she tries to collect herself. Then she forces a breathy laugh before looking at me through her lashes.

"So you can apologize, but I can't?"

I smile. "The last thing I want to do is make you

uncomfortable, Aurora. You didn't do anything wrong, so if something I said made you doubt that, then I'm sorry for it."

"You didn't."

I tilt my head to the side. "Foundation of truth, remember?"

She sighs. "Okay, fine, you did. But I deserved it."

"Hard disagree." I lean back against the wall and scan her face again. The flush is fading, but the little lines between her eyebrows are still present. "It's instinctual for you, isn't it?"

"What is?"

"Apologizing."

Her mouth pops open, and I wait as she visibly struggles for a response. When her mouth closes again, I take it she's decided not to respond at all. I also take it that I was correct, so I change the subject.

"Yes, Sav was talking about my girlfriend. You'll meet her in Auckland." I pause as something dawns on me. "Actually, have you signed an NDA? Most everyone has to, but I don't know if you're exempt since you're related to the boss."

"Oh, no. I mean, yes. I mean, I *have* signed the non-disclosure. No way Uncle Wade would break protocol on my account. He's far too professional. Everything by the book and all that."

"True. But Ham's been known to bend a few rules from time to time."

She smiles knowingly, and it makes me wonder what rules he's bent for her. I almost ask, but she speaks up, and I file the question away for a later conversation.

"I'd never share anything with the tabloids or anything like that. I respect the band's privacy. You don't have to worry about me."

"Good to know."

Aurora's brow furrows. Her next statement comes out slow and curious, prodding for information. She'd make a terrible spy.

"I actually had no idea you were dating anyone."

"It's not public knowledge."

"Why not?"

"My girlfriend's a very private person. She prefers that we keep our relationship out of the public eye."

"Do you?"

"Do I what?"

"You said that's what *she* prefers. Do you prefer it also?"

I'm taken aback for a moment, and I almost deflect again, but something about the genuine interest in those wide eyes pulls an answer from me instead.

"It's not what I prefer, actually. I like privacy, yeah, but I don't like having to hide my relationship from everyone."

"So why do you do it?"

I break our eye contact, fixing my attention over her shoulder on the cinderblock wall across the wide hallway. I sigh and shrug.

"Relationships require compromise."

My gaze returns to her when she gives me a quiet, almost sad laugh.

"Yeah. Yeah, I guess sometimes they do."

When she looks at me again, those hazel green irises penetrate in a way that makes me feel exposed, but not in a bad way. In a way that almost resembles relief. I hear the understanding in her voice, see it in the crease of her brow and the slight downturn of her pouty lips. I see sorrow there, too.

I want to ask *how* she understands. Why? I want to ask her about her own love life, about who she's compromised for, but I bite my tongue. I want to ask, but I don't think I want to know. Not yet.

"Well, I agree with Sav."

Aurora's words come out hushed, so I keep my voice low when I respond.

"About what?"

She sucks her lower lip between her teeth, then releases it slowly, turning it a darker pink and glistening with her saliva. On impulse, I wet my own lower lip, then lock my eyes with hers again.

"You deserve to be a priority. And if your girlfriend wanted to, she would."

My heart thuds hard into my rib cage as my breath catches in my throat. My lips part, but no words come. I don't know when we got so close, but I can see every fleck of green and gold in her irises. A bit of blue, too. Her lashes are long and dark blonde. When she blinks, they flutter against her curtain bangs. There's a single freckle just beneath her left eye. When she exhales, her breath feathers across my cheeks.

She'd be taller than me if I weren't wearing these platforms. Taller than Sav, but shorter than Kat. Aurora might be the perfect height, actually.

Goose bumps rise on the back of my neck and over my arms. I find myself wanting to lean even closer. To see how we'd fit if I closed the distance entirely. But then something down the hall crashes, and we both jump to look toward the noise.

"A ladder," I say, shaking my head to clear the fog. "Someone dropped a ladder."

My pulse is still thrumming rapidly, my nipples are peaked against my tight white shirt, and I try not to think about how easily I could have kissed her.

She's Hammond's niece, I remind myself. *And Kat.*

I'm *in love* with *Kat.*

I kick off the wall and head to the dressing room, changing the subject to something safe.

"Where will you be watching the show?"

Aurora falls in step beside me, her bare arm just an inch from brushing up against mine.

"Uncle Wade has me in the VIP tent."

"Are you excited?"

"Yeah. It's been a long time since I've been to a concert. It's been a long time since I've done much of anything fun, actually." She laughs and flashes a glance at me. "The last time I heard live music was when I was sixteen. My parents took me to see The Hometown Heartless in Phoenix."

"Jesus," I say on a surprised exhale. "I forgot what a baby you are."

Sixteen.

Aurora saw us in concert when she was sixteen years old. It's like a bucket of cold water over my head.

When I was sixteen, I was already on the run. That was the year I met Sav. We were living in Nashville and working as buskers and pickpockets for this guy named Oscar. He taught us how to play instruments, and for a while, he kept a roof over our heads and food in our stomachs, but the guy was an asshole who made a living off scared, vulnerable kids.

Fuck, that feels like a lifetime ago.

Sixteen.

"I'm not a baby," Aurora says, pulling me from my thoughts. "I'm twenty-three."

We stop outside the dressing room door, and I turn to face her.

"Trust me, compared to me, you're basically a toddler."

Her brows slant and her eyes narrow. "You're not that much older than me."

I smile, but I don't argue. "Are you coming in?"

She shakes her head and gestures down the hall. "I have to meet up with my uncle."

"Well, if I don't see you before the show, I'll look for you in the VIP."

She nods. "Okay. See you later."

As Aurora walks away, I can't ignore the strange pull in my chest. One that almost wants to follow her. *It's been a long time since I've done much of anything fun,* she'd said. She looks so small in this large hallway. She looks so alone. I *hate* being alone.

Before I think better of it, I call after her.

"Hey, Aurora." The skirt of her dress flares out as she spins around to face me. "Want to do something after?"

Her brows jump. "Like what?"

I shrug and pull a suggestion out of thin air, but as it leaves my mouth, it sounds like the best idea I've ever had.

"There's this restaurant. The rooftop bar is open late, and they always have live music. Jazz or blues, usually, but it's chill. We used to go every time we were in Melbourne, but I haven't been in a while. Savvy can't really go anywhere anymore—not without prior notice so we can either rent the place or stack it with security —but you and I could go tonight."

She smiles, and even from the distance, I can see a tint of pink color her cheeks. It's the good kind of blush. The one that makes my pulse kick up, and I find myself holding my breath as I wait for an answer.

"Okay. That sounds like good. I mean fun. I mean..." She pauses, takes a deep breath, then starts over. "Yes. That sounds fun. I would like that."

I have to work to keep my grin from stretching wider. "I'll see you after the show."

She laughs, light and tinkling, then nods. "See you after."

I resist the urge to watch as she leaves and head into the dressing room, taking smooth, even breaths to calm the fluttering in my stomach.

There's a nagging voice in the back of my mind telling me to be careful. To watch what I say and how I act. It's been there since yesterday morning in Aurora's hotel room, and while I possibly took the teasing too far with the yogurt, it was innocent. She's just too fun to poke, is all. Her reactions are fascinating, but it's nothing. It's harmless teasing.

And what just happened in the hallway...

I take a deep breath and blink away the thoughts.

It's *innocent.*

She's new here, and I want her to feel welcome. I could use the company, and she seems like she could use a friend.

It's been a long time since I've done much of anything fun, actually.

I'm just going to show her some fun, is all.

It's all *totally* innocent.

•　•　•

By the time we're stepping on stage, I'm vibrating with excitement.

The promise of music, of a loudly cheering crowd full of diehard fans, soothes the ever-present itch that sits just under my skin. It's like this for every show, and I'm fucking relieved the dread I'd felt during sound check didn't stick around.

I take my place behind my set, adjust my in-ears, and grab one of my three pairs of drumsticks. I listen for the click track to start, and when Jonah plays the first chords to our opening song, I ready my sticks. The crowd goes wild, but I can hear my band perfectly through my earpieces, and when the stage lights turn on —right on cue—I close my eyes and play. I don't open them again until the final notes fade and Sav greets the crowd.

"How you doin' tonight, Melbourne?" Sav's husky voice booms through the stadium, and the audience erupts. She turns to look at me. "That's what we like to hear, isn't it, Mabes?"

I pound out a quick beat in agreement, and she laughs as the crowd grows louder.

"We're so fucking excited to be back here with you. It's been too long, hasn't it, guys?"

"Too fucking long," Torren says into his mic, and I roll my eyes when high-pitched screams of excitement come from the floor. Torren King, our resident heartthrob.

"We took a little time off to make this new album. It's called Riot She Wrote. Have you heard of it?" Sav cups her hand to her ear as the crowd roars, and she smirks as she leans into her mic. "Oh, so you *have* heard of it. Well, if it's all right with you guys, we'd like to play that album for you tonight."

When we launch into our title track, they cheer so loud that, I swear, the walls of the stadium shake. Sav's the ultimate performer, and our fans might as well be an extension of her guitar. She knows exactly what to say, and just watching her for a few minutes is all the explanation needed for our global popularity. Sav Loveless is a fucking showboat, and our fans eat it up, then beg for more every single time.

If I could bottle this feeling, collect every ounce of adoration and love emanating from this crowd and store it away, I'd do it. It's impossible to feel alone when you're holding the attention of thousands of people, and while their eyes are trained on Sav or the guys, I'm still a part of it; that's all I need. I'm in the background, an undercurrent instead of a focus, but it's worth it. It's worth it just to be part of something bigger than myself.

I seek out the VIP tent. Aurora said it had been a long time since she'd been to a concert, and I want to know if she's enjoying herself. I *need* to know if she's buzzing from this energy, too. The moment I find her, her eyes are already on me.

Not Sav. Not Torren or Jo. *Me.*

I smile and incline my head, nodding at her. Her own smile stretches wide as she brings her hand up and waves. It's one of those cute, coquettish finger waves, her delicate wrist adorned with a stack of beaded bracelets, and for a moment, I think I feel a blush color my own cheeks.

I can only see her from the waist up, but I can tell she's changed clothes. Instead of the blue cotton dress she had on in the hallway, she's wearing something black and strapless. Her blonde hair is pulled back into a sleek ponytail, with her curtain bangs framing her heart-shaped face. I squint, trying to refine my view. I want to see her eyes. Her lips. The slope of her shoulders where they meet her neck. I find myself interested in every little detail. She's got a necklace decorating her collarbone, and I'm studying the jewelry when movement just behind her snags my attention.

I flinch and my stomach drops. A feeling I can't process overwhelms me, and for the first time in years, I fumble the beat.

I tear my gaze from the VIPs and focus on my floor tom. I adjust my grip on my sticks, then close my eyes to reorient my body with the music in my ear monitors. I take several deep breaths to get my shit together, and when I'm certain I'm seeing clearly, I cast my attention back toward the VIP tent.

Kat.

I blink again.

She's still there. Standing behind Aurora, scrolling on her phone. She's absolutely impossible to miss now that I know she's there. I'm not sure how I didn't see her to begin with.

I bring my attention back to my drum set, careful to skip right over my manager's twenty-three-year-old niece and her sexy, bare shoulders.

Kat's here.

My girlfriend's here in Melbourne, when she wasn't supposed to come until Auckland. She must have cancelled her other events. She must have cancelled them so she could come early. She cancelled them *for me.*

Sav said if Kat wanted to, she would.

Aurora said it, too.

And now, Kat has. She's done something to make me a priority, and for the fucking life of me, I can't ignore the sinking feeling in my stomach.

9

AURORA

I'm FLOATING on a cloud of shared euphoria.

A high induced by the drug that is The Hometown Heartless.

When I was sixteen, I walked out of their concert in Phoenix changed in ways I couldn't put into words. I swore I could feel the vibrations of their energy in the air for weeks after that concert, and the world seemed brighter, more vibrant, somehow. I felt more alive than I ever had. I'd lost that feeling for a while, and I didn't even realize it until tonight.

"Thanks so much for having us, Melbourne. You've been absolutely beautiful."

Everyone around me cheers as Sav's voice carries throughout the stadium. I pull my eyes away from Mabel and fix them on Sav. She's grinning at the audience as her skin glistens with sweat. She looks like she's glowing. Like she's living, breathing neon.

"This was just what we needed to kick things off for the Riot She Wrote Tour, and you definitely set the bar high."

A drumbeat sounds—Mabel expressing her agreement with Sav's statement—and my eyes dart back to her. Back to where they've been for most of the show. There's no questioning that Sav Loveless is the one who draws the crowds. With a voice and attitude like hers, how can she not be? But I'd be lying if I said she was the center of my attention tonight.

I bite the inside of my cheek to keep from grinning as I look at Mabel. I can't even see her that well because of the drums, but I can hear her. I've heard her over everything else. She's integral. Sav Loveless may be the frontwoman of this world-famous rock band, but Mabel Rossi is the heartbeat.

I'll see you after the show, she'd said.

I replay her voice in my head and count the backflips that take place in my stomach. It takes Sav's husky voice to bring me back to the present. When I look at the lead singer, I find her grinning conspiratorially as if she's in on a secret with the audience. When she speaks, it all makes sense.

"Melbourne, even though we're saying good night..."

Her voice cuts off as the crowd responds immediately, "It's not goodbye!"

"But just in case, so you don't forget us, back there is Mabel on drums, we've got Jonah here on guitar, this is Torren on bass, my name is Sav Loveless, and we're The Hometown Heartless. Thank you so fucking much, Melbourne! We love you. Have a great night."

The stage lights dim, and shadowy figures of the band leave one by one, but no one in the audience moves. In fact, the moment the darkened stage is empty, the chanting begins.

Encore, encore, encore.

I can feel the words echoing in my chest. The stadium floor vibrates under my feet from the force of the crowd's stomping, too. I read that Heartless concerts regularly cause earthquake-like activity. I bet it's happening right now.

My face hurts from the size of my smile. I'm so engrossed in the excitement that I barely notice the security guard approaching.

"Mrs. Sinclair, did you want to stay for the encore, or do you want to come backstage now and miss the crowd?"

I focus on the man in front of me. I recognize him. He's been standing off to the side of the VIP tent the whole show, but I don't know his name.

"I'd like to stay, if that's all right," I say, my voice raised so he can hear me over the chanting.

He nods. "Mr. Hammond requests that you not leave this area without an escort, so wait here after the encore, and I'll come get you."

"Okay. Thank you."

He nods, then moves back to his earlier position, and I turn my attention back to the stage. Someone brushes past me with an *excuse me* as she leaves the VIP tent. She smells faintly of orange blossom, but I don't look away from the stage.

"It's okay," I say absently, but she's already walking away.

Then the lights come back up and the audience screams so loudly that I have to cover my ears. The band comes back on stage, and Sav picks up her guitar and leans into the mic.

"You want a few more, then?" The response is deafening cheers, and she laughs again. "Okay, Melbourne. We hear you."

The Hometown Heartless plays three more songs, and I dance and sing along with ninety thousand other fans. By the time the stadium lights turn on for good, I'm sweaty and exhausted, but I'm still buzzing with energy.

They say a Heartless concert is a religious experience, but it's more than that. It's not religion. It's a revival. I felt it when I was sixteen. I feel it now. It's no wonder their fandom stretches the globe.

My smile stays wide, my cheeks almost aching as I watch fans filter out of the stadium. I stay put just as my uncle requested, and to his credit, the security guard arrives promptly.

"Are you ready, Mrs. Sinclair?"

I flinch. He called me Mrs. Sinclair earlier, but now, with the house lights up and the noise level down, the title feels almost like a sharp pinch to the side.

"You can call me Aurora."

"Aurora. Are you ready? I can take you backstage now."

"I'm ready."

I follow the man from the VIP tent to an exit door. When I ask his name, he tells me it's Jones, but other than that, the walk is silent. He's not much for small talk, and the closer we get to the backstage area, the happier I am about it.

I'm so nervous that I feel a bit lightheaded.

I'll see you after the show.

It's after the show. I'm going to be going out with Mabel tonight. Just a matter of hours, probably. We'll be at a restaurant with a rooftop bar and *chill music*. Somewhere trendy. Somewhere cool.

I tug on the top of my flowy black dress, adjusting the strapless bra underneath. This is the sexiest thing I brought with me, and it's better suited for a day at the beach than a night out. It beats everything else I had in my suitcase, though. Cotton sundresses, mostly. Of all the things I packed, this is the most *rock and roll* I could come up with.

Chin up. Shoulders back.

I picture myself across from a pub table with Mabel, or perhaps seated beside her at a bar top. The promise of proximity makes my skin buzz in anticipation. The most delicious kind of excitement. I want to sprint to the dressing room, but I don't. I probably couldn't find it on my own even if I tried. This place is an absolute maze. I keep up with Jones, two of my strides to his one, and I chew on the inside of my cheek to keep from smiling too big.

It's just a night out with a new friend.

Just a few drinks and some chill music at a trendy rooftop bar with Mabel Rossi, drummer for The Hometown Heartless. I haven't had a friend in so long. That's why I'm excited.

I bite my lower lip and fist my hands in front of me.

Just be cool, I tell myself. *Act like this is no big deal.*

She's just a famous, gorgeous, flirtatious rock star.

A rock star *with a girlfriend.*

I straighten my shoulders and work to tame my smile.

Just a night out with a friend.

As we approach the hallway with the dressing rooms, Jones lifts a walkie-talkie and announces my arrival. A voice I recognize as my uncle's tells him to leave me with *the girls*, which I take to mean Mabel and Sav. Jones drops the walkie to his side and nods to the hall.

"Their suite's on the right. Just head in."

"Thanks."

He leaves, and I stare down the hallway. I didn't pay attention when I was here this afternoon. It took me four tries to find the room where I was supposed to meet Uncle Wade, and as I walk slowly toward the dressing room doors, my stomach starts to turn somersaults.

"Suite on the right," I whisper as I step in front of the first door and turn to face it. "Shoulders back. Chin up."

I turn the knob and open the door.

And then all oxygen is sucked from my lungs.

Run, my body screams. *Get out of here.*

But I can't. I can't move. I can't even blink. I just stand there, cemented to the spot with my hand superglued to the door handle, and watch as the scene before me becomes achingly clear and technicolor.

Mabel's with someone.

Someone tall, and glossy, and gorgeous. Long dark hair. Golden skin. They're wrapped together, lips locked, hands everywhere. I catch a glimpse of the woman's long, red-painted nails as they glide up Mabel's side. Mabel laughs, and it feels like a knife, sexy and serrated, right into my chest. The woman gasps, the sound strangled and thick with arousal. My nipples peak, and my stomach roils.

Then, just as I am finally able to rip my feet from the floor, the woman's eyes open and land right on me.

"Get out! Get the fuck out!"

Her screams jolt me from my daze, and I back away. "I'm sorry. I'm sorry—"

"Get the fuck out of here!"

I turn and bolt. The door shuts behind me, and I'm halfway down the hall, running to I have no idea where, when it opens again.

"Aurora, wait! Hold on."

I freeze, but I don't turn around. I listen to Mabel's footsteps as she gets closer, the sound surprisingly light considering the thick platforms. When her hand wraps around my bicep, I bring mine to my face.

"I'm sorry. Jones told me to go in. I'm so sorry. I didn't know. I should have knocked. I didn't—"

"Breathe." Mabel squeezes my arm. "Breathe. It's fine. It's not a big deal."

"But she—she sounded so..."

Pissed.

"It was my fault. I should have locked the door. Honestly. It's not your fault. Are you okay?"

I drop my arms to my sides, tipping my head up toward the ceiling. I can't look at her yet. My face burns with embarrassment. Visions of Mabel and that woman flash behind my eyelids. My heart stays racing. My nipples stay peaked. My nausea increases.

"I'm fine. I just...God. I'm just really sorry. I really *did not* want to see that."

Mabel chuckles, but then the distance between our bodies shrinks. Despite my thoughts from just moments earlier, this proximity brings no excitement. It's all wrong. She smells like orange blossom and something muskier. Not the fun and flirty gardenia and fruit blend I've come to associate with her. No. This is a sexy smell. Sensual. It clouds the thoughts in my head until I can feel my heartbeat in my temples.

"Look...I trust you, okay? I do. But Kat wants me to make absolute certain you aren't going to tell anyone about this."

"Kat?" I open my eyes and fix them on her face, but her smudged lipstick makes me wince, so I look away again. "Kat Hughes? Your girlfriend is Kat Hughes?"

As I say the name, my mind sharpens the blurry parts of the memory. Slender and lithe. Sharp angles and elegance. My shoulders fall. Of course. She's a supermodel. Mabel's dating a supermodel, and for some reason, I find this news even more wrenching than the scene of them making out. I reach for the pendant of my necklace and rub the worn metal disc with my thumb. I can't remember the last time I was this uncomfortable.

"Yeah. And like I said before, it's important that it doesn't make it to the press."

"I'm not going to tell anyone, Mabel." I make eye contact and hold it, careful not to look at the way her lipstick is smudged over her full lips. "I promise. It's not my secret to share."

Mabel's eyes bounce between mine, searching for the truth in my words. When she finds what she's looking for, she nods.

"Look, I'm really sorry. I know we had plans, but I wasn't expecting Kat to show up. It was a surprise, so—"

"It's fine. I understand."

"Rain check?"

"Yeah, sure."

She nods once, her expression tight, and I can tell she feels bad. She shouldn't, though. That's her girlfriend. Of course she should cancel on me. Of course she should be with her. I know this. I *know*, but I can't fend off the disappointment.

Then she gives me a fake smile and nods in the direction of the dressing room. "Do you want to come back? I can introduce you. Kat's nice when she's not screaming *get the fuck out*. I promise."

I choke out a laugh. Her suggestion sounds about as appealing as cuddling with a cactus.

"I'm actually going to go back to the hotel. I'm not feeling well."

Her jaw ticks. "Is that the truth?"

I glance away. I don't answer her, but I don't walk back on my statement, either. Mabel sighs.

"Okay. I really am sorry, Aurora."

"Yeah, I know. You wouldn't say it if you weren't."

I wish I could read whatever emotion passes over her face. She pauses as if she's considering saying something else, but then she changes her mind. She gives me another small, fake smile and shrugs.

"See you tomorrow?"

"Tomorrow."

I jerk out one more nod, return her tight, forced smile, then head back the way I came. I keep my eyes fixed on the ground in front of me, despite the pull to stare at the closed door of the dressing room suite as I pass by.

I try to keep my cool the whole way back to the hotel, but the images keep circling. The gasps. The laughter. The smudged lipstick. The scent. I press my thighs together as my head swims. I don't know what I'm feeling. Jealousy? Anger? Disappointment?

Something else?

I close my eyes and shake my head, trying to clear the thoughts from my mind, but they don't budge. They just circle faster.

"Are you all right, Ms. Sinclair?"

"Yes. Just a headache."

My voice comes out weak, and he turns to look at me. "Do you need a medic?"

"No. No. Just sleep, thank you."

We make the rest of the drive in silence, and by the time I get to my room, my entire body is flushed and hot. I lock the door and pace the room, running my fingers through my hair.

"Stop it. Stop it."

But I can't stop. I see their arms tangled. I see her hands grasping and tugging. I see their lips locked, and then my imagination goes rogue. I hear moans and gasps that never happened. I see roaming hands I never witnessed.

I see *me*.

Me in Kat's place. Me wrapped up with Mabel. My lips. My gasps. My skin.

My breasts are heavy. My core aches. I'm buzzing with an

energy I've never felt before. My clit and nipples are so sensitive that even my cotton underwear feels tight. My heart thuds rapidly. Each inhale shakes with need. My body feels *alive*. I'm aroused, but it's more than that. This pressing, insistent *need*.

Desire, I realize. This must be desire, and it's completely foreign to me.

I can't be feeling this now. Not with her. I have a husband. I should be feeling this with my husband. Why, why, why have I never felt this with him? With *anyone*?

I shake my head again. I try to force it away. But I can't. I can't. I can't.

And then I realize that I don't want to.

Quickly, as if this moment is a forbidden, stolen thing, I pull off my strapless dress, then drop my bra to the floor beside it. I cup my aching breasts with trembling hands and brush my thumbs over my nipples. I whimper, the sound barely audible, but I swear it echoes in the darkness. I slide one hand into my panties and gasp at the wetness I find there. There's a twinge of shame, of embarrassment, and then it's gone. Incinerated by this pressing, heady need. Without a second thought, I climb into bed and crawl under the duvet.

Safely under the covers, I waste no time returning my hand between my legs, and the moment I brush my clit, my whole body shudders.

"Oh God," I gasp out, then I do it again.

Tentative, soft touches, exploring myself in a way I haven't in years. Only in my mind, it's not my hand.

It's Mabel's.

I watch, eyes shut and mouth agape, as her delicate fingers rub my clit. Her short, glittery black-painted fingernails sparkle as she moves over me. As she glides lower and swipes through me. As she pulses at my entrance.

"Oh, God," I cry again, my hips bucking, fingers slipping into my pussy just a little. "Oh my God."

I squeeze my breast, pinch my nipple, then dip my right hand into my panties to rub my clit as my left sinks into my wet, aching pussy. I writhe on the bed. The duvet tangles around my legs, and I imagine it's Mabel's legs instead.

Her thighs and calves wrapped with mine. Her mouth on my skin. Her fingers thrusting into my pussy, rubbing at my clit, making my muscles shake with the impending release.

My body bows when I come, and I choke out a strangled, almost silent moan. I'm sweating and panting. The bedsheets beneath my ass are wet with my cum. My pussy throbs with the hot blood coursing through my veins. I'm floating, floating, floating.

And then I crash.

My muscles tighten, the shame returning with a vicious vengeance, and I want to be swallowed up by the mattress. I want to disappear.

I just masturbated to Mabel Rossi.

I'm married. I'm in love with *Brady*. I'm not into Mabel. I'm not. But I just masturbated with her face in my mind and her name on my breath, and my orgasm was so strong I saw white.

"Oh God."

Once more, my whispered words echo in the darkness.

But this time, all I hear is dread.

10

AURORA

"WAIT."

Brynnlee scans the words on the page, her brows slanted so harshly I worry she'll give herself a headache.

"I thought this was supposed to be a love story? They die. They are *literally* dead. RIP them. This is depressing as hell."

"Common misconception."

She brings her wide eyes to meet mine.

"How? There is *nothing* romantic about this! They are *dead* at the end. They literally die by suicide. How can the misconception be common when it literally ends with their funeral?"

It takes everything in me not to laugh at her exasperation.

"Well, it is a *tragic* love story, but it's not *just* a tragic love story, and people often forget that."

"Or they haven't read it."

"Or that."

Brynn huffs and drops the paperback onto the couch beside her.

"I thought Romeo and Juliet were supposed to be bastions of true love? Taylor Swift even wrote a whole song about them. But why? They're idiots."

"What makes you say that?"

She arches a brow. "Well, for starters, maybe if they would have thought things through before going off half-cocked on some harebrained plan, they'd both still be alive. *Or if Romeo would have just waited ten minutes before drinking the poison, he'd have found out that Juliet wasn't actually dead, and they'd both still be alive.* Or, at the very least, Juliet could have said *oh bummer, he's dead, but I'm young and will get over it,* and then just *not* impaled herself on a stupid dagger, then *she'd* still be alive."

I bite my lip and nod, my eyes twitching from how hard I'm trying not to laugh.

"Valid critiques."

"Oh, and you know what else?"

"Tell me."

"I know Juliet didn't want to marry that one guy. What's his name? Ferris?"

"Paris."

"Right, him. I know she didn't want to marry that guy, but Romeo? Really? He was in love with that Rosa girl like an hour before he met Juliet, but Rosa wouldn't sleep with him, so then he sees Juliet and suddenly thinks he's in love with her? He's so capricious! He's so fickle! Frankly—and excuse me for this but Sav says that if a word applies contextually and isn't being used to dehumanize someone, then it's okay to say, and Romeo is fictional, so I don't have to feel guilty for insulting him—it's fuck boy behavior. He's not someone you *marry*. He's someone you avoid. This is why children shouldn't be making important decisions. Their brains are underdeveloped, and their hormones make them morons. This is why I've decided not to date until I'm eighteen."

I smile. I don't miss how she said *she's* decided, not her dad or Sav, which fits with the girl I've gotten to know. She knows her own mind, and I envy that about her. She's got a spark that I recognize, and I hope nothing ever happens to snuff it out.

"Actually," I say slowly, "Romeo is believed to be around twenty-one."

Brynn blinks. "But Juliet is thirteen."

"That's right."

"She's thirteen and he's twenty-one?" I nod, and Brynn's lip curls in disgust. "Ew, Aurora."

I can't hold it back anymore. I laugh.

"In our society today, it is definitely ew. But in fourteenth century Italy, age gaps like that were the norm. Count Paris was probably in his late teens to early twenties, too."

"Yeah, and I thought that was why Juliet was so desperate to avoid marrying him." Brynn throws herself onto the couch dramatically and stares at the ceiling. "I can't believe this play is so popular. It's just a creepy old guy trying to groom a child, and then they both die." She turns to look at me. "*That's* the misconception. It's not a love story. It's a cautionary tale about miscommunication, rash behavior, and pedophilia."

"You feel pretty strongly about that, huh?" I ask with a grin.

"Absolutely."

"Strongly enough to write a five-page paper?"

She pushes herself up with a groan. "If I must."

"Would you like help with the outline?"

"You know, I could probably just write it without the outline..."

"Well, unfortunately, the outline—"

"Is required by the program," she finishes with a sigh. "I know. Oh, but maybe I could write the paper and then fill in the outline after? They'll never know."

I smirk. "How about we do the first few the proper way. If you do them well, I'll let you try it your way."

Her answering grin makes me feel like I just struck a deal with the devil. She looks so much like Sav in this moment that I almost forget they're not blood related.

"I'm holding you to that," she says, and I nod.

"I'm a woman of my word."

Brynn turns on her tablet and gets to work completing the outline template required by her homeschool program, so I stand from the couch and make my way toward the kitchenette area of the suite. Sav ordered a continental breakfast of sorts, which from what I'm learning is the norm. Since I've been here this morning, Torren, Callie, and Claire have all filtered in and out, snagging food. I haven't seen Mabel, though. I've been watching.

"How's it going?" Levi looks up at me from a tablet of his own, a stylus in his hand and something resembling construction blueprints on the screen. "She giving you hell?"

I grin and grab a glass to pour myself some orange juice.

"It's going well. She might not like the subject matter, but she's very smart. I don't think she's going to struggle much, if at all."

He sets his stylus on the table. "When it comes to academics, if something doesn't click immediately for Boss, it makes her uncomfortable. She'll gladly work her ass off at anything else—guitar, drawing, skateboarding—but when it comes to school, she's either all in or all out."

"I can see that. It seems like the interpretation stuff is what gets her. Clear correct and incorrect, she can do no problem, but when the answer is up for interpretation? She doesn't like that."

Levi nods. "Nailed it."

"We'll get through it," I say confidently, then gesture to the tablet. "Work?"

"Yeah, kind of. I'm consulting on a project for a buddy of mine. A mansion on the coast, but the client has some big ideas, so I'm helping make sure they're carried out safely."

"Is the client someone famous? A name I'd recognize?"

He flares his eyes. "It's a name everyone would recognize. That's why it's also top secret."

"Intriguing."

"Don't try to get it out of him," Sav says as she saunters into the kitchen. "He won't even tell me."

"You'll tell Mabel," Levi says dryly.

Sav flashes me a smirk and a roll of her eyes, but she doesn't deny it. I watch her survey the breakfast spread, then snag a mini blueberry muffin.

Last night, she had on a full face of makeup and this open-back leather and lace ensemble that hugged every curve and showed off a tattoo of dahlias down her spine. This morning, she's in baggy sweats and an oversized shirt that says East Coast Contracting on the breast pocket. Her face is bare. Her hair is ratty and piled on top of her head in a sloppy bun. Two very different sides to the rock star, but both fit her effortlessly.

Everyone in this band seems so comfortable in their own skin. Even Brynnlee, and she's only twelve. It makes me envious. Envious and itchy, as if my own skin is too tight or too dry. I fiddle with the skirt of my dress and resist the urge to adjust the sleeves. Until a few years ago, I never wore dresses. Now my closet is full of them. I can't for the life of me remember how that happened. Brady likes them, though.

I frown and redirect my train of thought.

"What time do you have to be at the venue for sound check?" I take a sip of my juice and bounce my eyes between Sav and Levi. "I think I'd like to do some exploring before the show."

"I'll have to ask Ham—"

The door to the suite swings wide, revealing Mabel in full glam, and I stop breathing.

"Good morning, family. I'm here for breakfast."

Levi raises a brow at Sav, then rolls his head toward Mabel.

"This is late for you, Mabes. Busy night?"

Mabel hums, but as she opens her mouth to speak, her eyes fall on me, and she stops short. Her lips purse momentarily, but then the flicker of concern is gone.

"Something like that." She gives me a soft smile before picking up a plate and piling it with fruit. "Morning, Roar."

I return her smile, then check out the table in an effort to quell the blush triggered by her presence and the nickname on her tongue. Maybe it will be easier if I'm not looking directly at her.

"Good morning."

"She's still here, then?" Sav's tone is flat, and when I bring my attention to her face, her expression matches.

"Yep." Mabel's response is clipped. Her voice is pitched like she's trying to come off cheerful and failing. "Here for the week."

They're talking about Kat, and all at once, the images of her wrapped around Mabel flood my head. Those images plagued my dreams, only instead of Kat and Mabel, it was me and Mabel. I don't understand where it came from or how it happened, but the memory makes me blush hot with guilt and embarrassment. With *arousal*. It's all so confusing, my feelings muddled and indecipherable. I try to force them away, but the truth of what I did remains.

I'd managed to dam up these thoughts while I was working with Brynn, but now that dam has busted, and I'm drowning. I'll choke on them and die. My palms start to sweat, and my heart starts to race.

I need to get out of here.

Sav hums, and Levi pushes himself up from the table, picking up his tablet and empty plate. He flares his eyes at me, then leaves the kitchen area without another word. In his absence, the tension in the air thickens, and if leaving didn't require me walking right through Sav and Mabel's stare off, I'd sneak out just like Levi.

"Should we re-brief the Caveat boys, then?" Sav asks cryptically.

"Ham took care of it."

"Then why is she hiding in your room while you bring her breakfast? Still doesn't want to be spotted?"

Mabel scoffs. "No. It's because she knows you're pissed, and she doesn't want to deal with your glares."

"Excuse me. I won an Oscar. I can pretend to be civil."

"Please. You might have won an Oscar for acting, but you can't lie for shit."

Sav smirks and gives Mabel a nonchalant shrug, but then her expression shifts to something kinder. When she speaks, her voice is soft, and her tone is genuine.

"I'm glad she showed up for you. I'll be nice. I promise. Tell her to come eat breakfast with us." Mabel squints to study Sav's face, making Sav bark out a laugh. "I'm serious. Here, I'll even invite her myself."

As Sav takes out her phone to send a text, my heart starts to pound. When I look at Mabel, she's staring at Sav, but I get the distinct feeling she's also paying attention to me. I stand up straighter and clear my throat.

"Right, well, I'm going to head back to my room. I'll see you all for the show."

"Wait, Aurora," Brynn calls from the couch. "Can you come here? I'm a little stuck."

I look from Brynn to Mabel and back. God, I don't want to be here when Kat Hughes struts in, all glitz and glam in her supermodel body, but helping Brynnlee is my literal job at the moment. She is why I'm here.

I'm taking a seat on the couch next to Brynn when there's a knock on the door. I keep my eyes pinned on the computer screen, but I still see Mabel open the door in my periphery. I can still see the blurry, shadowy figure of Kat Hughes walk in, too. It might all be in my head, but I swear the encroaching scent of musk and orange blossom taints the oxygen in the room. I clear my throat and stifle a cough.

I fidget once more with my dress. It takes effort to keep my shoulders back and my chin up when everything inside me is screaming to bolt. Greetings take place between Sav and Kat. I can't make out the words. I can't analyze the tone. My heart is too loud in my head.

Then the figures in my periphery grow closer, until I can feel them standing only feet from me.

"Aurora and Brynn, this is Kat. Kat, this is Sav and Levi's daughter Brynnlee, and her tutor, Aurora."

I glance up at them. Kat's smiling, but it's tight, as if she's nervous. Even with the unnatural expression, though, she's beautiful. Almost lethally so. Like a spy in a blockbuster movie. Like a Bond girl. No doubt a face like hers could con someone out of nuclear codes or convince them to open a top secret safe. Not a shiny hair out of place. Not a wrinkle or blemish to be seen on her golden skin. She might actually be perfectly symmetrical. It makes my skin prickle with jealousy. I think I hate her.

"Hey." I raise my hand in an awkward wave, but I can't bring myself to stand. Not yet. "Nice to meet you."

"Hi," Brynn says, and thankfully she stays seated too. "I've seen you on a billboard for a perfume."

Kat laughs. "It's nice to meet you both."

Ugh. And her voice is smooth and sweet, like syrup. I frown before I can stop myself. I do hate her, and I never hate anyone.

"Are you Mabel's girlfriend?"

Brynn's forward question has Kat glancing nervously at Mabel, so I turn my attention to her as well. Mabel gives Brynn a small smile, and when she answers, her eyes collide with mine.

"Yes, Kat is my girlfriend."

Her words aren't surprising, but I still have to fight off a wince. Despite Mabel being the one to answer, Brynn's attention stays on Kat.

"How long are you staying? We're going to see koalas in Sydney. Will you be coming for that?"

Kat and Mabel answer at the same time.

"For the week."

"Just for today."

My eyes widen as Mabel whips her attention to Kat, forehead creased and jaw tight.

"Just today?"

Kat frowns. "I was going to tell you."

"An hour ago, you were staying for the week."

Kat looks quickly between me and Brynn before turning back to Mabel. "Let's take breakfast back to your room."

Mabel blinks, and I watch as her body seems to deflate with defeat.

"Fine." She looks back to me and Brynn. "See you later."

As they turn to leave, the door to the suite swings wide once more. My uncle walks through and the male members of Caveat Lover follow.

Uncle Wade told me they'd be on this tour, too. They've taken over the music scene in recent years, but I've been a little out of touch with pop culture, so I researched them. In this moment, I'm almost sorry I did. Nothing makes you feel small and unremarkable quite like being in the presence of global superstars.

The hotel suite seems to grow smaller as I watch them file in one by one. Rocky Hallstrom, the lead guitarist, is first, followed closely by Becket Walker, the bassist, Ezra Hawke, the drummer, and Crue, the mysterious rhythm guitarist without a surname. Well, I'm sure he *has* a surname. I just couldn't find it.

And then, when the door closes behind them, realization makes my skin itch. I'm officially in a room with half of The Hometown Heartless and almost all of Caveat Lover.

Brynn groans, then grumbles under her breath, "Caveat boys."

As if summoned, Ezra Hawke turns toward us. From what I've read, the media has dubbed him Caveat Lover's prankster and playboy. His eyes lock on Brynn, and a big, good-natured smile curves his lips. He saunters over toward the couch, looking just like a big brother prepping to cause trouble. Grief swells in my chest, but so does joy, and I can't help but want to smile with him.

"Boss," he croons. "What's the word?"

"Ezra." Brynn lets out a loud, exasperated sigh. "*Vexatious.* Adjective. Causing or tending to cause annoyance, frustration, or worry."

Ezra laughs. "I know where you're going with this one, kid. Nice try but—"

"I got it." Crue steps up, dropping his arm over Ezra's shoulder and winking at Brynn. "The little girl found the immature drummer to be extremely *vexatious.*"

Brynn rolls her eyes. "B plus, Crue."

Crue's jaw drops, and Ezra barks out a laugh.

"What do you mean *B plus*?" Crue says, whining in his English accent. "Don't be cheeky, Brynnlee. I went to an all-boys prep school. I will fight for top marks."

Brynn shrugs. "You called me little. I'm twelve."

I let out a small laugh at her tone, but then immediately wish I hadn't. The noise draws both pairs of eyes my way until the guys are peering down at me, and it takes everything I have not to get up and run. I'm so nervous that I almost forget that Kat and Mabel are looming beside me. *Almost.*

"The niece," Ezra says, and his smile morphs into something a little less *prankster* and a lot more *playboy.* "You must be Aurora. Ham's told us all about you."

The guys are standing so close that craning my neck is almost painful, so I reluctantly leave my protective cocoon of couch pillows and stand. I wipe my hand on my dress before jutting it out between us.

"Hi. Yes. I'm Aurora."

"Ezra Hawke." He takes my hand in both of his and brings it to his lips, pressing a soft kiss to my knuckles. "It's a pleasure."

Brynn makes a loud retching noise on the couch, breaking the tension, and I bite my cheek to keep from laughing again. Ezra sends her a side-eyed smirk, then drops my hand.

"I'm Crue." The guitarist nods in my direction, but he doesn't offer his hand, so I nod back. "And what Hawke means is that Ham's warned us off you."

I laugh awkwardly, fidgeting under their attention.

"Nice to meet you."

My cheeks and neck grow warmer until thankfully Mabel interrupts.

"Boys, this is my girlfriend, Kat. Kat, this is Ezra and Crue of Caveat Lover."

Both guys turn toward Mabel, and my shoulders fall with relief. Now that their focus is no longer on me, I lower myself back onto the couch beside Brynn. When I glance at her, she shakes her head and rolls her eyes, engaging me in a wordless conversation expressing her annoyance, and I grin. Vexatious indeed. I might be uncomfortable, but at least it's a bonding moment.

"Sorry, Rossi. We missed you there. You're just so tiny," Ezra teases.

Mabel narrows her eyes and smirks, but then Ezra's mouth goes slack before turning up into another wide, toothy grin. He looks from Kat to Mabel and back.

"Kat Hughes? *You're* Secret Girlfriend?"

Ezra elbows Crue as if he hasn't been part of the conversation all along.

"Dude, look. Secret Girlfriend is Kat Hughes." He puts out his hand, palm up. "I win, wanker."

"Fuck," Crue grumbles and pulls out his wallet.

"What did you fuckers bet on?" Mabel asks as Crue slaps a one-hundred-dollar bill in Ezra's hand.

"I thought Secret Girlfriend would be more masc," Crue admits on a sigh. "I just pictured you with a butch lesbian, Mabes." He turns to Kat and gives her a chagrinned smile. "No offense, Kat Hughes. You make a smashing Secret Girlfriend as well."

"None taken," Kat says flatly, her tone suggesting she does in fact take offense, but neither of the guys seems to notice. Or care.

"Wait," Crue says, head tilted in consideration. "Kat Hughes, I thought you were dating that Kaz fellow. With the blond hair and skinny jeans from that one show on the streaming platform."

"Great description," Ezra taunts.

Crue punches him in the shoulder without looking away from Kat.

Kat flicks her eyes from Crue to Mabel, her expression one of pure discomfort, so Mabel steps in front of her and gives Crue's chest a little nudge.

"Okay, boys. Enough questions. Go eat food or something."

"Actually," Crue says, spinning away from Mabel, eyes returning to me. My spine goes ramrod straight. "Ez, I think you need to give me back that Benjamin."

Then Ezra turns to look at me, smile slipping from his face. He tips his head to the ceiling and groans.

"What?" I ask, brows furrowed as Crue snatches the money from Ezra's fingers. "What did I do?"

Ezra sighs. "You've got Ham's genes."

I have no idea what that means, and my face must show it because Crue clarifies for me.

"Ham's hot. Must run in the family."

Before I have a chance to respond, Ezra drops onto the couch beside me, arm stretching across the back. He smells fresh and clean, like laundry detergent, and I'm dwarfed by the sheer size of his frame. I'm not short, but I didn't realize Ezra Hawke was so broad until just now.

"Scoot, Boss," Crue says, and it's all the warning he gives Brynn before he's plopping down on the other side of me.

"You're going to scare off my tutor," Brynn says, giving Crue's shoulder a shove. "She's not used to your brand of stupidity."

"Then we must expose ourselves to her."

I choke on a laugh as Crue's eyes widen the moment he realizes what he said.

"Apologies. That came out wrong."

"Good God, Crue," Mabel says on a groan, and Ezra snorts, but I keep my attention on the guitarist.

"It's fine," I say, my tone belying the humor I feel. "I know what you meant."

"Don't tell them that. They'll never shut up now."

Ezra leans over me to grin at Brynn. "Don't act like you don't love us, Boss."

"I find you loathsome."

I bark out another laugh, and the guys glance at me again. Then they look at each other as if sharing thoughts.

"What?"

"Even your laugh is hot," Ezra says.

I laugh again before I can stop myself, my hand shooting up to cover my mouth.

"You two are dangerous for my ego," I mumble between my fingers.

Ezra drapes his arm over my shoulders. "Or maybe we're just what you—"

"Hands off, Hawke."

My uncle's stern eyes are set on Ezra.

"I'm just saying hello, Ham. Introducing myself."

Uncle Wade arches a bored brow. He sees right through Ezra, and Ezra knows it. He sighs dramatically and reluctantly slides his arm off my shoulders like a scolded child. It's beyond amusing to watch my uncle wield this authority over people who, just moments ago, felt larger than life. I'm smiling so big my cheeks hurt, the discomfort from earlier rapidly dissipating until...

"I don't think her husband would approve."

My eyes widen at my uncle's words, spoken so plainly, yet the result feels like a slice on my skin. Like a betrayal, despite their truth. Uncle Wade's brows furrow slightly, and I work quickly to wipe my expression away. It doesn't matter, though. He saw.

"Husband," Mabel says. I whip my head toward her and find her staring at me. Face blank. Voice even. I can't tell what she's thinking. "You're married."

I nod once, and she drops her eyes to my hand.

"Where's your ring?"

"Oh." I fold my hands in my lap so I don't shove them under my thighs. "It hurts." I wince and add quickly, "I mean, it's uncomfortable because it's too small, and my fingers have swelled with the travel, so it hurts a little. I need to get it resized."

Slowly, Mabel drags her eyes back up to mine, and our gazes lock. She doesn't say anything else, but I can't look away. Not even when I know we've held the stare too long. Not even when I know the others have noticed. I feel the energy in the air shift into something tense and strange, but I still can't look away. Not until my uncle clears his throat, effectively yanking my attention to him. He's got two little lines between his eyes, and his jaw ticks as he studies me.

Whatever he's thinking, it needs to stop.

I shoot to my feet, plaster on a fake smile, and avoid eye contact with everyone.

"Sorry. I'm sorry. Anyway. I had some stuff I wanted to do. To get done. So, um, I'll...I'll see you all...Um. Bye."

I walk past Ezra and Crue and Brynn. Past Mabel and Kat. I keep my eyes on the ground in front of me. I'm steps from freedom when my uncle wraps his hand around my bicep, halting me in my tracks. Reluctantly, I look up into his face.

"Yes?"

His hazel eyes bounce between mine, and I plead silently with him.

Don't ask me anything. Don't say anything. Please, please, please. Just let me leave.

Finally, he jerks out a small nod, and relief surges through me.

"Jones will be accompanying—"

"Oh, that's okay. I don't need—"

He arches that eyebrow again, and I shut my mouth. There's no way he'll let me out of the hotel without a security detail, anyway, and I don't want to waste time arguing with him. I just need to get out of this suite.

"He'll meet you at your room in an hour."

"Okay."

He releases my arm and steps back, opening my path to the door.

"Have fun today, Aurora. You're young and fearless. Act it."

He smiles. It's small, but it's real, and it pulls a matching smile to my own face.

"Thanks, Uncle Wade," I say quietly, and then I speedwalk out of the suite.

11

MABEL

"Wow."

The word comes out in a whisper drenched in awe as I climb out of the SUV, then I spin in a slow circle, taking everything in. Rolling green vineyards and wild eucalyptus stretch for miles, their silvery-green leaves shimmering in the afternoon light.

And the scent.

I close my eyes and inhale. Crushed herbs, woodsmoke, the faint sweetness of flowering gums. It smells clean and untouched. *Unburdened.* It's so different from the air back home.

I turn to Sav. I knew she was up to something the moment we stepped off the jet, but renting out a luxury eco-lodge on top of Adelaide's Mount Lofty isn't at all what I expected.

"Do you have surprises like this up your sleeve for the whole tour?"

She smiles, almost shyly, and shrugs. "You like it? You wouldn't rather be in a five-star hotel?"

I huff out a breathy laugh. "Savannah. This is fucking gorgeous. It's perfect. Seriously. I feel like we've stayed in so many hotels that they blend together at this point, but this..."

I trail off and shake my head, lost for words as I admire the romantic façade of our home for the next week. It's all native stone, warm timber, and sweeping glass. Modern, but not sterile, and it feels almost as if the building wasn't built on the hillside, but rather molded from it.

"Yeah," Sav says, "that's what I was thinking, too. I never got to go on a vacation as a kid. I know you and Tor really didn't either, and Jo...Well, nothing he did with his family was ever a good experience. Now that we've got Brynn and Teddy...I don't know. I want to make it good for them, you know? Memorable. We're able to do something most people only dream about, and I want to make the most of it. For them and for us."

Her voice cracks, and my eyes sting with the hint of tears. I glance at her with a smile.

"Family vacations from now on?"

She meets my eyes with a smile of her own. "From now on."

One of the unforeseen perks of our front woman also being the CEO of our record label is the intentionality she puts into everything. No more long, grueling tour schedules with no time to breathe or sleep between shows. Now we get to enjoy the travel. We get to rest and adventure and *experience* everything.

Family vacations from now on.

"Thanks, Savvy."

She smirks. "The Caveat Boys don't know how good they have it."

On cue, Ezra whoops as he hops out of their SUV, and then he grunts as if someone socked him in the gut.

"You should have put them up in a hotel."

She sighs. "Probably, but I didn't want to separate them from Callie. Band bonding and all that." She turns to look at me. "I'm sorry Kat couldn't stay."

I shrug but I say nothing. I don't even know if *I'm* sorry she couldn't stay. We fought before she left. Things were tense, and I'm still not sure how I feel about all of it. This weird friendship with Kaz has always weighed on me, but it's been feeling heavier lately. More crushing and harder to carry.

I'm questioning if it's all worth it.

If she wanted to, she would.

But do I want her to? The answer evades me. I'm not sure what I want right now.

My eyes drift to Aurora. She's standing between Hammond and Payton Jones, her newly appointed security guard, and they're chatting about something I can't hear.

I'm certain she's been avoiding me, and while that bothers me, I'd be lying if I didn't say I was a bit relieved, too. In her absence, I didn't have to analyze things I wasn't comfortable acknowledging. I could pretend that it didn't sting to hear that she was married. That I wasn't hit with a wave of disappointment so strong that I was momentarily shocked.

This morning, though...

This morning, I woke up feeling...I don't know...*Pulled* to her, I guess. I couldn't ignore the itch to talk to her. To see her. She sat next to Ham on the jet, then rode in an SUV with him and Jones, so I haven't had a chance to talk to her. I haven't seen her since Friday morning in Sav's suite, and now it's like I can't stop looking at her.

She's wearing another dress—this one maroon with capped sleeves—her hair is in a loose French braid, and she's got her orchid held snuggly in her arms. I smile. *Arthur Orchidaceae.* It might be the lighting, but he's looking a little greener than he did last time I saw him.

Then she laughs at something her security detail says, and I feel another prickle of jealousy. Jones is a tall guy with curly brown hair and tattooed sleeves. He's one of our more attractive guards. I wonder if this is her type. A guy who is lean and toned with full lips and a strong jaw. A young guy. Someone closer to her age.

I bristle and tell myself to stop being ridiculous. Aurora is married. She's not interested in Jones. Then I frown. *Married.*

She's married, and I'm in a committed relationship.

None of it should bother me.

All of it does.

When she catches me staring, I wipe away my frown and replace it with a small smile. She smiles back, and I find my feet moving before I can think better of it. I reach her side just as our group starts walking toward the lodge entrance.

"Are you feeling better?"

She glances at me quickly, then looks away. "What do you mean?"

"You weren't at the shows this weekend. I haven't seen you."

It's not fair to bring this up, but I can't help it. She shrugs.

"Yes. I'm feeling fine."

I study the side of her face. She'd be taller than me if I were barefooted, but not by much. It would be a comfortable height difference. Kat's taller than me, and she hates it. Says she'd be forced to wear flats if we were ever out in public. I wonder if Aurora would hate it, too.

"How tall are you?" I ask, and her lips quirk up.

"I'm five-seven. How tall are you?"

"How tall do you think I am?"

She looks at me, and it makes me nervous in an exciting way. Her eyes drag from the top of my head to the bottom of my platform combat boots. Then, she looks from her shoulder to mine and back. She purses her lips and thinks for a moment before speaking.

"Five-one?"

"Five-two."

"I was close." She drops her eyes to my shoes again. "I'd fall on my face if I wore those."

"I have, like, fifteen years of practice."

Aurora huffs a soft laugh, and I change the subject.

"Is it just me, or is Arthur looking happier?"

"Oh, no, it's not just you." Her answering grin is contagious. "He's definitely perked up, which is surprising, you know, because I thought I would have trouble regulating the humidity and temperature being in hotels and such, but so far—judging from Arthur, of course—I guess it's not been hard at all. His leaves are greener and plumper, see? And if you look at his roots—well you can't see them while he's in the planter, but I can show you in a second if you want—they're finally getting that healthy silvery green color. He's been waffling between, like, yellows and browns and papery whites. Like too dry and too wet, you know? But he's doing good right now. And Uncle Wade said that this lodge has really precise climate controls in the suites, and the sunlight is perfectly filtered outside, too, so I think he'll be able to spend some time in the fresh air. Oh, and look!"

She holds the planter out so it's inches from my face, then points at one of the stems.

"See that bud there? I think it's growing. Just a little. Usually, by this point, he'd droop and lose the bud. That's called a bud blast. It's so disappointing, but I've gotten used to it. It's not happening right now, though. At least not yet."

She pulls the planter back to her chest and beams up at me with a wide smile. She's beautiful when she smiles like this, and I can't help but smile too. Her cheeks are flushed, her blonde hair is wisping around her head like a halo, and the green in her hazel irises seems to sparkle. She's breathtaking, actually. She's radiating joy.

"I like when you talk about your orchid."

Aurora's brows jump at my confession, the flush on her cheeks grows darker, and she folds her lips between her teeth as if trying to tame a smile. Her eyes bounce between mine, and when she speaks, her voice has lowered. Spoken just between us.

"Why?"

"You light up. Your smile is unbidden. You're not self-conscious. You seem *real*."

Her lips part, and she blinks several times before she breaks our eye contact, dropping her gaze to the ground in front of us. The mood shifts, and my shoulders fall when I see hers droop.

"Oh."

"Hey. What did I say? What's wrong?"

"I don't know, actually." She shrugs, but she won't look at me again as she forces out a quiet, almost sad laugh. "I don't know anything right now."

I have no idea what to say to that. I want to touch or hug her. I want to make her talk to me. I do none of it. Then Ham's voice breaks into our bubble, and we both turn to face him as he addresses the group.

"All right, listen up. We've got the whole lodge for the week. It's just us, so you have access to all of it. The restaurant is staffed from six a.m. to eleven p.m. for us, and they'll be stocking refrigerators in the lounge for after hours. The spa is also staffed, but they do ask that you make an appointment if you want to use their services. The estate is thirty acres. On the grounds, there are six spring-fed hot pools, an infinity pool, a wildlife enclosure, several walking trails, and a tennis court. You can book tours with the front desk or explore the estate on your own, but if you want to leave the grounds, check in with me first and take security with you. I'll give you a map and an information sheet with the key to your suite."

He focuses his attention on someone behind me, and I don't have to look to know it's Ezra and Crue.

"Look at the map and information sheet *before* texting me with your questions, and just because we're the only guests here, doesn't mean we don't have to act with decorum. You're still public figures. You still need to be professional. You still need to be respectful of the staff, the grounds, and each other. I do not want another incident like we had in Amsterdam. Do you understand?"

I smirk as the Caveat boys grumble their agreement, and I bet Crue and Ezra resemble scolded puppies.

In Amsterdam, the two of them got fucked up on mushrooms and somehow dyed the water in the pool and hot tub blue. They have no recollection of how they did it, but Ham found them in the sauna giggling like idiot smurfs with their skin dyed bright blue from the nipples down—dicks and all—five hours before their show.

Rock Loveless Records, Sav's label, had to fork out a fuck ton of money to replace the hot tub, fix the pool, and keep the staff from running to the tabloids. The boys earned themselves another security guard after that. Sav was less pissed than Ham, but that's because she's no stranger to making dumb decisions. I told her this is karma for her pre-sobriety days, and she just laughed.

In the boys' defense, they didn't expect the mushrooms to be that strong.

And also, they're morons.

"You'll have your usual roommates," Ham continues, and I feel Aurora stiffen beside me. Then Ham looks at me, and I understand why. "Rossi, I put you with Aurora. I already spoke to her about it."

It's not unlike Ham to do things like this without consulting us. He definitely lives by the *ask for forgiveness, not permission* philosophy. Though, he doesn't ask for forgiveness, either, come to think of it. He just changes things and expects a thank you.

I give him a thumbs-up, then glance at Aurora.

"You good, roomie?"

Her throat contracts with a swallow. "Yep. Good."

I nod. "Great. Me too."

That foundation of truth is feeling a little unsteady under my feet.

12

MABEL

THE LETTERS on the screen blur as I stare at them, my cursor flashing impatiently in the blank reply box.

I've already typed and deleted my email greeting three times. It shouldn't be this hard to commit, but it is. I either agree to schedule a phone call with my lawyer or I don't. If I don't, the thousands of dollars I've already paid her goes to waste, which makes me sick to my stomach. But if I do...

Well, that makes me nauseous as well.

I close my eyes and bring my fingers up to pinch the bridge of my nose.

Which choice is easier to live with? I think I know the answer, but I don't think I like it.

"Are you okay?"

Aurora's voice halts the back and forth inside my head, and I snap my eyes open to find her standing in the doorway to the bedroom.

Our *shared* bedroom.

That's another detail I've yet to fully process.

She's wearing a pair of shorts, a tank top, and tennis shoes, and I can't help but do a double take. I haven't seen her in anything besides loose-fitting sundresses, so my eyes dart from her body in the doorway to my laptop, then back before I can stop myself.

Her tank top is the kind with thin straps and a built-in bra. It's not tight around her torso, but it leaves little to the imagination. And the way her shorts sit on her wide hips...The way the fabric stretches and smooths over her skin and curves I shouldn't be noticing...

I glance at her left hand, but there's still no ring, then I force my eyes to her face and smile.

"Yeah, I'm good. Just obligations I'd rather ignore." I close my laptop and set it on the couch beside me. "Are you heading out?"

"Yeah. I wanted to check out the walking trails." She waves the map Ham gave us in the air between us. "Do a little exploring."

"That sounds like fun."

She reaches up and toys with the pendant on her necklace, and I follow the movement. I'm admiring the way the silver chain decorates the soft spot where her shoulders meet her neck when she surprises me.

"Do you want to come with? It could help you ignore those obligations a little longer."

My eyes meet hers, and it's the shy hope I see that has me standing from the couch.

"I'd like that. Just give me a second to change."

"You mean you don't want to hike in a tutu and platform combat boots?'

Her lips twitch into a smirk, and my heart kicks up at the playfulness in her tone.

"Not unless you want to give me a piggyback ride."

"I probably could, honestly."

I laugh, lowering my voice as I pass her. "Don't tempt me with that apple, Eve. I just might bite."

Her small gasp makes my smile widen as I shut the bedroom door, and it serves as a quiet reminder of how easily I could cross lines with her without even trying.

Married, I remind myself. She's married. Flirting isn't harmless when there are other people involved.

I change into a pair of leggings, a sports bra, and a cropped shirt, then pull on my only pair of tennis shoes. I throw my hair into a ponytail, touch up my eyeliner and lipstick, then grab a pair of sunglasses before heading back into the main room of our shared suite.

"Ready?" she asks, and I nod.

"Lead the way."

I follow Aurora to the lodge lounge, where we pick up two waters, then out onto the grounds, and for a long while, we don't talk. We just exist peacefully side by side, appreciating the wild beauty around us. I inhale deeply, filling my lungs with the scent of eucalyptus and sweet gums as I take it all in.

The trail is earthy beneath my sneakers, and the farther we walk, the more decorated it becomes with fallen leaves and bark. Colorful birds flash through the trees, their songs echoing like laughter, and every step makes me feel lighter. Like each exhale relieves me of an invisible weight, and each inhale fills the open space with something fresh and new. Something clean and unburdened. It's exactly what I've been needing.

"It's perfect."

Aurora gives voice to my thoughts, her tone almost dreamy. I turn and find her gazing up at the canopy with a small smile playing on her plump lips. She looks like something out of a fairy tale. Magical and alluring and effortless.

The sunlight filtering through the trees casts a patchwork of glittery shadows on her bare shoulders, the silver chain of her necklace shimmers when it catches the light, and there's a smear of sunscreen on her collarbone that I didn't notice before. My pulse stutters, and I fist my hands to keep from reaching out. To fight the urge to rub it into her skin.

I should be thinking about elevation and trail markers, not how she would feel beneath my fingertips. I should be admiring the natural beauty of Mount Lofty and the Adelaide Hills, but I can't bring myself to look away from her. The way the light dances along her cheekbones, the softness of her mouth, the sparkle of green in her eyes. She's not even trying to hold my attention, and that almost makes it worse.

Married. She's married. I'm dating someone. I repeat it in my head three times and look away from her before I reply.

"It is. And Sav was worried we'd prefer a five-star hotel over this."

"I still can't believe I'm here. I used to want to travel when I was younger, but I kind of gave up on that dream. I didn't think it was possible."

My brows fold inward. "You're only twenty-three, Aurora."

Twenty-three.

To think of her giving up on any dream makes my chest ache with sorrow, especially at twenty-three. She reaches up and rubs the circular pendant on her necklace.

"You sound like my uncle."

"Oh God." I laugh. "Ham might be a hard-ass, but I think he's right about this one."

She shrugs. "I don't know. I guess it just doesn't fit into my life plan anymore."

My eyes fall to her left hand again. No ring.

I reach out and brush my fingers down her forearm, and when she looks at me, I have to suppress a shiver. This isn't a stage. There's no audience out here. But something about Aurora's attention feels better than any concert. More thrilling than any spotlight.

"Life is full of changes. No plan is set in stone."

My fingertips tingle from the fleeting caress, and I hold her gaze for a few more breaths. I commit every fleck of green and gold and brown in her eyes to memory, and then I look away.

"What else did you use to want? Before now."

"A greenhouse and poetry."

I feel her eyes on me, assessing my reaction—searching for any hint of judgment—so I smile.

"Tell me more."

In the silence that passes, I almost expect her not to answer, but then she surprises me.

"I went to school for creative writing. I wanted to be a published poet. I didn't have delusions of grandeur, though. I didn't think I'd become famous or anything like that. I just wanted to see my words in print with my name on the book cover. I wanted to create something that would last."

Something that would last.

I feel that statement in my bones. It's why I clung so hard to this band, even when everything was falling apart. For so long, nothing in my life was stable. Nothing was certain or true. Nothing was built to last. But this band, this family. We had staying power. I knew it. I believed it as fiercely as I believed my own heartbeat, and I couldn't let go.

"I get that," I say honestly. "It's one of the reasons Heartless is so important to me. I've helped create something that will last long after we're all gone. And the greenhouse? You want to grow flowers?"

"Yeah. Flowers. Vegetables. Greenery. Everything. Anything. I want to grow it all. I think I like plants more than people."

I laugh at the smile I hear in her voice, and when I look at her, I can see proof of the truth in her words. Here, surrounded by things that grow wild and untamed, she's glowing. She belongs.

"I think you need to rework that life plan, Roar."

Her eyes shoot to mine. "Why?"

I twirl my fingers in a circle around her face. "Because anything that makes you smile like this should be a priority. You should look like this all the time."

She blinks, her voice dropping to a whisper that nearly blends in with the breeze.

"Like what?"

"Alive."

Her lips part, that same expression from earlier passing over her features. Like she's been found, but she doesn't know how to handle it. Like she doesn't know if she wants to return to hiding or not.

When she doesn't speak, I give in to temptation and brush my fingers over the sunscreen on her collarbone. She sucks in a sharp breath, but she doesn't move away. Her lashes flutter, like she's fighting the urge to shut them, and she ever so slightly leans into my touch as I rub until the white cream disappears.

"Sunscreen," I whisper. "You missed some."

"Thank you."

The hushed rasp of her voice makes goose bumps appear on my arms and chest. I step back, filling my lungs once more with the clean, calming scent of eucalyptus in hopes that it will slow my galloping pulse. It doesn't.

I don't trust myself not to do something I shouldn't, so I turn back to the trail and start walking. After three steps, she follows, and I catch her toying with her necklace again.

"What's on your necklace?"

Aurora drops her hand and offers me a small smile.

"More personal questions, Mabel?"

She tosses my own evasive words back at me, and damn if it doesn't make my stomach flip. She's being playful, and I want more of it. I let out a laugh that dances between us. It lightens the mood, but it doesn't lessen the tension. It almost seems to grow thicker, crackling, drawing me closer to her.

"Too much too soon?"

She shrugs coyly. "That depends."

"On what?"

She purses her lips and taps her chin with her index finger as she scans my face. I narrow my eyes.

"What's going on in that head of yours?"

"I'm considering my options." She laughs, light and melodic, then drops her attention back to the trail. "What was your guardian's name?"

The smile falls from my face before I can stop it, and my brows shoot toward my hairline. It seems like such an innocuous topic, but it hits hard and shakes my composure. I should have expected her to circle back to it—I did tell her to ask a different question last time— but I'm caught off guard, and I'm not used to being caught off guard.

In the pause, concern passes over her face.

A dozen practiced responses flash rapid fire through my head. A dozen tried-and-true ways to change the subject. I could laugh it off. I could make something up. I could distract her with a teasing, flirty comment. I'm a pro at avoiding this topic.

But Aurora is right. I've been asking her a lot of personal questions, and she's been giving me a lot of personal answers. Truthfully, I plan to ask her many more, because I want to know much more about her. And right now, as strange as it feels, I want her to know more about me, too.

So I go against fifteen years of instinct, and I answer.

"Mabel."

My jaw tightens in anticipation, waiting for my confession to hit the ground and explode like a bomb. My ears train on the birds and the breeze, waiting for the sound of paparazzi shouting and shutters snapping. I brace myself for all of my fears to come alive.

None of it happens.

Instead, Aurora breaks into a wide, surprised smile.

"Wait, what? Your guardian's name was Mabel, or is this some joke about how you're your own guardian?"

God, she's cute. Her nose scrunches up and the green in her eyes sparkles, and I can't help but laugh. The anxiety fades away until not even a whisper remains.

"Foundation of truth?" I ask, and she nods.

"Obviously."

I lean in and lower my voice. "Bubble of trust?"

"Of course," she says, smile still playing on her lips as confusion mixes with her interest. "I won't tell a soul. I promise."

I wait for another few breaths to consider her words, but I

believe her. I believed her even before she'd finished speaking. It might not be smart, but it's where I am right now.

"My guardian's name was Mabel. I called her Ms. Mabel. She died when I was fifteen, and I was sent to a group home. I lasted two weeks. When I ran away, I started using her name."

Aurora's jaw drops and her eyes go as wide as frisbees. "You stole her identity?"

I shrug. "I mean, kind of, but not really. I didn't use her social security number or anything like that. I just started telling people my name was Mabel Rossi. When we signed our first record contract, I had to get all new legal documents, so I used her name and birthday for that, too."

"What's your real name?"

I smirk. "Mabel."

"Okay, but who were you before you were Mabel?"

"Which time?"

"What do you mean *which time*?"

I laugh again. If I knew everyone would react in this way, I'd tell this story all the time. I don't think Aurora has even blinked. She's just staring at me with an amused, awestruck smile on her face, and I'm loving it.

"Well, I'm not sure if I was given a name at birth. I was surrendered at a fire station when I was a couple weeks old."

"A couple weeks? You must have had a name if your birth parents kept you for a couple of weeks."

A familiar pain shoots through me. She's said what's plagued me for years. Almost my whole life. It's a question that's been running through my mind a lot more recently. With my bandmates all pairing off and making new families, how can it not?

I was healthy when the firefighter found me. Fed and clean and happy. I was wrapped in a brand-new blanket and left with a bottle, diapers, and a can of baby formula. I must have had a name. I must have been wanted, even if just a little. I must have been loved...

I stave off the spiral—now is not the time or place—and shrug.

"Maybe. It's possible. But the foster agency called me Susan. I was Susan until I was about three, then a foster family started calling me Ainsley. I went by Ainsley until I was fifteen and started going by Mabel."

"Wow." Aurora shakes her head. "How many lives have you lived, Susan Ainsley Mabel Rossi?"

"One for every name, at least," I say wryly. "A different variation for every foster placement, too, probably. I had to try a few on before I found one that fit. But isn't that the point?"

"What is? Trying on lives?"

"Finding one that fits."

"I never thought of it that way." She hums, the sound pensive, and when I look at her, she's staring thoughtfully up into the canopy of branches. "So three, probably four names. How many foster placements?"

"A lot." *Too many.* "Only two that mattered, though."

It's the truth. All the others run together, but two of them will stay with me forever, for better or worse.

"Will you tell me which two?"

"I will," I say with a grin.

When I don't elaborate, she laughs again and amends her question.

"Mabel, which two foster placements mattered and why?"

"Better."

She rolls her eyes, and I have to suppress a giggle. An actual *giggle.* What the hell? I take a deep breath and refocus, bringing my hand up so I can tick off my fingers.

"Okay, so the two that mattered. First, the family that called me Ainsley. I was young when I was placed with them, but I remember liking them. They were nice. They almost adopted me."

"Almost? What happened?"

"I don't know everything that went into it, but the lady got pregnant with twins and soon after that, I was back in the system.

By that point, though, I'd gotten used to being called Ainsley, so it stuck."

I feel her eyes on me again, but I keep mine pointed forward. When she speaks, her voice is soft, and though we're not touching, I can imagine being held. Comforted.

"That must have been hard."

"I was young."

"Yeah, and it must have been hard." She bumps my arm with hers. "Foundation of truth."

Now it's my turn for a playful eye roll, then I sigh.

"Yeah, it was hard. I spent the next few years trying to be what I thought my new placements wanted me to be. Like, if I could make myself into what they wanted, I'd get to stay in one place, you know? It never worked. Not until Ms. Mabel, which is ironic because by the time I got to her, I was a mess."

Aurora laughs. "You were a troublemaker?"

"No, not really, but I had an attitude. I could get mean."

"I don't know if I believe that."

"Oh, believe it. I was an asshole."

I think back to my first weekend with Ms. Mabel and can't help but smile. I told her my new bed was trash and so was her cooking, so she erected a tent for me in the living room and we ate pizza five nights in a row. When I complained about my new school clothes, she took me to the mall and let me buy three new outfits. And when I woke up in the middle of the night crying from a nightmare, she played with my hair and hummed lullabies until I fell back asleep.

"Every time I lashed out, she responded with nothing but love and understanding. Didn't matter what I said or how I behaved, she was this steady, calming presence. It took me a year to really get comfortable, but once I did..."

I pause and breathe in through my nose, fighting the sting of tears.

"She was the first person I ever remember really feeling like *home*. Not the house or the room or the neighborhood. *Her*. She was everything I needed at that time in my life. I've thought about it a lot, and I really don't know where I'd be if not for her. She died right after my fifteenth birthday, and as much as it fucking hurt, threw everything into a tailspin, I still feel lucky I was placed with her. She changed my life."

"My mom would have called your Mabel a *passing comet*. Brief and brilliant. Not meant to stay, but to blaze through and leave your sky rearranged."

I smile. "I like that."

"Yeah. My mom could liken anything to astronomy. She was a big nerd."

"Is that where your name comes from? The Aurora Borealis?"

"It is indeed."

"Have you seen it? The Northern Lights?"

"No. We were actually supposed to go after I graduated, but then they died..." She shakes her head with a heavy sigh, then shrugs. "Someday, maybe. We'll see."

They.

She said when *they* died.

She's mentioned her mother's death, but Aurora is shouldering the grief of more than one loss. When did they die? For how long has she been hurting like this? Her voice holds so much pain that it makes my chest ache. It's a sound that I recognize, and I don't know how I missed it before.

I stop walking, and she does the same. When she turns to face me, she's clutching the pendant on her necklace, and I reach for it slowly. Instead of removing her hand, she settles it on my wrist as I take the disc between my thumb and index finger. The circular pendant is etched with lines and dots, and the metal is worn in places from her touch. I turn it over to find a similar design on the back.

"Are these constellations?"

I bring my gaze to her face, but her eyes have fallen shut. Every time she inhales, her chest rises toward my hand, barely grazing my knuckles. When she answers, her whispered words kiss my cheeks. My lips.

"It's the sky from the night I was born."

"And the back?"

"My brother. It's his night sky."

I run the pad of my thumb over the design, over her night sky, just like she probably does.

Her brother. Her mother.

Her father, too?

"I worry that I'm letting them down by not doing all the things I'd said I'd do. The things we were going to do together before the accident. They died, but what if I'm the one who stopped living?"

God, I hurt for her.

"You're in Australia on a rock and roll tour. I think that counts as living," I say teasingly, and it brings a small, sad smile to her lips. I brush my fingers up her jaw, then rest my hand on her cheek as she leans into my touch. "You're not letting them down. You're just in recovery mode. You'll get there, Roar."

I hope like hell she hears the honesty in my words. The conviction. She *will* get there. I know it. Maybe not to see the Northern Lights, but to a place where it doesn't hurt so much. To a place where she's not afraid to dream again, whatever that might look like.

She opens her eyes and holds my gaze, but she doesn't speak. Then she nods once, and I drop my hand and step back, giving her space. Giving *me* space.

We walk back to the lodge in comfortable silence, stopping every so often so Aurora can photograph a plant or a bird. Later in the afternoon, I catch her inspecting her orchid closely with a furrowed brow. I don't know what she's thinking. I wish I did.

I stand beside her and focus on Arthur's tiny bud, trying to see what she sees.

"Maybe he just needs to feel safe," I say, my voice low.

Her shoulder moves with a sigh, then I feel her eyes on me.

"We'll get there."

I don't ask if she means only the flower, or if she somehow means herself as well.

13

AURORA

I PACE the floor of the bathroom, gnawing on my fingernails as Brady chatters on the other end of the phone.

As the clock in my head ticks down loudly from five minutes to zero.

My husband's voice is particularly upbeat. He's just returned to our house from playing a round of golf and having lunch with some of the higher-ups at work. He thinks this means he's closer to a promotion, and it very well might, but I'm too preoccupied to be excited for him. It's hard to be excited about anything when you've been woken up at 6 a.m. and urged to take a pregnancy test. Thanks to the travel, I've been *forgetting* to take one. Or at least, that's been my excuse.

"I think I really impressed them, Auri. They even talked about some big investors. This is, like, top inside info, and they shared it with me. I'm sure it helped that I played one of the best games of my life."

"Wow, B." I keep my voice low and dart my eyes to the door as if I can see Mabel asleep under her duvet. "That's great."

"You don't sound excited."

"I am. I just haven't fully woken up yet."

"This could be my big break. You could at least pretend to be stoked."

I close my eyes and pinch the bridge of my nose. "You're right. I'm sorry. It's the jet lag."

"It's been over two weeks. You should be adjusted by now."

I huff a dry laugh. "Probably."

"Are you, like, okay? You sound moody as hell."

"I'm sorry."

My shoulders droop. He's right. I'm being rude. He doesn't deserve this. I open my mouth to apologize again, but I hear a timer sound on his end. The test.

"Time's up. What's it say?"

I stare hard at the door and work to control my breathing as his two words echo in my head. *Time's up.* His voice is eager, but it rings ominous in my ears.

Time's up.

Time's up.

Time's up.

Twice, I try to force myself to look at the bathroom counter. Twice, I fail.

"Aurora. Hello? What's it say?"

I clamp my eyes shut and shake my head, my hand tightening around the phone clutched to my ear.

"It says..." I turn slowly, eyes still closed toward the bathroom counter. *Time's up.* "Um..."

He sighs, loud and annoyed, and I flinch.

"Two lines mean pregnant, Auri, even if the second line is faint. It's not that hard. I told you we should have done a video call."

My lungs hurt, and I force myself to breathe. *That's the one,* he'd said. The last time we had sex, he was certain. *That's the one.* What if he was right? What if I am? What now?

Time's up, he said.

What if it is?

I shouldn't be feeling this way. I shouldn't feel like I'm

drowning. Like the padlock to my cage is about to be welded shut. I shouldn't. I know I shouldn't. But I do. I do, and it hurts so badly.

My inhale is shaky when I force myself to open my eyes. Tears well as I stare into the mirror at my reflection. What a mess. I swipe at my cheeks with the hand not threatening to crush the cell phone.

What have I done?

Suffocating.

I'm suffocating.

"Aurora. What the hell. Are you there? What's it say?"

I clear my throat. "I'm here."

"Hold on. I'm going to video call."

"No." I clear my throat again. "No, it's okay. I can read it."

"If you're struggling, then I can—"

"No." The word comes out louder and more forceful than I intended, and I rush to fix it. "It's fine. It's okay. I said I can read it."

"Fine. So what does it say?"

I search my reflection as if searching for a way out. I find none. My face has drained of color; the green in my watery eyes pops against the red rims, and all I see is loss. My stomach falls to my feet, and I finally turn my attention to the pregnancy test.

I focus on the narrow blue end first and count the grooves in the plastic. Four, with a slight, rounded indentation for a thumb to grip. User-friendly design, I suppose.

Then I move to the brand logo displayed on the white. The gray block lettering is plain and inoffensive, but it brings a scowl to my face. Resentment bubbles inside me, bile climbing in my throat, and I feel like I might vomit.

Brady groans, and I flinch. As if his voice serves as a physical shove, my eyes jerk forward, stumbling to the two small rectangles meant to deliver my sentence. Judge and jury.

I'm not ready, but who am I kidding? I'll never be ready.

I exhale slowly through my nose and let my eyes focus on the results. I read them twice through the water in my eyes. I fit my thumb into the perfect indentation on the narrow, blue end, and bring the test closer to my face, blinking to clear my vision of tears so I can read the results a third time before they blur again. I make certain I'm reading it correctly. Make certain my tear-flooded eyes aren't playing tricks on me.

"One line." It escapes on an exhale that's followed by a choked sob. "Negative. I'm not pregnant."

Brady swears on the other end of the phone, but I barely hear him over the sound of my rapid heartbeat and labored breathing. With trembling fingers, I bury the test at the bottom of the bathroom trash and pile a handful of tissues on top of it for good measure. As soon as it is out of view, I drop into a squat and put my head between my knees.

One line. Negative.

Time's not up.

I still have time.

"It's okay, Auri."

Brady's voice fades in and out as I work to settle myself, the adrenaline of my panic bleeding from my body like air leaking from a punctured tire. My hands shake and my cheeks start to cool as the tears slow.

"Don't cry. It's okay. It's not your fault."

He doesn't mean it. I've heard this tone hundreds of times before. Like the people who used to tell me my family's accident wasn't my fault. Placating, borderline patronizing, and completely fake.

It makes me feel worse for a multitude of reasons, but the most jarring is I'm not crying because I'm sad. I'm crying because I'm relieved, and he has no idea.

"I'm fine. I'm fine."

I wipe my eyes again and take steadying breaths through my nose. Guilt, once again, swirls in my stomach, and I try to fight off the nausea. I'm a terrible wife. I shouldn't be feeling this way, especially not when he thinks I'm feeling the opposite.

"I'm okay, B. Really."

"Maybe we should see a nutritionist? You don't always eat the best. You should cut back on sugar and starches. I've been doing some research, and if we want to get pregnant, you have to take better care of yourself."

I frown and stare hard at the tile floor as I attempt to process what he just said.

He can't mean...

"You just said it isn't my fault."

He sighs. "It's not. But it's *your* body. Have you thought of working out?"

I scoff. It's quiet, nearly a mere puff of air, but he hears it, and he sighs again. Louder. More frustrated. Angry.

"This isn't a joke, Aurora."

"I'm not laughing."

"I'm just saying that if this was something you really wanted for us, you'd be watching what you eat and working out more."

I drop back onto my butt, the cold floor seeping through the thin fabric of my pajama pants, and stare at the brown wooden shelves under the sink.

"How do you know it's not you?" I ask, defeat and defensiveness warring in my head.

"I drink protein shakes. I take supplements. I work out."

"Watching sports on television doesn't make you an athlete, Brady. You can't work out by osmosis."

I don't realize how harsh I sound until the words have already left me. My husband goes silent, and regret fills me. I squeeze my eyes shut and run my fingers through my sleep-mussed hair.

"I'm sorry. That was mean."

"Yeah, it was. You don't have to take your guilt out on me."

My eyes snap open. *Guilt.*

He knows? He knows I'm relieved? That I'm having second thoughts?

"What do you mean?" I ask tentatively, my voice choked with

nerves. He must pick up on my worry because his next statement is soft and gentle. Like how you'd speak to a child.

"I get that you feel bad for not taking this seriously and letting yourself go, but you're being unfair to me."

"What? Unfair to you? Letting myself go?"

"Auri, come on. You know what I'm saying."

"I don't, actually. Please elaborate."

He sighs yet again. "Don't make me say it."

"Say it. Say it, Brady."

"You've gained a lot of weight since we got married. Really since we got engaged, but even more since we got married."

I feel like I've been punched, and all it does is make me want to swing back harder.

"I've gained twenty pounds, and part of that is regaining what I lost after my parents and brother died. Remember that? When they fucking *died*, and I was *depressed* and *stopped fucking eating*?"

"You don't have to swear at me, Aurora."

"Oh, I'll say whatever the fuck I want, Brady."

"Jesus, if I knew you'd react like this, I wouldn't have said anything."

"How the fuck did you think I'd react when my husband, someone who is supposed to love me unconditionally, someone who knows everything I've been through, told me I'd *let myself go*?"

"I thought you'd apologize and see reason, not make excuses. The weight you've gained isn't just from what you lost when you were sad. You're bigger than you ever were, and it's been years. It sucks that they were in an accident, but you can't blame that anymore."

When I was sad.

When. I. Was. *Sad*.

I grit my teeth as tears once again flood my eyes, falling into tracks that haven't yet dried. These tears are different, though. They're hot and angry. They burn. If I wasn't huddled on the floor of this bathroom in a suite I'm sharing with someone else, I'd probably be shouting. I'd probably be pacing and irate. I take a deep breath, but my voice is still shaking when I speak in a harsh, strained whisper.

"I wasn't just sad, Brady. I was depressed. And it wasn't just *an accident*. My whole family fucking died. They're dead. I will never see them or speak to them again. I lost everything—"

"You didn't lose everything. Don't be dramatic. We gave you everything you needed."

"You weren't my family, Brady! Your parents are great, but they aren't *my* parents. It's not the same thing."

"Wow. Wow, Aurora. Not your family? That's a fucked-up thing to say, considering my parents put a roof over your head and paid for everything you needed."

"Oh, please. Your parents didn't pay for shit. Uncle Wade paid for everything."

He scoffs. "I don't even know who I'm talking to right now. You've only been with those rock stars for a couple weeks and you're already a totally different person. You're so ungrateful. After everything we did for you? You're being cruel."

At first, I want to scream. I want to reach through the phone and shake him. I want to thrash against every chain of obligation and grief that has been weighing me down for the last few years. But then his words crash through the fog of rage surrounding me, and I crumple. My muscles seize, my body hunches in on itself, and I feel terrible.

What am I doing? What am I even saying?

I don't want to be cruel. I don't want him to think I'm ungrateful. I'm grateful for everything the Sinclairs did for me. I am. I love his parents. If it weren't for their kindness, the changes would have been so much more drastic.

The Sinclairs saved me. *Brady* saved me.

God, I'm terrible. I'm so fucking terrible.

"I'm sorry." The words escape on a choked sob. "I'm so sorry. You're right. I'm sorry."

He doesn't say anything, and as the silence stretches, my thoughts grow louder.

I'm so terrible. My parents and brother would be disappointed. The Sinclairs' hearts would be broken. I *am* cruel and ungrateful. He doesn't deserve this.

My husband expels another sigh. It's long, drawn-out, and cuts like a knife.

"I'll send you the information about diet and exercise that I found. Just...I don't know. We'll talk later."

He hangs up. No goodbye. No I love you. No forgiveness.

I drop the phone to the floor and cover my mouth with my hand. I try to quiet my sobs, but they grow more violent, shaking my body and stealing my breath. Anger, fear, and guilt tangle into knots in my stomach, and I curl myself into a ball along with them. I lie on the floor and press my cheek to the cool tile, feeling it pool with my tears. I press my hand harder against my lips, but every ragged inhale cracks and suctions, and every forceful exhale refuses to be contained.

I don't want to feel like this. I don't want to *be* like this. I don't want any of it, and that makes me cry harder. Brady deserves better. He's my best friend. He's my *only* friend. I'm terrible. I love him. I don't want to get pregnant. I love him, but I don't want him. I owe him. He's my family. I feel trapped.

He deserves better than this, but don't I, also?

I'm terrible.

I'm suffocating.

"Hey, hey. What's wrong? Are you okay?"

A gentle hand brushes my hair from my face, then settles on my back. I open my eyes and run right into warm, amber gemstones full of concern.

"Do I need to call Ham?"

Mabel's lying beside me on the bathroom floor, and I'm awash with both gratitude and shame. I woke her. I'm embarrassed. But I'm also really glad she's here. Her kindness is a soothing balm, and the painful pounding of my thoughts starts to dull.

I swallow roughly, then shake my head. "No. It's fine. I'll be fine."

"What happened? You want to talk about it?"

I shake my head again. "I'm sorry I woke you."

"You didn't. I have to pee," she says it with a smirk, and I huff out a laugh as her fingers trail from my back to my head. She pushes a few strands of hair behind my ear, gaze falling to my tear-painted lips. "That's better. Is there anything I can do?"

I run my eyes over her bare face. I retreated to the bedroom almost immediately after dinner last night. Caveat and Heartless had a tour meeting. I had a date with a book and my pillow. I fell asleep before Mabel made it back to the suite. The last time I saw her, she had a full face of makeup. Now, there's not a stich of cosmetics to be seen, and it feels intimate. Vulnerable. *Real.* Even first thing in the morning, she's strikingly beautiful, and it takes me a moment to realize she'd asked me a question.

"No. I'm okay."

She arches a brow, and I roll my eyes with another laugh.

"Fine. I'm not okay, but I will be. I don't want to talk about it. Not yet."

Mabel purses her lips, then smiles. It's soft and heartbreakingly sweet.

"I'm no stranger to the occasional crash out, Roar. I'm here if you need me, okay? Even if you just want to vent. I'll nod and agree with everything you say." Her eyes narrow playfully. "Unless you start talking shit about yourself. Then we'll have to tussle."

I laugh for a third time, this one fuller and even more genuine than the last. Somehow, in just sixty seconds, she's made everything hurt less.

I'm here if you need me, she said. It's been a while since I've heard those words. Even longer since I've believed them. Right now, on this cold tile floor in Adelaide, I believe Mabel. I nod and wipe my eyes.

"Thank you, Susan Ainsley Mabel Rossi," I say with a smile. "That means a lot."

It means more than you could possibly know.

"Anytime, Aurora...Hey, wait. What's your full name?"

"Aurora Jade Hammond."

I answer on impulse, and I don't realize I gave her my maiden name until she frowns. Her next question comes out tentatively, with a forced lightness that makes my skin prickle.

"Did you not change your last name? You're married, right?"

"Oh." I break our eye contact, bouncing my attention to her ear, her forehead, her chin. Anywhere but those warm amber irises. Anywhere but her pouty pink lips. "No. I mean, yes. Yes, I changed my name."

I didn't want to change my last name. It was a tie to my family that I didn't want to sever after their deaths, but it was important to Brady.

I'm your family now, he'd said. *You need to move forward with me.*

I try so hard not to look at Mabel, but I can feel her eyes on me —fixed intently, searching—as if she can see the confessions screaming from inside my head. Like a magnet, my eyes are drawn to hers, and when our stares snap together, goose bumps rise on my skin. She trails her fingers up and down my back, her bare arm resting on mine, and when she speaks, the question doesn't fit her tone. Her voice is soft and kind, but the words *feel* hostile.

"What's your husband's last name, then? The one on your passport."

I swallow, take a deep breath, then whisper, "Sinclair."

Brady was right. Keeping my last name wouldn't bring my parents and brother back, but I miss being a Hammond. I've never felt like a Sinclair. Not really.

"Aurora Jade Sinclair. That's pretty."

I shrug. "Yeah."

I bite my tongue against what I want to say, caging the truth behind my teeth.

I don't like it. I don't want it. I'm suffocating.

Then she smirks.

"This floor is cold as fuck. If we lie here any longer, my piercings are going to turn to ice and freeze my nipples off."

My jaw drops, and she laughs.

"What?"

"You have your nipples pierced?"

She arches a teasing brow. "Yeah. Is that surprising?"

I shake my head slowly. "Not at all. I don't even know why I'm shocked. It's not surprising at all."

Mabel laughs again, then sits up, so I do the same. When she starts to stand, I freeze.

She's wearing a pink and black pajama set. Spaghetti straps and short shorts. Silk fabric. Lace trim. I didn't notice it before, but I do now, and my stomach flips. I can feel a blush start to spread, so I avert my gaze to the ground. It doesn't help. Her feet are bare, and her nails are painted white, with a little silver ring on her middle toe and a silver chain around her delicate ankle.

My pulse speeds up. My mouth goes dry. I'm reeling from the rapid change of my emotions in such a short period of time. Then her hand extends in my periphery, and my eyes are drawn upward. I nearly swallow my tongue.

She's so hot it hurts. Pink, sleep-tousled hair frames her face and rests on her bare shoulders. Her tattooed sleeve pops dramatically in the bathroom lighting, and the shiny silk pajama top flows over her curves like water. The elegant fabric is thin enough that I can see the outline of her nipples, and my eyes stick on the indentation of two dots on either side of each of them.

Her piercings.

My own nipples pebble under my oversized sweatshirt and I ache to press my thighs together. She's so sensual, so sexy, and that same feeling of desire is so overwhelming that I can almost taste it. Dark, rich honey, the color of her eyes. Sweet and heady. Twenty-three years of never knowing this feeling, and suddenly I'm craving it so deeply that my mouth waters.

"Want to see them?"

She asks it with a smirk, and my face flames hotter as I choke on a rapid inhale.

"Kidding. I'm kidding. You know, unless you do want to see them, in which case the offer stands."

I open my mouth twice to speak, and all I can manage is *okay.* Then her smirk softens, and she wiggles her fingers at me.

"C'mon. Family breakfast."

I place my hands in hers and allow her to pull me to my feet. The position changes, and our closeness leaves me dizzy. Her chin tilts up and mine tilts down, mere inches between us.

"Thank you," I whisper, the words barely more than an exhale.

"Always. You good now?"

I nod. "Yeah."

"Good." Her smile grows. "I still need to pee."

A snort of laughter escapes me, which draws laughter from Mabel, too. I shake my head and walk toward the door.

"I'll get dressed."

"I'll pee."

I laugh again, then let myself out of the bathroom. My smile makes my cheeks hurt, and my emotions have shifted so drastically that I can almost forget about my complete meltdown from moments earlier.

I grab a dress from my suitcase, then pause and look back at my selection of clothes. They're all neatly folded in piles, mostly dresses and cardigans, but my eyes settle on the few new items I bought when I went exploring in Melbourne. It's nothing crazy, but there isn't a single cotton dress in the stack, and a couple of the pieces are a bit out of my comfort zone. Things I'd admire in magazines or on other women but would never buy for myself. Things Brady would call weird or ugly.

I frown and consider the clothing for a few more seconds, then exchange the dress for a new pair of wide-leg jeans and a cute little mosaic crocheted top. I bought them to wear, after all, and Brady's not here to tell me to change.

I'm tugging the top down my torso when the bathroom door opens, and I turn to find Mabel grinning at me.

"I was wondering if you owned anything besides dresses."

I shift my weight between my feet. "I got these in Melbourne."

"I love them."

"Yeah?"

"Yeah. The whole outfit is adorable, and those jeans hug your hips perfectly. You look amazing."

My cheeks heat and I smooth my hands down the fabric of my jeans. "Thanks. I like them, too."

"I'll change fast, and then we can go."

When she disappears back into the bathroom, I turn to look at my reflection in the wall mirror. I run my eyes over my body, then settle on the flare of my hips. Mabel was right. These jeans fit perfectly, and this top is adorable. It's white with little red and pink strawberries on it, and it sits just above the waistband of my jeans, showing a peek of my stomach. I turn from side to side, assessing myself from each angle, and as I do, my smile grows.

I *do* look great. I love this outfit. I don't care that Brady would say it was ugly, or that the hint of skin that shows between my jeans and top is inappropriate. I like it, and that's all that matters.

Then, as if my husband could feel my good mood, my phone buzzes with a text that threatens to torpedo everything.

BRADY

I emailed you the stuff from the nutritionist. Daily exercises to implement and a list of good and bad foods to look over. There's a digital food and exercise journal you should start filling out too. Don't worry, Auri. I know you'll fix this. You just have to try harder.

BRADY

Oh, and what is this charge for a Melbourne boutique on the credit card? Making money doesn't mean you don't have to run things by me first. We're still a partnership.

I frown at my phone screen. I don't even know what to say to him. When I don't respond right away, he sends me another text. This one is just three question marks, and it makes me even angrier. I feel my eyes start to sting again, and my jaw aches from how hard I'm gritting my teeth. Then my phone rings, and his contact photo fills the screen. I stare at it, but I make no move to answer.

"You good?"

My head jerks toward Mabel. She's in another of her stage-ready ensembles, with a full face of makeup. I deflect.

"You look like a rock star."

"Well, if the platform combat boot fits..."

She winks, drawing a genuine laugh from me. I type out a quick *Okay, will talk later* to Brady, then shove the phone in my pocket.

"Family breakfast?" I ask brightly.

She nods. "Let's go before the Caveat boys eat all the pastries."

14

MABEL

As the phone rings, I check under the stalls for the tenth time to make sure I'm actually alone.

I *am* alone. I made sure of it before dialing the number, but I'm also a little paranoid right now. If this were to get out to the media...I cringe. It would be a circus, and the tiny bit of privacy I've managed to cling to would go up in smoke. My palms start to sweat just thinking about it. Fuck, it's the last thing I want—

"Hello, this is Alaina Caldwell."

My back stiffens immediately, and I force a swallow before responding.

"Ms. Caldwell. Hi. It's Mabel Rossi."

"Yes, hello, Ms. Rossi. How is your tour?"

"Good so far. We're in Adelaide this weekend, so the venue is smaller than we're used to. I'm looking forward to the more intimate setting."

"More intimate meaning eleven thousand people instead of ninety thousand?"

"Exactly," I say with a laugh. I always forget how different our situation is from so many other artists. I shake my head with a smile and switch gears. "I want to thank you for accommodating me with the time difference. I know it's early in New York."

"It's not a problem. I'm glad we can make it work. I was beginning to worry you'd had second thoughts."

I glance at my reflection in the bathroom mirror and sigh. "Honestly, I did."

And third. And fourth.

It was my conversation with Aurora that finally solidified my decision. I've been replaying it over and over in my mind. The way she talked about her family. How much pain I heard in her voice when she spoke of them. She loved them fiercely, and they were taken from her. She can't see them, or hug them, or laugh with them ever again. There are no future plans. No birthdays. No vacations. The chance for those opportunities is gone, and my heart broke for her.

And then...

You must have had a name, she said.

Is that true? If they'd kept me for a few weeks, they must have named me. Right?

I watch my brows bunch together in the mirror as the questions in my head grow louder.

What if I did have a name? What if I was more than just an abandoned baby? What if I was *wanted*? What if *my* chance isn't gone? My chance for plans and birthdays and vacations. What if it's all right in front of me, and I'm wasting it?

"Well, I'm glad to hear you didn't completely change course because I've got some news."

My lawyer's voice is positive despite it being four-thirty in the morning where she is, and it stokes the embers of nerves in my chest. Excitement. Anxiety. I'm feeling it all, so I cut right to the point.

"Did the private investigator find my birth mother?"

I can hear the smile when she answers.

"She did."

My head is in a fog as I leave the bathroom.

My birth mother is a vet tech living in Georgia with her husband and two kids. And she's young. That's the part that has shaken me the most. My birth mother is only forty-four, meaning she was only fourteen when she had me. She was practically a kid.

Fourteen. That's the age of her oldest daughter. Well...

Her second oldest daughter, I guess.

I have two sisters. Fourteen and twelve. Brynn's age. Would they be friends? Cousins, sort of, I guess. Do my sisters look like me? Do they know about me? Do they listen to my music?

My thoughts are spinning.

I have a mom and two sisters who are out there living happily in Georgia. The private investigator gave my lawyer all their information. Address, phone numbers, emails. I know where my mom works. I know where my sisters go to school. I know one of them plays basketball and one plays piano. I know all of it. I could call them right now if I want to. Could fire up the jet and show up on their doorstep.

But is that what I should do? Is that what I want to do?

Would they even want to hear from me?

They could have found me, too. They could have hired the PI just like I did. They could have searched.

If they wanted to, they would have. But...

God, there are so many unknowns. So many moving parts. No matter what I do, it's a leap into darkness. There's a best possible and a worst possible outcome, and both are equally probable. Both are equally terrifying.

I've never cared so much about odds before.

What if I was wanted?

But what if I wasn't?

I take a deep breath and attempt to shove my anxious thoughts aside as I get closer to the dressing room. Maybe I shouldn't have done this right before a show, but I was hoping the energy on stage would help to clear my mind. Now I'm not so sure.

I let myself in and smile at Red as Ziggy attacks my legs.

"Ooof, beast." I scratch between her ears. "I love you, too."

My eyes scan the room, seeking Aurora out without my permission. My eyes skip right over Sav and Claire to find her, and when they do, the knot of nerves in my stomach loosens slightly. I grab a mineral water from the minifridge and join the three of them on the small leather sectional. They're mid-conversation as I sit down next to Sav.

Claire gives me a smile and a wave, but she doesn't stop talking to Aurora. When I hear the topic of discussion, I'm glad she doesn't.

"So where did you and Brady meet?"

"Is Brady your husband?" I butt in, trying my best to sound normal. Trying my best not to frown, which is difficult.

There's no denying the jealousy burning inside me. The attraction is bad enough. But add in jealousy? That's a recipe for fucking disaster. Doesn't stop me from needing her answer, though.

Flicking her eyes to me, Aurora nods. "Yes, Brady is my husband."

Brady is a dumb name, but I don't say that out loud. She looks back at Claire with an uncomfortable smile.

"I've known him my whole life. He was one of my brother's best friends."

"Were you high school sweethearts?"

"No, actually. We didn't date until college."

"And you've been married for how long?"

I could kiss Claire for asking these questions. The answers might irritate me, but I'm salivating for them. Aurora darts her eyes from Claire to me and back.

"Eighteen months."

A year and a half. That means she probably got married around twenty-one. And if he's her older brother's friend...

"How old is Brady?"

Surprise passes over Aurora's face at my question, and she blinks twice before she answers.

"He just turned twenty-nine."

My lips tighten. It takes restraint not to unleash a deluge of questions, but I don't. I can't because Sav interjects, and I *know* it was on purpose.

"Well, I can't wait to meet him. Has he said anything about my offer?"

I whip my eyes to her. "What offer?"

"I told Aurora I'd fly Brady out anytime he wanted to visit. Fuck, I offered to let him come on tour, even."

A frown takes over before I can stop it, and Sav lifts an eyebrow. I fix my face and give her a saccharine smile.

"How benevolent of you."

Sav's eyes narrow as they scan my face, reading me in that annoying way that she does. I turn my forced smile on Aurora.

"Well? Will the hubs be joining us?"

Aurora laughs awkwardly and keeps her eyes trained on her lap. She's deliberately avoiding looking at me. I know it.

"No, he won't be coming to visit. He won't take the time off work."

To say I'm sad I won't get to meet Brady is a lie, but my frown still returns. Aurora didn't say he *can't* take time off work. She said he *won't*. I say the next thing before I can stop myself.

"He won't take time off work for an all-expenses-paid international trip with his wife? It would be like a second honeymoon."

"We didn't go on a honeymoon." She shifts her weight on the couch cushion and shrugs. "Anyway, he's trying to get a promotion. It's important."

I feel Sav's and Claire's eyes on me, but I don't take mine off Aurora. The topic obviously makes her uncomfortable, but I can't quite tell why. Her face, normally so expressive, isn't usually this difficult to decode. Is she upset her husband won't take time off work to visit? Is that why she was crying in the bathroom? Or is there something more behind the stiff posture and timid tone?

I drop my eyes to her bare left hand again. Still no ring. *It hurts*, she'd said. What did she mean by that? Is it truly because the ring is too small, or is there another reason?

The skin on the back of my neck prickles with awareness. There's something more here. Something concerning, yet less visible.

Just what kind of relationship does Aurora have with her husband?

She doesn't talk about him unless asked. I haven't seen her text or call him even once. And then the constant apologizing. It's habitual. An immediate impulse response. I think back to our conversation during our hike.

It's instinctual for you, isn't it?

What?

Apologizing.

To my knowledge, Hammond hasn't taken time off to visit her in a while. Not in a year, at least. *It hurts*, she said.

My stomach tightens.

"You said he was your brother's friend?"

She brings her eyes to mine slowly. "Yes."

"And when was the accident?"

I swear I can hear the air in the room crackle. Sav's disapproving stare burns into the side of my face, but I'll deal with her later. I need to know. There's something here. I know it. I'm just missing some pieces...

"Four years ago."

Her words are a whisper, and I mentally fumble through her answers. Eighteen months. Four years. Her brother's best friend. They didn't date until college—until *she* was in college, because he's five years older than she is—and likely not until after she'd lost her family.

There's something here. Something bigger. I just can't—

A knock on the dressing room door breaks our silent stare off, and we all turn to find Jonah walking in with Teddy in his arms. Claire jumps up and meets them. She takes Teddy, then Jonah cups Claire's face and kisses her deeply. Their daughter giggles and Sav groans.

"Not in front of my niece," she teases, then she pushes up from the couch and takes Teddy from Claire. "We don't want to see those smoochy kisses, do we, Teddy girl?"

Claire rolls her eyes and peers up at Jonah. "I'll stay for the first few songs, okay?"

Jonah grabs one of Claire's stray curls and tugs on it, straightening it out, only to have it spring back up.

"You don't have to, Trouble. Take her back to the lodge and get some sleep. I know you've been tired."

Claire's lips turn up into a small smile. "I'm fine. Just a few songs, and then sleep."

Jonah traces his thumb over Claire's jaw, then leans in for another kiss. The moment their lips touch, Sav playfully covers Teddy's eyes, making her giggle again and grasp onto Sav's fingers.

"Smoochy kisses," Sav sings. "Eeeew."

Jonah ends the kiss and turns a blank stare on Sav. "I'm flipping you off in my head."

Sav pokes her lip out in a pout. "Ouch. That hurts, Papa Jo."

Claire laughs and pushes on Jonah's chest, leading him to the door. "Now out of the girl party, please. If I'm asleep when you get back, wake me."

Jonah steps into the hall, and I catch him wink at her. "Not a chance."

The moment the door shuts, I smirk. "You're pregnant again."

Claire's eyes widen. "I am not."

"You sure? Being tired is a symptom of pregnancy." Sav tickles Teddy. "You want to be a big sister, Teddy Baby?"

"Being tired is also a symptom of jetlag, smart-ass." Claire throws herself onto the couch, then shakes her head slowly. "Besides, could you even imagine? Another baby on tour?"

"So we'll take another year or two off." I hook a thumb toward Sav. "I've got pull with the label and can work something out."

Sav grins. "I can also hire an au pair or something. We'll need to do it anyway if Callie and Torren decide to spawn."

I bark out a laugh. "I bet you could get Glory to do it."

"Ah, yes, another nepotism hire," Claire teases, and Sav waves her off with a roll of her eyes.

"Who is Glory?"

I turn to find Aurora looking totally lost, and I give her a smile. "Glory Bell is Callie's younger sister."

"And she would come nanny?"

Sav shrugs. "If we needed her, she might. She's currently attempting the production assistant temp thing in LA."

"Yeah, and Cal is not happy about it," Claire says with a laugh.

Aurora's eyes widen. "Why?"

"Because Glor turned down a basketball scholarship to do it." Claire's face turns pensive. "Honestly, I bet she'd be a great nanny."

I fling my finger at her. "You're pregnant!"

"I'm not! I swear."

"But you're not opposed to it," Sav adds.

Claire gives us a shrug and smirks. "I mean, if Callie and Torren are going to do it..."

We laugh, but when I glance at Aurora, her expression's tight and uncomfortable. When she catches me looking, the discomfort is wiped away and replaced with a bright, cheery, fake as fuck smile.

"What about you, Sav?"

The forced levity in Aurora's tone has my smile flickering, but Sav is too busy snuggling Teddy to notice.

"What about me?"

"Do you have baby fever?"

The terror that passes over Savannah's face has me snort laughing. She shakes her head and hands Teddy back to Claire.

"Take her. I don't want to get infected."

She's so dramatic. Teddy giggles and Claire laughs, but Aurora looks shocked.

"What does that mean?"

Sav's eyes flare. "My maternal instincts are nonexistent. My desire for a baby is at negative one hundred."

"Oh. Well, that would change."

"Trust me. It won't. One of my favorite things about Ted is that I can give her back when she cries or poops. I'll be on birth control until I die."

Aurora's smile fades and she shakes her head slowly. "Okay, but that would be different if it was your baby. Don't you want to have a child with your fiancé?"

I can practically see Sav's defenses shoot up, and the air in the room grows tense.

"We have one. Her name is Brynn."

"No, of course. But I mean, you know, a child who is biologically yours?"

Sav glances between Claire and me before looking back at Aurora. Aurora must not know that Brynn technically isn't Levi's biological child, either, or that she's just stumbled on a topic that can get Sav extremely heated. I can practically see the protective streak flashing like lightning in her storm gray irises.

"Biology doesn't matter to me. Shared genetics or not, Brynn's my kid, and I don't want another one. The thought of getting pregnant, growing a human, pushing that human out of my vagina, and then having to, like, feed it and change it and raise it and all that? Hard pass." Sav turns to Claire. "No offense."

Claire laughs. "Zero offense taken."

"I am baby free by choice. The universe did me a solid with Brynn because she's practically a miniature adult. I'd be a shit mom to anyone else."

As if to prove Sav's point, Teddy shouts *Shit!* and Sav grins.

"See? I'm a much better fun auntie."

I turn back to Aurora, expecting a smile, but instead she looks lost. Confused. Almost scared. Like the foundation beneath her feet is shifting, and she doesn't know how to keep her balance. Her expression changes as she mentally grasps for something, anything, to ground her. I'd help if I could, but I can't. I don't know how.

"I don't...I mean..." She swallows and fidgets with her fingers. "I mean, doesn't Levi want you to have his baby? What if you regret not having a baby, and then it's too late? That's what everyone wants, right? Isn't it? It's what everyone should want. Right?"

My eyes widen, and I dart my attention between the two of them.

Sav's jaw is tight. Paps love to shout these types of questions at her. *Sav, when will you start a family? Sav, do you plan to get pregnant? Sav, will you be putting music on hold when you become a mother?* It's her least favorite topic, tied only with anything questioning her sobriety. Her answer is always the same—*No comment*—and then she rants to us afterward about how she'd much rather tell everyone to fuck all the way off. Right now, though, I can tell she's considering her response carefully. Aurora is not the paparazzi, and she's not trying to get a headline for a gossip mag.

As the silence stretches, Aurora wrings her hands in her lap. Her cheeks go red, and I want to reach for her. Rub her back or hold her hand. Anything to help ease the embarrassment crashing through her.

"I'm sorry," she whispers. "That was far too personal and very out of line. I'm so, so sorry."

"No, it's fine," Sav says. She looks from me to Claire, and back to Aurora, then she leans in and softens her voice. "Aurora, Levi wants what I want because we're a team. I love my life and my family just as they are. We both do, and we don't want to change it. I'm fulfilled. I'm happy. I won't regret my decision to not have a baby. Ever."

Aurora scans Sav's face, then drops her attention to her lap. She nods and forces a smile.

"Right. Of course. I'm...I'm happy for you."

The way Aurora folds in on herself has me moving on instinct. I sit beside her on the couch and put my hand on her knee.

"Hey. It's okay, all right? Everyone is fine."

She nods again. "Okay."

I squeeze her leg lightly. "Sav's fine. Aren't you, Sav?"

"I am," Sav says, but I don't look away from Aurora.

My chest aches with the need to comfort her, and my mind swirls with questions. With theories. Nothing about this makes sense yet, but I'm certain of one thing. Aurora isn't happy. She's been shoved into a box and told what to want. How to act and think. And from what I can tell, she's outgrowing that box, and she's terrified.

A familiar chiming noise grabs my attention, and I reluctantly look away from Aurora to Sav. She's already scrolling on her phone.

"Did the Caveat boys do something stupid, or are you stalking someone new?"

I ask the question to lighten the mood, take some of the attention off Aurora, but I'm curious, too. Sav has internet alerts set for all of us, so she gets notified about any new media stories. Recently, she's also been setting alerts for bands she's considering signing to her label. Anything other than positive news about Heartless is rare these days, but the way Sav's face contorts as she reads her phone screen has me sitting up straighter.

"Shit. What did they do?"

I'm half expecting her to tell me Ezra and Crue got arrested, but then Claire glances at the phone screen, too, and they both look at me with pity.

"What? What happened?"

I'm reaching for Sav's phone before either of them says anything. Did the tabloids find out about my birth mother? Did someone overhear my conversation with my lawyer? I hold my breath as I flip the phone over and take in the article on the screen, then all the oxygen leaves me in one violent *woosh*.

Pictures of my girlfriend are plastered all over a popular gossip blog. They're blurry, obviously taken from a distance, but it's not hard to see what's happening.

Kat is locked in a passionate kiss with Kaz. Hands and lips in a tangle, I can't tell where she ends and he begins. I blink several times, but the images don't change. They just become more *real*.

"I'm so fucking sorry, Mabes."

I drag my eyes from the screen to Sav's face. Her expression must mirror mine. Shock and pain, but there's anger there, too. Anger I wish I could feel. It would be better than this. This throbbing heartache. This violent, stabbing sense of betrayal. I can almost taste it, copper and blood-like on my tongue.

Just once, just fucking *once*, I'd like to be first. I'd like to be *enough*. I don't think that's asking too much.

I manage a tight smile and push to standing, handing Sav's phone back to her as I grab mine from the couch cushion.

"Excuse me, guys. I have to make a call."

15

MABEL

"I can explain."

Kat doesn't even say hello when she answers. It's nearly two in the morning in Los Angeles, so the fact that the phone only rang twice tells me she was waiting for my call. Doesn't matter if she was sleeping or partying. She was ready, and from her tone, she's already annoyed.

I drop my eyes to the ring on my middle finger and make a fist. The gem glints under the florescent lighting. It might as well be mocking me. I take a deep breath and push my toes into the soles of my platforms.

"Explain, then."

"Kaz and I decided to be in a fake relationship. You know, to really lean into the public fascination. Give the people what they want, right? My agent is submitting me for this new runway competition show, and I could use the media attention. I'm pretending to date Kaz for op—"

I huff a laugh, cutting her off. "Right. For optics."

"It is. It's all for appearances. Just until I get selected for the show."

I lean against the wall and drop my head back on the cool brick. Caveat Lover's set is ending, meaning it's almost time for

Heartless to take the stage. Instead of warming up or getting ready, though, I'm listening to my girlfriend attempt to explain away pictures of her with her tongue down some guy's throat. The same guy she's always claimed was *just a friend*. She always made me feel crazy for being jealous of him. For being suspicious of him. It was *my* problem. *My* insecurities. Always me.

My eyes sting, and I breathe through it, willing the tears away. My emotions have been through hell and back in the last twelve hours, and I'm so fucking overwhelmed. I have a mom. I have sisters. I have so many unanswered questions and unmade decisions. And now, I'm about to have an *ex*-girlfriend.

I wipe my sweaty palm on my leather skirt and close my eyes.

"Kat, I know a thing or two about contract relationships, okay? Those pap pictures weren't staged for the media. If they were, they'd have been crisp, clear, and in public. The pictures I just saw were of a private moment between two people who had no idea they were being photographed."

"It wasn't like that. We were just practicing."

Kat stumbles over her words as she speaks, her voice high-pitched and defensive. But me? My words come out sounding tired. Defeated. I swallow back a sigh and pinch the bridge of my nose.

Practicing.

They were just *practicing.*

The lie hurts more than the pictures, and a tear breaches my lash line and rolls down my cheek.

"Three years," I whisper. "We were together for three years. You could at least respect me enough to be honest."

She gasps, then sniffs. "I do respect you!"

I roll my head back and forth against the brick. "No. If you did, you'd have told me about the relationship contract as soon as it was floated as an option. I wouldn't have found out from a gossip blog moments before I'm supposed to play a show. If you respected me, there wouldn't be pap photos of you and Kaz *practicing*. I wouldn't be blindsided. I would have known."

I also want to add that if she respected me, she'd have consulted me first. I don't, though. It's pointless.

She clicks her tongue and huffs. "I don't know what you want me to say, Mabel. You know how important my career is to me. I thought you supported me."

I can picture her thin brows slanted and her overlined lips pointed downward in a frown. Indignant and ready to argue. I bet she has her hand on her hip, too. In the beginning, I'd have found it cute. Admirable, even. The way she never backs down. The way she never admits fault or owns her mistakes. But now? Now I'm just...

Over it.

My exhale is slow as another tear trails down my cheek. "And what about after?"

Kat pauses. "After what?"

"This runway show. Let's say you get on it. What happens then?"

"What do you mean *what happens*? Then I compete, and I win. What else?"

"Will you still need to be in this fake relationship with Kaz once you get on the show? How long is the contract for?"

"Oh. Well...We haven't really signed a contract."

I bite back a groan. No contract. No parameters. Just *practicing* in the dark. I don't bother pointing out how fucked up it all is. It doesn't matter. She won't listen, anyway.

I ask the next question already knowing the answer. I don't even know why I do it. Maybe I need to be sure. I need it to hurt more before I take it seriously.

"So when you win, will we be able to go public? No more press appearances with Kaz. No more handsy photos or flirty videos. No more practicing kissing in dark corners. Instead, it will be you and me doing red carpets and events, right? You and me in the media. No more hiding. No more secrets. It will finally be how we've talked about. Right?"

I hate myself for the small bud of hope that starts to bloom in my chest as I speak. The way my mind creates vivid, colorful images of each scenario before they even leave my tongue. Scenarios I've imagined hundreds of times over the last three years. The outfits and the music and the glam. Flash photography and smiles. Her hand in mine. Us laughing and posing together on every tabloid cover in the magazine rack. Us in love, loud and proud. *Us.*

Even now, in the wake of this deep ache, I can't help but long for it just a little. I don't even want it anymore, but muscle memory is a bitch. And what's the heart if not just an annoying fucking muscle?

"Mabel. Sweetie. Don't do this. You know it's not that easy. It's just not the right time."

I huff another strangled laugh and wipe at my cheeks. She's not saying anything new, but this time...God, this time, I hear it for what it is, and it fucking hurts.

"When will it be the right time, Kat?"

When she doesn't answer, Sav's words from last week ring in my ears.

There is always something more important, or more urgent, or more exciting than you.

I swallow roughly, then lick my lips. They taste salty from my tears.

"I want to break up."

I say it clearly and calmly, resolute in my decision. I'm expecting Kat to agree, but when she snaps back, I actually flinch.

"Are you fucking kidding me right now? This is for my career, Mabel! It's not even a real relationship. It's for my career and you're making it about you."

I'm at fault again. Always me.

I shake my head. "It's not just about Kaz, Kat. It's not just about the fake relationship or the kiss."

"So what the fuck is it about?"

I shrug. "I don't want to be a secret anymore. I don't want to have to constantly hide my relationship from everyone."

Kat scoffs. "So now you're punishing me? You're breaking up with me because I'm not ready to let the world know I'm dating you? Because I'm not ready to sacrifice my career?"

"No," I say with a sigh. "I'm not punishing you. I'm standing up for myself. You're not ready, and I respect that. I'm not going to force you to do anything you don't want to do. But I don't want to do this anymore. I *can't* do this anymore, and I'm asking you for the same respect."

"This is bullshit, Mabel. You're overreacting."

My laugh is little more than a gurgle, and I squeeze my eyes shut against another wave of tears. I'm going to have to wear sunglasses on stage because I don't have time to redo my makeup.

"Kat, I've spent the last three years on your back burner. Being your second choice, your dirty secret, always hiding in the darkness while watching you parade around in the light with someone else, and I'm so fucking tired of hurting. I deserve better. I deserve dates and public outings and shared friendships. I deserve a partner who is *proud* to be with me, not ashamed. I deserve forever, Kat. An open, honest forever. Not one shrouded in secrets and lies. I deserve that, and so do you."

"I can give you that. I can! We can have it together. It's just not—"

"The right time. I know."

"Sweetie, you just have to be patient with me. Please. I thought you loved me?"

Her last sentence pounds against the inside of my skull as noise from the venue grows louder. Caveat's set is over. I have to go be a carefree rock star now. I kick off the wall and stand straight, swiping under my eyes once more. My fingers come back black with my destroyed eyeliner.

"I can't keep waiting for the right time when we both know it will never come," I say calmly. "I did love you. Part of me probably always will, but I have to love myself, too, and loving myself means recognizing that I deserve more than you can give me." I take one last deep inhale and blow it out slowly through my nose. "I'm breaking up with you, Kat. I wish you all the best, okay?"

Kat laughs, mocking and cruel. "Whatever, Mabel. I'll talk to you in a week when you come to your senses."

Then she hangs up.

I stand unblinking, with my mouth half open, staring at the wall across from me. She hung up on me after dismissing everything I'd said. No apology. No *I love you*. No recognition of the truth in my words or the devastation in my tone. Nothing except accusations and excuses.

You're making this about you, she'd said.

And therein lies the problem. For once, I centered myself. I put my feelings first, and Kat couldn't handle it. That's not love. Maybe it never was.

I turn to walk back to the dressing room and stop short when I find Sav leaning on the wall, mascara tear tracks drying on her own cheeks. I give her a sad smile and a shrug.

"It's over. I don't want to talk about it."

She closes the distance between us in three strides, and then she's wrapping me up in her arms and I'm collapsing against her. Sobs shake my body, and she pulls me in tighter.

"I love you," she whispers into my hair. "I love you so fucking much, Mabes. Anyone with any ounce of sense would be proud to call you theirs. Kat's a dumb cunt."

I snort a laugh and rest my forehead on Sav's shoulder. "She's not a cunt. She's just—"

"She's a cunt, Mabes, and you deserve better."

I shake my head, but I don't fight my smile.

"I know it hurts right now, but I'm proud of you for standing up for yourself. You'll find your one. I know it. They're out there."

More tears flood my eyes, but I nod. "Yeah."

I drop my arms and step back, then I laugh when I look at Sav. We must look terrifying, what with black eyeliner and mascara pooling under our eyes and streaking down our cheeks. I wave my finger around her face in a circle.

"This would be great for a Halloween show."

"Noted." She laughs, and then her smile softens. "Is there anything I can do?"

I purse my lips, consider her question, then give her a half smile. "We could go dancing?"

Sav smirks and arches an eyebrow.

I arch a brow back. "What did you do?"

"Oh, nothing much..." She shrugs, then turns back to the dressing room. "Just had Ham rent out part of a club downtown for us. We should be good to go after the show."

I roll my eyes with a laugh. "Of course you did."

"I have this new wig I want to try out." Sav threads her fingers through mine and squeezes. "And I know my sister."

I squeeze back. She's right, and I'm so fucking grateful. We walk hand in hand back to the dressing room, and when we enter, it's empty.

"Claire and Aurora went back to the lodge." Sav plops in front of the vanity mirror and takes a makeup wipe to her face. "They'll be with us tonight. Callie, too, but I told the boys they have to stay home."

"Cool."

I grab one of her makeup wipes and start on my own mess of a face, ignoring the flicker of excitement that's ignited in my chest. I tell myself it's for a night of dancing with my friends. A night where I don't have to worry about my girlfriend getting angry that I went out, or about her guilt trips built precariously atop her double standards. That's all. I'm excited for dancing and laughter and friendship and *freedom*.

It has nothing to do with Aurora. Of course it doesn't. I just broke up with my girlfriend and Aurora is *married*. A crush would be fucking stupid, and I'm done being stupid with my heart.

Absolutely *done*.

16

AURORA

"Nervous?"

I glance up at Callie and stick my hands under my thighs to halt my fidgeting fingers. She's wearing this skin-tight green dress that I could never pull off, and her red hair is falling in waves around her face. Add in her dark red lipstick and shimmering gold eyeshadow, and she looks like someone straight off a Hollywood red carpet.

I swallow back a laugh.

Of course she does. They all do. They're celebrities. They practically *are* straight off a Hollywood red carpet.

I smile and nod. "A little. I haven't been out like this in...well...ever, actually."

Her eyes widen. "Really? Never been out clubbing with girlfriends?"

I shake my head. "Nope. Never."

"And here I thought that's what all college kids did." She grins. "I never went, though, so all of my knowledge comes from shows and movies."

"The closest I've been to going out with girlfriends was homecoming dances and bonfires in high school." I shrug. "I wasn't very social in college."

"Well, we don't go out much either, so this is a rare experience." Callie waggles her eyebrows. "Things might get a little wild."

My laugh is awkward, my nerves flipping around in my stomach like a fish out of water, and I press my hand to my chest to feel my rapid heartbeat.

Wild has never been a word I'd use to describe myself, yet here I am, going dancing with a group of rock stars. They're all dressed in bodycon and sequins, and I'm *so* out of my element.

"Can't wait."

I flick my eyes toward Sav. She's wearing a purple balayage wig and a black faux leather minidress. There's a see-through mesh gap that stretches from her collarbone to her navel, then two more on both of her sides, running from the top hem to the bottom hem. So much *skin*. Side boob. Butt cheek. She looks, in Callie's words, *hot as fuck*, but I could only dream of having the confidence to wear something like that.

For the hundredth time since climbing into this SUV, I adjust the skirt on the dress I borrowed from Claire. Sav offered me something from her wardrobe, but I almost passed out when I saw the options. Everything was so risqué and edgy. Perfect for her. Not so much for me.

Thankfully Claire's selection offered more, uh, *coverage*. The black dress is still tight and short, but the sleeves are capped, there are no cut-outs or see-through details, and the hem reaches past the curve of my butt. And, the best part, I can wear black ballet flats.

Thank God. I don't think I'd survive if I had to also wear heels.

I cast my attention out the tinted window and cement it there, letting my eyes unfocus until I see nothing but dark, blurry images rolling past. I've been a chaotic mess of cyclical thoughts since my outburst in the dressing room—since the negative pregnancy test, truly—and I haven't had a chance to calm down. So much has happened in such a short period of time, one massive thing after another, like a totem pole of ground-shaking revelations. I haven't processed. I *need* to process.

I don't want to have a baby right now. I might not want to have a baby *ever*.

And maybe...

Maybe that doesn't make me a terrible person.

Sav's words from earlier keep echoing in my head, loud and soft, fast and slow. Haunting and repetitive. She's *baby-free by choice*. She *won't regret it*.

Ever.

I'm happy, she'd said. *I'm fulfilled,* she'd said.

She doesn't *need* to have a baby with Levi. She doesn't *want* to have a baby with him.

And then...

Levi wants what I want because we're a team.

I want to laugh at myself. The idea of Brady *ever* wanting what I want, of being a team with him, feels so unrealistic. I've spent so long being led, being told, being spoken for, that I've all but forgotten how to use my own voice. How to recognize my own wants and needs. But if I told him how I felt...

My chest contracts and my stomach tightens. I grit my teeth and remind myself to breathe. I feel dizzy and unsteady. I feel lost. But also...

I feel like I'm standing on the edge of a thick fog. Just a few more steps, and the air will be clear. The haze lifted. The light bright. It's as exhilarating as it is terrifying. This fog has been my home for years now. A tight little cocoon of manufactured safety and security. And while it's starting to feel constricting, I don't know if I can survive without it.

I blink out of my daze and settle my attention on the reflection in the glass. It's clear in the semidarkness. Pink hair and a mischievous smirk.

Mabel.

I've worked to keep my eyes off her, but I've not had the same control over my other senses. I can feel her energy emanating from the bench seat behind me. I can smell her flirty blend of fruit and flowers with each inhale. I can hear her every move, word, breath.

After she left the dressing room, I went to the internet and found the pictures of Kat Hughes and Kaz Storm. My heart broke for Mabel, and from the bits of conversation I've heard, she has ended things with Kat.

I don't know what I was expecting when I first saw her after the show. A sobbing, distraught mess, maybe? Instead, I found a brave face and a forced smile.

I just need to dance it out, she told me.

Then she emerged from the bathroom in a red sequined bralette, tight black skirt, and six-inch stilettos. The stilettos did me in, and I don't even know why. I keep picturing those dainty feet with her white polished pedicure inside those sky-high heels, and it makes my heart beat faster.

How is she going to dance in those? Will she have to take them off? Won't the balls of her feet hurt? Is she still wearing the toe ring?

I dig my fingers into the leather seat and will my heated cheeks to cool. I take out my phone and scroll through pictures of my garden, picturing my own feet and hands in the dirt until my pulse has calmed. I don't look up from my screen for the rest of the ride.

When we get to the club, we're lead through a back door and up a roped-off stairway into a private upper level. It has its own dance floor and bar while overlooking the main dance floor on the lower level. When I peer over the railing, I find hundreds of people staring up at me, and I immediately take several steps backward.

"Weird, right?"

I whip around and come eye to eye with Mabel. "Huh?"

She smirks. "Being up here while they're all down there, staring up at us like we're animals in a zoo."

"Is that how it always is? Being famous?"

"Pretty much. Especially if I'm with the others. They attract the attention, but I can sort of blend in from time to time if I'm on my own."

She glances over my shoulder toward the main dance floor again, and I don't miss the way her smile falters, revealing the sadness underneath. I speak without thinking.

"I could find you in any crowd."

She flicks her eyes to mine, something intense and almost painful flashing in those amber irises.

"You might be the only one."

I do a quick scan of the venue, noting several people with their attention set on Mabel. It's no surprise to me that people are looking. She's gorgeous and charismatic. People are always going to look. Something akin to jealousy stirs in my stomach, but I force a small smile and shake my head.

"No. Definitely not the only one."

I'm not sure if it's the lighting from the DJ booth or my eyes playing tricks, but Mabel's cheeks seem to color with a flush before that smirk of hers is back.

"Well, maybe I'll try to slip down there later and find someone to feed my ego."

She winks at me, then walks away, leaving me with my stomach at my feet and my heart in my throat.

Help feed her ego?

What does that mean? Dancing? It's got to be dancing, right? She wants to find someone to dance with. I'm not completely certain what kind of dancing happens in dark nightclubs after midnight, but something tells me it's not the kind I did at high school prom. It's probably a lot of touching. Groping. Grinding? I wince.

Wait.

Or does she mean she wants to *hook up* with someone? That's a rock star thing to do, right? Hook up with someone you meet while clubbing? Would it be another supermodel? A woman like

Kat Hughes? Someone tall and thin with more sex appeal in their left earlobe than I have in my entire body?

Oh God.

Will she be bringing them back to the suite?

I might throw up.

I don't know that I've ever felt this intense blend of emotions before. Jealousy and anger and sadness. It's overwhelming. It's unbearable. It's...

Well, it's stupid, is what it is.

I shouldn't care if she hooks up with someone tonight. I *don't* care. It doesn't matter to me because I'm not gay, and I don't have any feelings, whatsoever, for Mabel Rossi.

I shake my head as if I can rattle loose my ridiculous thoughts, and then I zero in on the bar. Callie said that tonight is bound to get wild. I might as well jump in headfirst.

Shoulders back. Chin up.

I manage half the distance between myself and the bar before my shoulders start to slump, and I grip my purse a little tighter. The text I got from Brady earlier flashes in my head.

Making money doesn't mean you don't have to run things by me first.

My brows furrow, and I practice the excuses under my breath.

"It was just one drink. I didn't even finish it. I just wanted something to hold. I didn't want to text you and bother you over a single drink."

By the time I'm stepping up to the bar, my stomach is in knots. I'm already dreading the conversation I'll likely have to have with Brady. And after the Melbourne boutique and the clothes?

Ugh.

I close my eyes and inhale slowly, then I open my clutch to fish out my wallet. I just want a buffer. I want something to take the edge off. To quiet my questions and slow down my brain. That's all. What's a cocktail go for these days? Twenty bucks? Just twenty dollars. Twenty dollars won't upset him.

"One drink. It's just one."

"A'right, just one, then." The bartender's voice is playful as I meet his eyes, his lips curled into a conspiratorial grin. "But if ya fancy another, I won't stop ya."

He winks, and I can't help the laugh that bubbles out of me.

"Careful flashin' that smile. I might forget how to pour."

I laugh again. He's cute. Long blond hair and a clean-shaven, sharp jaw. I bet customers swoon over him every night. Too bad it won't work on me.

"Are your drinks as strong as your flirt game?"

"Stronger." He smirks and leans closer, resting his arms on the bar top. "What's your poison?"

I hesitate. I don't even know what to order. I don't think I've ever ordered a drink at a bar before. What do people drink at nightclubs? I say the first beverage that comes to mind.

"A martini? Please."

"Gin or vodka?"

"...Gin?"

"You like it dirty?"

I blink. "Excuse me?"

The bartender laughs, then leans even closer. "Ya ever had a martini?"

I blink again, feeling my face flame red, then shake my head no. "I don't drink much, honestly."

"Ah. Just one, then." He nods knowingly, his face softening. "D'you trust me, love?"

"No. I just met you."

He barks out another laugh. "Fair enough. No worries, though. I'll fix ya right up."

I watch as he grabs a tall silver tumbler and gets to work *fixin' me right up*. He mushes up a lime wedge and some other sort of orange fruit, adds a clear syrup, vodka, and some orange liqueur to the tumbler, then puts another silver tumbler on top of that one and shakes it up. He slides a cocktail glass in front of me, plunks in some ice, and pours his tumbler mixture over it. It's yellow and smells sweet.

"Passion Fruit Caipiroska for the lady." He pops a lime wheel onto the side of the glass, then gives me a wink. "G'head. Try it."

I pick up the cool glass and bring it to my lips, and my eyes flutter shut the moment the sweet cocktail hits my tongue.

"See? I mix as good as I flirt, yeah?"

I smile and nod. "Better."

I take a deep breath and give him my credit card, eyes trained on it the entire time he runs my payment. One drink. Just one. Twenty bucks, tops. That's it. It's just one—

"Did you just pay for that?"

I turn and find Sav beside me. "Uh...yes?"

The bartender slaps my card down in front of me, and Sav turns to him.

"Hey, anything else she orders can go on my tab. Stephanie Lynn."

He blinks at her, his mouth popping open a bit. "Are you...You're not..."

"I'm not. I get that all the time, though." Sav smiles and bats her eyelashes. "People always tell me I should do one of those DNA tests or something. Maybe we could be sisters. Could you imagine? I'd be able to buy a Corvette."

He scans her face, blinking rapidly. "You sure?"

Sav laughs that iconic, world-famous laugh, and the bartender's eyes widen. She's got to be doing it on purpose. She's won an Oscar, so surely, she's capable of acting less *Sav Loveless*. I bite my cheek to tame my smile, but my lips twitch with the need to laugh with her.

"I think I know who I am, champ." She winks, then knocks on the bar in front of him with her knuckles. "Stephanie Lynn from now on."

She saunters away, and I lose the battle with my smile as the bartender's face grows more confused.

"Did you short-circuit?" I ask, and he flicks his eyes to me.

"You're on her tab?"

I shrug. "Guess so."

"Doesn't she look just like that rock star? Sav Loveless? The Hometown Heartless."

He turns back to Sav and tilts his head to the side. I take another sip from my drink. She looks just like herself. It's a terrible disguise. Even in a wig and colored contacts, she stands out, but I shake my head anyway.

"I don't see it."

I spot Callie and Claire in the back, so after a goodbye nod to the bartender, I weave through bodies to stand next to them. They're both holding glasses, one of something clear and one of something dark brown.

"Whatchya got?" Claire asks, nodding to my cocktail.

"Oh. Um...passion fruit something or other? I don't know. The bartender made it." I take a sip and smile. "It's good. Fruity. What do you have?"

Callie holds up her glass. "Vodka soda. Not as fun as yours."

"Mine's just a cola," Claire adds, and I raise my brows. She laughs. "No, I am *not* pregnant."

I wince. "Sorry for earlier. I'm so embarrassed. I never should have gone off like that on you guys. I can only imagine how awkward it was for you."

I put my palm on my cheek in an attempt to chase away the heat. The fact that Callie doesn't ask what the hell I'm talking about tells me she's already been filled in on my unhinged interrogation.

Claire gives me a genuine smile. "No worries. It's already forgotten."

I doubt it—I will certainly *never* forget it—but she's sweet for saying that. I nod and take another sip of my cocktail, then the air vibrates around me. A breath later, Mabel and Sav step into our group. My eyes are drawn upward, connecting with shimmering amber magnets, and Mabel smirks.

"You coming?"

I don't know where she's going, but I nod anyway. "Yes."

She takes my hand and leads me down the stairs onto the

lower-level dance floor. Callie might follow. Claire and Sav might stay in the VIP section. I can't be sure because my entire focus has zeroed in on Mabel's hand in mine. I don't look away from the contact until we're in the middle of the dance floor, surrounded by strangers, and she turns to face me.

Her plump pink lips are curled up at the side with a little half smile that makes my stomach flip. Then, without a word, she closes her eyes and starts to dance. For a moment, all I can do is watch. I stand there like a dazed fool, and I watch as she moves to the music.

The lights from the DJ booth shimmer off the sequins on her bralette, refracting glittering starbursts over the bare skin of her collarbones and shoulders. When she raises her arms above her head, her colorful tattoos serve as the most captivating frame. Her smile widens slowly, almost dreamily, and it's like I can see the tension evaporating from her body. Her heartache being soothed by the music and the movement. She's pure joy. She's bliss. She's freedom.

She's *everything*.

Mabel Rossi is beautiful and fun and alluring and *everything*, and it hits me like a tidal wave. I sway on my feet from the force. I try to tell myself it's the music, the atmosphere, the alcohol, but it's not. It's her. It's *all* her.

The realization makes my mouth suddenly uncomfortably dry. I force a swallow and finish my cocktail just as Mabel's eyes open. Those amber gemstones hold me hostage, sucking my breath from my chest. When she catches me staring, her lashes flutter, and she darts her gaze away and back. I should smile or apologize. I should look away. I should do something, anything, but I can't. I just watch.

The music changes, something sexy and slow, and then her smirk returns, softer this time. Tentative. Shy. My stomach clenches and aches. Something stirs low inside me, and I suck my lower lip between my teeth. She steps toward me, and my breath comes more rapidly. Every inhale makes my chest tight, pressing my breasts uncomfortably against the bodice of my dress. She takes the empty cocktail glass from my grip and hands it to someone beside her. A security guard. I hadn't even noticed him. I open my mouth to say thank you, but she moves her hand to my waist, and all words die on my tongue.

She leans in, putting her mouth to my ear, and I'm entrenched in gardenia and pear. Something sweeter. Brown sugar, maybe? I want to fill my lungs with the scent of her. My head tilts on its own, my nose brushing her hair, her skin, and I inhale.

"Dance, Roar."

Her voice tickles the shell of my ear, and my exhale trembles when she squeezes my waist. Gently, she urges me to move with her, so I do. She's a snake charmer, and my body mimics hers on impulse. On *instinct*, despite having never danced like this before. Not with someone like her.

Mabel leans back and locks her gaze with mine, but something has changed in her eyes. There's an intensity, a heat, that I don't recognize. I don't understand it, but I crave it. She smirks, then brings her lips back to my ear, this time erasing more of the distance between us. I can feel her body heat kissing my skin.

"There we go," she purrs. "Just like that. Just move with me. Let go."

Chill bumps coat my skin as her breath skates over my neck. I close my eyes and let my fingers trail down her arm. Energy dances over me from the contact, shooting up to my shoulders, then down my spine. My hand splays on her rib cage, my thumb and forefinger resting on the rough sequined fabric of her top while the rest press into her warm exposed torso, and it's all I can do not to pull her closer. It's all I can do to remember to breathe, let alone dance. Let alone stay upright.

The bass from the music pulsates up through my ballet flats. The DJ's lights paint the backs of my eyelids in vibrant colors. One drink, just one, but I feel like I'm floating. Drunk on this moment. On the scent of her. On the closeness. A buzzing hum of *more, more, more* thrums in my veins, and a need for something I don't understand drives my every decision.

Slowly, I lean forward and press my forehead against hers. I almost whimper when her hand wraps around the back of my neck, holding me to her. In my head, I picture her lips. I lick my own, threading my arms around her waist. She's soft and warm and smooth. I want to run my hands over her. I want her hands on me. I want, I don't even know. *Everything.*

I want everything.

Then the music changes, and she releases me.

Cool air hits my chest, and my eyes fly open so fast that I flinch. Mabel's laughter mingles with the song, and I blink several times to bring the scene before me into focus.

She's still here. She's still dancing with one hand on my waist. She's still just inches away. But now, her other hand is wrapped around someone else's neck. Someone who is pressed up behind her with his large hand spread wide across the bare skin of her abdomen. I stare at that hand, at the way he flexes his long, thick fingers into her skin. The way the tips slip just slightly into the band of her skirt. If she's wearing underwear, I bet he can feel them. If she's not wearing underwear...

I force my attention to the ground, landing right on their feet. Mabel's stilettos look so small bracketed by this stranger's giant shoes. It's a strange, unexpected punch to the stomach.

I take a step back, out of Mabel's reach, and her eyes meet mine when her hand falls away from me. Her smile falters, but before she can ask, I hook my thumb toward the bar.

"Gonna get another drink," I shout over the music. "You want anything?"

She shakes her head, concern lingering behind her smile. "I'm good."

I nod and turn away without saying anything else.

At the bar, the guy asks for my ID. I try to remember the name of the cocktail the bartender upstairs made for me, but when I can't, I order a vodka soda and tell him to put it on Stephanie

Lynn's tab. I take one sip and regret the drink, but I squeeze the lime garnish into the glass and pretend that I like it. Then, because I can still see Mabel dancing with that giant man twice her size, I weave my way through the bodies and head back upstairs.

"How was it?" Claire grins at me from her place at a tall pub table with Sav.

"How was what?"

"Your first clubbing experience. You weren't down there very long."

I flare my eyes. She must have heard me tell Callie I'd never been out dancing. That or Callie told her. It doesn't matter. I take a drink and shrug.

"It was fine. Sweaty. I don't think I missed out on much in college."

Sav laughs. "I'm not much of a fan, but Callie and Mabel will shut the place down if we let them."

"Those two love to dance," Claire adds.

I force a small laugh and let my eyes trail back toward the dance floor. Back to Mabel.

"I can see that."

I wasn't kidding when I said I could pick her out of any crowd. Even now, in the dim light of this club, with a hundred people dancing on the floor below me, I find her easily. I wish I hadn't.

She's still dancing with that guy. And while Callie is there, too, dancing and laughing alongside them, I can't stop looking at the guy. At every place his body touches Mabel's. His hands are all over her. His attention is only for her. She's eating it up.

It doesn't make sense. Not the way my stomach roils or my chest burns. Not the way she smiles up at him like he's special. Not the way I'd felt just moments earlier when her hands were on me. When her body was against mine...

None of it makes sense, but even though it hurts, even though I shouldn't care, I can't keep my eyes from darting back to them at every opportunity. I keep up the conversation with Sav and

Claire. I laugh and smile when appropriate. I even order two more cocktails and finish them without wincing. And whenever possible, I sneak glances at Mabel and tell myself that I don't care.

I don't care that she's dancing with this Australian cover model. I don't care that his hands have grazed and groped every inch of her skin he can reach. That his body has nearly folded itself over hers. That she's very obviously enjoying every second of it.

She told me this was what she wanted, right? Someone to *feed her ego*? Well, judging from her smile and her own roaming hands, she's definitely gotten that. He's fed her ego, all right. I bet he'll feed her something else tonight, too. In the suite that we share. In the bed right beside mine. It will sound like sex and smell like sex and—

I grit my teeth. I finish off my cocktail.

I do not care.

Because I have no feelings whatsoever for Mabel Rossi.

I repeat this over and over in my head. A mantra. A spell. I almost believe it. But then he kisses her, and I see red.

17

AURORA

I AM FEELING something for Mabel Rossi.

I'm not sure what it is. It might be anger. It might be more. I can't tell, but I'm definitely feeling *something*, and I don't like it.

He kissed her.

I watched him kiss her.

This big, stupid ape of a man kissed her right on her neck as his hand grazed the underside of her freaking boob. He practically had to bend in half to do it, and he looked completely ridiculous, too. Like a humpback whale. Like a...like a snail. The invasive kind. The kind you're supposed to stomp on sight, or they'll destroy your garden and spread disease to your animals. Or, you know, like an idiot Australian underwear model who will probably be having sex with Mabel tonight. I scowl.

"Are you okay?"

I blink out of my haze and dart my eyes to Sav. She and Claire are both staring at me with furrowed brows. Awesome. I'm a spectacle again. They must think I'm so strange.

"Yep. Great. I just...I have to pee. Bye."

I stand quickly and walk in the direction of the bathroom before either of them can say anything else, but instead of turning down the hall to the bathrooms, I take the stairs that lead to the lower level. I don't consciously make the decision. I'm running on autopilot and adrenaline.

As soon as my ballet flats hit the floor, I point them toward the spot where I last saw Mabel. The spot where that massive giant of a man was feeling her up. With his hands and his mouth and probably *other* appendages as well.

I clench my fists and weave through bodies, bumping and being bumped. Thankfully, I don't have to go far before the catalyst for my surging emotions pops up in front of me.

Ugh. And she's all sparkling with sweat and her hair is mussed and her face is flushed and she's just...*hot*. The thought brings on a jolt of confusion, but I can't focus on it through the haze of *other* feelings. I'm a mess, and she's so damn hot, and I hate all of it. It's dumb.

I check behind Mabel, but there's no attractive behemoth Australian. There's probably a security guard trailing her, but I don't bother trying to pick him out. I don't care about him. Just ol' Mr. Handsy Hands with the suction snail lips.

"Hey! Did you come back to dance?"

Her question is shouted over the music, drawing my attention back to her face. When my gaze locks with hers, she must see something in my expression because her smile drops, and she steps closer.

"What's wrong? Is everything okay?"

"I thought you liked women."

Her eyes widen, and she blinks a few times. I should apologize, but for the life of me, I can't remember how at the moment.

"What?"

"That giant man was feeling you up and kissed you on your neck, and you let him, and I thought you liked women. Right? But he's not a woman. He's very much a man."

My nose scrunches on the last sentence, and Mabel's lips twitch like she's trying not to laugh. Then she grabs my wrist and leads me to a back wall, away from the crowd, where the music seems less loud and the lights less bright.

"Okay, this is better." She folds her arms over her chest and leans casually on the wall. "What was your question?"

I huff, the dim lighting making me bolder. More confident. Reckless.

"I thought you liked women."

She smirks. "That's not a question."

My eyes narrow. "Why would you let that man kiss you if you like women?"

She arches a brow. "I do like women. Unfortunately for me, I am also attracted to men."

"And you were attracted to *him*?"

"Sure, he was attractive, but you don't have to be attracted to someone to enjoy dancing with them."

"But he kissed you!"

"He did."

"And you let him."

Mabel's head tilts just slightly. "I didn't, actually. He just did it."

"You didn't stop him."

"I didn't stop that one, no. But I left, didn't I?"

"You left?"

"You ran right into me as I was heading back upstairs."

"Oh." I clasp my hands in front of me, my eyes falling to the floor between us. "Oh, right. Right. Well...I'm sor—"

Mabel presses her finger to my mouth, silencing the apology before I can finish speaking.

"Don't do it, Roar."

I purse my lips against her skin and bring my narrowed eyes back to meet hers. I'm sure mine look wild, unhinged, yet hers are sparkling with humor. I bristle and move my hands to my hips, but I don't speak, and I don't remove her hand. She smirks.

"Jealousy is a completely normal emotion."

My jaw drops, and her hand falls away. "I am not jealous!"

When her smirk widens but she doesn't speak, I start to

ramble. My inability to shut the hell up around her is my fatal flaw. I'll die in this hallway, mid-run-on sentence, from lack of oxygen.

"I was just worried, is all. Because of Kat, of course, and I didn't want you to make any rash decisions because I thought you were, like, attracted to tall, skinny, sexy celebrities, and I didn't want you to bring that giant Australian underwear model back to the suite and bang him on the bed next to mine and then regret it in the morning. That's all. I was just looking out for you, is all. That's all. I'm not jealous. I'm not."

I'm nearly out of breath when I finish, and the intensity of Mabel's gaze makes my ears burn.

"What?" I ask aggressively.

Too aggressively. I almost apologize, but I bite my tongue. Mabel sighs.

"Well, that's a lot to unpack. First, thank you for looking out for me."

"You're welcome," I say curtly.

She smirks *again*. "Second, I broke up with Kat, so you don't have to worry about her. *I'm* not worried about her. Neither of us has to consider her feelings at all. Okay?"

My eyes flare before I can stop them.

She broke up with Kat.

She broke up with *her*.

Mabel isn't dating Kat anymore, and the reminder makes me want to smile right before I force myself to frown.

I am *not* happy.

I mean, I *am* happy. But for Mabel. I'm happy for Mabel. Good for her. I saw those pictures. She doesn't deserve to be treated like that. That's why I'm happy. That's all.

I flatten my hand over my stomach and attempt a nonchalant shrug. "Okay."

"*And* I would never bring someone back to the suite we're sharing. It's disrespectful. I wouldn't do it."

I shrug again. "I wouldn't care. It's fine."

It's a terrible, obvious lie. I drop my attention back to the floor, but then Mabel crooks her fingers under my chin and tilts my face back to hers so we're eye to eye once more.

"I wouldn't do it," she insists. "I don't want to do it."

My swallow is rough, and I lick my lips to wet them. Her eyes follow the movement, then slowly drag back up. Her next words are low, carried on an exhale that I feel more than hear.

"And I'm not *only* attracted to sexy celebrities."

"You're not?" I whisper, and her gaze is pulled back to my lips. "Who else are you attracted to?"

She forces her eyes to mine once more.

"I'm attracted to sexy *normal* people, too. I'm attracted to people who are full of energy and light. Creativity and confidence. To the passion I can see and feel in another person. It's not just physical for me, Aurora. It's deeper."

My face falls. It's stupid, I *know* it's stupid, but her admission fills me with disappointment. Sexy? Creativity and confidence? Passion? I don't know what I was hoping she'd say, not really, but it wasn't that.

It wasn't the exact opposite of *me*.

It shouldn't matter. None of this should matter. But God, it does, and I don't understand why. None of this makes sense. I am such an idiot.

My eyes start to sting, so I pull away from her. I don't want her to see me cry. Not over this. It's all just so stupid and ridiculous, and I am *such* an idiot.

"Hey. Hey." Mabel steps forward and grabs my shoulders, holding me in place. "What just happened?"

I blink away the threat of tears and clear my throat.

"Nothing. Nothing. I swear, nothing. I just...I'm just tired. I'm not used to being out this late. I'm not used to drinking. I'm just...I'm just feeling really raw right now, and I think I need to leave."

Her eyes scan my face, and I watch her own expression change from one of concern to one of anger.

"God, what has he done to you?"

"What?" I shake my head. "Who?"

She huffs, then runs her hand through her hair. Her jaw pops and her nostrils flare.

I don't know why she's agitated. I don't know what I did wrong, but it must have been bad. I never should have said anything. I never should have come downstairs after her or asked her any questions. I never should have even come tonight. I should have just gone back to the lodge.

Now I've made her angry. She's mad at me, and I don't want her to be mad at me. What if she never forgives me? If I've ruined this friendship, this one thing that's been giving me joy...

I shake my head again and wring my hands.

"Mabel, I'm sorry. Please don't be mad. I shouldn't have said anything. It's none of my business. It's not—"

She cups my face in her hands, and my words evaporate between us. I can't move. I can scarcely breathe as her amber eyes —eyes so full of emotion that it physically hurts—hold me in place. She opens her mouth twice without speaking as if warring with herself over something, and then her expression softens with resignation.

"*You* are light, Aurora Jade. *You* are energy. You're creative and passionate, and I know there is confidence here. I've seen it. It's been beaten back too fucking far, but it's not lost. Do you understand? It's not gone."

Her words decimate me. I hear them. I feel them. I want to believe them. I want to so badly that I grow dizzy. When tears begin to roll down my cheeks, her thumb brushes them away, but she never lets me go.

"*You're* not gone, Roar."

She whispers the words, and they serve as a tether. A tug right at my chest that pulls me through the last of the thick fog and right off a cliff.

I don't remember making the decision to move, but my mouth falls into hers perfectly. When she gasps, it's a shot of adrenaline, and I feel more alive than I have in a long, long time. Her fingers tighten on my face as mine reach for her, needing to touch her. Needing an anchor. A reminder that she's real. I run my palms over her smooth arms. Trail my hands up her delicate neck. Thread my fingers into her soft hair. *This* is real. It must be. It has to be, but it's unlike anything I've ever felt before.

It's free-falling. It's flying. It's perfect.

On instinct, I trace my tongue along the seam of her lips. Mercifully, she parts them, and then our tongues are colliding. Dancing. Tangling. Hungry and desperate, but still graceful and soft. So, so soft. Just how I imagined it would be.

Mabel's hand wraps around the side of my neck as her other hand grips my waist, pulling my body into hers. I whimper the moment we press together, but it's not close enough. I want to be closer. My fingers tighten in her hair, and she moans into my mouth. I can feel her chest vibrate with it, and it makes every muscle in my body tremble. That spot between my thighs aches. My heart pounds so hard that I fear it might burst. And I want more. I want her. I want everything.

And then she's gone.

Just like on the dance floor earlier, I'm hit with a wall of cool air in her absence, and I have to blink away the fuzz that's all but filled my head. My hands stay open, suspended in the air, but now she's out of reach. Steps away, staring wide-eyed at me in a way that makes me both proud and self-conscious. I don't understand. I don't know what's happened.

"We can't do that," she says finally, and it knocks the air from my chest. I start to panic.

"Oh my God. I'm sorry. Of course. Of course you wouldn't want to kiss me. Oh my God, I am so sorry." I grab my hair and pull. I look everywhere but at her. "I shouldn't have done that. I shouldn't. I'm sorry. I never should have assumed. I don't even know why...I wasn't...It was so stupid. I am such an idiot."

"Hey. Stop it. You're not an idiot. You're not."

"I shouldn't have kissed you."

"I kissed you back."

My breath hitches. She *did* kiss me back. She did. It *was* real, then. It wasn't just in my head. But, God, why does she look so sad? What did I do wrong?

"Then why...then what..."

I trail off, and Mabel huffs a tired laugh. "You're drunk."

"I'm not. I'm not drunk. I only had two. Or maybe three. I'm not...at least I don't think..."

"And I'm older than you. I'm in a position of power. I don't want to take advantage of you when—"

"You're not in a position of power," I interrupt. "You're not my boss. Sav is. And you're not that much older than me. Seven-ish years is basically nothing. You're not taking advantage. I started it. I wanted it."

Mabel smiles a soft, sad smile, then she takes a step forward, grabs my left hand and rubs my naked ring finger.

"You're married, Aurora."

There it is.

I stepped out of the fog, fell over the cliff, and this is where I crash right into the ground. I can practically hear the crunch of bone. I can absolutely feel it.

Brady.

I'm married.

I'm married, but I just kissed someone else. My husband was so far from my mind that he practically didn't exist. I didn't consider him once. Not once.

I'm a horrible wife. I'm a terrible person.

I'm married, but I just kissed Mabel Rossi, and God help me, but I want to do it again. I have never, ever wanted to do anything more in my whole life. In this moment, I would burn my whole life to the ground to touch her one more time, and it's terrifying.

I pull my hand from her grip and take several steps back, my heartbeat growing louder in my ears, my breath coming in pants. I'm going to cry. I'm going to pass out. I need to get out of here.

"I have to go."

She steps toward me. "No, look, it's okay. We should probably talk—"

"No. No." I shake my head frantically and widen the distance between us again. "I have to go. I have to think. Please. Just stay here and have fun. Find Kangaroo Jack and, you know, dance with him again or whatever. I'm fine. I'm fine. I just...I'll...I'll see you in the morning."

Mabel's smile is more of a wince as she nods. "Sure. I'll see you in the morning."

I turn and flee.

I'm ashamed and embarrassed. I'm going to start sobbing. I can feel it. I need to leave. I need to get the hell out of here. The lights are suddenly blinding, and the music is too loud, and the people are—

I run smack into a tall, hard body. His large hands close gently on my shoulders. When I look up into the face of my security guard, I cringe. Jones. And he looks so damn *awkward*.

Shit.

"Tell me you haven't been here the whole time."

His wincing smile mirrors Mabel's. "Sorry, Mrs. Sinclair. It's my job."

Mrs. Sinclair. God, it's like a slap to the face. I swallow roughly, take a deep breath, and beg.

"Please, please don't tell anyone. Not my uncle or Sav. No one. Please."

He nods. "I promise."

We ride back to the lodge in silence. He doesn't speak, doesn't even turn on the radio, and I'm so grateful for it. All I can do is stare out the window and replay every amazing, confusing, terrible moment with Mabel in that club. She was *everything*, and I'm...I'm...

I'm so screwed.

What the hell am I going to do?

Jones says something about the others and transportation, but it doesn't make it through the thick fog that's once again descended in my head. I amble through the suite, take a quick, freezing shower to wash away the buzz, and climb into bed. I'm plugging my phone in when I notice three missed calls from Brady and a series of texts.

My heart races once more, guilt and fear stabbing at my skin. Does he know? Were we seen? Oh God, not yet. He can't know yet. Not before I know what to do.

I hold my breath as I open and read the texts.

BRADY

What the hell is this 30-dollar charge at a bar?
What the fuck are you doing at a bar at 2 in the fucking morning?

BRADY

Answer the fucking phone, Aurora.

BRADY

Call me. Now.

I can hear Brady's voice. Raised and angry. Past condescending. Past patronizing. Nothing but ire.

Every message is like a backhanded slap, and my cheek stings with each word. I flinch and grit my teeth, imagining the phantom handprint blooming on my skin.

He's hit me twice before. Twice, in quick succession.

Only twice, he'd said the next morning. *It's not like I beat you.*

Only twice, and it was enough.

Enough to intimidate me into submission. Enough to shove me back into the darkness I'd been fighting against. To keep me down, quiet, and obedient.

The realization hits me like a punch to the gut.

This isn't normal. This isn't how it's supposed to be. *Nothing* about this is how it's supposed to be.

I think of Sav and what she said about her relationship. *Levi wants what I want because we're a team.* She went out tonight wearing an outfit that revealed more skin than it covered, and I watched him kiss her goodbye and tell her to have fun. No judgment or jealousy or strong-armed attempt to control her. He respects her and he trusts her. That would never happen with me and Brady.

What Brady and I have...

It's not healthy. It's harmful. It's not how it's supposed to be.

I bet Callie and Claire don't get texts from their partners that feel like physical blows. I bet they don't have to think up pre-planned excuses before spending money. When Jonah came to the dressing room earlier, he didn't make Claire go home with the baby. He gave her the choice, and then he respected it.

It been years since I've witnessed relationships that work harmoniously. I almost forgot they existed. I forgot it could be different. That is *should* be different.

I don't have friends. I've all but cut off my relationship with my uncle. I don't talk to anyone outside of the Sinclairs, and as for them...

Well, Brady is just like his father. Do I want to end up just like his mother?

Then, as painful as it is, I think of my own parents. Their relationship was one of strength, trust, and love. They supported each other. They respected each other. Their marriage was like a team, and they were equal players.

What would they say about my marriage? What would they think of what I've let myself become?

Uncle Wade said on the tarmac, just before we left the States, that my family would be proud of me. But would they? Because if they read these texts from my husband. If they knew about the anxiety I feel on a daily basis. The fear that weighs me down at the mere thought of going against him...

I don't think they'd be proud. I think they'd be devastated and disappointed.

And then that kiss.

It wouldn't have happened if I were in love with my husband. It shouldn't have happened at all, but now that it has...

God, what am I going to do?

I turn off my phone and drop it beside the bed.

Then the tears come in one giant flood. For the second time in a matter of days, loud, hiccupping sobs rack my body. My muscles ache. My throat burns. I bury my face in my pillow, soaking it in tears and snot, and it takes all my self-control not to scream.

In hindsight, I can see it all so clearly. My misguided reasons and fearful excuses. My desperation. My vulnerability. I'd just lost my family. I was so terrified of being alone, so burdened with grief and guilt, that I numbly handed all the control over to the first person who wanted it.

What if by doing that, I let go of myself, too?

What am I doing? What have I done? Why did I let this happen? Mabel's voice is a whisper in my head, and it starts to make sense.

What has he done to you?

There is confidence here. It's not gone.

You're not gone.

"Not yet," I say out loud, my voice echoing through the dark room.

I'm not gone yet, but I'm trapped. I'm suffocating.

And if I don't change something soon, I'll disappear for good.

18

MABEL

"Do you think something is wrong with her?"

I glance up from my drum kit and into Sav's frowning face. I could tell she was distracted during sound check. Now she's staring backstage, but when I follow her gaze, the spot is empty. I know who she's talking about, though. I don't even have to guess.

"Maybe she's homesick." The suggestion tastes bitter on my tongue.

Two nights ago, in the back of a dark club, Aurora kissed me. My lips still tingle with the memory. It was a hungry, confident kiss. The way she touched me, *clung* to me, as if I was all she needed. As if she'd been waiting to kiss me her whole life. I have never been kissed like that, and I can't get it out of my head. I can't get the feel of her off my skin. I can't stop analyzing every breath and caress and whimper.

I can't stop wanting more, and I know how dangerous that is.

Not that it matters, I guess. She won't even look at me, let alone talk to me. My schedule is usually jam-packed once shows start, but I was hoping I'd get a moment alone with her since we're sharing a room. So far, I've had no luck. She's been gone before I wake up and already asleep when I come to bed.

I clench my fists and breathe deeply through the guilt that's been steadily building.

I tell myself it's for the best. It's safer right now. The distance is a good thing. She's married. She's young and obviously confused. I can't get tangled up in that, especially not right after ending a three-year relationship.

Everything about this is wrong. The timing. The circumstance. All of it, and I don't want to make things more difficult for either of us. She doesn't know what she wants. She can't.

But...

I'm no stranger to being a thrilling experiment for the bi-curious. Usually, I welcome it. I play along and have a little fun. But this thing with Aurora? This feels different. Everything about it feels different, and not just because the stakes are higher. I'd be lying to myself if I said I wasn't drawn to her from the beginning. The attraction and interest have been there since day one, and they're only getting stronger. If she leaves the tour because of it...

I force down the concern with a rough swallow, then clear my throat.

"How's she been with Boss?"

"Great. Honestly, I think Brynn might actually be liking the subject, which is a miracle, but after their last session, Aurora just disappeared." Sav purses her lips, the lines on her forehead deepening. "And she skipped family breakfast."

I watch Sav as she puzzles through it. I know she's running through every interaction she's had with Aurora, analyzing every word and expression. From the look on her face, she's not liking whatever conclusion she's coming to. Then she finally brings her eyes to mine, and her brows are slanted with concern.

"How much has she told you about her husband?"

"Not much. Why?"

"I don't know. You seemed irritated when I mentioned bringing him on tour. Thought you knew something."

I shake my head. "Nope. I know what you know."

It's not a lie. Aurora has told me next to nothing. All I know for sure is what she told us in the dressing room. I'm starting to suspect something is wrong, though. I don't say it out loud, but I don't have to. I can tell Sav's thinking the same.

She hums and looks back out into the venue. "Everything seemed to go downhill after that baby conversation. It was just...bizarre. It was bizarre, right? You think I said the wrong thing? Did I upset her?"

My lips twitch with a sad smile. "Is *the* Sav Loveless second-guessing herself? Loud and cocksure Sav Loveless?"

She flips me off, and I laugh.

"No, Savvy. I don't think you said the wrong thing. And I don't think you upset her. I think..."

I trail off and drop my attention to my kit. A huge part of me wants to tell her about the kiss. About the tension that's been mounting between Aurora and me. The chemistry. The *pull*.

In any other circumstance, with any other person, Sav would be the first person I told. But right now, I just can't do it. I can't move past the feeling that it would be betraying Aurora. Whatever she's going through...Well, that's her story to tell.

I sigh and shrug, then give Sav the most honest answer I can without spilling everything.

"I think she's still figuring out what she wants in life, and that can be hard."

Sav hums again and nods. We sit in the quiet for a few moments, and I see the second she decides to change the subject. She arches a brow and looks back at me.

"Have you heard from Kat the Cunt?"

I roll my eyes. "It doesn't matter. It's over."

"Yeah, well, it's been over a few times before, but that didn't stop her from sending you gifts and late-night *I miss you* texts and nudes and showing up unannounced, et cetera, et cetera."

I flare my eyes. Sav's not wrong. That was always Kat's MO, and this time it's been more of the same.

I think back to the text she sent last night. A mirror selfie wearing a sheer white negligee that I bought her two years ago in

France. I didn't even let my eyes focus on the photo before I deleted it. In a few days, a piece of jewelry or a bouquet of flowers will likely show up at the hotel for me. It's the same tired playbook. In the past, those things worked. They filled me with just enough hope, made me feel *just* loved enough that I'd fall back into her.

Not this time.

"Doesn't matter what she's done or is doing, Sav. It's over for me."

"I know."

My brows rise. "You know?"

"You're different this time." Sav smirks. "So if Kat keeps bothering you, I know a place that will let us ship her elephant shit anonymously. You know, to help her get the message."

I huff a laugh. "I'll let you know."

I stand from my drums and turn to follow Sav offstage, but my attention falls to Hammond standing in the wings. I know for a fact he's talked to Aurora. I've seen it. Right now, though, he's alone.

"Hey, I'll catch you at the lodge. I have to talk to Ham."

Sav nods. "Sure. I need to meet with Caveat anyway. Label CEO duties and such."

We part ways once we hit the hall, her toward the dressing room and me straight to Hammond. When I step up to him, he's frowning and typing furiously on his phone.

"Everything okay?" I ask casually, and he harrumphs.

"I'm about to get a bank manager fired."

I quirk a brow. "Yeah? What for?"

Hammond sighs, but he doesn't look up from his phone.

"I set up a new account for Aurora yesterday, had a card overnighted for her, but now she's been flagged for fraud because these fucking idiots didn't consider that if I had the card shipped to fucking Australia, then it would be used in Australia despite the California billing address."

I can't help but grin. Hammond cussing is a rare occurrence. I almost feel bad for the bank manager. Then my brain latches onto the core of what he said, and I pounce on it.

"Why'd you have to set up a new account for Aurora?"

He finally looks up from his phone and hits me with narrowed, suspicious eyes. No doubt he's realized he gave me more information than he'd intended while in the throes of angry emailing.

"What do you want, Rossi?"

I shrug. "Just wanted to ask where Aurora is."

"She's your roommate."

"Our schedules haven't aligned for the last couple of days. I haven't had a chance to talk to her since the girls' night, and I wanted to check in."

Hammond surveys my face, so I smile and bat my eyelashes just to irritate him. To throw him off any other conclusions he might be coming to. Then, thankfully, he returns to his phone. My shoulders sag.

"She was shopping with Jones, but she's finished. She's at the lodge."

"Great. Thanks."

I turn to leave, but his voice stops me. "When you see her, exchange phone numbers. I don't want to be arranging your playdates."

My eyes widen and I feel the color drain from my face, but he doesn't notice. He's typing up another angry email, and I've been dismissed.

When I get back to the room, I can't ignore my nerves. My stomach is flipping over on itself, and I hold my breath as I push open the door. I'm expecting to see Aurora inside—*hoping*—but instead, the room is empty. The only proof that she'd been here at all are the shopping bags sitting atop her made bed.

Curiosity draws me to the bags, and despite being alone, I tiptoe cautiously. When I reach her bed, I hold my breath again, listening to the silence. Checking once more that I'm the only one in the suite.

When I'm certain I won't get caught, with my heart racing like a child stealing cookies before dinner, I reach my hand into one of the bags and run my fingers over soft, cool fabric. I peer inside and find clothes. I smile.

Despite knowing I shouldn't, I start pulling the items out of the bags, and each piece makes my smile widen.

Two pairs of jeans. A few pairs of denim shorts. A pair of corduroy overalls with cute little flower patches on them. Tank tops. T-shirts. A long, flowy skirt. A pair of tennis shoes. A pair of sandals. A few pieces of jewelry. Every item follows a similar style from the other day, when she wore the wide-legged jeans and crocheted top, and it doesn't escape me that there isn't a single cotton dress among them. It feels significant, but I don't fixate on it.

I turn my attention to the small outdoor patio, and my eyes fall on Aurora's orchid. It's sitting on the same little table in the dappled sunlight where it's been since we got to the lodge. It doesn't look like Aurora's moved it at all, so I step out onto the patio and crouch down beside it.

The orchid looks healthier than it did last time I looked at it. A darker, more vibrant green. Firm, shiny, plump leaves. And maybe it's just wishful thinking, but the bud, tiny as it may be, appears to be growing. No bud blast yet, as Aurora called it.

"Are you coming out of recovery mode, Arthur?"

Carefully, I trail my fingertips along the leaves, then inhale, filling my lungs with the fresh air. It's so peaceful here. I think it could bring anyone back to life. I close my eyes and listen to the breeze. The bird songs. I try my best to clear my head of everything that's been causing me stress, and I just breathe.

"What are you doing out here?"

I whip around and find Aurora standing in the doorway. Her hair is wet and hanging down her shoulders, and she's wrapped in a large, fluffy white towel.

"Were you in the shower?"

She shakes her head. "No. I just came back from one of the hot pools."

"Oh."

I stand quickly and run my eyes over her face, searching for any hint of regret or shame, and my throat tightens. I didn't realize how much I missed her presence. Her voice. It's been a matter of days, but I missed her so much that my eyes nearly devour her, searching every feature as if I've not seen her for years. The longer I stare at her without speaking, the pinker her cheeks tint, so I break the silence.

"How was it? The hot pool, I mean."

"Good. Nice and, um, hot."

"Cool. Good. I should try one before we leave."

"You should."

I nod, and another uncomfortable pause stretches. She glances back into the room, probably searching for an escape route, so I gesture to her orchid, grasping for any topic that will keep her here. I'm not ready for her to leave again.

"He looks good," I say, and her eyes drift to the flower.

"Yeah. I feel bad, though. I haven't really been tending to him, but he doesn't seem to mind."

"Maybe he just needed space."

"Maybe." She flicks her eyes back to mine. "How was sound check?"

"Good. It was good. All sounds were checked. How was shopping?"

"Good."

"Cool."

"Yeah."

"I saw your bags." I nod toward the bed. "You did some damage."

She winces and lets out a forced laugh. "Yeah, I guess."

Another painfully awkward pause follows. I try to think of anything else to talk about—anything safe and easy—but I come up short. Aurora and I don't really do small talk. We haven't stuck to safe, easy topics, and this stilted conversation actually hurts. I hate it. There's no sign of the warmth or playfulness that's colored all our other interactions. There's no familiarity. That strong connection I feel with her, it's flickering—fading in and out—and I feel anxious. Panicky. As if I don't do something soon, it will disappear, and I'll question if it was ever real at all.

I grab my ring and spin it around on my finger. I shift my weight from one foot to the other. The tension mounts until I can't take it anymore, and then I blurt out the first thing that comes to mind.

"I found my birth mom."

When her eyes widen, and her lips curl into a surprised smile, I'm immediately relieved. I've been itching to talk about this with someone, but I realize now that it wasn't just anyone I wanted to share it with. It was her. With just a few words, just one intimate secret, we're *us* again, and I feel like I can finally breathe.

"Really? How? Where? How do you feel?"

"Really. I hired a law firm and had them hire a private investigator. She's in Georgia. And to be honest, I don't know how I feel yet."

She nods, her smile softening. "I understand that. It's a lot to process. Do you think you'll meet her?"

"I haven't decided. What if she doesn't want to know me?"

"Then she's a fool."

The conviction in her voice makes my heart ache, and I huff a small laugh.

"Maybe, but it wouldn't make it hurt less," I confess. "She gave me up and made no attempt to find me. It's not unreasonable to think she wouldn't want me just showing up on her doorstep."

"Are you sure?"

Aurora's head is tilted to the side, her question posed so plainly that it takes me a minute to understand it.

"Am I sure what?"

"That your birth mom didn't try to find you. Are you sure?"

I think about it for a moment, blinking at the open, interested, completely unjudgmental expression on her beautiful face. And then I shake my head.

"No, I guess not. I just, I don't know, I assumed since no one came knocking on my door in the last thirty years that they haven't looked."

She smiles again, this one more playful. More *her*, and it makes my throat tight.

"You've tried on a lot of lives, Susan Ainsley Mabel Rossi. I don't know that it would be easy to find you if someone didn't know where to look."

"You said you could find me in any crowd."

I hadn't realized how strongly I'd been clinging to those words, to her meaning behind them, until they escape my lips and float between us. In the seconds following, I hold my breath. I wait for her to flee. To apologize. I watch as shock and embarrassment pass over her face, and then it's awash in something like sadness.

"I could"—her voice is a whisper, and I lean closer—"but that's different."

"How?"

"Because I don't do it on purpose. I just *know*."

It's like she's reached right into my chest, grabbed onto my heart, and squeezed. It brings tears to my eyes, but I don't look away from her. I can't. I see everything I'm feeling in her expression. Every ounce of longing and confusion. The frustration of being so inexplicably drawn to someone you can't have.

The pain.

God, she looks like she's in physical pain, and I reach for her. I take her hand in mine, and I hold on tight.

"Are you okay, Roar?"

The question comes out innocent enough, but I can tell she knows I'm asking about more than just the kiss.

The apologizing. The crying. The dressing room outburst. Even the cotton dresses, the shopping sprees, and the new bank account. It's all pieces of a larger puzzle, and I need to figure out how they fit together. I know in my bones that something isn't right. I know it. I just need her to confirm it.

When she speaks, her voice shakes, but not in a frightened or uncertain way. It's like she's been keeping this bottled up for so long that she has to release it slowly or risk erupting.

"A truth for a truth?"

19

MABEL

I NOD ONCE and hold her gaze as I respond.

"Always. Only honesty here."

Her eyes search mine, misty and conflicted, and I rub my thumb over the back of her hand. *Tell me,* I plead silently. *You can trust me. Tell me, please.*

When she finally speaks, it's one of the bravest and most difficult things I've ever witnessed.

"Grief is a strange thing, you know? It can change you in ways you never expected. Turn you into someone you never thought you'd be without you even noticing. It's like this...this thick, dark cloud. It's sticky and heavy and coats everything. It makes it hard to see clearly. Hard to think. Makes you physically ache. Makes you feel like you're drowning, or being buried alive, until you're...you're desperate. Until you'll latch onto the first thing that offers refuge, even if..."

She closes her eyes and takes a deep breath, then blows it out slowly.

"Even if deep down, you know it's bad for you."

She pauses again, but I don't try to fill the silence. I just rub her hand and wait with her until she's ready to continue. And when she does, my heart breaks.

"The accident happened on a Tuesday. My graduation day. I was pissed off because Paul wasn't coming home for it. He was in grad school out of state and doing this internship thing, and he said his car was acting up. He told me he couldn't come for the ceremony, but he would *try* to get a flight out that weekend for the party. We'd gotten into a fight the day before. I told him he was a shitty brother. Said I'd spent my whole life being dragged to all his stuff, and he couldn't at least make it home for *the biggest day of my life."*

She lets out a sad laugh and shakes her head, wiping away a few tears.

"God, I was so melodramatic. The biggest day of my life. I actually threw the phone after I hung up on him, and then I blocked his number. I was being such a selfish brat. The next morning, when my parents dropped me off—I had to be at the venue, like, three hours early—I wouldn't even speak to them. I didn't say goodbye. I didn't tell them I loved them. I just slammed the car door and marched off without looking back. I was determined to be a bitch, you know? My feelings were hurt, and I took it out on them."

Her gaze drifts behind me—to the orchid, I realize—and then they go unfocused. I watch her pained expression, and it becomes clear to me that she's picturing it. That day. She's reliving everything, and it's agonizing.

I don't resist the urge to take her other hand. I cup hers in mine and bring them to my chest, pressing them against my skin. I hope she can feel my heart beating. Feel my chest rising and falling with each breath. I hope she uses it as an anchor. So if she gets lost inside that memory, in that pain, she can use me to find her way back out again.

"I kept my phone off. I met up with my class advisors and my friends, and then the excitement kind of took over. I stopped being angry. I realized that I'd been unfair and immature. I turned my phone back on and unblocked Paul. Sent a text to the group chat with my parents and told them I was sorry. I said I wasn't mad anymore, and I loved them. And then I put my phone in my pocket, got in my alphabetical place in line, and waited.

"I knew something was wrong when we got into the commencement hall. I couldn't find my parents anywhere. I kept checking where they were supposed to be sitting, and the seats were empty. I texted and asked where they were. They didn't answer. I texted the group chat. I texted Paul separately. Nothing. When the ceremony started, I was officially panicking. I knew something was wrong—I knew it—so I checked their locations."

Her face crumples and her next inhale is ragged. Her lips tremble. Tears flood her cheeks. I have to blink away my own so I can see her clearly. I don't dare let go of her hands to wipe my eyes. I don't dare take away her anchor. I just hold on tight, and I listen, and I hope it's enough.

"It showed them on the highway. All three of them. And they'd been there, unmoving, for over an hour. It didn't make sense. My parents were supposed to be at the commencement hall. My brother was supposed to be out of state at school. They weren't supposed to be on a highway together. It was wrong. It was all wrong.

"I left immediately. I ran to the lobby and called Uncle Wade. We were only allowed ceremony tickets for immediate family, so he was still in LA and was planning to come for the party. I told him my parents weren't answering their phones. Told him about their locations. He said to stay put and he made some calls, and then...then..."

She sucks in a harsh breath and starts to sob. I wrap my arms around her, and she collapses against me. Her tears soak through my shirt, my shoulder and collarbone wet with them, and I rub her back. I hum and kiss her hair and slowly, I lower us to the ground, until she no longer has to support herself. Until I'm supporting us both. And then I let her cry.

I don't try to quiet her. I don't give her platitudes or reassurances. I do the only thing I know how to do. I let her *feel*, and because I don't want her to be alone, I feel with her.

I don't know how long we sit on the patio. I don't know how long we cry together, but when her tears slow and her breathing calms, I don't release her. When she speaks again, it's a steady, strong whisper, but she doesn't take her head off my shoulder. I feel every word on my neck. In my chest.

"Paul had decided after our fight to come home. He felt bad. I made him feel bad, and he drove all night. Then his car died on the side of the road, so he called my parents to pick him up. On the way back, another driver fell asleep at the wheel. Went off the road and over-corrected. Crossed the median. There were four cars involved in the accident. Nine people total. Only three fatalities."

Only three fatalities.

Her family.

On a day that was supposed to be a celebration, she lost her entire family. Everything she knew changed in an instant, and along with grief, she's been harboring guilt. Four years of agony. I can't even imagine how heavy that must be. I can't imagine how exhausted she is from carrying it.

I almost tell her it's going to be okay, that it will get easier, but I stop myself. That's not what she needs to hear. More condolences and false promises. I can't tell her something I don't know to be true. I press another kiss to her head and instead say what feels necessary. I give her honesty.

"It wasn't your fault."

"I've spent so long believing that it was."

"It was a terrible, horrible accident, Aurora, and it wasn't your fault. Not only that, but your parents and brother loved you, and they knew you loved them."

She shakes her head. "The last thing I told my brother was to go to hell. I slammed the car door on my parents as they were telling me they loved me. That's my last memory of them. Their last memory of me..."

"My apology came too late. They never saw my texts. By the time I stopped being a brat and sent them, my family was already dead. Now they'll never know how sorry I am. They'll never know I didn't mean what I said. I was too late."

Her apology came too late.

It makes sense, now. The constant apologizing. That must be why she's so quick to say she's sorry. For everything, all the time, even when she's done nothing wrong.

I hold her tighter and press my face into her hair, willing my words to penetrate her skin. To burrow into her. To become permanent.

"They knew you loved them. They did. I promise you, they did. Foundation of truth, remember? I wouldn't lie to you."

Aurora sniffles and nods, but she doesn't say anything. Instead, she sits up, and chill bumps rise on my arms from the air when it hits my shoulder, replacing her warmth and cooling my skin that's still wet from her tears.

I loosen my hold on her, but I don't let go. I don't wipe my face of my own tears, and I don't hide from her pain. I don't want her to hide from it either.

Her eyes bounce between mine, and she chews on her lower lip before folding it between her teeth. Her brows furrow, and I hold my breath for whatever she's going to say next. Then she huffs out a small laugh. It's quiet and tired, but it's still such a sweet sound.

"Second time in a week you've found me sobbing on a floor."

I smile. "To be fair, you found me this time. And we weren't on the floor to start with. Or sobbing."

"I suppose that's true."

She leans back onto the sliding glass door, cheeks flushed and glistening with slowly drying tear tracks. Her lashes are matted, and her eyes are red-rimmed, but I can't look away from her. She's a mess—we both are—and she's beautiful. Raw, real, vulnerable. Beautiful. Her attention moves back to the orchid, and her frown returns.

"Uncle Wade wanted me to move to L.A. with him until the college semester started, but I didn't want to leave my hometown.

We sold my house, but my friends, memories of my family, everything I'd ever known was in that town. I couldn't go through another huge change. I couldn't."

She shakes her head and sighs, slow and defeated. Then she shrugs. "Enter Brady."

My spine straightens at the mention of her husband, and I can't fight the downward turn of my lips or the slant to my brow. Her shoulders droop. I can see her regret in the way her body deflates. In the crease of her forehead and the tone of her voice.

If I could turn back time—if I had the power to change one thing about the past—I'd change this for her. Fuck all the shit I've been through, all my mistakes. They can all stay. But this pain she feels? This regret and guilt? Aurora doesn't deserve it. I'd erase it all.

"Paul and Brady were best friends. He was at our house a lot. I kind of grew up with him, and my brother thought of the Sinclairs like a second family. When they offered to let me stay with them, I jumped at the chance. I clung to it. I was desperate. Brady had all these stories about Paul. All these pictures. He was so comforting. In a way, it was almost like having Paul back. Like having my family back. I told Uncle Wade to go back to L.A., and while he called and checked in every day, he wasn't there, you know? And my friends didn't understand. They tried, but they had lives. They all went off to college. I only had Brady.

"When he suggested I defer my university acceptance and go to the local community college, I did it. I didn't think twice. The thought of being on my own so soon was debilitating. I thought I needed the Sinclairs. I thought I needed Brady. When he asked me out, I was happy for the companionship. He offered me a comfort I desperately needed, and at the time, I didn't see it for what it was. A crutch. A bribe. A trap."

Aurora drops her head to the glass door and peers up into the tree canopy. The dappled sunlight dances across her flushed skin, and for a moment, it's like I can see her gaining strength from it.

She's fascinating and resilient. The more I learn about her, the more in awe I become.

"You are one of the strongest people I've ever met," I say, giving her hand a squeeze, but she shakes her head and keeps her eyes on the trees.

"I've spent the last four years willfully blind and closed off. I've lost direction and control. I couldn't handle my reality, so I allowed Brady to change everything to better suit him."

She blows out a slow breath and tips her head toward me, finally connecting our gazes once more.

"I was so numb that I stopped caring about everything. I let him take the reins, and now I'm stuck in a life I never wanted. Now I'm stuck in a marriage with a controlling, manipulative man who I don't love. That's not strong. That's pathetic."

Controlling. Manipulative. Pathetic.

She states the words with such matter-of-fact precision that I get angry. Angry at the universe for putting her through such a tragedy. Angry with Brady for taking advantage of her when she was vulnerable. Angry with Hammond for abandoning her when she needed him most. And though I understand how irrational it is, I'm angry with myself.

If only I could have found her sooner. She was so close. Mere miles separated us. How many times was I in the room when Ham was texting her? How often did the voice on the other end of his phone belong to her? How did I not know that his family had gone through this? That *he* had gone through this?

He lost his brother and sister-in-law. His nephew. He almost lost his niece.

If I'd just shut up. If I'd just listened. He never told, but I never asked. Maybe if I had, I could have stepped in and prevented it from getting this far. I could have been the safe space Aurora needed. I could have helped her heal.

I feel so close to her now, it's hard to believe she was ever in such pain, and I didn't feel it, too.

God, it's all so fucking unfair. I could have been there, but I wasn't.

I wasn't, but I am now.

I hold her gaze and speak clearly, pouring everything I'm feeling into my voice, hoping she can hear it. Hoping she can feel it.

"You are not pathetic, Roar. You were nineteen, heartbroken and traumatized. You were in recovery mode, and you were vulnerable, and someone you thought you could trust took advantage of you. That's not your fault. You did nothing wrong. That's all on Brady. You *are* strong."

She swallows and licks her lips, her voice thick with sorrow.

"It doesn't change where I am now. I'm stuck."

"You're *here* now. You're here with me. You're not stuck."

She shrugs. "He won't let me get a job. He monitors my bank account. I can't have friends or hobbies that involve leaving the house. He even dictates the way I dress. Honestly, I think the only reason he let me come here was so he could use it against me later. He didn't think I would last. He said I'd get fired or come home early. He let me do it so that for years to come, when I'm three kids in and miserable, he can throw it in my face to keep me in line."

I nearly flinch when the realization hits me. *Three kids in and miserable.* Suddenly, her outburst in the dressing room replays in my head, and the reasoning behind it becomes clear.

That's what everyone wants, right? It's what everyone should want.

She'd said it so frantically, asked the questions so desperately, like she was trying to make herself believe them. Like she needed someone other than Brady to tell her what she should want. After four years of not trusting herself—four years of living in darkness and letting Brady control everything—it makes sense that waking up to reality would be scary.

She wanted reassurance that the life she'd been living was her only option, that desiring something else was pointless, and she didn't get it.

Three kids in and miserable.

That's what everyone wants, right?

But not her.

A harrowing possibility sinks into my stomach and makes my insides churn. Is that why she was crying in the bathroom, too? Is there more to her desperation? A catalyst that's pushed her over the edge?

I force a swallow to calm the quiver in my voice before I ask.

"Are you pregnant?"

She shakes her head rapidly, and a bit of my concern eases. But then she speaks, and it fills me with anger.

"I'm not pregnant, but Brady wants me to be. He's been trying. If I don't get pregnant in the next few months, he wants to see a fertility doctor. He wants his first kid before he's thirty."

He's trying. *He* wants. *His* kid.

It's all him, and I hate him.

I hate him more than I've ever hated anyone, and it takes everything in me not to let that hatred show in my face and voice. The last thing Aurora needs right now is to worry about my feelings, too.

"Do *you* want any of this?"

Her eyes fill with tears once more, and she shakes her head again. Her confession comes out whispered and quaking, like speaking it aloud is dangerous, and maybe it is. Truths, once revealed, can't be taken back.

"I don't. Not now. Maybe not ever. But definitely not now, and not with him."

"Leave him."

"I don't know if I can."

"You can. You have to."

"I have no job. No money. No family or friends."

"You have a job. Brynn needs a tutor, so there's your job. Your money. And you have Ham. You have me. You have support. You can't stay with him, Aurora. He's not good for you."

"It's been my entire life for four years, Mabel. It's all I know."

"So? Maybe it's time to try on a new one."

She clamps her eyes shut again and pinches the bridge of her nose. The creases in her forehead deepen. Her frown becomes more pronounced. I can feel the despair rolling from her in waves.

"I've let everything get so messed up. I don't know how to fix it. I don't know where to start. What if I screw it up? What if I just make everything worse? I don't even know what I would do. I feel like I'm trapped under the rubble of my mistakes, and I have no idea how to get free."

"Be light."

Her eyebrows scrunch. "What?"

"If you feel like you're trapped under rubble, then be light and push through the cracks. A little bit at a time. You don't have to know everything right now. You've got time to figure shit out. Travel. Write poetry. Work at a greenhouse. Go see The Northern Lights."

I grab her necklace and rub my thumb over the worn pendant, then press my palm to her chest, right above her heart. I feel it racing under my touch. The *thump, thump, thump,* pounding into my skin so familiar, it could be my own.

"Follow *this*. Don't be afraid. Don't settle. There are no wrong answers, Roar. Mistakes are inevitable, but sometimes, to find yourself, you have to let yourself get a little lost."

She looks at me with those hazel eyes in a way that makes my chest tight and my throat burn. No one has ever looked at me the way she does. Like I'm brilliant and valuable. Like my words hold weight and meaning. Like I'm the only thing in the room. It makes me want to keep her, and then my heart aches because I know I can't. She doesn't need another keeper. She deserves to be free.

"How did you get so wise, Susan Ainsley Mabel Rossi?"

I smirk. "I've tried on a lot of lives, Aurora Jade Hammond."

Her eyes drop to my lips, then drag back up, and I feel it on every inch of my skin.

"Did you ever get lost?"

"More times than I can count." I lean closer and lower my voice to a whisper. "But you know what?"

"What?"

"I always found myself again. You will too."

"Promise?"

I smile, and because I need to touch her, I tuck a strand of hair behind her ear, allowing my hand to linger there, so I can feel the heat from her skin. So I can soak up some of the light I see inside her. I know it's there. I need her to know it, too.

"I promise. Only honesty here."

20

AURORA

Be light.

Be light and push through the cracks.

I watch the clouds through the window of the jet and repeat the words over and over in my head like a mantra. I can do that. I can be light. I can get myself out of this mess. I just need to have courage, even if I have to fake it.

I can do it. I can be light.

I run my palm over the smooth cover of my new notebook. Hand-bound, brown vegan leather, and deckled edges. I bought it from a small stationery boutique in Adelaide, and the purchase felt like a promise. A promise that maybe the dreams I'd once had could be revived. Like there was still hope in who I used to be. Who I could maybe become, if I just tried. But then later that afternoon, I stared at the blank page for an hour before sliding it back into my bag without writing a thing. My new pen never graced the page.

The words are there. I can hear them at the edge of my consciousness, but I can't grasp them. Not yet. It's frustrating, but it's also exciting. It's been a long time since poetry was even a whisper in my mind, and right now, it's humming. Buzzing. Out of reach, but louder and more present than it's been in four years. It's not much, but it's something.

I lean back against the headrest and close my eyes. My breathing is calm and steady. I focus on that. On how much better I've gotten at flying. Every flight has been a little easier. I'm adjusting, and it's proof that I can grow. I'm proud of myself for that. I pull confidence from it, as much as possible, and I hold on as tightly as I can.

Again, it's not much, but it's better than nothing, and I'm going to need all the help I can get.

"Fuckin' ace, innit?"

Crue's arm lands heavily around my shoulders as we stand on the stone-paved path, staring up at the three-story beachfront villa Sav rented for our stay in Sydney. It's gorgeous and huge, and just like with the lodge in Adelaide, it almost doesn't feel real.

"Yeah," I breathe out. "Ace."

"Think we can get surfboards?"

I look toward the voice beside me and find the lead guitarist for Caveat Lover peering at us through aviator sunglasses.

"You can surf?"

He grins. "I could surf before I could walk."

I narrow my eyes in question and tilt my head to the side. "I don't think that's physically possible."

"It is if you're surfing Santa Monica beaches."

Beckett Walker, Caveat Lover's bassist, steps in front of us, smirking at Rocky.

"Fuck you." Rocky sings the words, then lifts his hand and brandishes his middle finger inches from Beckett's face. "You don't get an opinion, Walker. You spend all your beach time worrying about tan lines."

Beckett puckers his lips and kisses Rocky's finger. "You like my tan lines."

I have half a second to analyze their interaction before Ezra pushes his way between them and wraps his arms around their necks.

"You guys can't surf here. Don't you know about the sharks? Shark attacks are disproportionately high in Australia compared to other countries. You want to lose a leg?"

"I could still play without a leg," Rocky says, and Ezra groans.

"You want to lose an arm?"

"You're more likely to be killed by a kangaroo than a shark, dummy," Brynn says from behind us, and we all turn to face her. She's scowling at Ezra before turning a kinder expression on Rocky. "Don't listen to him. Odds of a shark attack are low, and Dad already said I could go if you went with me."

Rocky laughs, shrugs out of Ezra's hold, and walks to Brynn. He reaches out and ruffles her hair. She pretends to gag, but she doesn't push him away.

"C'mon, kid. Let's go find some boards."

"Yes!"

As they leave, she turns and sticks her tongue out at Ezra, and I watch him do the same in return.

"If you lose an arm, I'm not going to feel sorry for you, Boss!" He shakes his head with a sigh. "No one ever listens to me."

"Last time I listened to you, I singed off my eyebrows and eyelashes," Crue deadpans.

"You prove my point, wanker. If you'd *listened* to me, that wouldn't have happened." Ezra waves him off, then takes off at a jog toward the house. "I call dibs on the primary!"

I look between Crue and Beckett. "Is it always chaotic like this?"

"Yes."

"Nah."

They speak at the same time, and I smile. "Perfect answer."

We head into the house, and everyone disperses down hallways and up staircases. I stop in the foyer and stare awkwardly. We were given no direction like at the lodge. No room assignments. Am I supposed to just *call dibs*? The thought makes me nervous. That might work for Ezra, but there's no way I could do that. I'd just as soon sleep outside and take my chances with a kangaroo.

"Hey. You good?"

I turn around and find Mabel standing in the doorway. I shrug.

"What exactly am I supposed to do?"

"Well, it's a bit of a free for all at the moment, but everyone is claiming rooms."

My shoulders slump, and she smiles before stepping beside me and jutting her chin toward the staircase.

"C'mon. We can do it together. The house is huge, and there's a pool house, too. That's where the Caveat boys will stay."

"But Ezra called dibs on the primary bedroom."

Mabel laughs. "He'll be corralled."

On the upper level, I find Claire, Jonah, and their daughter already in one room, then another room occupied by Brynnlee. Mabel leans closer and lowers her voice.

"The trick is knowing who is safe to room beside."

"What do you mean?"

"Well, if you're next to Claire and Jo, you risk hearing Teddy in the middle of the night. She's usually a pretty good sleeper, but it's always a gamble."

I nod. "Okay."

"Brynn is always safe, and so are Sav and Levi. Ziggy will bark sometimes in the morning when she needs to pee, but not often. You want to avoid Callie and Torren at all costs, though. Hopefully there's a lower-level room they can stay in."

"What? Why?"

"That way they can fuck without us having to hear it."

I snort an awkward laugh and try to act cool despite the heat rushing to my cheeks. "So? I can wear my headphones for fifteen minutes."

Mabel smirks. "Try *all night*."

I'm nearly bowled over with shock, and my next sentence escapes in a squeaky, whispered rush.

"They have sex all night?"

I can feel my eyebrows practically in my hairline, and Mabel glances at me curiously.

"Yeah. Headboard banging and moaning you can hear through a cinderblock wall."

The look on my face must be a doozy because she steps closer and lowers her voice.

"What? You look shocked as hell."

I dart my eyes around the hallway to make sure we're alone—I hadn't even noticed we'd turned a corner—and try not to dwell on the fact that the tips of my ears are on fire.

I wouldn't be able to confess this to anyone else, but Mabel has never once judged me. In fact, I feel more comfortable with her than I have with anyone else in years. Maybe with anyone else *ever*. She knows more about me than even my own husband, and she makes me feel safe and normal. It makes me want to tell her everything just to hear her confirm that I'm not a complete failure of a human.

Unlike Brady, Mabel doesn't get condescending when I ask questions or get confused. She doesn't jump on opportunities to patronize or belittle me. She makes me feel heard and seen. She makes me feel *worthy*, and it's something I didn't know I'd been needing.

I take a step closer, check the hallway once again to be absolutely certain no one will overhear, and lower my voice.

"I just...I guess I didn't know people actually *did that*."

"Did what? Have sex?"

"No, I know people have sex. But for that long? And so loud people can hear you? Hours? Headboards banging? That's movie and book stuff. That's not real life."

Mabel's face is blank as she blinks at me before lifting her eyes over my shoulder.

"Here." She pushes past me and opens a door, then steps into an unoccupied, lavishly decorated bedroom. "This conversation needs privacy."

I follow her in and let her close the door behind me, then she plops onto the bed and pats the mattress beside her.

"Sit, Roar. Let's chat."

"I sound terribly stupid, don't I?" I say on a sigh as I take a seat on the bed next to her.

"No." She shakes her head adamantly and holds eye contact. "Not stupid. Never stupid. Inexperienced? Yeah, sure. But not stupid."

I roll my eyes "Right. That's why you're about to give me a birds and bees lecture."

She purses her lips, hesitating, and I sigh again.

"Go ahead. It's fine."

"I'm going to ask you a deeply personal question."

A laugh bubbles out of me. As if I need a warning. "Haven't all of our conversations been deeply personal?"

She smiles and continues. "I know you've had sex, but have you ever *enjoyed* sex?"

I don't even have to think about my answer. "No."

"Have you only had sex with your husband?"

I shake my head. "No. I had a boyfriend in high school."

She pauses, and I don't miss the slight crease on her forehead. I brace myself for the next question I know is coming.

"Have you ever had an orgasm?"

I nod. "Yes."

"Have either of those men brought you to orgasm?"

I think of my encounter with Brady right before I left to come on tour. He'd gone down on me, and I came. The first and only time it's ever happened during sex. But if I'm going to be honest with myself, I was pretending it wasn't him. Can I really say he brought me to orgasm? I don't actually know the answer, so I shrug.

"Kind of? Maybe?"

Mabel's lips curve downward, and mine follow.

"That's not normal, is it."

"Actually, unfortunately, it *is* pretty normal." I feel relief for a split second before she adds, "But it doesn't have to be."

My eyes widen. "It doesn't?"

It might be my imagination, but I swear her pupils widen as she leans even closer. There might also be a slight flush coloring her cheeks, a deeper red than the shimmering pink blush she uses. I fist my hands in my lap and turn toward her a little more, until our thighs barely touch.

"Sex feels good—*really* good—if you're with someone who knows what they're doing. If that person cares about your pleasure as much as they care about their own."

The back of my neck prickles with sweat, and I fist my hands tighter in my lap. She's said next to nothing, but I can already feel my heartbeat pulsing between my thighs. Suddenly, my clothes feel too tight, and the air feels too thick.

I shouldn't ask any questions. I shouldn't continue this conversation, I *know* I shouldn't, but I want her to keep talking—something inside me *needs* it—so I do it anyway. I exhale slowly, releasing my words with it.

"What do you mean?"

Her plump pink lips curl into that smirk that does strange things to my insides, and when she speaks next, her voice is a purr, so sensual and sexy that chills dance over my heated skin.

"A good partner wants you to feel good, Aurora. They take the time to learn your body. Pay attention to your reactions so they know what you like. So they know how to make you come."

"Wh-what kind of reactions?"

"All kinds." She scans my face with those amber gems, bouncing between my eyes and my mouth, then to my rapidly rising and falling chest. "There are physical signs. You pupils dilate. Your breathing accelerates. Your skin erupts in goose bumps. Bodies talk, Roar. A good partner listens."

Oh God.

My nipples pebble against the fabric of my bra. The spot

between my thighs grows damp. My muscles ache, and I wonder if she knows. Can she tell? Is my body talking to her right now?

My throat tightens, and I have to swallow twice before I can get words out.

"Are you a good partner?"

Her grin is positively wicked, and she sinks her teeth into her bottom lip as she nods slowly.

"I'm a *very* good partner, Aurora, because I'm a *very* good listener, and I won't stop until I'm certain I've wrung every last ounce of pleasure from your body."

My breath hitches. "Me?"

She shrugs slowly. "If I were the one in your bed."

I picture it. I don't even have to try. The image is immediate and as crisp as a movie scene. She and I, tangled in bedsheets. Touching. Kissing.

Our moment at the club flashes once more in my head, and I relive all of it. Her lips. Her tongue. Her hands. Her body. The way she tasted. The way she smelled. The way she made me feel.

I want it all over again, and the pull between us is so strong that I almost close the distance. I almost kiss her for a second time, but when I lean a fraction of a centimeter forward, my weight shifts on the mattress, and suddenly, I become very aware of where I am.

I'm in a bedroom—on a bed—with Mabel Rossi.

Mabel Rossi, who just told me in no uncertain terms that she's a sex goddess who could make me orgasm until I black out.

I would let her, and I would enjoy it.

Terror seizes my chest, and I shoot to my feet.

"You, um, you can take this room. I'll, uh, I'll be down the street. Or the house. The hall. I mean the hall. I'll be down the hall. Okay, uh, thanks. Bye."

I'm out of the room before I even finish talking, and I swear I hear her chuckle as I pull the door closed behind me. I don't breathe until I'm opening another door and tucking myself safely inside the next bedroom. I close my eyes, lean my forehead on the door and shakily fill my lungs with air.

"Oh my God, calm down. Just calm down."

"Name three things you can hear."

I jump and spin around, seconds from releasing a terrified scream, but I swallow it back when I find Ezra Hawke splayed across the made bed.

"Ezra," I gasp out, my palm pressed to my chest, and he grins.

"There's one thing. Now do two more."

I shake my head. "What are you doing in here?"

"Hendrix kicked me out of the primary bedroom."

Every room in this house that I've seen has had an ensuite bathroom and a walk-in closet, so I'm not sure what he thinks makes the primary bedroom, but I don't bother asking.

"You're supposed to be in the pool house."

"No shit? Is that where my band is?"

"Probably?"

He hops up and struts toward me. "Looks like you can have this one then, Lil Ham."

I groan. "Please do not call me that."

Ezra winks, ruffles my hair the same way Rocky did to Brynnlee earlier, and disappears back into the hallway without another word.

I wait thirty seconds and listen closely for any sound coming from the hallway and the bedroom. When I'm met with silence, I walk slowly to the bed, faceplant right onto the mattress, and let out a muffled, near-silent scream.

"I'm married," I say into the plush comforter. "I'm married. I don't love my husband and I'm pretty sure he secretly hates me, but I'm *still* married."

I keep repeating the word—*married, married, married*—but Mabel's voice is still louder in my mind.

I'm a very good partner.

I'm a very good listener.

I wouldn't stop.

If I were the one in your bed.

I groan and flop over onto my back so I can stare at the white ceiling.

It doesn't matter. None of it matters. None of it means anything. She was speaking hypothetically. Empty words to prove a point.

"It means nothing."

I say the words out loud, willing them to calm my racing heart and cool my heated blood, but the moment they reach in my ears, I know I'm screwed. Even I can hear the blatant lie in my voice. Even I can tell I'm full of crap.

I might be feeling something for Mabel Rossi, and it definitely doesn't mean nothing.

21

MABEL

I RAISE my hand to knock, hold it there for a few seconds, then drop it back to my side.

I wait, staring at the door as if I can see through the wood, but I can't. When my vision starts to go unfocused, I blink and cast my gaze to the ceiling.

This is a bad idea.

I should leave her alone for a while. For her sake but also for mine. My heart hasn't stopped racing since she left my bedroom two hours ago. Her flushed face and wide hazel-green eyes have stayed at the forefront of my mind.

The way she looks at me. The way she makes me feel...

No one has ever looked at me that way. No one has ever had this kind of effect on me before. Not even Kat, and we dated for years. I thought Kat was my forever, but she never once made me feel the way I do when I'm with Aurora. Needy and needed. Valuable and worthy. Wild and fearless.

I know how dangerous this is.

I know how stupid I'm being.

I don't need complications. I don't need *mess*, and nothing but mess would come from acting on whatever emotions are barreling through my body right now.

I should keep my distance. I know this. I *know* it.

I know it, but I knock anyway, and the moment Aurora opens the door, all the warning signals silence.

"Hey. What's up?"

Just seeing her makes me smile. Her hair is wet like she's showered, and she's changed clothes. I recognize the outfit from her shopping bags in Adelaide.

"Nothing. Just saying hi."

"Oh." Her lips curl into a soft smile that makes my skin heat. "Well. Hi."

"Have you settled in?"

"Yeah, mostly. Jones brought my suitcases up. I was just checking out our little terrace thing."

I tilt my head to the side. "Our?"

"Oh. Yeah. Have you not seen it? Since our rooms are side by side, I think we share the terrace. I saw another set of doors when I was out there just now."

"The terrace connects our rooms?"

"I think so, yeah. Come look."

Well, shit.

She swings the door wide and gestures into her room, so I follow her to the open French doors that lead to the terrace. I have an identical set of doors in my room, but I haven't opened them to explore yet. I was too busy fixating on the conversation we'd had when she admitted to not enjoying sex and probably never having a real orgasm with a man.

The boyfriend gets a pass because it was high school, but I'm certain her husband is a fucking loser. The guy is a full ass adult and can't make his wife come? Huge fucking loser.

I almost searched him up on social media to see what he looks like, but I stopped myself. I don't know if I want to know. I don't know if I want him to be *real* yet, and that's another thing that makes this situation dangerous.

I force the thought from my head and step out onto the terrace after Aurora. Sure enough, when I peer into the other pair of French doors, I can see right into my room.

Goddamn it.

I realize the terrace is basically just an outside hallway, but something about it feels different. It feels intimate and secretive. Romantic. Sexy, even. I almost groan.

Dangerous. This is all so very dangerous.

"See? That's your room, right?"

I force a smile and nod. "Yep, it sure is."

"Well, we have a great view, right?"

I turn and look over the glass half wall. Directly below is an infinity pool with a swim-up bar and a hot tub. Past that is a sliver of yard full of bright green grass, a deck with modern lounge furniture, and a firepit. Then, just beyond that, down a small hill, the grass gives way to a sandy beach that leads to the ocean. This house backs up directly to the beach, and it's beautiful.

"Wow."

I scan the horizon, then close my eyes and inhale, the briny air filling my lungs as the ocean waves create the most relaxing background music.

How lucky am I that this is my life now?

Last week, I was in a luxury hilltop lodge in Adelaide. This week it's an oceanfront mansion in Sydney. And in a few days, I'll be playing another sold-out show for thousands of people who love my band. They'll dance and sing along to music I helped create, and I'll leave that stage feeling alive and loved and immeasurably happy.

It's almost perfect.

As close to perfect as I could get, anyway, and not for the first time, I wonder how it would have been different if I'd not been left at that fire station. The question has been occurring more frequently since learning about my birth mom. It's been so persistent that it's in my dreams, as if even my subconscious needs to weigh the pros and cons of meeting her.

What would it change? Nothing? Everything? I don't know which outcome I fear more.

Who would I be if she'd kept me? Would Mabel Rossi even exist? Would The Hometown Heartless? Would I have ever learned to play drums or met Sav and the guys? It's hard to imagine myself without the music. Without my band. My family.

Family.

If my birth mother had kept me, I might not have gone through all those foster homes. I wouldn't have found Ms. Mabel's lifeless body. Wouldn't have run away at fifteen, been recruited into Oscar's gang of lost kids, and become a busking pickpocket. There are so many difficult, painful memories from the last thirty years of my life that I could do without. That I likely wouldn't have had to endure had my mother kept me.

But if I'd not endured them, would I still be *me*?

"I think it's called Whale Beach."

Aurora's voice pulls me from my thoughts, and when I look at her, she's studying the GPS on her phone.

"And apparently there's a rock pool"—she glances up and points into the distance—"that way down the beach."

"A rock pool?"

"Yeah. As far as I can tell, it's like a pool carved out of the rock that sits just off the ocean. Here."

She hands her phone to me, the screen full of images of Sydney rock pools. I click on the first one to enlarge it, but before the photo can load, her phone rings, and the screen fills with a video chat request from Brady.

My eyes dart to Aurora, and what I see fills me with anger.

The color has leeched from her cheeks, and she's staring wide-eyed at the phone. She is the picture of dread, and I can feel her fear in my gut. It spikes my adrenalin so my fingers tremble. I fist my hand and try to stay calm.

"I can leave so you can talk if you want?"

Her attention jumps to my face, and she shakes her head. "No. Stay. Stay."

I nod and hand her the phone. I watch her take two deep inhales and exhales before plastering on a fake smile and answering.

I hate his voice immediately.

"Hey, Br—"

"Oh, so you can answer the phone."

She flinches. "I told you I was flying."

"Your location says you've been in Sydney for almost three hours."

"Yeah, but I've been unpacking. I took a shower. I'm sor—"

"I just wanted to make sure you weren't in some club doing God knows what."

"Brady, it's eleven in the morning."

The asshole on the other end sighs, and I watch as Aurora chews on the inside of her cheek. If she weren't holding the phone, I bet she'd be wringing her hands right now. Instead, she's clutching the pendant on her necklace like a life preserver, and she's holding the phone so tightly that her knuckles are turning white.

I've never wanted to hit a man so much in my life. And that's saying something, considering I'm on tour with the Caveat boys, and I had to put up with Jonah in his pre-sobriety era.

"How am I supposed to know what those depraved rock stars have you doing? It seems like getting drunk at all hours of the day and blowing all your money is standard these days."

Aurora drops her voice lower and her shoulders slump. She visibly shrinks into herself, and I get the distinct feeling she's trying to hide.

From him? From me?

Maybe I should leave and give her some privacy. This is a personal conversation between spouses, and maybe it's disrespectful for me to witness it.

But fuck that man.

I don't owe him respect, and I'm not leaving her right now. I do, however, turn my attention to the ocean and hope that it makes her feel a little less uncomfortable. I'm a calming presence, not a gawker. I'll just be here if she needs me.

"It was only thirty dollars. One drink. We talked about this."

"Thirty dollars at a bar. One hundred dollars at some bullshit store in Melbourne. You're being irresponsible, Aurora."

This fucking bastard. Now the separate account makes sense. She's here working, getting paid to be Brynn's tutor, and he's flipping out over one hundred and thirty dollars? I hate him.

"I already apologized for that. You don't have to keep bringing it up."

"You don't belong there. You need to come home."

I whip my head around, and I'm sure my anger is apparent on my face. Aurora flicks her eyes quickly to me, then back to the phone, but I don't miss the slight shake of her head warning me not to interfere.

I grit my teeth and fist my hands, but I don't turn back around. I glare at that phone and hope that he can feel it. He should be ashamed of himself.

"The tour isn't over yet, Brady. I'm supposed to be—"

"You're supposed to be home. You've got responsibilities as my wife that you're neglecting, and now that you're not answering my calls—"

"I was on a pla—"

"Do not interrupt me!"

That's it. I've heard enough. My feet launch me forward with zero thoughts in my head except to put a stop to this conversation. Aurora gapes at me, her lips parting on a small gasp, but the fuckhead on the other end doesn't notice. He just keeps going, spewing verbal abuse like it's as natural as breathing. Speaking to her like this is a common occurrence. It all makes fucking sense now.

"For fuck's sake, Aurora, I have no idea what those assholes in The Hometown Heartless are doing to you, but you need to—"

"Hey there!"

He flinches when I cut him off, and I take a second to study him. He looks just like how I thought he would. Like an entitled, tech bro douche. Blond hair, blue eyes, and a navy quilted vest over a blue checkered Oxford. I bet he's wearing chinos, chukkas, and a mixed metal Rolex, too. And I bet he's a "serious" golfer. He's got that look. That pretentious, competitive asshole look.

"This is a private conversation," he snaps in a tone so patronizing I have to stop myself from rolling my eyes. Instead, I smile brightly and speak with a sarcastic kind of cheer.

"You're Brandy, right? I'm Mabel, one of the assholes in The Hometown Heartless you seem to think is corrupting Aurora. Listen, Brandy—"

"It's Bra—"

"I'm speaking."

Aurora's hand digs into my forearm, but I don't take my glare away from the moron on the screen. His mouth snaps shut, and his face turns a delightful shade of puce. Good. Maybe he'll have a heart attack and die.

"Exactly. Now what was I saying? Oh, right. So yeah, I am an asshole. So is most of my band. Apparently, so are you. You know who isn't, though? Aurora. And she certainly doesn't deserve the way you're speaking to her right now."

"She is my wife—"

"A *wife* is not property, Brody. A *wife* should be treated with decency and respect, not whatever vile bullshit you're spitting at her. Do you speak to her this way all the time? Because I have to say, if you do, that's fucking disgusting."

"Mabel, it's fine." Aurora's voice quivers as she pleads with me, her hand tugging lightly on my arm. "It's not a big deal."

"It absolutely is not fine, Roar. This is verbal abuse. He is abusive."

"I am not abus—"

"I said I am speaking, Brad!"

I'm pretty sure he growls at me like a rabid dog, which just fuels the flames of my ire.

Gently, I take the phone from Aurora, then turn my body, so

her face is no longer in the frame. It's just me and the douche now, and I do my best to speak calmly. I keep my tone direct and straightforward, leaving no room for argument. You can't reason with people like him, and I have no desire to try.

"You listen to me, and you listen good. You should be fucking ashamed of your behavior right now. A grown man throwing a tantrum and bullying his own wife? It's pathetic, and despite what you want to tell yourself, it *is* abusive. Now I am going to give you the benefit of the doubt and assume this is a one-off. Maybe you're hungry or tired, and like most fucking toddlers, you're struggling to regulate your emotions. Fine. But this conversation ends now. You're done talking to Aurora. You're done looking at her. You won't try to call back. You won't send any text messages. You're going to hang up, and you're going to think long and hard about your behavior. Tomorrow, when you realize what you've done wrong, you will call and apologize. Do you understand?"

He scoffs. Fucker. "Or what? You don't have authority over me."

"I have more power and connections than you realize, Brandon. You want to fuck around and find out?"

His jaw pops and his nostrils flare, but he doesn't try to interject again.

I don't like pulling the *do you know who I am* card, but I'm glad I did. This guy looks like he listens to money, and people always associate celebrity with money. If I have to, I'll flex all the way to the bank to shut him up.

Forcing another tight smile that doesn't reach my eyes, I give him a curt nod.

"Glad we're in agreement. Have the night you deserve."

Then I hang up.

I take a few breaths before meeting Aurora's eyes, and when I do, I feel worse than I did moments ago. Her expression is one of shock, and there are silent tears running down her cheeks. Fuck. I set the phone on the small patio table and step toward her, cupping her face in my hands. She immediately reaches up and wraps her fingers around my wrists.

"I'm sorry," I whisper, swiping at her tears with my thumbs. "I'm so sorry. I didn't want to upset you."

She shakes her head. "No. No, it's not that. You didn't." She closes her eyes and leans her face into my palm. "It's just...I don't know." She licks her lips, and her throat contracts on a rough swallow. "No one has ever stood up for me like that."

My heart fucking breaks. I can't even imagine what she's been through. To be so alone, so isolated, and subject to treatment like that from her own husband? She'd told me he was controlling, but to see him in action? To actually witness the terrible way he speaks to her?

God, no wonder her confidence flickers. No wonder she's scared. Every puzzle piece is more devastating than the last, and I just want to hold her. I want to protect her. I want to treat her the way she deserves to be treated.

"Thank you," she whispers, tears slipping through her lashes and trickling down her cheeks.

I press my forehead to hers. My heart is still racing. I move my fingertips to the tender spot just below her jaw and feel for her pulse, finding it thrumming rapidly, just like mine.

"Always," I whisper, and I mean it. "Always."

We stand like that, eyes closed, breathing each other in, for I don't know how long. I just know that I can't leave her. I don't want to. I could stand here all day. All night. I'm not ready for this embrace to end, and I can tell she isn't either.

And then I'm hit with a realization that shakes me to my core.

I sense her emotions as strongly and as deeply as if they were my own. I feel protective of her in a way I never have before. Not with Kat. Not even with Sav. It's like Aurora is part of me. Like her pain is my pain. Her heart is my heart. Whatever is happening between us, whatever this is, it's not something I'll be able to move past. Not easily, anyway. Maybe not ever.

I don't need complications. I don't want mess.

I'm afraid I've found both, anyway, and I don't know where to go from here.

So I stand with her on this terrace, the warm, salty breeze kissing our skin and the soothing ocean tides easing the tension, and I wait for whatever comes next.

I wait, and I hope like hell that I'm strong enough to handle it.

22

AURORA

THE MOMENT the French doors open, my eyes snap up from my notebook.

I knew she'd come. I didn't have the courage to knock, but something in me knew that I wouldn't have to. I was right. I've only been out here ten minutes, and already, she's here.

"Good morning."

Mabel's voice is still sleepy as she pads on bare feet toward me. I let myself look her over, and the sight both quickens my breath and calms my mind. She's in a pink silk robe that hits her midthigh, the neckline open just enough to show pajamas with lace trim. Her face is bare. No thick, black eyeliner. No bright pink lipstick. Just Mabel.

This was the worst part of sharing a room with her in Adelaide. Seeing her dressed down and real. It made me feel things I didn't understand—truthfully, I still don't understand them—yet I still craved it. Now I miss it. I miss it so much that now that she's here, I can't bring myself to look away. Not even when she catches me staring. Her naked lashes flutter and she sucks her bottom lip into her mouth before setting a latte cup on the table, toffee from the smell of it, and taking a seat across from me.

She gives me a small, almost shy smile, and nods to the notebook in front of me.

"What's that? Are you writing poetry?"

I drag my eyes off her long enough to glance at the open page filled with my loopy handwriting.

"Journaling."

Not poetry. Not yet. But journaling is a start.

"About your Tour du Australia?"

"Well, right now I'm making a list of places I want to visit. If I get the chance."

"Yeah?" Her mouth curls into an excited smile that I can't help but mirror. "Can I know what's on the list?"

"They're pretty generic travel destinations, I think."

"Tell me anyway."

She lifts her latte to her lips and takes a sip without breaking eye contact, and there's something so intimate about it that I nearly lose my breath. I avert my eyes to my notebook and read.

"Paris. Rome. London."

"Good choices. Where else?"

"Marrakech."

"Oh, Morrocco. Nice."

I glance up at her and find her brows raised with interest.

"I've never been there. Why Marrakech?"

"There's a garden there," I say slowly. *"Jardin Majorelle.* I'd like to visit it."

"Like a botanical garden?"

"Yeah. But kind of different."

"Different how?"

I try to sound nonchalant, try not to geek out over it, but she's so genuinely interested that my excitement boils over, and I start to ramble.

"Well, it was designed by a French painter, Jacques Majorelle, over the course of forty years. It was a lifelong passion project of his, with every single detail and plant being thoughtfully selected by him, but then he had to sell it in the 1950s. It was actually going to be bulldozed in the '80s, but then Yves Saint Laurent and Pierre Bergé bought it and restored it. Can you imagine? Botanical gardens designed by an artist and a fashion designer icon? It's got these vibrant blue walls, and exquisite architectural details, and over two acres of exotic plants from all around the world. It's supposed to be absolutely gorgeous."

Mabel smirks and arches an eyebrow. "How many other gardens are on your list?"

"Only a few." I fold my lips between my teeth to tame my smile and give her a shrug. "It's not the whole list."

"Liar." She laughs. "Tell me."

I scrunch my nose and purse my lips, hesitating briefly. "You sure?"

Her eyebrow arches again, higher this time, and I laugh out loud. Morning coffee and conversation in your pajamas. Is this how it's supposed to be? Fun and light. No anxiety. No judgment. Just *peace.*

"Okay," I singsong playfully. "But remember, you asked for this."

"I did. Now ramble about your gardens, plant nerd. I want to hear all about them."

"Okay, so, there's The Garden of Cosmic Speculation in Dunfries, Scotland. It's like plants and science combined, and it's only open to the public one day a year."

"Cool name."

"Right? Very cool name."

"What else?"

"Well, there's one at the base of Corcovado Mountain in Rio de Janeiro, and there are royal palms, and orchid houses, and giant Amazonian lilies, and even marmosets and parrots. Sometimes even toucans."

"So, paradise. You've described paradise."

"Exactly," I say, nodding emphatically. "Exactly paradise. Then there's the gardens at *Château de Villandry* in Loire Valley, France. It was built during the Renaissance, and it's got these big, ornamental hornbeam hedge mazes. And, you know, if I make it to France—"

"*When* you make it to France," Mabel interjects, her voice soft and encouraging, and I pause, words escaping me for a moment.

When.

When I make it.

She's so certain that I amend my statement without questioning it.

"*When* I get there, I'll have to see the Palace of Versailles gardens, too."

"Of course. You can't miss those. Do you have more?"

I laugh. "Mabel, there are like twenty places on this list, and I haven't even scratched the surface." I run my fingers over the letters on the page feeling the slight indentation from the pen and drop my voice lower. "It would take years to see them all."

Years, and I haven't even begun. I don't know if I ever will.

Suddenly, the mood shifts, and I feel the grief start to creep in. It's always there, just on the edges of my mind, waiting. I can fend it off for a while, sometimes for days or even weeks, but it always comes back. And now, with the haze lifting, the grief is even more painful, because reality is so much worse than I realized. My hand goes to my necklace on instinct, and I clutch the metal pendant, rubbing it with my thumb.

My parents and brother would be so disappointed in me. In what I've become. In what I've allowed to happen.

For my birthday one year, Paul bought me a world map and a tin of red thumbtacks. He said it was for documenting my travels. I don't know where that map is now. I wouldn't be surprised to learn that Brady trashed it with the rest of my things when I moved in with the Sinclairs.

Even the paper under my fingertips burns, and I have to fight off an overwhelming sense of shame. My mom loved my poetry. She saved all my notebooks filled with poems since kindergarten. Now I've been reduced to writing lists of places I'll probably never see.

They're gone. They're dead. Their last memories of me were horrible, and even in their death, I've let them down. I'm trapped. I'm suffocating. I did this to myself.

I sigh and close my notebook. I have every intention of excusing myself, but then Mabel speaks up.

"You know there are a few botanical gardens near here, right?"

"I do know that."

I try to keep my attention on my notebook, but like pulled by magnets, my eyes are drawn up again until they snap together with hers. Amber irises full of warmth and acceptance. I would dive into them if I could. I'd wrap myself in her confidence, in her optimism, and I'd never let go.

"Would you like to visit one with me?"

Her question catches me off guard, and for a breath, all I can do is blink at her. When she smirks, I give my head a little shake and speak slowly, hoping my voice doesn't belie the butterfly-type nerves that have erupted in my stomach.

"Really? You would want to do that?"

"Absolutely. I love watching you geek out over plants. Going to a botanical garden with you is exactly my idea of a good time."

Her tone is light and playful, like she's fighting off a laugh, and her eyes sparkle with that flirtatious glint that sets my heart racing. I nod once. Twice. Several times, rapidly, unable to tame my excitement any longer.

"Okay. Okay, yes. Yes, I would love to. I would absolutely love to."

"Cool. It's a date."

I force a swallow, my throat suddenly bone-dry.

"Yeah," I croak out. "A date. When should we—"

There's a banging on my bedroom door that makes us jump, and we both whip our heads around to stare into the room.

"Koalas," a voice shouts in an English accent. "Koalas, Lil' Ham!!!"

Then the same banging sounds from Mabel's room, and the voice shouts again.

"Koalas! Wake up, Rossi! Koalas!"

And then he's gone.

Mabel and I look at each other, then we both laugh.

Crue.

"Well," Mabel says, pushing up from her chair. "Better get dressed, *Lil' Ham*. Sounds like we're going to meet some koalas."

I groan as she saunters across the terrace toward her French doors.

"Please don't call me that."

She laughs once more before disappearing into her bedroom, so I collect my things and head through my own doors.

Today, koalas with the bands, and then later this week, a botanical garden date with Mabel.

A date.

I smile to myself as I pick out an outfit for the day. Someone showing interest in something I love, showing interest simply because I love it, is something I haven't had in such a long time. Brady hates plants. He hates when I talk about plants. Aside from my mom's orchid, he doesn't let me have house plants at all, and he tolerates my time in the garden only as long as I'm still playing the doting wife and housemaid.

But with Mabel...

Going to a botanical garden with you is exactly my idea of a good time, she'd said. She listens. She cares. And it's genuine. I know it.

To feel seen is such a heady, addicting experience, and I find myself craving it more and more as the days pass. I find myself longing for Mabel, for the way I feel when she's around. Needing her eyes and voice and scent. Needing her playful, calming presence. Needing *her*.

She's earned a starring role in my thoughts, dreams, and fantasies, and I can no longer ignore the way she makes my stomach flip and my heart squeeze in my chest. I can't ignore the way I want her, but I still try. Despite our foundation of truth, I lie to myself.

I tell myself that the way I feel for her is simply a normal, innocent reaction to kindness. It's just been so long, that I've forgotten what it feels like. My connection with Mabel is nothing more than a harmless, innocent friendship. It's normal. It's harmless.

"It's innocent," I say out loud.

Even though I know, for me, it's anything but.

23

MABEL

Scrolling through the photos on my laptop makes me feel sleezy.

They didn't know these pictures were being taken. They didn't ask for this. It's a violation of their privacy, and I'm no better than the paparazzi.

These are the thoughts cycling through my head, but I still click from one image to the next. I still stare, unblinkingly, at each one. Analyzing every feature. Every expression. Every detail.

She's got my eyes.

Or, rather, *I* have *her* eyes, I guess. And her heart-shaped face. Her stature. Her hair. Honestly, if I wanted a preview of myself in fifteen years, I could probably just look at these pictures. Genetics are wild, and my sisters are also little carbon copies of me, too.

The older daughter, Calliope, reminds me of Sav when I first met her, right down to the messy hair, ratty old jeans, and dirty skate shoes. A type B ball of unfettered energy. She even has the same glint in her eye. The one that always got Sav and me in so much trouble.

I grin as I zoom in on a picture of her. She's walking down the street with a backpack hanging open and slung over her shoulder and a smirk on her lips. I bet she's a handful. I bet we'd get along.

Amelia, the younger of the two, seems more easygoing. The

calm to her sister's chaos. Her backpack is always zipped. Her shoes are always tied and clean. She's usually holding a book, and she's always sporting a wide, genuine smile. Always.

They seem so different, so uniquely themselves, and I'm certain that means their mom is a good mom.

Our mom.

Is this how I would have been at their age? Confident and carefree. Secure and loved. It took me a long time to settle into myself. To feel comfortable and safe in my own skin. Sav and I always say that we saved each other. But if I'd been kept, would I have needed saving?

I snap my laptop closed and drop my head back against the wall. I close my eyes and breathe.

Why is this so hard?

Why can't I just make a decision and stick with it?

Is my hesitancy based on fear or intuition? Maybe both?

If nothing else, this process has revealed something that I'd rather not have known. Deep down, that insecure little girl is still alive and well. I thought I'd grown out of it. I thought I'd healed. But I'm still terrified of people leaving, of being unwanted and alone. Thirty years and dozens of lives later, yet not much has changed.

What life would I be living now if I'd just been *enough* from the beginning?

I push my palms into my eyes to stave off the tears, but they come anyway.

Every feeling of inadequacy, of loss, comes crashing down on me until I'm overwhelmed by them. I was just a baby. I was innocent and helpless. I wasn't enough.

How long did it take before I knew love? Until I was able to hold it firmly in my hands without it being torn from my grip? Right now, it feels like I still can't. Not really.

My birth mother. My foster families. Ms. Mabel. Kat. In one way or another, they all left. I always end up alone in the end.

Even Sav and the guys haven't always been stable. I love them.

They're the only true family I've ever known, but dynamics are changing. They're moving forward without me. They've got their own families and facets of their lives that don't include me, and it hurts.

I know I'm always welcome in their homes, in their lives. I *know* I am, but right now, I don't feel it. Right now, I feel like the cycle is repeating itself. I feel like I'll end up alone again. Right now, I feel sad and scared. I feel helpless.

I feel like I'm not enough.

I drop my head between my knees and breathe. Tears drip onto my thighs and down my calves. I press my toes into the floor. Try to remind myself that I'm on solid ground. I'm safe and in control, even if I feel like I'm plummeting.

Between my shaking inhales and exhales, I strain to hear the waves ebbing and flowing on the beach. The sound is carried through my French doors on the evening's ocean breeze. I try to fill my lungs with that breeze. I try to pretend the salt I taste is from the air and not my tears.

I can't make my hands stop trembling. I thread them through my hair, push my fingers into my scalp, but still, they quiver against my skin. I swear I can hear my bones and joints rattling as the floor shifts beneath me.

"I'm here," I tell myself. "I'm sitting still. I'm not spinning out. I'm not abandoned. I'm not alone."

I am not alone.

I repeat it over and over, but my anxiety is a talented liar, and my body doesn't recognize the truth through the pain.

I tug at the roots of my hair. I count backward from one hundred. I recite lyrics to Heartless's very first chart topper. I try to time my breaths with the slow, steady rhythm of the waves. None of it works.

Desperately, I reach for the first calming image I can find and focus on it.

Aurora.

Aurora with her little crocheted tops, wide-legged jeans, and glittery tennis shoes. Aurora with her orchid and the way she gets so excited talking about plants that she forgets to breathe. The way she looks at me. Like it's physically difficult to look away. Like I'm the most fascinating thing in the room. Aurora and the way she's literally bursting at the seams with light and energy. I'm witnessing her confidence come out little by little. She's like a sunrise. A blooming flower. A brilliant, beautiful, wonderful act of nature.

At the wildlife sanctuary, we got to feed quokkas. One of them absolutely loved Aurora. I replay her laughter in my mind. I picture her smile, so big and wide that it transformed her whole face. Her nose scrunched up. Her hazel eyes sparkled. Her cheeks flushed with life and color. We took a selfie with that little quokka, and he looked like he was smiling right along with us. I made it the wallpaper on my phone.

Normally, when I start to feel unsteady on my own feet, when my mind starts to play tricks to convince me that the ground is shattering, I find Sav. It's automatic. My legs carry me to her without thought. Tonight, though, she's not who I want. She's not who I *need*.

Tonight, I let my body lead me through the French doors and onto the terrace.

I let myself find Aurora.

I stand outside her room for a moment, noting the low hum of the television. It's late. She might be asleep. Maybe I shouldn't be here. I shouldn't—

"Hey. I thought I felt you out here."

My muscles relax at the sound of her voice. It's such a relief that more tears break through my lashes. When I tilt my face to hers, her smile fades, and she brings her palms gently to my cheeks.

"What's wrong? What happened?"

I close my eyes. "I'm just having a moment."

"What can I do?" Her thumbs caress my cheeks, the touch so grounding and safe that I lean into it. "What can I do, Mabel?"

"I don't know."

She goes quiet, but the silence isn't awkward. It's comforting. When she moves her hands to my shoulders and guides me into her room, I let her. We sit on the edge of her bed. She rubs her hand up and down my back. She does for me what I did for her. She gives me space to feel, and she feels with me. And when the spinning slows and the ground stills, I open my eyes and let them find hers.

"I look just like them."

My whispered words are ragged, my body emotionally exhausted from the overwhelming anxiety. She doesn't ask who I'm talking about. She doesn't have to. Instead, she brushes a strand of hair behind my ear and nods.

"An attractive family, then."

That brings a small smile to my lips before I push forward.

"My lawyer sent me photos. It makes them more real now, you know? It makes *everything* real, and I feel rushed. I feel all this pressure to decide if I want to meet them or not. I don't know what to do. I don't know what I want to do or what I should do. It's just...it just all got so *heavy*. I couldn't carry it."

"That sounds really daunting," she says, her eyes holding mine. "It makes sense that the decision would feel heavy, but you don't have to make it right now. There's no time limit, right?"

I shake my head. "No, there's no time limit."

Just saying the words helps relieve a little more of my anxiety. There's no rush. I don't have to make the decision today or tomorrow. I don't have to do anything until I'm ready.

But what if I'm *never* ready?

Will they go back to being strangers? To abstract figures in the back of my mind? I don't know if that's possible. I can't unsee their faces. I can't unlearn their names. I can't bury it all back up again.

"I thought I was prepared. I wasn't," I confess. "I knew she was out there. I thought I was ready, but I didn't consider all the feelings it would dig up."

"What kind of feelings?"

I drop my eyes to my hand and spin my ring around on my finger.

"Inadequacy, I guess. I mean, I knew there was a possibility she'd have a family, but I didn't realize how much it would hurt."

I pause when my voice cracks. I breathe in and out, in and out, trying and failing to keep another wave of tears at bay. I feel the shift of the Earth beneath me as it threatens to knock me off balance. I fear it will start spinning again. That I will spiral and fall.

But then Aurora puts her hand on my knee, and it all halts.

I release my ring and lace my fingers with hers. I wrap my other hand around her wrist and press two fingers to her pulse point. I feel her heartbeat. I hear it in my head. I imagine my pulse syncing with hers. Then, with tears streaming down my face, I force another rough swallow and continue.

"She has two girls, and they look just like me. Just like me, Roar. Same hair and eyes and face. Same everything. And I know it's not rational, I know it's not, but I can't stop thinking that they were her do-over, you know? Like she got it wrong with me but right with them. They get the birthdays, and the vacations, and the back-to-school photos, and I got dumped at a fucking fire station with a blanket and a bottle. Why are they enough, but I wasn't? Why did they deserve the happy family fairy tale, and I didn't? What was wrong with me? Why wasn't I enough for her?"

Aurora lifts her hands, still entwined with mine, to my chin and tilts it until our gazes lock.

"You are *more* than enough, Mabel. I can't speak for why your mom did what she did, but I can say with absolute certainty that it wasn't because of anything wrong with you. There is *nothing* wrong with you. You are beautiful, and smart, and kind, and strong, and you are *more than enough*."

She leans in and presses her forehead to mine, our noses grazing as she releases my hands and slides her palms to the sides of my neck.

"You are more than enough, Susan Ainsley Mabel Rossi. In every single life and every single version, you are more than enough. I swear it. Only honesty here."

She wrecks me. The measly dam I'd been trying to maintain breaks, and tears flood down my cheeks. I squeeze my eyes shut. I try to stop them, but it's futile. I want to believe her. When she says it, she sounds so sure, and I almost do. But thirty years of these feelings, these questions...

I bite my cheek and try to stifle a sob. It shoves violently through, anyway. My body shakes. My head pounds. My balance falters. I'm spinning. I'm falling.

Then she's wrapping her arms around me, hugging me so tightly, and I cling to her. I anchor myself to her. She's steady and strong and grounding. I hold onto her until I'm no longer dizzy. Until my tears slow to a trickle. Until I can breathe without my chest aching. And even then, it takes effort to loosen my hold.

"You are more than enough," she whispers once again, her lips moving against my hair. "I swear it. Okay?"

I will her words to soak into my skin and stay there. I want to be able to replay her voice and this statement whenever I need it. Whenever I doubt it. Until I believe it for real.

"Okay."

Slowly, reluctantly, I release her and put space between us. Her arms fall from my body, and I miss the contact instantly. I don't want to let go. I don't want to leave the comfort of her touch.

I meet her eyes to find them glassy and red. Tear tracks that mirror mine are shimmering on her cheeks. It hurts in a whole new way. Like I've finally found what I've been missing, but it can never be mine.

She's married. She's Ham's niece. I hate it.

I want to pull her back into me, but I don't.

Instead, I shrug and change the subject.

"I'm sorry for waking you."

Aurora smirks and arches an eyebrow. It takes a second to realize she's mimicking me, but when I do, I can't help but laugh.

"You didn't wake me." She gestures to the television. "I was watching a movie."

Sure enough, there's a movie paused on the screen, and I immediately recognize the frozen image. My jaw drops, and I whip my attention back to her.

"Is that what I think it is?"

"All I Wanna Do." A smile stretches across her face. "You know it?"

"I've watched it no less than ten times. Have you seen it before?"

She nods. "It's my comfort movie. It's so underrated."

"So underrated. I haven't seen it in years."

I shake my head and blink at the television. God, what are the odds? I used to be obsessed with this movie. I used to force Sav to watch it with me at least once a month. I tried to watch it once with Kat, but she hated it. I haven't seen it since, and here's Aurora calling it her comfort movie.

"Do you want to stay? I can start it over. I don't mind." She gestures to her bed. "I have snacks."

I didn't even notice the bag of popcorn and package of TimTams, but when I see them, I laugh again. I don't know what I did in a past life to deserve the temptation that is Aurora Jade Hammond, but she might actually be perfect. It's agonizing, but I'm done fighting it, at least for tonight. I don't have any strength left in my body.

"It's hard to turn down TimTams," I say with a dramatic sigh.

"Oh my God, they're so good, right? I think I've eaten my weight in them three times over since Melbourne. I already told Uncle Wade he has to ship me boxes from now on every time you guys tour here."

I smile with her despite the pang of loss that radiates through me.

The statement was meant to be fun and light, but I hear the stark reality screaming from between her words.

She won't be here for long.

When we tour again, she won't be with us.

Soon, she'll return to whatever life she was living before this.

She'll return to Brady, and she'll leave me.

I twist my ring around on my finger and press my toes into the floor again. I direct my attention back to the television and decide to focus on that. On the movie and the snacks and the company. I refuse to ruin this moment with the truth. I don't want to cry more. I don't want to feel lonely.

For now, I just want to enjoy the present. I want to watch one of my favorite movies with one of my new favorite people while snacking on TimTams in this ocean front mansion in Sydney. I want to be *here* and ignore everything else.

I put on a smile and allow myself to pretend. Just for tonight. Just for a little bit. I just want to be happy, even if it's all a lie, and I really, really don't want to be alone.

"Are you sure it's okay if I stay for a bit? I know it's late."

Aurora rolls her eyes. "Absolutely. Movie nights are better with company."

I round the bed and climb onto the side with the unrumpled covers. When she climbs in beside me, the mattress dips under her weight, and my stomach dips with it. I grab a TimTam and shove it into my mouth to distract myself from the way my heart flutters in my chest.

It's just a movie. Nothing more.

I keep my eyes on the screen as she starts the movie over, her arm raised in my periphery with the remote in her hand. She pushes play, drops the remote to the bedspread between us, then hands me the popcorn.

"I'm glad you're here," she says, drawing my attention back to her face.

God, she's beautiful.

Her eyes are like starbursts. If I stare into them long enough, I'm sure I'd find sparkling constellations in those hazel irises. She's filled with every green and gold and blue cosmic wonder of the universe.

And then it hits me.

Aurora is my passing comet.

Brief and brilliant.

Not meant to stay, but to blaze through and leave my sky rearranged.

I want to cry all over again, but I won't let reality ruin it. I fist one hand in the duvet and grab a few pieces of popcorn with the other. I force a smile, give her a nod, and speak the only truth I can utter for now.

"There's no place I'd rather be."

24

MABEL

My eyes flutter open and the room, lit by the faint glow of the television, comes into focus slowly.

With it, comes Aurora.

Our gazes lock. We're so close that I could count the freckles on her cheeks. I can see each eyelash. Each fleck of gold and green in her eyes. Waking up to her fills me with warmth and sets my blood racing.

I don't know how long I've been asleep. I don't know how long she's been awake. But we're here, facing each other with our heads on the soft white pillows, and I wish I could stop time so we never have to leave this bed.

"Can I ask you a question?"

Her whispered words fan softly over my lips, and I nod.

"Anything."

"Why did you come to me?"

"What do you mean?"

"Earlier. Why did you come here? Why not go to Sav or Callie or Claire? Why me?"

I don't miss the hint of nerves in her voice, and for a moment, I swear I can read her thoughts. Did I come to her because she was the closest, because she was convenient, or was it something more?

With Aurora, I'm learning, it will always be *more*.

I consider my answer, rolling her question over in my head. Why *did* I come here? I don't know if I can explain it. Coming to her wasn't exactly a conscious decision. It was more visceral. Instinctual. Need-driven and immediate.

What do I even say to her? I came here because my body brought me to you? Because I needed you? Because I was desperate for the type of calm I've only ever found in you?

Each answer is more jarring than the last, and the more I think about it, the more it scares me. I've promised her honesty, but the truth is becoming dangerous. I should be careful. I should lie. It would be easier for both of us if I did. But as I stare into her eyes, wide and hopeful, I can't bring myself to do it.

I sigh and shrug. "I just went where my body led me, I guess."

The understanding I see pass over her face gives me chills, and she releases a small puff of laughter.

"Yeah. Yeah, I get that."

My pulse speeds up as something like hope thrums through my veins. "You do?"

"Yeah. You know how I said I could find you in any crowd?"

I nod, but I can't bring myself to speak.

"Well, it's because I feel you." Aurora brings her hand to her chest and taps twice. "I feel you *here*."

Her words wrap around my heart and squeeze until time slows to a crawl. I don't understand the emotions that flood me. I can barely breathe through the wave of longing that threatens to pull me under. I have no thoughts except her. Except Aurora. And when she leans toward me, I close the distance without hesitation.

Her lips are just as soft as I remember, just as warm and plush, and they vibrate on a whimper that I feel all the way to my toes. I wrap my hand around her neck and pull her closer. She fists my shirt at my waist and tugs. Our bodies meet in the middle of the bed, and still, it's not close enough. Her tongue traces the seam of my lips, and I open for her on a groan.

Our kiss in Adelaide was hungry. Desperate and rushed. But this kiss...

This one is reverent.

It's just as eager, but it's slow. Savored. Like every swipe of her tongue is painting a memory. Every taste, every touch, is being stored away for future worship. I hold her closer. Kiss her deeper. I let myself *feel* her, and I know without a shadow of a doubt that I'm ruined. This kiss, this woman, has ruined me for all the rest, and there's no undoing it.

Somewhere in the back of my mind a voice is telling me to stop. It's whispering warnings, but I can't hear them over the pounding of my heart. Nothing matters outside of this moment. Outside of this kiss. Outside of her.

When her lips start to slow, my heart falls. I don't want this to end. I don't want to open my eyes and plummet back into reality, but I follow her lead. I move my hand from her neck to her shoulder and I shift my weight backward, so my body is no longer pressed up against hers.

She kisses me twice more, then rests her forehead against mine. Our breath comes in pants as we lie tangled in each other, and my mind starts to swirl with what she might say next.

It was a mistake.

It meant nothing.

We should pretend it didn't happen.

Anxiety creeps up my throat with each possibility, but then she giggles. It's a light, joyful sound that makes me smile, and I pull back so I can see her face.

"What?" I ask on my own laugh. "What are you giggling about?"

Her cute little nose scrunches up on a grin before she shakes her head and gives me a shrug.

"I don't know. I just...I've never felt like this. Kind of bubbly. Excited. I feel like I need to giggle."

I trace her cheeks with my fingertips, then run my thumb lightly over her glowing smile.

"You mean happy?" I tease. "You've never felt happy before?"

Her smile falters and sadness flashes in her eyes as she shrugs, then shakes her head.

"Not like this, Mabel. Not like with you."

I don't know what to say. I don't know how to tell her everything that I'm feeling when I can't make sense of it myself. I understand her, and it's not fair. She makes me happy, too. It's not fair. None of it is. How can it feel so right with her if everything about it is wrong? I can't find the right words to say any of it, so I say nothing.

Instead, I kiss her.

I kiss her, and I don't stop until the sun rises.

"Are you even listening to me?"

I tear my attention away from Aurora's French doors and look toward Sav. She's got her sunglasses perched on top of her head and a towel wrapped around her waist. I didn't even realize she'd gotten out of the pool.

"What?"

She narrows her eyes. "Who is it?"

"Who is who?"

"Who are you going all dopey over?" She waves her finger in a circle around my face. "I know this look. This hazy, brain fog, first crush look. Who is it? Do I know them?"

I push up from the lounge chair and make my way to the mini fridge. I hope like hell she doesn't see the blush heating my neck and chest. This fucking bikini hides nothing. I can't lie to her—Sav's like a bloodhound when it comes to sniffing out dishonesty—but I can't tell her the truth either. I go for something in the middle.

"I don't want to jinx it."

"Are you going to tell me who it is?"

"Nope."

I keep my back to her as I pull a mineral water from the fridge, uncap it and take a long drink while she groans. When I turn to face her again, she's got her hands on her hips and her head tilted to the side.

"I know it's not Kat."

"That's correct."

"I know it's a woman, though."

My eyes flare. Thank God I'm wearing sunglasses. "Why?"

"You've never caught feelings for a guy."

"Who says I've caught feelings?"

Sav arches a brow, and I bark out a laugh to throw her off.

"Whatever. It *could* be a guy. There's a first time for everything."

"There is, but it's not. It's definitely a woman."

I don't respond. Instead, I roll my eyes, grab my towel from the lounge chair, and head toward the house. I have every intention of escaping further conversation, but Sav keeps talking.

"How long?"

"What?"

"How long have you been talking to this mystery woman? It must have been building for a while if you already look like this, which means it started *during* your relationship with Kat. Is that why you finally broke it off with her? Someone else wanted to and actually did?"

I stop in my tracks and drop my eyes to the stone pavers as her barrage of questions pelts the back of my head.

I don't keep secrets from Sav. I never have, but now I've got two big things I'm hiding from her, and it just feels wrong. I don't even know why I haven't told her about my birth mom, but this thing with Aurora, it could be bad for all of us.

Still, I have to actively fight the urge to give Sav an answer. I have to force myself not to turn around and tell her everything about everything. The desire to analyze my feelings with my best friend is strong. I want to know what she sees and what she thinks. I want to hear her opinion. I want her to tell me I'm not fucking crazy for getting tangled up in this...this...whatever *this* is.

I want so badly to confess it all, but I don't. I can't. Not just out of respect for Aurora, but also out of fear. I'm scared that Sav will give me the same unfiltered honesty she always does. Scared that she'll remind me of the reality that I'm willfully ignoring, and this *hazy, brain fog, first crush* feeling will disappear.

I'm still floating on the high of my night with Aurora days ago. I'm still replaying every look and subtle touch that's happened since. When I'm with her, I'm trying my best not to stare. When I'm not with her, I'm thinking about her.

Even now, she went to lunch with Ham, and I've been buzzing with anticipation for the moment she returns. For two hours, I've been stealing glances at our terrace, willing her to come out. Hoping for her to come join us at the pool.

Aurora Hammond has consumed my every thought. She's taken over my brain and body, and I can't take back control. I don't *want* to take back control. I just want to enjoy the excitement of the freefall. It's such a welcome change.

I spent the last three years in an unhealthy, one-sided relationship with a person who was always half out the door. Kat made me question my worth. She made me feel like loving me was something to be ashamed of. Like I would never be enough for her.

With Aurora, it's different. She makes me feel like the sun, and after so many years of being kept as a secret, of being hidden in darkness, I can't get enough of the light. She looks at me like I'm worth something, and I crave it so badly that it outshines everything else. All the reasons why I shouldn't no longer exist. All the truths that I'm ignoring are erased. Everything, every thought and emotion, revolves around her.

Then, as if summoned, her French doors open, and Aurora steps onto the terrace. No matter where she is, that place becomes the center of the universe. My eyes snap up, and they're immediately met with hers. She smiles, and I start walking.

"I said I don't want to jinx it," I call over my shoulder to Sav, throwing up a peace sign before opening the door to the house. "See you later."

I don't turn around to see the look on her face, but I don't have to. I can practically feel the irritation and curiosity rolling off her in waves. It should bother me. I know her, and I know she won't leave it alone. She'll be paying attention now. I should probably be careful, but the farther I get from her, the less it concerns me. My focus is on the woman upstairs.

I keep walking until I'm at Aurora's bedroom door, and when I get there, I don't even have to knock. She swings the door open and welcomes me in with a smile.

Thanks to this house being packed with people, we haven't had a minute alone, and the second the door shuts behind me, the air sparks with an electric charge that crackles around us. We stare at each other for a few breaths, neither of us moving, until her eyes drop down my body. They linger on my breasts, my navel, the apex of my thighs. Her gaze tickles my skin with a featherlight touch, and my nipples pebble beneath my thin bikini top. It makes my pulse stutter as need courses through my veins.

People have looked at me with lust-filled eyes many times in my life. Never once has anyone affected me the way Aurora does. I love the way she stares. I love what looking at me does to her.

I watch as a flush spreads from her ears to her collarbone, and her breath quickens. It's such a powerful reaction, and I'm just in a bathing suit.

It reminds me of that morning in Adelaide, when I was wearing silk pajamas and her eyes stuck on the imprints of my piercings. That morning, I'd thought maybe I'd embarrassed her. Now, I see it for what it is: *desire.* And being the object of her desire makes me feel alive.

When she forces a swallow and fists her hands at her sides, I step closer.

"You can touch me. If you want."

Her eyes jump to mine and her flush deepens. "What?"

I smirk and rub my fingertips over her pinkened cheeks, savoring her warmth. "You're looking at me like you want to touch me. If you're curious, if you want to touch me, you can."

For a moment I think she might decline. A hint of fear flashes in her hazel irises, but it's no match for the hunger. Her white teeth sink into her plush lower lip as her gaze dips once more. To my mouth. To my collarbone. To my chest, rising and falling with my quickened breaths.

When she meets my eyes again, my heart is thudding so hard I'm sure she can hear it. Her pupils are blown wide and her lashes flutter nervously as she nods once. Gently, I trace my knuckles down her arm and take her hand. I look to her for confirmation, and she nods again, so I raise her hand and place it on the exposed skin just above my breasts.

"Your heart is pounding," she whispers.

I smirk again, but my voice quakes with anticipation as I respond.

"That's my body talking, Roar." I release my hold on her hand, giving her the power to choose what happens next. "Are you listening?"

Aurora licks her lips, and for seconds that feel like hours, neither of us moves. Her eyes bounce between my mouth and my chest before finally, *finally*, she rubs her thumb softly over my sensitive skin. Goose bumps prickle my arms and stomach, and I exhale slowly.

She pulses her fingertips against me a few times before inching lower. She cups my breast and pulses again—the lightest of touches—and my breath hitches. She's barely touched me, but my pussy throbs.

My nipple hardens to a peak beneath her palm, and her gaze flies to meet mine. She watches my face as she presses her hand into me, and when my lips part on a silent gasp, her eyes flare.

"Does that...does that feel good?"

I nod once. "They're sensitive."

She sucks her lower lip between her teeth, then shifts her hand so she can rub her thumb around my nipple in a circle. A whimper escapes me, and she rubs again, this time with a little more pressure.

"You like that?"

"Yes."

"What else do you like?"

My eyes flutter shut, images of everything I want to do with her flashing in quick succession in my mind, and I release another shaky exhale before I respond.

"Pinch it," I rasp. "I like when they're pinched."

"Like this?"

She pinches my nipple between her thumb and forefinger, and another whimper falls from my mouth as I nod. She does it again, and my hands shoot to her waist. My bikini bottoms are soaked with my arousal, and I press my thighs together, resisting the urge to kiss her. To move this along faster.

Then, without my urging, she slips her hands into the cups of my bikini top and palms my naked breasts. The moan that escapes me is ragged, and my eyes fly open to find her staring hungrily at me.

I can't fight it anymore. I kiss her, and she kisses me back eagerly.

Her hand wraps around my torso, slides down my back, and slips into the side of my bikini bottoms. My entire body is covered in goose bumps. My nipples and clit are throbbing. I've never been so aroused in my life. I remind myself to go slow, to let her lead, but when her soft hand squeezes my ass cheek, I grow dizzy. I moan into her mouth and drag my lips to her ear.

"Let's move to the bed."

Aurora freezes for a moment, but she doesn't let go of me. I wait as she processes my words, and then release a small, relieved exhale when she nods.

We sit on the edge of the mattress and face each other. She's a breathtaking sight to see with her lips swollen and her eyes bright. She's so damn beautiful that it hurts.

"Well..." She darts her eyes to the pillows and back to me. "What do we do now?"

I can't help the way my lips curve up at the corners, my cheek twitching against my fight to tame what I'm sure would be a wicked grin.

"What do you want to do now?"

Her throat contracts on a swallow before she shrugs. "What do *you* want to do?"

The hold I've been keeping on my grin snaps, and my smile widens, slow and suggestive, across my face. I need to touch her. I need it like I need air. So, I tilt my head to the side, bounce my eyes between hers, and return her shrug.

"How about I show you?"

25

AURORA

Mabel's words, though spoken like a low hum, echo loudly in my ears.

My rib cage rattles from the pounding of my heart. I'm trying so hard not to pant that each breath in and out quakes almost violently. Every part of my body aches to touch and be touched. And her smile, sexy and mischievous, has set my blood to boiling.

I don't know what to do with these feelings. I don't know how to make sense of this overpowering need. It's jumbled all my thoughts until only one is clear.

I want her—I want her so badly—but I have no idea what I'm doing.

Standing felt safer for some reason. It was less scary, less intimidating. But now we're on a bed. We're on a bed, she's in glorified underwear, and I know what her naked breasts feel like in my hands.

I clench my fingers into a fist at the mental image. Her piercings were cold and smooth against my palm. Her skin was soft and warm. At the thought, my eyes drop back to her chest, and my breath hitches. Her bikini top has come untied. She's bare from the waist up.

I zero in on her small, brown areolas, then on the shiny pink metal jewelry pierced through each of her peaked nipples. She has a small smattering of brown freckles on her left breast, and I picture myself kissing it.

My mouth waters. My panties grow more damp. Then her hands come into view, and she rolls both nipples between her slender fingers.

Seeing the pink jewelry pinched between her short, black-polished fingernails makes my own breasts ache, and I find myself mirroring her. Cupping my own breasts through my shirt and bra, wishing the fabric was gone and that my hands were hers.

"What do you say, Roar?"

My eyes snap back to her face, and I'm floored by what I see. Mabel said that bodies talk. If that's true, hers must be screaming for me. Her cheeks are a deep pink, her lips are puffy and glistening, and her eyes. Those amber gemstones are just a thin, sparkling ring around wide, depthless pupils.

She wants me. She wants me as badly as I want her. But still...

"I...I want to, but..."

"But?"

I try to force back the insecurity that is clawing its way into the forefront of my mind, but there is no quieting it. I'm so out of my element. I am so inexperienced. But I have never wanted anything more in my life. I drop my attention to the bedspread and shrug.

"I don't know what to do."

"You don't have to worry about that." Mabel cups my cheek and tilts my face until I'm once again looking into her eyes. "I'll do everything."

I blink, my brows furrowing slightly as I shake my head. "But I want to make you feel good."

She smirks, and the muscles in my lower belly clench with desire. She kisses me, sucking my lower lip into her mouth and biting lightly before pulling away too soon.

"Making you feel good will make me feel good. I'm a giver, Aurora. So, lie back, and enjoy what I have to give."

I stare at her, scanning her face for any hint of a lie. I'm scared —terrified, really—but the temptation is greater. The curiosity. The need.

I've never had these feelings with anyone, and I want to explore them. I want to fall headfirst into them. I've also never been with someone who actually cared about my enjoyment. And then her words from a few days ago float back into my consciousness.

I won't stop until I'm certain I've wrung every last ounce of pleasure from your body.

My desire battles with my insecurities, and I clear my throat. "What if I'm bad at it?"

Her expression softens, and she shakes her head. "That's impossible. Do you trust me?"

"Completely."

Mabel kisses me again, then moves to take off my shirt. I don't hesitate, raising my arms up to allow her to pull the fabric over my head, then drop it onto the floor. The impulse to fold my arms over my chest, to hide myself from her, evaporates the moment she drags her lips down my neck, kissing her way to my collarbone and shoulders.

"You are so beautiful."

Her voice vibrates against my heated skin, and I glow under her praise. Beautiful. *She* thinks *I'm* beautiful. It boosts my confidence and soothes my anxiety, and when she nips at the swell of my breast, I don't have space left in my brain to be self-conscious. My nipples are so hard they hurt, and I arch my back in an attempt to rub them against the cotton fabric of my bra. By the time Mabel's fingers find the clasp, I'm dying to be rid of it, but she pauses.

"Can I take this off?"

"Yes."

I sigh when the bra falls down my arms, but then Mabel leans in, closing the space between us, and I groan the moment her skin meets mine. When her piercings rub against me, cold and hard on my stiff nipples, I feel the contact on my clit. The apex of my thighs throbs in time with my heartbeat, fluttering quickly as the blood rushes through my veins.

I almost pass out from the sight of her delicate hands on my body. Her fingers pulsing into my flesh, pinching and massaging. Then she bows her head and takes one of my nipples into her mouth. She bites lightly, and I drop my head back on a moan as another rush of wetness collects between my legs.

"Oh, shit," I pant out, squirming on the mattress. My hands fist into the duvet and she bites again. "Oh, shit."

She chuckles, urging me backward until I'm lying flat across the bed, and she's suspended above me. Peering up into her face, I can hardly believe what I'm seeing is real. I blink several times to make sure it's not a dream.

Her hair curtains around her face, and the pink ends tickle my skin as my chest rises and falls rapidly with my breathing. I shift my shoulders and peer down my body to marvel at all the places where our naked skin is pressed together. It is the sexiest thing I have ever seen. An actual fantasy come to life.

She's an actual fantasy come to life.

"Are you comfortable?" she asks, voice low, as she trails her fingers up and down my stomach. I suck in a sharp breath as goose bumps pop up in the wake of her touch.

"Yes," I say honestly. "Nervous, but comfortable."

Mabel drags her fingers lower and traces them along the band of my jeans.

"Can I touch you?"

I don't have to ask what she means, but when she dips under the denim, I'm certain. Every ounce of my attention is on her slender fingers, just inches from me. From *touching me*. Right now, nothing exists outside of this room and this bed. Nothing exists except her and me.

I nod. "Yes. Please."

When she doesn't move or speak, I raise my eyes to hers to find her staring at me with the most sinful smirk on her swollen lips.

"What?"

She shakes her head once. "I like watching you." She pops the button on my jeans, my eyes flare, and her smirk grows. "I'm going to enjoy this."

My tongue goes numb when she rises onto her knees and grips my jeans.

"Lift your hips for me."

I do as she asks, and she doesn't look away from my face as she takes off my jeans and underwear and drops them to the ground. In seconds, I'm completely naked, but I'm too turned on to be self-conscious. I can barely think over the sound of my panting breaths and pounding heart.

Every inch of my skin is sensitive and tingling. I can feel the charged air buzzing against me as adrenalin and pure, unadulterated need pump through my body. Still, she doesn't break eye contact. She doesn't lower herself over me. She waits, stretching out the anticipation, until I'm nearly squirming and desperate to be touched.

Finally, she drags her fingers down both my thighs, and a needy whimper escapes me. She sinks her teeth into her lower lip and grins.

"Fuck, Roar, I'm *really* going to enjoy this."

Gently, she grips the back of my knee and bends it up so she can move between my legs. Cool air kisses my clit when my thighs part, making me whimper again, and her eyes fill with hunger.

The sight of her kneeling between my legs and looking at me like that is enough to make me lightheaded. The confidence she exudes. The control. The sex appeal. I never want to forget this moment, this picture. Mabel Rossi is a work of art, and I can't look away.

"What are you thinking?"

Her voice is thick with desire, and I shift my hips again. Needing friction or pressure. Needing relief. I clear my throat.

"I think you're the sexiest thing I have ever seen, and I am so turned on that I might combust."

Her lips twitch into another trouble making smirk, and she drags her nails down the insides of my thighs. The groan that leaves me is carnal. I feel the heat of her gaze as she slowly moves her eyes down my torso. She doesn't even have to touch me. Just having her eyes on me is like a jolt of electricity to my most sensitive parts.

"You have a beautiful body, Aurora. Do you know that?"

She runs her thumbs along the sides of my breasts, before cupping them and flicking my nipples with her thumbs. My answer is strangled.

"No."

"You do. You're so soft and supple. I love your curves. Your skin. I could look at you for hours."

"You could?"

"Mmm. It was hard not to stare before, but now that I know all of you, I won't be able to stop myself. Every time I look at you, I'll remember you like this."

I want to return the compliment, to tell her I feel the same. That I've never seen anyone or anything more beautiful, but she touches me again, and my tongue stops working. My lips can't form coherent words. Only sounds.

Her fingers circle around my belly button, and I feel like I might die from the wait. I'm certain I've made a mess of the bedspread from how aroused I am. I can feel wetness dripping from me, running down my thighs and collecting beneath me. I might be embarrassed if I could think straight.

"Can you open your legs all the way for me?"

I do it without hesitation or pause. I spread my legs wide, and when she finally drops her attention between my thighs, the look on her face makes my stomach clench with desire.

She looks starved for me. She looks like she needs me. And

God, I need her to take what she wants. I need it so badly that it hurts.

I prop myself up on my elbows so I can watch her, but then she runs her fingers through my short patch of hair, and I'm jolted out of the moment. My cheeks burn with shame when I remember I haven't shaved.

I clamp my eyes shut, and my body tenses as a familiar male voice sounds in my head. Berating me for being dirty. Belittling me for not meeting his standards.

For a second, I want to cover myself. I want to run into the bathroom and shower. I want to apologize. I open my mouth, ready to say *I'm sorry*, ready to make excuses for my negligence, but then Mabel speaks, sweet and sensual, and it all disappears.

"Fuck, you're so beautiful. And this—" She tugs lightly on my pubic hair "—is fucking sexy."

My eyes fly open to meet hers, and I find no lies. No reason to be ashamed. She finds me sexy, and she's being honest. It's all I need to reorient and bring myself back to this moment with her and only her.

"You have a perfect pussy. So pretty and wet." Her eyes drop back down, and she runs her tongue along her bottom lip. "Does it taste as sweet as it looks?"

My brain goes fuzzy again. Hearing Mabel say *pussy*, knowing she's thinking about *tasting* me. I can't handle it. I can't take it anymore. I shift my hips again, arching my body into the mattress, needing something, *anything* she's willing to give me. Then she laughs, and my pussy throbs.

"Please," I whisper. "Please."

"Please what, Roar?" She runs her knuckle up between my pussy lips, and I groan. I try to arch into her, but her other hand grips my hip and shoves me into the mattress. "Do you want me to touch you?"

"Yes. Yes, I do."

"Do you want me to taste this pretty pussy?"

"Please, yes. Yes. Please."

She doesn't say another word. She just lowers herself between my legs and places her hands on either side of my pussy. Her face is inches from me, so close that when she exhales through puckered lips, I feel the cool air on my clit, and I hiss. Then she presses a soft kiss to the sensitive spot, and I moan.

"I love how responsive you are." She kisses me again, and my hips buck slightly. "Are you ready for me?"

"Ye—*ohh*."

I don't get the whole word out before her mouth covers me, and I melt into the bed. Her tongue swipes through me before sucking my swollen clit between her lips. She hums, and one of my hands threads into her hair while the other fists the duvet until I'm sure my knuckles turn white.

When she sucks on my clit again, silver sparks flash at the edge of my vision. Part of me wants to close my eyes, but I can't bring myself to look away from her. She looks so damn hot between my legs. Her dark eyelashes fluttering with every lick and flick of her tongue. Her hand rubbing up and down my thigh. When she looks up at me before licking up my pussy once more, I almost die.

I will never forget the image of Mabel Rossi's mouth on my body. I hope I see it every time I close my eyes.

She covers my pussy again with her mouth, and a carnal groan claws its way out of my throat. My body tries to move against her, to rub myself on her, but her tattooed forearm presses against my hips, stilling me. She hums on a laugh and her mouth vibrates on my skin, making me moan again, and then my muscles start to pulse.

"Mabel, I think...I think..."

I think I'm going to orgasm. I'm so close, right on the precipice, toeing the edge. And then Mabel's body shifts and she snakes her hand beneath herself. It takes a breath for me to realize what's happening, but when I do...

She's touching herself.

She's got her hands on her body while her mouth is on my body, and that's all it takes to shove me over the edge.

A high, breathy moan tears from my throat, the sound so unfamiliar that it's hard to believe it's come from me. My body starts to spasm, but Mabel doesn't let up. Her tongue continues to torture me, determined to drain me of all sanity with her talented mouth.

My hands fist into her hair, the duvet, my own skin. I grip and tug to find purchase, to find balance, as the room spins and electricity shoots from my core out to the tips of my fingers and toes. My eyes clamp shut and colors flash in the darkness. Starbursts and sunbursts and fireworks.

I feel like I've been shocked repeatedly, but in the most delicious way. My body goes rigid, and then contracts. My thighs try to close, and when Mabel finally takes mercy on me, my stomach muscles bunch as I nearly fold myself into a ball.

"Oh my God, oh my God, oh my God," I chant breathlessly. "I can't...I can't..."

"You can't what?"

Jesus, that voice. It's enough to bring me to orgasm all over again.

I open my eyes and blink rapidly to bring the room back into focus, then peer up into Mabel's smirking face. A face that is *glistening* with what I'm assuming is my arousal. Add that to the fact that her hair is mussed, no doubt from my hands, and her skin is flushed red, and she looks like a literal wet dream.

"How are you feeling?"

A laugh escapes me at her question. "How am I feeling?"

She grins, then slides her palms down her sides, stopping at the ties on her bikini bottoms.

"Yeah. You good to keep going? I want to try something else with you."

My pulse starts racing again as all my nerve endings fire back to life. *Keep going? Try something else?* She wasn't kidding. She won't stop until I'm well and truly spent.

I might die, but I'll die happy.

All I can do is nod eagerly and stare as she pulls on the cloth ties and her bikini bottoms fall to the bed. And then my jaw drops.

Jesus.

Not only is Mabel's pubic hair trimmed into the shape of a heart, but she has a pink metal piercing in her clitoral hood. I look from it to the piercings in her nipples and back.

"They match," I muse, and she laughs.

"I'm just a girl who likes pretty things, Roar."

A giggle bubbles out of me, then another. My hand flies to my mouth to try to stifle it, but I can't. Then she giggles too, until we're both laughing gleefully. It's ridiculous and silly, and I love it. Never has a sexual encounter left me feeling this giddy. I feel sex drunk. Effervescent. I feel alive.

I smile up into her face and let the reality of this moment soak into my skin. The sun has started to set, casting the room in a warm, orange hue, and she looks almost alight from the inside. It fills me with a thick, warm feeling that I can't quite describe. I just know that I don't want it to end.

When our giggles have calmed, Mabel holds up a finger. "Do you need anything? Hydration? Pee break?"

I laugh again but shake my head. "I'm okay, thanks."

"Good. Stay."

She winks at me before climbing off the bed, snagging my bathrobe from the back of the door, and dashing out onto the terrace. My curiosity is thoroughly piqued, and she's back in less than a minute with a box in hand and a devilish smirk.

Mabel slips off the robe, then saunters toward me in slow motion with a confidence that makes my mouth water. When she reaches the bed, she places the box on the mattress and flips it open. I don't know what I was expecting, but a bottle of lubricant and a massage wand was not it. Then she flips a switch, making the wand buzz to life.

My jaw drops on a gasp. "Oh, God."

She smirks. "Goddess, baby. A man could never."

26

AURORA

My heart stutters as I read the note again.

I've read it probably twenty times since finding it on my nightstand this morning. I could close my eyes and picture it perfectly.

She has the most elegant handwriting. Each word is written in flowing, loopy cursive, and if I didn't know her, I might be surprised. I might expect something more edgy and chaotic, something more *rock and roll*, but that's just not Mabel Rossi. Her voice from last night plays in my ears, and my blood heats at the images that come with it.

I'm just a girl who likes pretty things.

The sultry makeup. The pink lace and leather. The matching piercings.

She's so hot that it hurts.

I drop my face into my hands and groan. I can't get a handle on my emotions. I keep jumping from *oh my God, I can't believe that happened* giddy giggles to *oh my God, I can't believe that happened* anxious panic. It's been a chaotic morning for my nervous system, and I haven't even left the room yet.

But seriously. I cannot believe it actually happened.

I keep waiting to wake up and discover it was just a dream. Just another of the X-rated fantasies that have been popping up in my head lately. But no, the delicious ache of my muscles and the technicolor film reel of memories flashing on repeat in my mind say otherwise.

I read the note one more time before sliding it into the back of my leather journal, then press my hand over my heart, feeling the *thump thump* against my palm.

I *am* awake. It *did* happen. Every touch. Every kiss. Every amazing, blissful, terrifying moment. It was *all* real.

I was completely naked in this bed with Mabel Rossi last night. She tasted and caressed every part of my body, and I enjoyed it. She brought me to orgasm multiple times, and never once did she expect anything from me in return.

That's the part that has rocked me the most, I think. How is that possible? Sex has never not been a chore for me. A quid pro quo, heavy on the quo. Or is it the quid? Whatever. Usually, my pleasure is the very last priority, so how could Mabel spend hours focusing on me, and then be just fine when I passed out from exhaustion without returning the favor?

I mean, thank God she didn't expect anything from me, because I would have freaked out. I'm freaking out a little now just thinking about it. I don't know what the heck I'm doing. I'd screw it up. I'd make a fool of myself. I have no idea how to please a woman. Just because I have a vagina doesn't mean I know what to do with one sexually.

I groan again and squeeze my eyes shut.

But I *want* to please her. I want to make her feel good. I want to do for her what she did for me. I want to, but I don't know if I can.

I push to standing and start to pace, then my eyes catch on my journal on the bedspread, and I think of her note again. She called me Sleeping Beauty and said I looked pretty. I can't remember the last time someone called me pretty or made me feel special. I don't know when, if ever, I was put first in a relationship.

My eyes widen the second the word forms in my head. *Relationship*.

Why would I think that? This isn't a relationship. It's not. It can't be. Right? What happened last night wasn't that big of a deal, was it? It felt like a big deal for me, but was it for her? She's a rock star. People throw themselves at her. I literally watched that guy at the club in Adelaide do it. She's experienced. She's not hurting for attention. She probably hooks up with people all the time.

Are we just hooking up, too?

Is that what I want?

Yes.

No.

I don't know.

God, I am such a mess. I don't know what I want. I don't even know if I am allowed to want what I might want even if I knew what I wanted. Do I even *like* women?

I mean, I like Mabel. That much is obvious. After last night, I can't really deny that anymore. So does this mean I'm gay?

The question gives me pause and makes me a little dizzy at the same time.

No.

I'm twenty-three. I would have known by now, right?

I guess I've always appreciated women. The more I think about it, the more I think I've always appreciated them more than men, to be honest. I had crushes on boys in high school, but I can't recall ever feeling truly attracted to a single one of them. Not physically, not emotionally, and certainly not like with Mabel. Not like this.

Was I conforming? Was I lacking in self-awareness?

Am I even self-aware right now?

I don't know.

I don't know, I don't know, I don't know.

But, God, it probably doesn't matter, anyway. A relationship with Mabel Rossi is totally unrealistic. It could never work. She's hot and famous and talented and everyone wants her, and I...I...

I drop back onto the bed as the final bit of bone crunching reality takes me out at the knees.

I have a husband.

The room goes silent, and I feel the oxygen being sucked out the window as my chest grows painfully tight.

I have a husband—I am legally married—and I never thought of him. Not once.

Instead, I'm crashing out about my probably non-existent relationship status with someone else. I have a husband, but I crossed many, many lines last night. I feel guilty. I feel terrible. I am a horrible, horrible person. Not just because of what I did, but because I can't stop wanting to do it again.

As if Brady sensed my dread and wanted to add to it, my phone buzzes from its place on the nightstand, and my whole body freezes with fear. I don't have to look at the caller ID to know it's him. I can tell just by the way my insides slither into an anxious, nauseous ball.

I *always* know.

I haven't spoken with him since Mabel hijacked his tirade on the terrace a few days ago. He hasn't reached out, and I've been content to chalk it up to good luck.

Foolish.

Foolish and naïve.

He wasn't giving me space. He was waiting for me to make

first contact. He wanted me to grovel, and his patience has run out.

I close my eyes and work to keep my breathing steady, but my fingers start to tremble anyway. The phone rings through to voicemail, and I count backwards from ten. I get to four before it inevitably rings again.

I do mental math. It's around seven in the morning back home, which means he's getting ready for work. He has no one around to pretend for. No reason to feign decency. No audience for whom to play the happy, healthy couple. It's just Brady, unchecked, and it makes the knot in my stomach pull tighter until I might actually throw up.

I don't want to answer.

God, I *really* don't want to answer.

But if I don't, he'll just continue to call back, and his mood will sour more every time my voicemail picks up.

I should have called him already.

I should have texted him an apology.

It never should have gotten to this point, but my mind has been on other things. On other *people*. Now, I have to deal with the fall out. If I don't, it will only get worse, so I unplug the phone from its charger, force a smile I don't feel, and accept the video call.

"Hey Bra—"

"Where the fuck have you been, Aurora?"

I flinch at the way his voice booms through the room. His face is already beet red and furious, and I frantically punch the button on the side of my phone to lower the volume out of habit. I'm alone, but I still don't want anyone to overhear.

"I've been work—"

"You've been ignoring me!"

I shake my head. "I haven't. You haven't called or texted—"

"I shouldn't have to! I shouldn't have to chase my wife around like a fucking dog. You let that bitch berate me, and then you ignore me for three fucking days."

I wince. "She's not a bitch—"

"You are coming home. You are getting on the next flight out, and you will make your uncle pay for it. If you don't tell him, I'll call him and demand it."

My breath catches in my throat. He can't talk to Uncle Wade. Uncle Wade can never know about Brady. About how he *really* is. He can't know how bad I've let it get. I shake my head rapidly and start to beg.

"No, please, I'm sorry. You can't call Uncle Wade, Brady. You can't. He doesn't—"

"Shut the fuck up, Aurora. For fuck's sake, just shut up. Do it. Now. Or I'll do it for you."

He hangs up, and I just sit there, staring blankly at the screen until it goes dark. I don't move, I barely breathe, until the screen lights up again.

It's my alarm reminding me of my session with Brynn in ten minutes. She's got a course-mandated test today, and I have to monitor to make sure she doesn't cheat. Despite everything that's just happened, the thought makes me want to smile. As if that child would ever.

Slowly, I stand from the bed and get dressed. I go to the en suite bathroom and splash water on my face. I take two ibuprofen, then step onto the terrace to stare at the ocean. I count to 100. I inhale the briny air through my nose and exhale it slowly through parted lips. When I'm certain I can socialize without crying, I leave the room and head down to the kitchen.

Just as my feet hit the last stair, my phone buzzes again. When I check it, it's a soothing balm, and the relief makes my eyes well with tears.

MABEL ROSSI

Can't wait to see you here.

She sent a picture of what I can only assume is the VIP section at the venue, and her hand is extended in the bottom of the frame, pointing to the barricaded section of seats. Her nails are a shimmery midnight blue, and her shiny bangle bracelets sparkle atop her colorful tattoos.

She's just a girl who likes pretty things.

I smile as I type out my reply.

ME

Me too. See you soon.

"Hey! You're getting a late start today."

Looking up from my phone, I'm shocked to see every member of Caveat Lover spread out in the open concept living room and kitchen, with Callie's bright smile directed at me.

"Oh. Um. Yes. I was up late last night." My cheeks flush, but I push forward. "I thought you had a long day today?"

"Heartless does. They're filming all the Sydney shows, so Hammond is running a tight ship. Me and the guys get the day to lounge."

"Oh. I forgot about the filming. Uncle Wade mentioned it when he picked me up from the bus station, but it must have slipped my mind."

"Understandable. A lot has happened since we left LA."

I nod. "I don't know how you guys do it."

"For the money, baby," Ezra chimes in from his place on the couch, and Callie rolls her eyes.

"You're full of shit," Callie says to him. "You'd be doing this even if we were still couch-surfing and living out of the van."

Ezra shrugs. "I knew we'd get here. I was playing the long game."

"Yeah. The fat paychecks make it all worth it," Crue adds, and Rocky barks out a laugh.

"Shut the fuck up, *Your Highness*. As if you didn't already have a treasury-sized bank roll."

I look back at Crue. "Your Highness?"

Crue waves him off but ducks his face into a book in his lap. "Rock's stoned."

I survey Rocky. He doesn't *look* stoned, but what do I know?

The hardest substances I've been around in years were the cocktails I consumed in Adelaide.

"Actually..." I glance around the room, then bring my attention back to Callie. "Now that I think of it, you guys have been surprisingly...*sober*."

Callie grins. "We pride ourselves on bucking those rock star stereotypes."

"She's not like other girls."

Ezra's tone is high-pitched and mocking, but aside from the middle finger she brandishes in his direction, Callie doesn't acknowledge him at all. I laugh, and she winks at me.

"Think of him like a pesky, annoying brother. He feeds off attention, so it's best to let him starve."

Her comment sends a wave of sorrow through me, and I can tell from her expression that she noticed. Her face softens with concern, and she lowers her voice so her next words can't be overheard.

"Are you okay?"

I give her a shrug. "My brother passed away a few years ago. Sometimes it still hurts."

She nods. "You'll grow around it. The grief, I mean."

"Yeah. I'm trying."

"Give yourself grace. You'll get there."

A moment of understanding passes between us, and it feels healing, in a way. Being seen without pity. Having my pain acknowledged and accepted without shame. It brings a genuine smile to my face, because *this* is what it's like to have friends. *This* is what it's like to be met where you are without expectation or judgment. *This* is what I've been missing.

The realization gives me courage, so I take a deep breath and step a little closer.

"Callie, can I ask you a question?"

"Of course."

"It might be kind of personal..."

She smiles. "That's fine. What's up?"

I shoot a quick glance to the guys to make sure no one is watching. They're occupied with each other, but I still turn my body so they can't see my face before I speak again.

"If Torren ever wanted you to do something, but you really didn't want to do it, how would you...I mean how would he..." I close my eyes and take a breath. "How would you handle that?"

"Oh, um...well, I guess it would kind of depend on what it was—"

"Something life-altering."

Her brows jump at my interruption, but she recovers quickly and nods.

"Well, I guess I would start by talking to him about it. I think once he knew about my feelings, he'd respect them."

I can't fight the frown that pulls at my lips. Torren would respect her feelings, but I'm certain Brady won't respect mine. I shake my head.

"And if he doesn't?"

Callie studies me with concern, her eyes scanning my face as if she's analyzing a painting. I get the feeling she's connecting dots, this conversation with the story of my dressing room outburst, and I don't miss the way she hesitates. She glances over my shoulder toward the guys, then back to me before she speaks.

"If it was important to me, if it was something I truly didn't want to do, and he didn't respect that, I'd probably end the relationship."

I don't know why it affects me so much. I shouldn't be surprised. She doesn't seem like someone who would let another person control her. But I've watched them together; they seem so in love. I guess I didn't think ending the relationship would be an option for her.

"You would?"

"Yeah, I would."

I fist my hands in front of me and shift my weight, dropping my eyes to the floor between us so I don't have to look at her. I can't for this part.

"What if you, like, *owed* him. Like, what if he had once helped you, and he did a lot for you, and now you feel like not doing what he wants would be...I don't know...would be...wrong? Unfair? Like it would make you a bad person?"

She's quiet for long enough that I can't help but raise my eyes back to her face just to gauge her mood. Did I cross a line? Did I say too much? Does she think I've completely lost it?

I find her watching me carefully, her face soft, and when we make eye contact, she gives me an almost sad smile.

"Torren and I have been through a lot together, actually. I almost died in a car accident a few years ago." She traces her fingers along the surgical scar on her forearm. "Without him, I probably would've given up on piano and my music career. I owe a lot of Caveat's success to Heartless, too. They'll never say that—they insist we're successful because we're talented—but I know the truth. Without the boost Sav and Torren gave us, Caveat Lover would've stayed a dusty memory, and I would still be working two jobs and living in a tiny apartment with my mom and sister. So, I know a bit about feeling like you owe someone a debt you can never repay."

"And you'd still...you'd still end it? You wouldn't compromise?"

Callie shrugs. "I don't want a love that comes with strings, or a relationship built on a foundation of obligation. I'm willing to compromise on a lot, but my bodily autonomy isn't one of them. If I really didn't want to do something big and life-altering, and Torren didn't respect my choice, I would absolutely end it."

I blink at her like an idiot as her confession settles around us. Torren helped her heal. He helped her professionally. They've been through a lot together.

Yet, she'd still end their relationship if her wishes weren't respected.

And she said *bodily autonomy*, which means she definitely has an idea of what I'm talking about. I'm not embarrassed, though.

I'm more...I don't know. Empowered, I guess. Validated. I feel stronger.

My phone goes off with another alarm just as Brynn comes bounding into the kitchen with her laptop.

"Well, I have to go. She has a test today," I say, nodding toward Brynn. "But thank you for being honest."

She smiles, and it's genuine. "Anytime, Aurora. Seriously."

I could get used to having friends.

27

MABEL

I CAN'T STOP SMILING.

I can't recall a thing my band said at breakfast. Sound check went by in a blur. All I can think about is Aurora. How she tastes. How she sounds when she comes. How she feels under my palms.

I'm a woman obsessed, and I don't even care. I've lost all good sense, but this giddy excitement is addicting. I'm literally counting down the seconds until I'm alone with her again.

"Rossi, pull your head out of the clouds, for fuck's sake."

I snap my attention up from my phone screen and blink at my manager. His eyebrow is arched, and his lips are pursed. It's a look I've seen many times, just never directed at me.

"What?"

"Did you hear a word I just said?"

"No."

"Are you ill?"

I blink, and my brows furrow. "Am I what?"

"You're not my problem child, Rossi, so either you're ill, or it's time for me to retire."

I blink again as I process his statement. I can feel my band's eyes on me, but I keep mine on Hammond as I slowly raise my hand to my mouth and fake a cough.

"I'm sick."

He's unamused, and I watch as he pulls his phone from his pocket, makes a call, and barks an order to whoever is on the other end.

"Rossi needs cough drops."

He hangs up, slides his phone back into his pocket, and hits me with another arched brow.

"Anything else?"

I shake my head. "Nope. Thanks, Dad."

He doesn't acknowledge me again, and I do my best to pretend to listen to what he's saying about calendars, show times, and set lists. We're filming all seven Sydney shows, and we have another fan meet and greet before the show tomorrow night. This is all stuff I already know, but Hammond is nothing if not thorough, and I don't make the mistake of looking at my phone again.

By the time our manager dismisses us, my phone has buzzed multiples times with texts, and I'm dying to see if they're from Aurora. Instead, though, I'm cornered by a suspicious looking Sav, and my hackles rise.

"You guys coming to grab food with us?" Jonah asks, but Sav doesn't look away from me as she answers.

"No. We'll order something."

I break my stare off with Sav to look at Jonah and Torren. They're both smirking.

"What?" I spit.

"It's just nice to see the golden child get in trouble, is all," Torren says with a laugh.

"Good thing, too. Can't have Ham thinking we've gone easy on him," Jo adds, and I roll my eyes.

"You are literally asleep by 10 p.m. every night there isn't a show, and you've replaced liquor with ginger tea."

Torren snorts a laugh, so I whip my attention to him.

"And you're just as boring, Mr. *Newspaper and Black Coffee at 5 a.m.* You're one pair of white sneakers away from a lawn care routine. *Easy* is an understatement."

"Exactly," Torren says, ignoring my weak jibe as he heads to the door. "That's why we're glad you're taking up the torch."

"If you need help on how to be the problem child, Mabes, I got you covered," Jo says.

I flip them both off and keep my middle fingers up until the door shuts behind them.

"We need to talk."

I turn my attention back to Sav and try to act unbothered by her cold tone. "Okay. Talk."

She leaves the exec suite without another word, so I release a loud, dramatic, *Sav Loveless*-coded sigh that she doesn't acknowledge as I reluctantly follow her.

We don't speak as we weave through the halls, and I don't bother catching up to her. I drag my feet and lag despite it being childish. I don't know what she wants—probably to assault me with more nosy questions—but I'm in no hurry to find out.

As we approach the dressing room though, I grow nervous. I hate lying to Sav. I hate having to dodge these conversations. Keeping a secret from your best friend is so fucking hard, and I hate doing it. I hate it so much. I'm so far in my own head, that when we walk through the door, I don't see her stop in front of me until I'm running smack into her.

"Fuck, Sav." I step back and rub my forehead. "What the hell?"

"Oh, sorry. You must have been too busy daydreaming about Ham's niece to see me."

I can feel the blood drain from my face until I'm sure I'm white as a sheet. The reaction is all the confirmation Sav needs, and she flings a finger in my direction.

"I fucking knew it. I knew it! Jesus, Mabes, what the actual fuck are you thinking? She's not just Ham's niece, she's married! Married!"

I clamp my eyes shut. I know she's right. Fuck, I know it. I just don't want to admit it.

"How did you know?"

"I could tell she was into you from the beginning. I just didn't think you'd fucking act on it. But then you got all crush-faced and spacey, and you both started disappearing at the same time, so it wasn't hard to put two and two together. Please tell me you're just hanging out."

I don't respond to her last sentence and instead blurt out the first thing that comes to my head. "What do you mean *you could tell* she was into me?"

Sav pinches the bridge of her nose. "For fuck's sake, Mabel."

"What do you mean, Savannah?"

She glares at me, but I wave my hands, signaling for her to spit it the fuck out because I am dying to know. She caves, thank God.

"She literally stalked you with her eyes every time you were in a room together. I'm sure she thought she was subtle, but—"

"But you noticed because you're a fucking annoying, nosy, pain in the ass?"

"Oh, shut up. You're not mad at me. You're just mad you got caught."

I groan and throw myself on the couch. She's not wrong, and I hate it.

"Please tell me it hasn't gone further than hanging out. You haven't crossed any physical lines, right?"

I can't tell her what she wants to hear, so I drop my head between my knees and say nothing. She releases a groan that mimics mine, then the couch dips as she plops down next to me.

"Okay," she says on a defeated sigh. "Okay. At least tell me it was just physical, and you haven't actually caught feelings. Just a harmless crush. Right? We can work with a harmless crush."

I *want* to tell her that. I want it to be true so badly, but I know myself better than that. I've definitely fallen for Aurora, and there's no point in lying. Sav would see right through me anyway.

When I don't speak up, the back of the couch bounces because she's dramatically thrown herself into it, and when I look at her, she's staring at the ceiling. We sit in the quiet for what feels like an hour, and when she finally breaks the silence, her voice has a morose tone that makes my whole body deflate.

"I just don't want you to get hurt, Mabes. I want whatever you want, but I honestly cannot picture an outcome that doesn't end in you getting your heart shattered."

I close my eyes again and lean back into the couch beside her. My eyes well with tears, but I don't let them breech my lashes. It won't help anything.

"I know," I whisper. And I *do* know. I've just been avoiding it. I've been lying to myself by refusing to take off the metaphorical rose-colored glasses. "I shouldn't have let this happen. I know that. But, God, Sav, I just..."

I trail off and shake my head.

How do I say this without sounding like an idiot? Without coming off as a completely naïve fool? I should have known better. I should have been more careful. I never should have let it get this far, but I just...I just...

My thoughts are reeling, searching frantically for a way to explain it, but then Sav takes my hand and squeezes.

"But the connection is so strong, you couldn't fight it," she says quietly, and I'm so fucking relieved to hear understanding in her voice.

Of course, she gets it. I never should have doubted her. Sav will always be on my side. I turn my head so I can see her, and I find her already looking at me.

"Yeah. It is."

"Well," she says, a small smirk forming on her lips. "Every person in this band would be fucking hypocrites if we criticized you for it."

A small, sad laugh bubbles out of me, and I nod. "That's true."

She squeezes my hand again. "I love you, Mabes. I'll back you in any way you need me to, okay? Even if me and Ham have to tussle. I got you."

I laugh again. "You barely reach Ham's nipples, Sav."

She waves me off. "I've had self-defense training for years. If I can take down Red, I can take down Wade Hammond. I'll just blitz attack him while he's sending a ragey email or bullying a frightened intern."

I *have* seen her take down Red, her giant bodyguard of over a decade, so she probably could take on our manager.

"That won't be necessary. I'll handle my shit."

"The offer stands."

"You're just looking for an excuse to knock Ham on his ass."

She waggles her brows. "Since I was eighteen, babe. I think I've earned the opportunity."

I roll my eyes. "I'll keep you on standby, then."

A knock has both our heads turning toward the door.

"Go away," Sav calls, but the door swings open anyway, and in walks our manager with a giant bouquet of flowers.

"Hey, Ham. You think I could take you in a fight?" she asks before standing and sauntering over to him.

He arches a brow. "You wish, Shaw."

Hammond hands her the flowers, then calls over his shoulder as he leaves.

"Those aren't for you. They're for Rossi. Don't forget your call time for tonight."

The door closes behind him, and Sav and I look at each other with wide eyes. I bound off the couch after her just as she clutches the bouquet to her chest and sprints into the attached bathroom, slamming the door behind her. Bitch.

"Savannah, open the door, damn it. Those aren't for you!"

I bang on the door and jiggle the handle. She's locked it.

"Open the door, you hoe! Those aren't for you! Open the door!"

She flings the door open just as I'm trying the handle for the tenth time, and her scowl is murderous. The gorgeous bouquet has been discarded in the sink, and she slaps the card in my hand.

"Say the word, and I'll order the shit."

I know even before I read the card that the flowers are from Kat, but nothing could have prepared me for the words she's written.

I miss you, sweetie.
I'm ready to go public.
Love, me

28

AURORA

THE BACKSTAGE HALLS are a hive of activity as I follow Jones to the band's dressing rooms.

Each step closer heightens my nerves. I haven't been in a dressing room since embarrassing myself in Adelaide. I've been avoiding them at all costs, but tonight, I'm driven by a strong desire to see Mabel in person.

I can't wait until after the show. It needs to be now.

I've spent all day thinking about her. Stewing. Panicking. Then grinning like a fool with every text she'd send.

Logically, I know it's quick. I know I shouldn't be basing huge life decisions on Mabel Rossi, famous drummer for the world's biggest band. But the more I think about it, the more I realize that it's been a long time coming.

I've been living in the dark for so long. Being away from Brady has brought me back into the light. It's not just Mabel's influence that's helped with that; it's been Sav, Callie, and Claire, too. I've witnessed healthy relationships and strong friendships. I've been treated with respect and compassion. I've been reminded that I matter. What I want matters.

Sav said she and Levi are a team. He wants what she wants. I deserve that kind of partnership.

Callie said she'd leave Torren. She said she wouldn't compromise her bodily autonomy for anyone. I shouldn't have to either.

I'm anxious. I'm nervous. I'm so, so scared. But for the first time in years, I'm feeling brave and confident, and I can't let those feelings fade back into the darkness.

"It's right here, Ms. Sinclair."

Jones's voice pulls me from my thoughts, and I look up to find him standing in front of a door. The dressing room. My nerves spike once more. I tear my eyes from the door and look back at Jones, stalling.

"You can call me Aurora," I remind him. "I really prefer it."

"Of course. Apologies."

"Actually, Payton is your first name, right?"

He shakes his head. "Yes, ma'am."

"Can I call you Payton?"

"Yes."

"Payton. Please, for the love of God, don't call me ma'am. Or Ms. Sinclair. I hate them both. It's just Aurora."

A rare smile crosses his face as he responds. "Okay, Aurora."

"Thank you." I nod toward the door. "I'll see you later?"

"I'll be back to escort you to the front before the show."

When he leaves, I turn to face the door again.

Shoulders back. Chin up. Suck it up, Aurora Jade. Be brave.

I take two deep breaths, then knock.

"Enter," Sav calls from the room, so I open the door and step inside.

My eyes find Mabel immediately, but they're pulled back to Sav when she speaks again.

"Oh, hey, Aurora." She gives me a weird, plastic smile that doesn't reach her eyes. "Did you come to hang out before the show?" She gestures to a spread of food where her bodyguard is casually picking grapes off a fruit tray. "You can help yourself. There are drinks in the fridge, too."

"No. Uh, thanks, but no." I flick my eyes back to Mabel. "Actually, I was hoping I could talk to you? In private?"

Mabel's smile doesn't reach her eyes either, and it makes uncomfortable chills skate down my spine. I frown, almost expecting her to turn me down, but she nods and stands from the vanity where she was sitting.

"Sure."

She walks toward the door without even looking at or acknowledging Sav. In fact, the room seems to be filled with an eerie, tense energy that I didn't notice at first, and I'm relieved to see Mabel heading into the hallway.

I follow her, but before I step out of the room, I look to Sav once more and raise my hand in an awkward wave.

"Do the good tonight." I cringe, because that didn't come out at all how I wanted it to. "I mean good luck tonight. Or break a leg? I hope it goes well. I mean that."

Her brows rise in amusement, and she gives me one of those *Sav Loveless* smirks.

"You, too."

I have no idea what she means by that.

You, too?

Why would I need good luck? What does she hope goes well for me? Does she know something I don't?

My brain attempts to go down a side quest spiral, but then Mabel is halting in front of a totally different room, so I follow her inside and let her shut the door behind us.

"What's up?"

Her voice is soft, and her tone is light, but I can still see the tense set to her shoulders and jaw. It gives me pause. I don't want to unload on her if she's already dealing with something, and suddenly my whole center shifts. I'm no longer worried about me. I'm concerned for her.

I shake my head. "Is everything okay? Did something happen with your birth mom? You seem stressed. We can talk about that first if you want."

It's like watching a balloon deflate slowly, the way the tension bleeds from her body, and she exhales as if my words have relieved her of something heavy. Then she smiles. It's timid and tired, but it feels like a hug, and brings a matching smile to my face.

"Thank you for that," she says. "That really means a lot. I'm okay, though. Everything is fine with my birth mom. Nothing new. Tell me what you wanted to talk about. That's more important to me right now."

I scan her face, but I find no lie there, so I take a deep breath and push forward.

"Right. Well, I just wanted to...I think that I'm going to...No, I *know* I am. I know. I know that I am going to..."

I start to fumble over myself, so I stop, close my eyes, and collect my thoughts. I inhale slowly, then let the confession be carried on my exhale.

"I'm going to tell Brady that I don't want to have a baby."

The room goes eerily still. I can't even hear breathing. When I open my eyes, I find Mabel staring at me, lips parted as if on a silent gasp.

"You are?" she whispers finally, and I nod.

"Yeah. And..."

I dart my tongue out to wet my now parched lips.

"And I'm going to tell him that I want a divorce."

Her expression shifts, and for the first time in a while, I can't read her. All emotion leaves her face until she's just a blank canvas. My heart starts to race.

"Mabel?"

She blinks several times, and then nods twice before whispering, "Why?"

I shake my head. "What? What do you mean why?"

"*Why* are you going to do that?"

Still no discernable tone. Still no readable expression. She's flat, blank, and cold, and in response, I start to ramble.

"Because I don't want to have a baby. I don't want to be

married to him. It's not fair to anyone. I don't love him, Mabel. He's manipulative and mean and controlling, and I actually think I might hate him. He speaks to me like I'm nothing. He makes me feel like I'm nothing. I can't be with someone like that. Not now that I know what it feels like to be with someone I actually have feelings for. Not now that I know how it feels to really connect...to really care about...to really *love* someone. I just can't. Being here with you, with your friends, it's shown me how much better it could be. How much better is *should* be. It's shown me what I really want, and that's not Brady. I don't want to be married to him or to be tied to him by a kid I don't want. I can't do it. I *won't* do it. I've wasted too much time already. I've let him take too much from me. I have to end it. I have to."

My breathing is elevated when I stop talking, and my pulse is pounding in my ears, but with the exception of two small lines forming between her brows, Mabel's expression hasn't changed. She's still stony. She's still cold. I start to panic.

"Mabel, say something. Please. You're starting to worry me."

I shake my head and take a step away from her.

"Did I upset you? Am I wrong? Do you not...are you not...is this bad? God, I shouldn't have said anything. It's not your problem. I'm sorry. I'm so sor—"

My apology is halted when her lips press against mine, and the surge of relief almost makes my knees buckle. Her hands cup my face, and I wrap my arms around her, clinging to her, kissing her desperately. Once again, she breathes life into me. She fills me with so much happiness and excitement and hope that I might burst with it.

I've never felt like this with anyone. Ever. I can question it all I want, but being with her makes it undeniable.

She pulls away and gazes into my eyes as her thumbs trace my jaw.

"Are you sure?"

I nod. "Yes."

She presses another soft kiss to my lips before resting her

forehead on mine. "I'm going to say something, but I don't want you to take it the wrong way. Okay?"

My lips pull into a frown. "Okay."

"I support you, and I agree that you shouldn't stay with Brady. I agree with everything you said. But I need to know that you're not doing this for me."

I jerk back so I can look at her.

"What? What do you mean?"

She hesitates, so I step backward, and her hands fall away from me.

"What do you mean, Mabel?"

"This is a huge decision, and you should be making it for yourself, and only yourself. Not for me. Not for anyone else. Only for yourself."

I feel like I've been scolded, and I break our eye contact so I can process what she's said. I know she's right. I *know* she is. But I expected happiness. Excitement, even. Not this insistence to remove herself from the decision. Not this attempt to remove herself from *me*. It hurts a lot. Probably more than it should.

"Please don't take this the wrong way."

"I thought you'd be happy."

She steps closer and takes my hands in hers. "I am. I *am* so, so happy. But I also know how dangerous it can be to make life-altering decisions based off someone else. You need to do this for you and only you. I promised that I'd always be honest with you. This is me doing that."

I drop my forehead to her shoulder and breathe her in. Gardenia and pear with a hint of brown sugar. I inhale deeply, letting her scent calm my spinning thoughts and racing heart.

She's right, and I am taking this too personally. She's being smart, and I'm being emotional. If I'm going to do this, I need to be honest with myself, and with her.

"I'd be lying if I said you aren't a big reason why I came to this realization," I say softly. "But the decision to leave is for me. He's chipped away at me for four years. If I stay, I know he won't stop until there is nothing left."

"Okay," she whispers.

Her lips ghost over my hair as she speaks, her breath warming my scalp. Then she wraps her arms around me in a hug and moves her hand to the soft spot behind my ear, right on my pulse point.

"I'm here for you in any way you need, Roar. Anything you need. I'm here."

"Thank you."

I hold her tightly, feeling her heart pound against my chest and listening to her soft inhales and exhales. I've never felt safer than I do when I'm wrapped up in Mabel's arms. I don't want to let go. I don't want to leave the comfort of her embrace.

But I know I have to.

Tonight, Mabel has a crowd of 80,000 people to dazzle.

Tomorrow, I have a life to ruin.

Only then, can I step into a better one.

"Sydney, Australia, how are we doing this evening?"

Sav's voice is swallowed up in the boom of cheers and screams from the crowd, then her laughter fills the stadium as she turns to her band.

"That's what we like to hear, isn't it guys?"

Mabel pounds on the drums as if to say *yes, it is*, and like an extension of her hands, her lips, I feel each beat on my skin.

The Hometown Heartless always puts on a phenomenal show, but this one feels different for me. It feels like I'm viewing it through new eyes, hearing it with new ears. I can't contain my giddy excitement, and I don't even try to tear my eyes away from the drummer. When Sav starts wooing the crowd some more and everyone's attention goes to her, mine stays on the back of the stage. On Mabel. She's all I see.

"Welcome to the Riot She Wrote tour, Sydney. We're so fucking excited to be back here sharing new music with you, and we hope you're excited too, because we've got a little surprise for you."

The ground vibrates beneath my feet as the audience goes nuts, and the cheering gets so loud that I'm sure my ears will be ringing tomorrow.

"You might have noticed some camera crews around the venue, and that's because we'll be filming every show while were here in Sydney, so we need you to bring the energy. You think you can do that?"

Sav laughs again as the audience erupts with cheers.

"I knew we could count on you."

Jonah strums his guitar, and Sav flashes him a smirk. "That's my cue."

She pauses, and in the silence, excitement rolls off the crowd in waves. She looks from Jonah, Torren, and then to Mabel before finally leaning back into the mic and casting her attention out at the crowd. Then she grins.

"Sydney, are you ready to fucking rock?"

I watch a smile take over Mabel's face as the crowd goes wild, but then she looks at me, and my breath hitches.

In all the chaos, with a crowd of 80,000 people, it's like we're the only two in the place. She winks and blows me a kiss, and I ride that high for the entire two-hour show. It's the exact thing I need to solidify my decision.

This is how it's supposed to feel. Fluttering butterflies and good chills. The bubbly, effervescent kind of nerves. Pure, thrilling happiness. That's what Mabel Rossi gives me. If I have to set fire to my entire life, I'll do it, because now that I know how this feels, I refuse to settle for anything less.

After the show, Payton escorts me back to the house we're renting, and instead of waiting for everyone else, I head straight to my bedroom.

I can do this. It needs to be done. There's nothing to be afraid of. His hateful words don't matter anymore, and since he's on another continent, when he tries to berate me, I'll hang up.

"Brady, I don't want to get pregnant," I say into the mirror. "I want a divorce."

I practice saying the words a few more times, changing the inflection and speed until I decide to stop stalling and just go for it.

"I can do this. Just be honest, and then hang up when he gets mean."

I repeat it out loud as I unlock my phone and pull up Brady's contact. I say it over and over in my head as the phone rings. When he doesn't answer, I hang up, and I call again. It's pretty early back home, but I know he's awake.

When the voice mail picks up a third time, I get annoyed. He would be livid if I let his call go to voicemail even once, let alone three times. He would leave me a raging, horrible message, then continue to call every few minutes until I finally answered. And then he would yell. It wouldn't matter if I was in the shower, in the garden, or had my hands full with dinner or laundry; he would scold and insult me until I apologized for missing his call.

The thought fills me with anger, hot and bubbling in my stomach. I haven't been this angry in a long time. I don't know if ever, honestly. I usually cower. I usually beg for forgiveness. Not anymore.

He truly does treat me so poorly. It's been years of abuse, and just thinking about it makes me wish I could time jump straight into a life without him. A life full of love, laughter, and light. I can't rewind, but I can start fresh. My eyes seek out my orchid and focus on the healthy bud. Rebirth and rebloom. I can do that. I *will* do that, and it will be so beautiful. I can hardly wait.

A sense of urgency fills me as his phone goes to voicemail yet again, but this time I don't hang up. This time, I dig my nails into my confidence, holding tight so it doesn't slip, and let my anger bolster it as I leave a message.

"Hi. It's Aurora. I didn't want to have to do this on your voicemail, but since you're not picking up, I guess I have to. Brady, I'm not leaving the tour. I'm going to stay and honor my commitment. And..."

I pause to collect myself. Do I tell him I want a divorce? That I'm leaving? For a moment, I almost do just to make it easier on myself, but then I think better of it. I don't want to give him any extra ammunition to throw at me.

"And we really need to talk. It's important, so please call me back when you get a chance. Goodbye."

I hang up, then sit for several minutes just staring at the phone. I wait with rigid muscles for it to ring, for him to return the call just to scream at me from across the ocean. When my phone buzzes with a text, I about jump out of my skin before I realize it's not from Brady. Immediately, my fear vanishes, and I'm filled with those fluttering butterflies.

MABEL

Open your door, Sleeping Beauty.

I rush to let her in, and it takes all my strength not to collapse into her as soon as we're alone.

She takes off her jacket and drops it on my bed, then sits to take off her boots. She's still in her concert clothes, so she must have come straight back to the house. I'm so glad she did. I'm jittery and bouncing with adrenaline, but she always makes me feel calm.

"Hey. You played a great show tonight," I say. "You all did, but especially you. I bet you got some great footage."

She gives me a tired smile. "You looked like you were having fun in the audience. I saw you dancing and singing."

"I had a blast. It was probably my favorite show of the tour so far."

She stands and steps closer, several inches shorter now that she's barefooted, and tucks a strand of my hair behind my ear.

"And how are you feeling? About what you said earlier, I mean. Second thoughts?"

I shake my head. "No second thoughts. I actually tried to do it tonight, but he didn't answer his phone."

Her brows rise. "Really?"

"Yeah. I'm serious about this, Mabel. I want it done. I want it over."

I want you, I almost add, but I bite my tongue. I told her that this decision wasn't about her, and I don't want her to doubt that.

She smiles softly, then leans in and presses her lips to mine. It's sweet and tender, but I want more, so I deepen the kiss. Slowly at first. Timid. But when she responds, I grow bolder.

I run my tongue along her lower lip, just like she's done to me, and she parts them. Our tongues glide together, and I swear I can feel it on every inch of my skin. My neck. My breasts. Between my thighs. I tug on her corset, pulling her closer, but she pulls away, and I'm left panting and confused.

"I'm going to shower, okay? After, if you're not too tired, maybe we can hang out? Watch a movie or something."

I try not to frown as I nod, and I watch her leave through the terrace French doors. Minutes later, the shower kicks on in her en suite bathroom. Then I start to pace.

Blood is pumping quickly through my body. My skin pulses with it. I'm still energized from the phone call, from the promise of my life without a cage, and after kissing Mabel, I can't settle. I don't want to settle. I want *her*.

An idea pops into my head, and with it are images that set my skin on fire. That same sense of urgency grows stronger, more frantic. I'm almost free. My new life is right at my fingertips, and I want it now. I'm so tired of wasting time. Of wasting *myself*. I want to close this dark chapter and start a new one. I want a life full of light.

I want Mabel Rossi, and I'm going to show her.

29

MABEL

I'm so far in my head as I step under the shower spray and let the warm water roll down my body.

I will it to take away some of the tension, but it doesn't. Kat's note is weighing heavily on me, and I'm not sure how to make it stop. All I keep thinking about is the advice I gave Aurora hours ago.

I can't make life-altering decisions based on someone else. I have to do what's best for me. I know this. But what is that?

I was with Kat for a long time. I invested so much time and energy into that relationship, and a month ago, that note would have made me fucking ecstatic. It was all I'd been wanting, to go public with her. To love and be loved in the open. And now she's saying I can have it, but is it what I want?

Then there's Aurora.

I've never felt for anyone what I feel for her. I could love her. I might already. I can't deny how amazing it felt to hear that word fall from her lips earlier. But am I setting myself up for heartbreak? Is this just a rebound crush after a breakup? It doesn't feel like that, but can I really trust my own judgment?

She's twenty-three, my manager's niece, and *married*. All of those are great reasons to stay away; instead, I dove in headfirst.

Sure, she said she's going to divorce that fucking abusive twat, and I'm thrilled for her. But that doesn't mean she'll still want me. We're in two very different stages of life. There's no guarantee we'd last. Can I take that risk again? Should I even try? Because if it doesn't work out, I know it will crush me worse than anything else has.

And then there's my birth mom. I still have that decision looming. When I'm not thinking about Aurora, I'm thinking about the birth family in Georgia that doesn't know I exist. I don't know what to do. I don't know the right answer.

I've never been this happy, but I've also never been this stressed. It's all so heavy, making my skin tight and itchy, and I can feel the floor shift beneath my feet.

I tilt my head up and let the water spray on my face, willing it to ground me. To fend off the spiral. I inhale the steam and hold it in my lungs, then count to a hundred. My heart still races. The stone floor still wobbles.

Then a noise draws my attention to the bathroom door, and through the foggy glass, I see Aurora's outline. She's blurry, almost abstract, and at first, I think my brain conjured her to calm me down. But when I wipe the condensation from the glass, she becomes clearer, and I know she's real.

She gives me a small, nervous smile, and then slowly, she pulls her shirt over her head. Now, my heart is racing for a different reason, and I can't tear my eyes off her.

The glass begins to steam over again, and I wipe it off quickly, just in time to see her hands slide to the band of her jeans. I watch with labored breaths as she undoes the button and pushes them down her thighs, until she's standing in the bathroom in just a white matching bra and panty set.

I've never been this turned on before. I blink several times to reassure myself that this isn't just a rogue fantasy, but it's not. She's here, half-naked, and she's getting into the shower with me.

We stand for a moment, inches apart, just staring at each other as steam fills the shower once more. The water hits her body, rendering her cotton underwear see-through, and I have to bite back a groan. She looks so sexy. I want to touch her, but I fist my hands at my sides.

"Hi," she says, her sweet voice floating over the pattering of the water hitting the stone floor. "I hope this is okay."

I nod. "Yes. Yes, this is okay. More than okay."

She sinks her teeth into her bottom lip, and I feel it on my already hardened nipples.

"Can I try something?"

I nod again. Slowly this time. "Anything."

Her lips twitch into a smile, excitement and nervousness dancing across her features as she steps closer, closing the distance until our bodies barely brush together. When my breasts graze hers, a shaky whimper escapes me. I'm trembling for her.

She kisses me, gentle at first, then a little deeper. She trails her fingers up and down my torso, then pinches my nipples just how I showed her last night. I hum into her mouth, and she breaks the kiss, pulling back to watch my face as she does it again.

She doesn't take her eyes off me as she bows her head and takes one of my nipples into her mouth, sucking first, then swirling her tongue around it, toying with my piercing before biting.

"Fuck, Aurora. That...that feels good."

I try to keep my voice low and even. I don't want to overwhelm her—I remember how scared I was the first time I touched a woman—but when she bites again, my hands grip her waist and my head tips back on a groan.

"Oh, fuck, yes."

I can feel her lips curve into a smile against my sensitive skin, before she moves a little lower, sucking on the underside of my breast just hard enough that my clit throbs. It'll leave a mark, and the thought makes me wetter.

It takes a minute for me to realize what she's doing, but when I do, my heart starts to pound hard enough that I might pass out. She lowers to her knees, her hands roving up and down my back, grazing my ass a little more each time as she kisses my stomach. She swirls the tip of her tongue around my navel, then shifts to my hip bone.

I have one flash of good sense as my legs tremble.

"Wait," I force out.

When she looks up at me, hazel irises nearly swallowed up by wide pupils, my pussy pulses.

Her chin rests just above my pelvis, her blonde hair is wet and pushed back off her pretty face, her soft skin glistens with sparkling water droplets, and the fabric of her bra is so transparent she might as well be naked.

I can see everything perfectly, and she looks like art. Like a painting I could spend hours appreciating. She's so inherently beautiful, so painfully sexy, and I can barely form words.

"A towel. You should..." I force a swallow, then raise my heavy hand to grab the towel hanging on the side of the shower. I drop it to the floor between us. "For your knees."

"Thank you." She shifts onto the towel, and her sweet smile makes me dizzy. "I've never done this before," she whispers. "I might need guidance."

Jesus, the way my stomach flips in anticipation. I smooth my hands over her hair and brush my thumbs over her cheek bones. I need to touch her everywhere and always.

"Of course. Anything you need."

She smirks and her eyes flash with heat as she licks her lips. "I need to be the giver tonight."

My breath hitches, and all I can do is nod in response.

"Can you widen your legs some more?"

Jesus fucking Christ, I can't handle it. My core is pulsing with every beat of my rapid heart. I nod again and take a wider stance as she requested, and then I can feel her eyes on me. Her gaze is just as powerful, as sensual, as her touch, and my fingers tremble in her hair as I wait.

She leans in and licks up my pussy slowly, her back arching in the sexiest way, and a moan sounds from deep in my chest.

She does it again, and my fingers sink a little deeper into her hair.

"Is that good?"

"Very good."

"Tell me what you like."

This is so hot. This is so fucking hot, I might die. I clear my throat.

"The jewelry. Just...just pla—Oh, fuck."

My knees threaten to buckle as she licks around my piercing, flicking the jewelry and then sucking my clit between her lips. My legs widen farther, and my hand tightens on her head as the other flings out to grip the shower wall for support.

"That's so good, Roar. Just like that."

She plays with my clit, alternating between sucking and licking, until I'm half mad. When she licks up my pussy again, her tongue presses deeper, probing my entrance, and my vision sparks. I fall back onto the shower ledge to support myself, and bottles of hair products fall to the ground. I barely notice.

"Good. Fuck, that's it. Do that again."

My leg lifts almost on reflex when she licks me, and she shifts to prop my leg on her shoulder. I want to stare, to watch, but she licks me a third time, sucking my clit into her mouth when she reaches it, and my head falls onto the shower wall.

"Can you come like this?"

I don't answer right away, and she pulls back to look up at me.

"What's wrong? Did I do something wrong?"

"No. No, definitely not. You're perfect."

Her brows furrow. "What do you need? Tell me."

"I don't want to make you do anything you're not ready for."

"You won't. Tell me."

I pause. I almost tell her no, but I'm so fucking turned on, and she's so sexy kneeling there, looking up at me with her back arched and her lips swollen from eating my pussy, that I just blurt it out.

"I need penetration."

She doesn't so much as flinch. Instead, she glides her hand up my inner thigh and rests her finger on my entrance.

"Tell me how."

Good God, I am definitely going to die. My heart is going to explode.

"Just push slowly. Pulse—oh, fuck, like that."

She eases into me, little by little, until I can feel her soft palm on my pussy lips, and I clench around her.

"Now?"

"Pulse, but curve, like a...a..."

I don't know how to describe it, so I do a *come here* motion with my index finger.

"Oh, fucking hell, Aurora," I moan as she does what I say. "Now can y—oh my God."

She moves to my clit, tending to it with her tongue as she fingers me, and all my restraint snaps. My hand clutches her hair, and I move on her, grinding against her, fucking her. I don't worry about scaring her or overwhelming her, I'm driven by pure need and spurred on by her talented mouth and fingers. She works me until I'm panting and twitching, and then she shoves me over the edge.

"I'm coming. I'm coming. Don't stop."

My body bucks and my muscles contract. I release a moan that vibrates through the steam, and when I can't take anymore, I pull away to break contact. When I look down at her she's grinning and proud with swollen lips and a flushed face.

"That was amazing," I pant out. "Oh my God, that was amazing."

She stands, and her wide grin shifts into a smirk. "Goddess, Mabel. A man could never."

I laugh out loud and kiss her deeply. Everything outside of this moment, outside of me and Aurora, has disappeared. We're all that matters now.

"C'mon," I say, leading her out of the shower. "Dry off. I need a snack, and then I'm taking you to bed and fucking you until you pass out."

30

AURORA

A BUZZING PENETRATES the warm cocoon of bedsheets and body heat currently wrapped around me.

The sound fades away, and I snuggle deeper into Mabel, burying my face into her hair to fall back asleep. The buzzing starts again, and I groan.

"If it's your uncle, tell him to fuck off," Mabel mumbles into my neck, and I laugh as I reluctantly wriggle out of her arms and climb out of bed to follow the sound.

The cool air kisses my body, bringing goosebumps to my bare skin as I search for my phone. It stops buzzing, so I wait until it starts again, then find it in my pile of clothing on the bathroom floor.

The moment I see the name on the screen, my heart drops to my feet. *Brady.*

I knew he'd be calling. I told him to. But having to deal with him immediately after waking up is not something I want to do. At all. Especially not while naked in another woman's bedroom after fooling around all night long.

My stomach roils as the phone rings out and his contact photo disappears, displaying ten missed calls and twenty text message notifications. All from him. But then something else catches my eye, and all the oxygen is sucked from the room.

A notification from our tracking app sits at the top of my phone screen.

Brady has his set up to alert him when I leave or arrive home, and when I complete a drive. It tells him my speed and if I've made any stops, and I've been trained to also text him photos several times a day.

For a while, I believed it was because he wanted me safe, but now I know better. Now I know it's for control, and I've slowly stopped sending those photos since Adelaide. Since the kiss.

My tracking app is only set up for one alert, though.

Brady will travel often for work. Sometimes to San Francisco or Seattle. Once or twice, he's had to go to New York. I am always left at home.

Since the accident, I sometimes get anxious when I know someone else is traveling. Because of this, I've set my app to alert me when Brady completes a flight safely. There's only one reason that notification would be on my phone screen right now, and I don't know of any business trips on the calendar.

With shaky fingers, I tap the notification, and the app pops up on my screen.

Brady Sinclair has landed safely in Sydney.

I blink several times to make sure I'm reading it correctly, but then it's replaced by his contact photo as he calls again.

I jump up and start putting on my clothes. I'm so frantic that I trip over my jeans and my phone crashes to the floor.

Mabel appears in the doorway in a silk robe with her hair still messy from sleep. She's smiling until she sees me, and then her face fills with concern.

"What's wrong? What happened?"

The phone, face down on the ground, starts to ring again, and she reaches for it.

"Don't! Don't answer it. It's Brady."

She looks confused. "I thought you were planning to talk—"

"He's here," I blurt, cutting her off. "He's in Sydney."

Her eyes go wide as she starts to feel what I'm feeling. "Where?"

I shake my head as I zip my jeans, then pull on my shirt. I don't bother with my underwear. I don't have time to look for them, and they're probably still wet, anyway.

"I don't know. If you pull up the purple tracking app, there's a map. You can zoom in."

It a matter of seconds, she looks up from the phone with a horrified expression. "Five minutes. He's less than five minutes away."

I run.

Out her French doors, on to the terrace, and into my room. I rip a brush through my hair and pull on a hoodie to hide the fact that I'm not wearing a bra. My hand is closing around the doorknob as Mabel comes rushing in through the terrace doors.

"Hey, take deep breaths. It's okay. We'll—"

"It's not okay. He's not supposed to be here."

"I know. But we can handle this together. We can talk—"

"No! No. No, you can't talk to him. You can't. I'm sorry, but you can't."

I rush out the door and down the stairs. I don't know what to do. I wasn't supposed to have to face him in person. On the phone. It was supposed to be on the phone, so I could hang up if he yelled. So I didn't have to listen to his hateful words.

Oh, God, what am I going to do?

Now he's angry. He must have heard my voicemail by now. He knows I'm not coming home. He's called ten times and texted twenty times, and I haven't answered a single one.

When I reach the main level, I grow even more apprehensive when I only see Callie, Claire, and Sav in the kitchen.

"Where are the guys? Uncle Wade?"

Sav looks up from a red notebook. "Surfing. Well, the guys and

Brynn are surfing. Ham is probably off somewhere snarling at small animals."

"No."

No, this isn't good.

He won't check himself if it's just women here. If the guys were here, maybe he'd pretend. But if it's just the girls...

I open my mouth to ask about the bodyguards, but my voice dies the moment a loud, forceful knock booms through the house. My eyes whip to the front door, and I freeze. I can't move, and I can't breathe. My muscles and organs are lead.

There is movement in my periphery, but I don't turn to see what it is. Instead, I watch in slow motion as the front door bangs open, and my husband steps inside.

His face is scrunched and ugly with fury, and his eyes scan the room, jumping over everyone until finally landing on me. My hand flies to the pendant of my necklace, clutching it tightly, as I act on muscle memory.

It's almost pathetic how my body moves on instinct. It's something I've done for years, only this time, it's like I'm watching it from above.

It's not *me* plastering on a smile and walking up to greet him. It's not *my* high-pitched, quivering, saccharine voice inviting him inside. It's some woman who looks like me, some actress in a movie or figment of my imagination. I can't stop it. I can't intervene. I can only watch in disgust.

"Brady! Hi. What a nice surprise."

He scowls at me, but I do my best to ignore it and go in for a hug. His body is rigid and wrong in my arms. Too hard. Too cold. I kiss him on the cheek and hide a wince when his stubble scratches my lips. He doesn't make a move to embrace me back, and I'm grateful for it.

I widen the distance and try to run damage control the only way I know how.

"I didn't know you were coming."

His jaw pops and his nostrils flare as he glares at me. "Maybe if you'd answer your phone, you wouldn't be surprised."

The bite in his tone makes me flinch, but I try my best to hide it with a bright smile.

"Oh, I can't find my phone. It must—"

"You had it last night when you called to say you weren't leaving the fucking tour."

I flinch again, and I dart my eyes to the kitchen where all the women, including Mabel, are now openly watching this embarrassing dumpster fire. I step a little closer and lower my voice.

"How about we go to lunch—"

"No, how about we talk about it right fucking now."

He hasn't raised his voice, but the barely contained anger is evident to me in every syllable. I reach with trembling fingers to brush his hand, but he smacks me away.

"I'd love to show you around. We can—"

"So, you lost your phone, Aurora? And you expect me to believe you're responsible enough to stay here? You can't even keep track of your own shit."

It's my impulse to nod, and despite trying to fight it, I apologize. "I'm sorry. I'll find it. I'm sure it's here somewhere."

He opens his mouth again, but snaps it shut when Sav slings her arm over my shoulder and Mabel steps up on my other side.

I look quickly between the two of them, and then at my husband. He's livid, and they're too close. I try to take a step back, to get them out of his reach, but their feet stay planted firmly in place. In fact, to my absolute horror, they're both glaring defiantly at him.

This is not good. This is very, very bad.

"What do you want?" Brady snaps, shifting his eyes between Sav and Mabel. "This is a private conversation."

"You're talking so loud the neighbors could hear you, bud," Sav says, voice all sass and snark. "I'm curious. Is this how you always speak to Aurora?"

"It is," Mabel says, and she's simmering with rage. "I've heard it before. Apparently, his role is to play the controlling, abusive asshole."

"This is none of your business."

Sav holds up a finger. "Yeah, no. You're not tall enough to use that attitude with me. Bring the audacity down until it matches your height, okay, buddy?"

I think Brady's head might explode. His height is his biggest insecurity, second only to his receding hairline. How Sav knew to hit on it is beyond me, but it just makes me more scared for her. I need to get him out of here.

"It's fine, Sav, he didn't mean to get loud." I look back at Brady. "Let's go to the beach, okay? We can talk there."

He turns his narrowed eyes on me, and I let him see the desperation in my face. I'm not above begging.

"Please," I whisper, and I feel Mabel stiffen beside me.

"If you leave this house, you're taking Red," Sav says, and Brady finally releases me from his glare to look at her.

"Who?"

"Me."

I whip my eyes to the voice and find Red with his giant, tree trunk arms folded across his barrel of a chest. I don't know when he got here, or how long he's been standing right behind Brady, but he eases my tension just a tiny amount.

"That's Sav's security guard," Callie says, and I turn around to find both her and Claire standing behind me. "He's trained in Muay Thai and Brazilian Jui Jitsu."

"And you should know that he also used to be a cage fighter," Claire adds with a smirk. "Just in case you try to get a little too big for your breeches."

"I'd send someone closer to your weight class, but my twelve-year-old is surfing with sharks."

Goddamn it, Sav.

She has no self-preservation. Brady is going to lose it if I don't get him out of here. I slide out from under her arm and inch my way to the stairs.

"I'm going to go get my shoes, and then we can go to the beach, okay? Please."

Brady tries to walk with me, but Red steps in his path. "She can go alone."

"I'll be right back," I say with a fake smile, and then I turn and sprint up the stairs.

I'm in my room for all of two seconds before Mabel comes rushing in behind me.

"Are you okay?" She pulls me in for a hug, and I inhale gardenia. "God, he's such a fucking prick. I texted Ham. He's on his way, and then we can get rid of that asshole."

I step back and let her arms fall away. "You texted my uncle?"

"Yeah. I figured we'd need—"

"You shouldn't have done that." I shake my head as I tug off yesterday's clothes and dig through my suitcase for a sundress. "I don't want Uncle Wade to get involved."

"Aurora, you're going to need his help if you're—wait, what are you doing?" I look over my shoulder and find her staring at me in disbelief. "You're not actually going to go anywhere with that asshole."

"I have to. I have to get him out of here before Sav starts something."

"Before *Sav* starts something? Are you kidding?"

"You know what I mean. She's deliberately pushing his buttons."

"Yeah. Good. He could stand to be knocked off his fucking high horse."

I sigh and pull my dress over my head quickly. "You don't understand."

"So, tell me. Help me understand."

I shake my head, but I stay quiet. I have one goal, and that's to get Brady out of this house as soon as I can.

"Aurora. You can't go with him. What if he hurts you?"

"Red will be there. It's fine." I drop to the floor and start looking for my sandals.

"It's not fine, Roar. Nothing about this is fine."

I find Mabel's boots under my bed, but not my shoes. Then see her jacket on the floor by the door, so I crawl quickly over there to see if my sandals are underneath it.

"I know you're worried, but you have to trust me."

Lifting Mabel's coat, I find my sandals, but then my eyes catch on a small, rectangular card on the floor beside them. It looks like the kind of card you'd get with a flower delivery. I remember a lot of those after the accident. This one isn't expressing *Deepest Sympathies*, though. It's got red hearts on it, and the print says...

My heart trips over itself as I read the card once, then twice, before turning to Mabel.

"What's this?"

Guilt transforms her face, and it's like a knife to the chest. It doesn't hurt, though. It just renders me numb. I've been a bundle of live wire nerves since waking up this morning, and my body can't handle any more. It just shuts off.

"She sent me flowers yesterday. I threw them away, but I still should have told you."

Yesterday.

Before or after I told her I wanted a divorce? Is that why she was so insistent that I not make the decision based on her?

Kat wants to go public. Kat misses her. This is what Mabel wanted. I close my eyes and breathe.

"You threw away the flowers but kept the card."

"It's not like that. I swear."

I push to standing and hold her eye contact. My heart might be breaking, but I'm too exhausted to feel it.

"Have you texted her since getting the flowers?"

"No."

"So not even to tell her you're not interested."

I watch sorrow flood her eyes, and that's the first pinch of pain. Since I've met her, Mabel has never looked at me with sympathy, with pity, until right now.

"Did you consider it? Her offer. She said she wants to go public. Have you considered it?"

She stays silent, and that turns the pinch into a cut.

"Foundation of truth, Mabel. Have you considered it?"

She exhales. "Yes."

My eyes fall shut as the word slices through me, and I imagine myself bleeding from my chest. I wish I could go back to the numb.

I turn toward the door, but she wraps her hand around my wrist and stops me.

"It's not like that, Aurora. I was going to contact her today. I just haven't had a chance."

Logically, it makes sense, but I'm struggling to think straight right now. Too much is going on. Too much is happening.

Kat misses her. Kat wants to go public. Mabel considered it. It's what Mabel wanted from the beginning.

Meanwhile, my husband, whom I don't love, is downstairs right now being insulted by Sav Loveless. I want to leave my husband. I've been fantasizing about a life without him. But Mabel, the one I have been picturing in his place, is considering an offer from her ex, the tall, gorgeous, famous model.

God, I can't even process it all. It's too much, too fast, and it hurts too much to think about, so I don't even try. I force a plastic smile and cue up my happy homemaker tone of voice.

"It's fine. You have to do what's right for you, right? I'm happy for you. You and Kat make a beautiful couple."

"Don't do that. Don't talk to me like I'm him."

"I don't know what you mean."

"You're acting like you don't care. You're lying. We don't lie, remember?"

I almost laugh. "But lying by omission is okay?"

Her frown deepens, and I see real regret in her eyes, so I turn away. I can't look at her anymore.

"I was going to tell you. I'm sorry."

Her hand brushes my arm, and I take a step away. I'm losing my grip on my composure. I need to get out of here before I start crying.

"You're getting what you want, and I'm happy for you. And you two make sense. Much more sense than we do. You're closer in age. You're in the same industry. She can make you happier than I can. You probably have more in common. My uncle would likely lose his mind if I dated you anyway. I mean, I'm married, for God's sake, and I'm not even gay, so of course you're going to consider going back to Kat. It makes sense. It does. It makes sense, and I'm not mad. It's okay. I'm fine. But I really have to go. I've taken too long as it is, and Brady doesn't like waiting."

When I look at her, she's staring at me like I've just slapped her, but I'm too busy trying not to fall apart to analyze it.

"Right," she breathes out, nodding. "Yeah. Okay. We'll, um, we'll talk when you get back."

She drops her eyes to the carpet, releasing me from their hold, so I leave quickly. If I don't do it now, I might never.

When I step back into the kitchen, it's eerily quiet, and everyone is staring at each other. I rush past Callie, Claire, and Sav, and take Brady's hand.

"Okay. Sorry for making you wait. I couldn't find my sandal."

He scowls. "Lost your phone and your sandal?"

I force a laugh and tug him toward the door, waving at the girls as I do. "I'll see you guys later."

"Red's coming with," Sav adds, and I nod.

"Okay."

Then she looks at Brady and twirls her finger around her own hairline.

"And bud, you might want to wear a hat on the beach. Australian sun is strong. You don't want those balding spots to burn."

Goddamn it, Sav.

31

MABEL

My head is in a fog as I make my way around the botanical gardens.

The tickets were nonrefundable, and since Aurora went back with dipshit to his hotel room, I made the stupid fucking decision to come alone. Now I'm having regrets. If I thought coming to a place full of plants would be a great way to take my mind off things, I was wrong.

I can't stop seeing her face when she found out he was in Sydney. Abject terror. There's no other way to describe it. She was terrified and panicking, but the way she changed when he walked through the door was like something out of a psychological thriller. The plastic smile. The calm, careful tone of voice. It was like watching her navigate a mine field, and her husband was the biggest bomb.

The minute he was in the room, he was her sole focus. She was constantly testing the temperature of his mood and trying her best to keep him from boiling over. She wasn't concerned for her own safety or happiness, only for him and minimizing any damage he might do. It was maddening and heartbreaking, and I couldn't do anything but watch.

I had suspicions that she'd been living in a domestic battle zone, but seeing proof put everything into perspective. Aurora has been living life in survival mode, and her husband is an absolute tyrant.

The only reason I didn't lose my shit last night when I learned she left with him was that both Ham and Red went with her. I haven't seen any of them since. Last night was the first concert in over a decade where Ham and Red weren't in attendance, and it just added to the sense of foreboding.

And then there's what she said right before she left. I can't stop hearing it.

I'm not even gay.

It probably shouldn't bother me the way it does. She was rambling and making excuses out of self-preservation. She was trying to convince herself that she'd be okay with me choosing Kat, and most of what came out of her mouth was a lie.

She's been kept in a box for so long. I know she needs to grow. I know she needs to find out who she is without Brady. I know that some aspects of self-discovery never end. I know all of this. But fuck, it still felt like a sharp slap across the face.

I left a three-year relationship because the woman I was with wouldn't come out publicly, and I was tired of being kept in the shadows. That relationship sucked the joy out of me, and I didn't even realize how bad it had gotten until I met Aurora. But hearing those words come from her mouth sent me spiraling back into that pain.

I rub my chest as if it's possible to massage away the ache, but I can't. I don't know how I let this happen. I don't know how or why I didn't see it, the risks, but I can't go through that again. I can't.

I slow when I come to a fork in the trail, so I pull my map out of my back pocket and look it over. There's an orchid house to the left, and though I know it's a terrible idea, that's the direction I head.

It's like stepping into another world when I push through the doors. The room is heavy with the scent of blooming flowers, and it's humid and warm, like a tropical forest after a rainstorm. The only sound I hear as I walk farther into the place is the distant trickling of water and the *tap tap* of my boots on the stone floor.

All around me, orchids of every shape, size, and color seem to float on the thick air. Perched in baskets, climbing up moss-covered branches, nestled among ferns. Everywhere I look are jewel-toned purples, electric pinks, and soft whites freckled with magenta or gold. When I stand in the middle of the room and turn in a slow circle, it's like a being in a giant kaleidoscope.

It's enchanting and peaceful, and Aurora would love it.

I wish she was here, and then I hurt all over again, because she's with her husband. I don't know what they're talking about. I don't know what's going to happen. Is she actually going to divorce him, or will I return to the house to discover that she's caved and gone back to him?

Maybe I'm just an experiment.

Maybe she was just exploring her sexuality, and I just happened to be the lucky plaything within reach.

It's not uncommon. People get a little bit of freedom—go to college, go on vacation, go on a rock and roll tour without their husbands—and their inhibitions loosen. It's like sampling at an all you can eat buffet. If it looks good, you try it. It happens all the time. Hell, it's happened to me many times over the years.

Maybe that's all I am to Aurora. A temporary excursion.

I frown.

No. That's not Aurora. That's not the kind of person she is.

But she did say she wasn't gay, and it's obvious that she doesn't know what she wants. How could she? She's been sheltered, and she's confused. She's spent four years being beat down by her fuckhead of a husband, and I was the first person to build her up.

What if she doesn't actually like *me*, she just likes the idea of me? She just likes the way I make her feel?

My shoulders droop with the thought, and I turn to leave, but my attention is caught by an older woman half hidden in a thick patch of ferns, and she's watching me. I smile awkwardly and give her a wave.

"How can someone be sad in the Orchid House? That's what I'd like to know." She waves her hand in the air, then points at me. "It's paradise in here. You can't be sad in paradise."

"Do you work here?"

"I tend to the orchids, and the orchids tend to my soul."

I huff a laugh and turn to leave, but then I think better of it, and walk toward her instead.

"Actually, could I ask you a question about that?"

"About orchids or souls?"

"Orchids."

"Ask."

"I have a friend who has a moth orchid that isn't doing very well. She can get it to bud, but not bloom. Do you have any advice?"

The lady's brow furrows in thought. "It's hard to tell without looking at it. How's the root system?"

I shrug. "Good, probably. My friend knows a lot about plants. She's doing everything she can to help this one thrive, but it refuses."

The lady hums and gives me a sage nod.

"Sometimes, they die because we love them too much. Sometimes, they bloom because we finally let them breathe." She gives me a wink and lowers her voice to a whisper. "And that goes for orchids and souls. You're welcome."

She leaves me standing amongst the ferns without another word, and I think about her advice for the rest of the day, and well into the next.

32

___

AURORA

Iᴛ's quiet in the car on the drive back to the house, and I keep my eyes out the dark window, watching the night woosh past.

I can't quit picking at my thumbs. I can't calm the racing of my heart. I can't be still, and I know it's annoying my uncle, because, for the third time in ten minutes, he places his palm on my knee to halt my bouncing. I send him an apologetic smile, then ask him the same question I've already asked him multiple times since we left Brady's hotel this morning.

"Did I do the right thing?"

He arches a brow. "Do *you* think you did the right thing?"

"Yes."

"Then it's the right thing."

I sigh. He's been giving me the same answer every time I ask, and I'm tired of it.

"Uncle Wade. I want to know what *you* think."

"Why?"

"Because. It's important to me."

He pauses, scanning my face with eyes that are so much like my father's that my chest aches. Then he takes my hand and folds it between both of his, and my eyes well with tears. My father used to do this exact thing, and in this moment, it's like he's here with me.

"I think it was the right decision," my uncle says finally, giving my hand a squeeze, "and your parents would think so, too."

I close my eyes and soak up his words, hoping they're true.

I didn't get married thinking I'd file for divorce eighteen months later, but I spent all day in a hotel board room video conferencing with divorce lawyers my uncle hired. I didn't agree to move in with the Sinclairs thinking I'd risk slipping into darkness, but here I am, four years later, fighting to claw myself back out of it. It feels like it's happening too fast, but not fast enough, and all I can do is go one step at a time.

"Thank you," I whisper. "I'm scared. Everything is going to change so drastically. I don't know if I can handle it."

"It's okay to be scared. Change can be very scary. What you did took courage, and I'm so damn proud of you for being scared and doing it anyway. You can do this, Aurora Jade. You deserve to be happy, and I'm glad we're going about it this way and not through a contract killer."

I hiccup on a laugh as tears start to fall down my face. "You want me to be happy even if I have to move into your basement?"

He arches a brow. "Even if you fall for my degenerate drummer."

I almost choke on my own spit with how violently my muscles freeze.

"What?"

My voice is barely a croak around the word, and a playful smile takes over my uncle's face.

"It's my job to know everything," he says, as if it's no big deal, and my jaw drops at his implication.

To know *everything*? What does that mean? Is he saying he knows I have feelings for Mabel, or is he saying he knows I had my face between her thighs a few nights ago? What exactly does he know? Should I ask? Do I want to know?

I shake my head to rattle away the thought. No, I definitely do not.

"Are you mad?"

"Rossi is a good kid."

"She's thirty, Uncle Wade."

My uncle's eyes flare. "Don't remind me, or I *will* be mad."

I fold my lips between my teeth to hide my smile and jerk out a nod. Then, just as we're pulling into the circle driveway, he squeezes my hand once more.

"You deserve happiness, Aurora. Whatever that looks like."

"Thank you. I love you, too."

Red parks the car and leads us into the dark house, and after a quick good night to both him and my uncle, I make my way upstairs to my bedroom. I change out of my clothes quickly, check myself in the mirror, and moments later, I let my feet carry me out onto the terrace.

I need to talk to Mabel, to tell her how I feel before it's too late, because our last conversation has been weighing heavily on my mind.

She's considering going back to Kat. I can't let that happen. I lied to her. I told her it was fine. I said we wouldn't work out. That I couldn't make her happy. I didn't mean it. I just needed to get my own problems under control, and now that I have, I need to set things right with Mabel.

It's dark in her room, and I debate knocking, but she makes the decision for me when she opens the door and gives me a tired smile.

"Hey. When did you get back?"

She takes a seat at the little patio table, so I follow her lead.

"Just a couple of minutes ago. Were you sleeping?"

"No."

"Oh. Well, I'm glad I didn't wake you, then."

She nods, casting her eyes out toward the ocean, and I can't tell if the cool chill is from her or the night air. I fist my hands in my lap and shift in my seat.

"I told him I want a divorce," I say, and she turns back to face me.

"How did that go?"

"Not good at first." I wince when I replay it in my head. "Thankfully Red and Uncle Wade were there. Brady got manipulative, pretended to be sad, he even cried a little. When that didn't work, he started making threats. *I'll be destitute. My brother would hate it. I'll never find a man who will want me.* That sort of thing. Which honestly is a little funny because I know the first two are lies, and I don't particularly care about that last one."

I laugh awkwardly, and her lips curve into a small smile that heightens my nerves. It doesn't reach her eyes. She's closed off and distant. This isn't how I saw this going.

"Anyway, Uncle Wade and Red were more intimidating, so Brady backed down pretty quick. Uncle Wade said he would sue him and file a restraining order, then threatened his job, which is probably the only thing Brady cares about. After that, he agreed to leave Australia immediately and accept my divorce filing uncontested."

"You think he will keep his word?"

I frown, then shake my head. I've thought about this a lot since Brady left for the airport.

"No, not right away. I think he'll go back to California and change his mind, and then Uncle Wade will have to make the threats all over again. Might even have to follow through on some of them, but..." I shrug. "In the end, he'll do it. And then I'll be free."

I feel Mabel's eyes on me, and I turn toward her. "I'm happy for you, Aurora. You deserve that freedom."

Her tone of voice makes me wary, but I tell myself she's just tired. That's it. Things couldn't have changed between us so drastically so quickly, right? But then I think of the card from Kat, and I start to doubt everything.

"Mabel, can I ask you a question?"

"Anything."

"Are you going to choose Kat?"

Her brow creases, and she shakes her head.

"No, Aurora. I called her yesterday and told her that it was really over, and that I had no interest in going public with her."

"Oh, good."

I release a sigh of relief, my tense shoulders drooping slightly with the exhale, then I reach across the table and take her hand.

"I was so worried I'd be too late. I was worried you'd choose her, but now we can be together. We don't have to hide or sneak around. I'm getting a divorce, and Kat knows you're not interested, and we can be together for real. Right?"

She doesn't answer right away, but she gently pulls her hand out of my gasp.

"Aurora, we need to talk."

No. I slump back in my chair as dread washes over me.

"You don't want me."

"It's not that. Trust me, it's not. But..."

She closes her eyes and drops her chin to her chest. I can feel her sorrow, and it's making this so much harder. I almost wish she'd be a bitch about it.

"But I think we need to take a little break from one another. Slow this down a bit."

I shake my head. "I don't understand. Why? Why do we need to slow down? I'm getting a divorce. That isn't a problem anymore. I'm getting a divorce, Mabel."

"I know, and I'm so happy for you. He was an asshole who treated you like shit, and I'm glad you're divorcing him."

"Then what's the problem," I ask, my voice raising slightly. "I just blew up my whole life so we could go full speed ahead and now you want to pump the breaks? Why? What did I do wrong?"

"Aurora."

My name floats on a pained exhale as she finally opens her eyes and looks at me again.

"I told you not to make that decision based on anyone else. You have to divorce Brady for *you*, not for me."

"It wasn't for you! It was for me so I could be with you. I love you. I love you, Mabel. I want to be with you."

"What if you don't, though, Roar? What if you don't love me? What if I'm just the first person to show you kindness in years, and you want to cling to that?"

My head jerks back like I've been slapped. "That's not what this is."

"You..."

She clamps her eyes shut, her voice quivering slightly like she's trying not to cry.

"You deserve freedom and independence. You deserve to live your own lives and to be your own light. You need to breathe so you can bloom, and you don't need another cage. I won't be another cage."

"You wouldn't cage me. You wouldn't."

"Not intentionally, but my life is in LA. It's established and structured. Are you just going to jump from Brady's routines right into mine? Without any of your own experiences? Without anything—"

"I don't want my own experiences! I don't care about any of that. I don't care."

"But I do, Aurora. I do. I *need* you to have them. I need you to, because I can't be another place holder. I can't be another body to explore until you realize that what you want isn't actually me. I couldn't handle it again. Not with you. Not when I..."

She runs her hands through her hair and tugs, shaking her head as tears finally break through her lashes in a steady stream. I track them with my eyes as they roll down her cheek and over her lips, catching in the seam between them before she licks them away.

This isn't happening. This isn't happening.

"I can't do it," she repeats, and this time, her voice shatters me. "My heart wouldn't survive it. Not unless I'm certain you're sure, and right now, I'm not."

I feel like I'm falling. Like I'm plummeting to the ground.

She's getting rid of me. She doesn't want me. I told her I love her, and she is pushing me away. Everything I saw, everything I hoped for, it's all going up in flames, and I can feel myself burning with it.

"I wouldn't do that. I'm not Kat."

"I know. You're *you*. You're energy and creativity and passion and light, and I love you, but I can't keep you."

It's a blissful high and a devastating low in the same breath. She loves me, but she can't keep me. She loves me, but she doesn't want me.

"Don't say that. You don't mean it. You don't. You love me. You *can* keep me. I'm right here."

I reach for her, but she leans away again, then she pushes up from her chair and crosses the terrace. Every step backward is a mile between us. A fracture, a crack, and the walls start to cave in around me.

"Come back," I beg. "Please. Please don't do this. I love you. You love me. Keep me. Please."

Her face falls, and she rests her hand on the doorknob to her room. It's over. I can tell it's over. There's nothing I can do or say to save us.

"Go try on some lives. Travel. Get lost in your gardens. Write poetry. Make mistakes. Kiss people. Be light. Do all the things you've wanted to do and couldn't. Try on some lives, Aurora Jade, and when you find one that fits, if there is room for me in it, I'll be waiting."

My heart breaks and falls to my feet, and I can hardly see through the tears flooding my eyes. I stand so quickly that my chair clatters to the floor, and I fist my hands at my sides.

"I love you," I say again, begging, pleading. "Please, please don't do this."

Her eyes flutter shut, her next inhale and exhale ragged, and she opens her mouth as if to speak. I hold my breath, waiting, hoping to God she'll take it all back.

But she doesn't.

Instead, she clamps her mouth shut again, caging her words behind clenched teeth, and I watch in slow motion as she opens her terrace door and disappears into her dark room without a sound.

I collapse to the ground and sob until the sky starts to pinken with the rising sun. Then I stand, stretch my aching muscles, and stare for several minutes at Mabel's room. Without thinking too hard about it, I unclasp my necklace and hang it over the knob of her French door.

"Don't forget me," I whisper, and then I retreat to my room.

Within thirty minutes, I've packed my things, apologized to Sav, and buckled myself and my orchid into the SUV so Uncle Wade can take me to the airport.

"Are you sure you want to do this?"

I don't lift my head from the passenger window as I nod. "Yes."

He pauses for a moment, and I can feel him looking at me, but I don't look back. Finally, he breaks the silence, and I'm grateful his tone is all business.

"I'll have a car at the airfield to pick you up when you land, and the penthouse will be prepared for you when you arrive."

"Thanks."

"And Jones will be coming with you." I sit up to argue, but he holds out a hand. "Don't even try."

Reluctantly, I drop my head back to the cool window and bite my tongue.

"Since you'll be back in the states, I'll set up a time for you to meet with your divorce lawyers in person. Proximity should make it easier to speed things along."

I nod again. "Kay."

"And Aurora?"

"Hmm?"

"I'm still proud of you."

I roll my eyes. "That makes one of us."

33

MABEL

THREE MONTHS LATER

"Is this the place?"

I glance out the window of the SUV at the white, two-story Colonial, my hand coming up to clutch the pendant on my necklace. I rub the worn, silver disk and nod.

"Looks right."

Sav whistles. "That's a nice house. You said she's a veterinarian?"

I nod again. "Vet tech. And I think her husband works construction."

"Construction workers are hot."

I roll my eyes as Callie and Claire laugh from the back, but I'm too nervous to join in. I've been a bit of a zombie these last few months, and I only decided to make the trip to Georgia a few days ago. Now that I'm here, I'm starting to think it was a mistake.

I should have emailed first. I should have called. This whole *fly to Georgia and scope it out without a plan* plan is feeling pretty ill-advised.

"We don't have to get out if you don't want," Claire says. "Red can just drive around the block, can't you, Red?"

"Sure can."

I sit in silence for a moment. God, this is so fucking weird. I'm sitting in a dark SUV with tinted windows outside my birth mother's home like some sort of stalker.

I know her name. I know what she looks like. I know where she lives. Yet, she knows nothing about me.

I don't know what I thought I would do when I got here. I just knew I was tired of moping around filled with regret and longing. I needed to stop pining for Aurora. I needed to *do something*.

But, fuck, I should have chosen something else, because staking out my birth mother's place of residence isn't it.

"Let's just leave," I mumble. "I need a toffee latte and a scone, stat."

Red puts a nearby coffee shop into the GPS and has us parallel parked in ten minutes. I twist my hair into a bun and pull on a baseball cap before climbing out of the SUV. I purposely dressed down today to be more inconspicuous, and it's so weird to wear jean shorts and flip flops that I almost trip over my own feet.

Then, leaving the two most noticeable in the SUV with Red, Claire and I make our way to the building.

"Coming here was a big deal. I'm proud of you."

I flash Claire a sardonic smile. "We parked outside the house for fifteen minutes before speeding away like criminals fleeing a bank robbery."

She shrugs. "Yeah, but you still did it, and I know it was difficult for you. Baby steps. Next time, maybe we'll park for twenty minutes, then drive away leisurely."

I laugh and roll my eyes, grabbing the door of the coffee shop and pulling it open. "Maybe, but we—oh, shit."

Someone runs smack into me. My hat is knocked backward, and my shirt is hit with something ice cold and wet. A toffee latte, from the smell of it.

"Oh, fuck, I'm sorry," a dark-haired woman says, brushing off her scrubs and bending to pick up the cups and napkins she dropped. "Goddamn it. This is not my day. I'm so sorry..."

She looks up and meets my gaze, and her voice trails off as her eyes widen. I imagine my face is a perfect reflection, because I'm just as shocked.

I'm standing in front of my birth mother, and judging by her expression, my disguise isn't as good as I thought. My hand shoots to my side, and I grab Claire's hand, squeezing tight. She knows who we've just run into. She's seen the pictures, and she squeezes back.

It's okay. I'm not doing this alone. I can handle this.

I try to prepare myself for the impending freak out, but I'm dreading it. I didn't realize it until now, but I don't want this to play out like a typical fan interaction. I've tried not to picture this moment, but I have, and never once did our first meeting include me signing an autograph for the woman who dropped me at a fire station as an infant.

I plaster on my meet and greet smile, then open my mouth to tell her it's okay, but she speaks first, and it about knocks me off my feet.

"Brooklyn?"

My mother's voice is almost dazed as she scans my makeup-free face, then her eyes start to shimmer. Goose bumps raise on my arms and the tiny hairs on the back of my neck lift as I squeeze Claire's hand hard. My fingers tremble anyway.

"No," I whisper, and the word feels raw. "No, I'm Mabel. Mabel."

Her expression shifts with a wave of disappointment. She shakes her head, but she doesn't look away from me. She doesn't stop studying my features, and I know what she's seeing. I know because I saw the same thing the first time my lawyer sent pictures.

Same eyes. Same nose. Same lips. It's like looking in a mirror, and just like the first time I saw her, she can't seem to look away.

"No, of course. I'm sorry. I thought you were...I thought you were someone else. You just look..." Her voice cracks, but she forces a smile. "You look familiar. I'm sorry."

Claire pulses her grip on my hand, and I glance at her. She

gives me an encouraging smile and a tiny, subtle nod. I nod back, exhale slowly and try to keep my tears from falling as I look back at my mom.

"Actually...um...are you Gianna Amato?"

Her eyes flash with hope. "I am, yes."

"I know you're probably on your way to work, but would you, maybe, want to grab a coffee with me? After?"

"I can do it now. We can do it now. I can call in."

"Oh, I don't want you to have to do that," I say quickly despite the way my heart leaps.

"It's no problem. Not at all." She smiles and sniffs as a single tear rolls down her cheek. "I want to. I've been..."

She closes her eyes and takes a few grounding, deep breaths as a few more tears escape her lashes, and then she nods again.

"I would love to get coffee with you right now. I live close, if you want. I'm sure I have a shirt you can change into, and I can wash that one. You...you look about my size."

I look back at Claire and find her crying, too.

"I can grab us new coffees," she says. "Toffee latte?"

"Yes."

"Yes, please."

My mom and I respond at the same time, and then we share a smile.

"And a scone?" I ask, and she nods.

"That would be lovely."

34

MABEL

TWO YEARS LATER

"How's the fam?" Sav asks as I make my way through her front door and into her kitchen.

"Good." I pat Zigs on the head as I rummage through the fridge. "Amelia got first place in the science fair, and Calliope snuck out and got picked up by the cops for toilet papering the neighbors' houses."

Sav barks out a laugh. "I love that kid."

"Yeah, she loves you too, and it's a problem."

"Are they going to come visit again?"

I open a yogurt and grab a spoon from her drawer. "I think so. The girls have a break from school soon, so I think they'll come then."

I haven't gone a day without talking to my family since the coffee shop, and it's been better than I could have imagined. It turns out, my mom and birth father are married. They met at a church camp, conceived me, lost contact with one another, then reconnected after high school. It's all very heartbreaking and romantic, and it explains why my sisters look exactly like me. We have the exact same DNA.

My father didn't even know I existed until years later. It was a rough patch for them, but he understood. My mother had no way of contacting him, and she hid the pregnancy from everyone, including her parents, because purity culture is a fucking trauma demon. Then, when she gave birth, rather than let the whole town know their daughter was a disgrace, her parents took me to the fire station.

My mom was a terrified child, and she had to navigate the whole pregnancy alone. And in the end, it wasn't even her choice to surrender me. The decision was made for her. I have no idea what I would do in that situation, and I'm not angry anymore. I just know that I'm glad to have her in my life now.

"Oh, before I forget, your mail is right there on the table."

"Thanks," I say around a spoonful of yogurt, then I shuffle through the pile.

I wouldn't expect it to be so big when I was only gone for two weeks, but I feel like I'm opening bills, packages, and fan mail for an hour. Then I get to the last package, a plain white bubble mailer with international postage, and a strange feeling fills me.

I recognize this handwriting.

I set the open, half-eaten yogurt on the table and start walking toward the door.

"Hey, Sav, I'm heading back to my house. See you later."

"Oh, okay. Well, nice to see you, bitch. Bye!"

I'm at my house in less than five minutes, and I tear open the package before I'm even through the door. When I have the contents in my hand, I start to cry.

It's a worn journal, brown leather with deckled edges, and it's so thick that the strip of leather keeping it closed is stretched tight.

My knees buckle, and I sit on the floor right in my foyer. I turn the package upside down, but there's no note. No card. Just the journal.

Aurora's journal.

My hands are shaking as I open it, and on the first page is a pressed flower, a pink moth orchid, and a poem written in purple pen. My hand flies to my pendant, and as I read the poem, my tears come faster.

Be Light, She said,
and the Dark will forget.
she found me (small
as a whisper) curled
in the elbow of Midnight,
deep in the crevice of Never.
Stuck.
Be Light, She said
and push through.
so i dared
to
burn
no trumpet Moon,
no skyshout Star.
just this Stubborn glow
barefoot, stumbling
through all the Shadow-Screams

& i dared to whisper
"i am"
which was the Loudest Light
i'd ever known.

Be Light, She said,
so I did.

and I was.
and I am.
and the dark forgot.
but I never will.

The poem takes my breath away.

It's about me. I know it is. I'm the *She*. I'm the one who told her to be light. I am so fucking happy to see that my words impacted her, because she made an impact on me. I read the poem three more times just to feel closer to her. Each time I do, her voice becomes stronger in my ears, as if she's reading it to me.

I flip to the next page and find a polaroid of a flower with *Jardin Majorelle, April 2nd* written across the bottom in black marker. There are several pressed flowers taped to the sides of the page, and a second poem in the middle written with the same purple pen as the first.

if the void has teeth
& you've fed it your voice
(all of your everything)
rest.
let silence hold
your throat
like petals hold
the morning dew
soft.
heal the breaks,
nurture the bud,
(tiny though it may be)
Then, when you're ready,
drop your jaw
and
ROAR
as if the void
never
learned
your
name.

My chest swells with pride, and I have to wipe away more tears before they fall onto the page.

"You got to Marrakech," I whisper, running my finger over the words, feeling the indentions in the paper.

She's so talented. I knew she would be, but it's so amazing to see. I can feel the emotion in her words, and I can imagine her, sitting on a bench in *Jardin Majorelle,* pouring her emotions into this notebook.

I turn to the next page and find it decorated with more pressed flowers, another poem, and another polaroid, this one with a new location and date. *Palace of Versailles Gardens, May 15th.*

It's a travel diary, I realize, and she sent it to me. It's full of memories, flowers, and poetry—full of *her*—and she wanted me to have it.

For the next few hours, I sit on the floor in my foyer, and I devour every single page. I run my fingers over every pressed flower. Study every single polaroid. Read, and reread every line of every poem. Aurora documented two years of travel—trips separated by mere days to a few months—in the way only she could, and it makes me ache with missing her.

I know Ham speaks to her regularly, and I'm pretty sure she stays at his penthouse from time to time, but I never ask him about her, and he never says a word. I still think of her every single day. I still long for her every night. It's never stopped, but it's been a while since these feelings were this visceral. To the point of a physical pain in my chest. I don't stop reading her diary though. I don't stop poring over every page like I'll be quizzed on it later. Like I need to tattoo every word and flower and image into my brain until I see it in my sleep.

I'll start dreaming of her again. It's going to hurt. But I welcome it if it means I'll get to see her face.

As I reach the last page, sadness starts to overwhelm me. I don't want it to be over. I don't want to have to say goodbye all over again. But then I get to the end, and the style has changed.

There's no poem. No polaroid. No pressed flowers.

Just FIND ME in black marker, followed by the name of a hotel in Iceland with a time and date. A date that is only two days from now.

My heart jolts in my chest, and I scramble for the package. It's post marked three weeks ago, so it must have been delivered just after I left for Georgia. It's been sitting under a pile of mail on Sav's counter for weeks, and if I don't hurry, I'll be out of time.

Quickly, I push to my feet and run to my room. I throw the journal and a few random articles of clothing into my carry-on—anything else I can buy when I get there—then shove my wallet and passport into my purse. I'm out the door and climbing into the car I rarely drive in less than five minutes. I plug the airfield into my GPS, then call Ham on the Bluetooth.

"Rossi."

"Ham, I need the jet."

"Why?"

"I need to go to Iceland."

He's doesn't respond right away, and I grow impatient.

"Hammond!" I shout, punctuating the word with a slap to the steering wheel. "I need the jet!"

"Calm down, Rossi. It's already fueled and waiting at the airfield."

I frown at his name on my car's display screen. "What?"

I could be totally losing it, but I swear I hear him try to cover a laugh with an annoyed sigh.

"It's my job to know everything," he says blandly, and then he hangs up.

"Fucking hell," I mumble, but I'm grinning so big that my cheeks hurt.

I'm coming, Aurora. I'm coming.

35

AURORA

As soon as my phone alarm alerts me that it's 10 p.m., I feel rather than see her.

My heart jumps to my throat, and I spin in circles, scanning the lobby, looking through the crowd of people waiting for our guided tour to begin. It takes all of ten seconds for my eyes to land on her, and she's already looking at me.

Slowly, she walks toward me, but I don't trust myself to move. I've thought I saw her before. Once in Portugal. Another time in Scotland. Both times my heart filled with hope before it shattered.

This time though, she doesn't disappear when I blink. She just gets closer and closer, until I swear I can smell the most hauntingly beautiful blend of gardenia, pear, and brown sugar.

She looks just as gorgeous as when I left her in Sydney in her platform combat boots and thick black tights under a distressed denim skirt. The coat she's wearing is bright pink and puffy, and it matches her black and pink stocking cap. She's bundled appropriately for viewing the Aurora Borealis on a November night in Iceland, and it makes me even happier.

She knew. She figured it out. She came.

I fold my lips between my teeth to tame my smile and taste tears. When she steps up in front of me, I inhale, filling my lungs with the scent of her. Confirming what I already knew but was too afraid to believe. It's real. She's here. She came.

Mabel reaches up, her hand covered in black, fingerless gloves, and wipes tears from my cheek while ignoring the steady stream of her own.

"Hey, Roar."

I laugh. "You found me," I say, my voice a trembling whisper.

She shakes her head, and lifts my journal, hugging it to her chest.

"No," she says. "You found you."

Then she kisses me, and everything is finally perfect.

Hours later, in my hotel bed, I snuggle into Mabel's warmth as she runs her fingers through my hair.

"I like it short," she says, toying with a single streak of purple. "It suits you."

"Thank you." I press a kiss to her breast, and she hums. "I like it, too. I can't wait to hear more about your family. Your mom, dad, and sisters. I'm so happy for you, Mabel."

"I'd like for you to meet them. If you're comfortable with that, I mean."

I smile against her. "I'd love that. As long as you don't think we're going too fast."

"I've been missing you for two years, Roar. I'm all in if you're all in." I feel her body tense. "Are you all in?"

"I'm more than all in." I can't help but giggle as I pull her tighter, lifting my leg up and over her hips so I'm clinging to her like a koala in a tree. "Should we have had this conversation before we fucked?"

When she laughs, the sound vibrates through her chest and tickles my ear. "Maybe. But the next best time is now."

"I'm all in, Brooklyn Susan Ainsley Mabel Rossi," I tell her firmly. "I fucking love you. No lies here."

She shifts and tilts my chin up so our lips meet, and she kisses me so deeply, I could sink into it.

"I fucking love you, Aurora Jade Hammond," she says into my mouth. "Foundation of truth."

I grin. "Thank God. This would all be so embarrassing if you didn't."

Mabel rolls her eyes playfully, then tucks me back into her side, and we lie together in the quiet for a while. I listen to her heartbeat. My breathing syncs with hers. I want this to be my life forever now. I never, ever want to lose her again.

"Your journal is beautiful." Her voice breaks the silence, and I can feel her words dancing through my hair. "I read every single page the moment I opened the package, and then I read it again on the jet. And your poetry, fuck, you're so talented, Roar. You should be published."

"I'm proud of it," I say, tracing my fingers along her stomach and marveling at the goose bumps that rise on her skin. The fact that she loves it just makes me love it more. "Actually, I have sort of a surprise."

"Yeah? What kind of surprise?"

"Well, my journal is being published. I wanted you to read it first."

She sits up quickly, making me fall into the pillow with a gasp, and then I laugh loudly when I see her gaping at me with the biggest smile I've ever seen on her face.

"Are you fucking kidding?"

I shake my head. "I'm very serious. It should be out next year."

"Oh my God, we have to celebrate. What do you want to do? We need to do something."

"I mean..." I smirk and drag my eyes over her naked body. "This kind of was my celebration."

She laughs and shakes her head. "Let's order room service. Champagne or something."

My stomach flips with an idea. I didn't plan to do this tonight.

I didn't know if I'd do it ever actually, but being with Mabel tonight, it's like no time has passed. I've changed, yes, but our connection hasn't. If anything, it's only gotten stronger, and I think my confidence has a lot to do with that. So, I wrangle the butterflies in my stomach and raise up to my knees.

"Actually, I kind of want to try something, if you're up to it."

Her eyes narrow with curiosity, and she tilts her head. "Anything."

I stand and walk toward my beat-up travel trunk. I've lugged it around with me for two years. It's covered in stickers and stamps and, with the exception of my important documents and a few mementos that I keep at my uncle's, it contains all my possessions.

"You can say no if you want. Don't feel obligated, okay?"

"Just tell me what it is."

I purse my lips, consider it again for just a second, then say fuck it, and dive into my trunk. I find what I'm looking for, then stand and show it to Mabel. She takes one look at it and barks out a laugh, but there's no hiding the heat that flashes in her eyes.

"You haven't seen me in two years, and you're busting out a glittery pink dildo?"

I can feel my cheeks flush, but I scrunch up my nose and give her a shrug.

"Depends. Are you still a girl who likes pretty things?"

She nods. "I am. I very much am."

"Oh, phew. That's good."

I mime wiping sweat off my brow, then upend the box, dropping everything on the bed. I stare at the leather harness, then at the glittery pink dildo, then I look at Mabel.

"I might need some guidance."

A night from years earlier flashes in my mind as soon as the words leave my mouth, and I have to give my head a shake to loosen the image of me on my knees in a shower in Sydney. I can still taste her, and it's not just from what we did earlier.

"Have you ever used one before?"

"Nope. Never." I shake my head and pick up a small piece of paper with instructions and squint at it. "This is actually brand new."

She goes quiet, and when I look up at her, she's staring at me in a way that makes my heart skip. Like she can't believe I'm real. I haven't exactly been celibate in the last two years. She basically told me not to be, and I'm not naïve enough to expect it from her either. But I wanted to save some experiences for her. For us. I wanted her to have more of my firsts, and from the way she's looking at me, I'm so glad that I did.

She clears her throat and gives her head a shake. "Okay, well, we should probably start by cleaning it."

"Oh, I did that already. With rubbing alcohol."

Her eyes go wide, and I smirk.

"Kidding. I used a toy cleaner."

"Funny." She rolls her eyes. "You want help?"

"Yes, please."

I hold the jockstrap harness out to her, and she helps me step into it before pulling it up and adjusting the buckles so it's secure, but not too tight.

"Is it comfortable to move?"

I bend my legs, one at a time, then drop into a squat, and we both start to giggle. I'm doing squats in a jockstrap harness while naked in a hotel in Iceland, and I'm giddy over it.

"It feels good." I stand, then hand her the dildo. "Dick me up."

Mabel snorts, and then I snort, and then we fall into laughter again, until I'm giggling so hard I have to bend over and support myself on the mattress until I catch my breath. It's the most fun I've had in a long time, and I'm just so damn elated that it's with her.

God, I've missed her so much.

When we've composed ourselves, I stand, and hand the dildo back to her.

"I like the color," she says as she fits it through the harness. "I'm partial to glittery pink things."

"Well, I bought it because it reminded me of you," I say on a laugh. "It was in a sex shop in Amsterdam, and I had to get it for you."

She freezes. "You were in Amsterdam over a year and a half ago."

I nod. "Yeah."

She locks her gaze with mine. "You bought this for me over a year ago?"

I hear the question within the question, and give her a small, shy smile.

"I was always going to come back to you, Mabel. It was just a question of whether you'd want me."

"I have always and will always want you." She rubs at her eyes and laughs. "I can't believe I'm crying over a dildo."

I shrug. "It *is* glittery pink."

"Facts." She taps my hip lightly, then takes a step back. "Finished."

I put my hands on my hips. "How do I look?"

I don't have to ask, though. Her face says it all. "This is the hottest thing I've ever seen."

A smile, sinful and mischievous, stretches slowly across my face, and I pull confidence from the way her breathing speeds up.

"Good." I take a few steps toward her, then drag my finger down the middle of her breasts. "Because I'm a giver, Mabel Rossi, so lie back and enjoy what I have to give."

EPILOGUE
MABEL

I CAN HEAR the music blaring from the backyard as soon as I get out of the car, and it brings a wide smile to my face.

I grab my bags from the backseat and head into the house, and I'm hit with the scent of florals as soon as I step into the foyer. I look around the lower level and laugh. There are fresh flower bouquets in every room. Coffee table, dining table, kitchen counter. There's even one on the landing at the top of the stairs.

My girlfriend is a real-life flower fairy, and I am obsessed with her.

Dropping my bags on the floor, I go to the kitchen and throw together a little plate of meat, cheese, crackers, and fruit. I also fill two glasses with water, because If I know my girl, she's covered in dirt and dehydrated.

When I'm sure I can walk without dropping or spilling something, I head out the back door and down the little stone path that leads to Aurora's greenhouse.

We built the greenhouse last year, about a month or so after she moved in, and it's become a sanctuary of sorts. It's teeming with flowers and foliage, vegetables and fruits, and there's even a desk in the back where she can write.

Well, when it's not littered with soil and propagations, anyway. Although, I guess that hasn't stopped her. I think half the stuff she turns into her editor is handwritten and covered in dirt.

When I push through the door, she sees me immediately and rushes to turn down the music.

"You're home early." She smiles brightly, pressing a kiss to my lips before taking the water glasses and plate of food and setting them on a table. "How was the flight? How as the trip? Did the boys behave? Tell me all the things."

I wrap my arms around her and kiss her again, smiling against her lips.

"I'm home on time, and the flight was fine."

She pulls back in surprise, then checks the clock on the wall. "Oh shit. I must have lost track of time."

"Time doesn't exist in the greenhouse," I tease, and she rolls her eyes. "Your uncle had to lay into Crue and Ezra for acting like idiots, but otherwise, the trip was uneventful."

"I wish I could have come. This deadline is kicking my ass."

I arch a brow. "Is that why you have dirt on your forehead and three new plants behind you?"

She gives me a sweet smile and bats her eyelashes. "It's my process, baby. You have to respect the process."

I shake my head. "Of course. I would never disrespect the process."

She grins and kisses me again. "Anyway, want to read what I've got so far?"

"Absolutely. How many new ones since I last looked at it."

Aurora scrunches up her nose in that cute way that I love and holds up a single finger. "One."

"This deadline *is* kicking your ass," I say on a laugh, but she waves me off and takes my hand, pulling me to her dirty, plant-covered desk.

She shuffles through some papers with scribbled writing and doodles, even picking up Arthur her orchid—careful not to disturb one of his seven beautiful flowers—to look underneath him until she finds what she's looking for.

"Got it," she says, handing me a piece of paper. "Be gentle. It's raw."

I refrain from making a *raw* joke, but I waggle my eyebrows at her and take pleasure in the way her cheeks flush with heat. She flares her eyes then nods to the sheet of paper.

"Go on. Read it."

I shake my head, and just like all the other times, I hold it back out to her.

"You read it to me. I like them in your voice."

She hesitates, narrows her eyes as if she finds me ridiculous but loves it, then plucks the paper from my hand. She straightens her shoulders, clears her throat, and reads.

I wore a thousand yesterdays
buttoned tight:
wrong sleeves,
inside-out dreams,
and shoes that blistered
souls
and feet
I tried on the quiet,
and danced in the loud.
I stitched a few maybes
into the hem of my now.
until a life,
both hers and mine
slipped over my shoulders
and down my thighs.
no bars
no walls
but fresh blooms
and deep breaths

> *of all the lives*
> *that I've traveled in,*
> *you are the perfect fit."*

She finishes and looks at me with a nervous smile.

"Again, it's rough. I tried with a rhyme scheme, and I kind of lose it in the end, so I have to rework it, but the premise stays the same."

I work to keep tears from my eyes, but I'm absolutely terrible at it. I always am.

"I love it," I say honestly, and she smiles.

"I love you."

I take her face in my hands and kiss her again, grateful that I have the freedom to do this whenever I want. Whenever I need to. Like water. Like air. Like *light*, she gives me everything I need to thrive, and like a flower to the sun, I will always reach for her. Always.

I rest my forehead on hers and smile against her lips.

"It's beautiful. I think you get better with every new poem."

"Yeah?"

"Yeah."

"Well, I guess you would know best."

"I would?"

"Yeah. My poems are my heart on the page, after all, and no one knows my heart better than you do."

I pull back and bounce my eyes between hers, hazel-green and filled with a galaxy of starbursts. I love her. I'm so damn in love with her that I could burst with it. I love her so deeply and infinitely that there aren't enough words in the English language for me to describe it. Yet, somehow, she manages to do it perfectly in just a few stanzas every time.

"What are you thinking, Brooklyn Susan Ainsely Mabel Rossi?"

I laugh lightly, then press one more kiss to her lips.

"I'm thinking that I've tried on a lot of lives, Aurora Jade Hammond, but this one, with you, is my favorite."

THE END
(for now)

AUTHOR'S NOTE

Well, I guess that's it.

The Hometown Heartless farewell tour is over. I'm officially leaving my rockstar era, and to be completely honest, I didn't expect to feel this emotional over typing *The End.*

Sav Loveless and the gang have been performing an extended residency of sorts in my brain since 2022. There hasn't been a single day in the last two and a half years where at least one of these characters wasn't talking to me—usually screaming and demanding my attention—and I almost don't know what I'll do with the quiet now that it's over.

What started as a standalone, second chance love story grew into a world tour of angst, heartache, and happily-ever-afters, and during that process, these characters, this band, became *real* to me. They became like family, and I think I'll miss them more than I realized. Especially now that Mabel's and Aurora's voices are so distinct and special.

I've loved Mabel Rossi from the moment I met her in that sketchy dive bar in Miami, and I know so many of you love her as well. Refining the details of her story was something I enjoyed thoroughly, but it was getting to know Aurora that left the biggest impact on me.

If you've been reading me for a while, you know how much I love writing about growth. Mabel Rossi knows who she is and what she wants out of life, and much of that work took place off page for her. For all intents and purposes, *The Temptation of Truth* starts in the middle of Mabel's story. But with Aurora Hammond, we meet her between a tumultuous ending and a beautiful beginning, and it was almost like creating two separate characters. Like drawing a picture, getting it near finished, then erasing it entirely and starting over. Crafting Aurora's character arc was equal parts daunting and rewarding, and I loved every second of it.

Self-love and self-discovery have been two recurring themes in this series, and ending with *The Temptation of Truth* feels like a fitting way to close it out. This book isn't just a story about two people meeting and falling in love; it's also a story about a woman meeting and falling in love with herself.

I wanted Aurora's transformation as a woman to feel just as dynamic and impactful as the romance, and I hope I accomplished that. I truly believe that she is the perfect partner for our beloved drummer, and the perfect addition to the Heartless family.

ACKNOWLEDGMENTS

The Temptation of Truth would not have been possible without the help of some wonderful people.

Since this book is my first queer romance, it was very important to me that I approached Mabel and Aurora's love story with care and respect. I was lucky to have two amazing authenticity readers on this project, and I owe much of the richness and beauty of this story to their influence.

Callie and Rosie, from the bottom of my heart, thank you for everything you did for this book and for these characters. Your commentary, advice, and suggestions were truly invaluable to me.

Rosie, thank you for always being willing to read through the chaotic, ever-changing Google Doc, and for being just a text away when I needed to send a rambling voice note.

Callie, thank you for the notes, feedback, and phone calls. Your love for this book series helped immensely when it came to staying true to Mabel's character and crafting a dynamic character arc for Aurora.

The relationship between Mabel and Aurora is complex and layered in a million beautiful ways, and I have you both to thank for that.

As always, **my team of beta and alpha readers** were key in keeping this story on track. Haley, Jessie, Caitlin, Mickey, Shauna, Bri, Sarah Beth, and Leticia, thank you so much for the feedback and suggestions. You pulled me out of more writer's block slumps than you realize, and I couldn't have done it without you.

To **my editing team**, Emily and Becky, I am forever in awe of your ability to polish up my chaos. I'm so grateful for your brains, skills, and patience. Thank you both so much.

And **Becky**, once again, you're the only reason I made it to the finish line. I love you, friend.

My design team is beyond talented, and they truly outdid themselves with this book.

Kate, the covers are absolutely gorgeous, and the full series together is a masterpiece. You did such a beautiful job, and I couldn't have dreamed up anything better.

Sarah Beth, you once again nailed the graphics and teasers, and they match the vibe of this story perfectly.

Thank you both for lending your talent to this book and this series. You helped make The Hometown Heartless the most attractive and aesthetically pleasing band out there.

Huge thank you to **The Author Agency**, the team of masterminds behind PR and Promo. Shauna, Becca, Emma, Ashley, Reema and Brooke, you played a pivotal role in getting this book out to the masses, and I am so grateful for the work you've done.

Shauna, you are the wind beneath my wings. Your love for these characters means more to me than you know. Thank you for always helping to get their stories into the hands of readers. I love you.

Thank you to **Brittney**, my audio fairy god mother, and the team at **Lyric Audio** for creating an absolutely gorgeous audiobook and for always making my narrator dreams come true.

Britt, I love you. Thank you for putting up with my BS for this entire series. Pizza and wine on me always.

Emma, I don't know how I survived before you. The Universe (see also: Shauna) sent you to me when I needed you most, and

I'm so grateful. I would probably have drowned this year without you. Truly. Thank you for everything.

To my **Street Team**, thank you so much for being the most supportive and encouraging group of hype-women. You're the best group of humans on the internet, and I am extremely grateful for each and every one of you.

Kristina, you've helped me more this year than you probably realize. I cannot express enough how thankful I am for you. You're a gem, and I'm lucky to know you.

No acknowledgements would be complete without a shout out to my ride-or-dies, my besties for the resties, my **Emotional Support Pirates**, Hales and Jessie. I love you both so very much, from the top of my head to the tips of my toes. Thank you for literally everything.

To **Jonathan**, whose unwavering support and encouragement make this possible. Thank you for everything you do and everything you are. You are the Nick to my Jess, the popcorn to my Reece's Pieces, the Ralph to my Vanellope, and I am obsessed with you. Thank you for being the only man I could ever love. You are the exception to every rule in every scenario, and I am forever grateful that our paths crossed. I love you so, so, so much. The absolute biggest.

To **Ophelia**, my orchid, who is determined to survive but not thrive. Thank you for inspiring Aurora's love of plants. I love you. Please don't die.

And last but not least, **to my readers,** thank you so much. Whether you're new to my books or you've been here since the beginning, I literally would not be able to do this without you. There are so many amazing books out there. The fact that you took the time to read one of mine means the world to me.

I'm going to miss this rag-tag band of runaways and misfits, and while I don't have any plans on the immediate horizon to revisit The Hometown Heartless, I'll never say never. So to sign off, I'll leave you with the legendary words of rock icon Sav Loveless:

While this might be goodnight, it's not goodbye. But just in case, so you don't forget me, I'm Brit Benson. Thank you for reading and loving these stories. I love you all.

—Brit

ABOUT THE AUTHOR

Brit Benson writes real, relatable romance. She likes outspoken, independent heroines, dirty talking, love-struck heroes, and plots that get you right in the feels. Brit would almost always rather be reading or writing. When she's not dreaming up her next swoony book boyfriend and fierce book bestie, she's getting lost in someone else's fictional world. When she's not doing that, she's probably marathoning a Netflix series or wandering aimlessly up and down the aisles in Homegoods, sniffing candles and touching things she'll never buy.

authorbritbenson.com

ALSO BY BRIT BENSON
AVAILABLE NOW

The Hometown Heartless

Between Never and Forever (Sav & Levi)

Of Heartbreak and Harmony (Callie & Torren)

For Wrath and Redemption (Claire & Jonah)

The Temptation of Truth (Aurora & Mabel)

Next Life

The Love of My Next Life (Lennon & Macon, pt. 1)

This Life and All the Rest (Lennon & Macon, pt. 2)

The Love You Fight For (Sam & Chris)

Better Love

Love You Better (Ivy & Kelley)

Better With You (Bailey & Riggs)

Nothing Feels Better (Jocelyn & Jesse)

Better Than the Beach (Cassie & Nolan)

To stay updated on future release dates and plans, follow Brit on Instagram and Facebook, and sign up for her newsletter.

www.ingramcontent.com/pod-product-compliance
Lightning Source LLC
Chambersburg PA
CBHW071344300726
48976CB00006B/1759